ENEMY
OF THE
STATE

BOOKS BY ROBERT SWARTWOOD

THE KILLING ROOM SERIES
The Killing Room
Enemy of the State

THE HOLLY LIN SERIES
No Shelter
First Kill
The Devil You Know
Hollow Point

THE NOVA BARTKOWSKI SERIES
Bullet Rain
Bullet Country

THE MAN OF WAX SERIES
Legion
Man of Wax
The Inner Circle
End Game

STANDALONE NOVELS
The Calling
Land of the Dead
The Serial Killer's Wife
Walk the Sky (with David B. Silva)
New Avalon
Abducted
Temple

AS EDITOR
Hint Fiction: An Anthology in Stories 25 Words or Fewer

WRITING AS AVERY BISHOP
Girl Gone Mad
One Year Gone
Dear Seraphina

USA TODAY BESTSELLING AUTHOR

ROBERT SWARTWOOD

ENEMY OF THE STATE

BLACK STONE
PUBLISHING

Copyright © 2024 by Robert Swartwood
Published in 2024 by Blackstone Publishing
Cover and book design by Alenka Vdovič Linaschke

All rights reserved. This book or any portion
thereof may not be reproduced or used in any manner
whatsoever without the express written permission
of the publisher except for the use of brief quotations
in a book review.

The characters and events in this book are fictitious.
Any similarity to real persons, living or dead, is coincidental
and not intended by the author.

Printed in the United States of America

First edition: 2024
ISBN 979-8-212-63813-5
Fiction / Thrillers / General

Version 1

Blackstone Publishing
31 Mistletoe Rd.
Ashland, OR 97520

www.BlackstonePublishing.com

For Douglas Clegg

Daniel Burke is about to die.

In the next sixteen minutes, to be exact, but that isn't anything anyone at The Office knows yet.

The Office—what Mitchell Hargrave and his team call the place they work.

An innocuous, simple, straightforward name.

The thing about The Office is that it has no centralized location. Control—the epicenter during an op—can be anywhere. Almost always in a subbasement of some random building in Washington, DC.

The government has several of these secret locations spread across the country—buildings with subbasements that can be used as safe houses or control centers or, in some cases, medical bays for individuals who need immediate attention but can't risk going to the hospital for one reason or another.

Today, The Office's location is a building in Dupont Park. Mitchell Hargrave is here, along with his second-in-command, Rita Salazar, and two techs, Theo and Julian.

In the dark room, a half dozen LED screens are lit up on the wall. One of the screens shows real-time imagery from an unmanned aerial vehicle flying thirty thousand feet above a building outside Erzurum, Turkey. It's nighttime there, but the UAV has the capability to read heat signatures, so they can see the outline of the buildings in the area and the people moving about outside.

The Alpha Team has been sent in to verify intelligence that a rebel faction within the Turkish government is planning an attack using nerve gas.

The op is being run by the usual team leader: Lucas Hancock. Dennis Rowe, Daniel Burke, and Noah LaSalle make up the rest of the team.

Typically, Theo and Julian can hack into any system, so if there are cameras nearby connected to a network, they can see what's happening on the ground.

But not tonight—the facility purposely doesn't have any security cameras, so right now the only way they can track the team's location is by the devices implanted subcutaneously in each of the team members.

The trackers are still highly experimental—monitoring a person's location as well as their vitals—and it's unclear whether there are any long-term adverse side effects, as seventy-two hours after the tracker is injected, it disintegrates and is absorbed by the body.

The team entered the location fifteen minutes ago, and based on the most recent situation report, everything should be wrapping up shortly. So far it appears this will be a clean mission: no bullets fired, no blood shed.

Lucas Hancock's voice issues from the tiny transmitters in everyone's ears.

"Control, we have the package and are headed out."

Standing with his arms crossed, watching the screens, Mitchell Hargrave says, "Good to hear it, Alpha One."

On the screens, they watch as Alphas One and Two—Hancock and Rowe—start out of the north side of the building. Alphas Three and Four—Burke and LaSalle—head out the south side.

Suddenly, gunfire erupts from the transmitters.

Noah LaSalle's voice: "Shit! I'm taking fire!"

Hancock: "We're headed back in."

Burke: "Negative. We can handle this."

Hargrave trades a look with Rita Salazar. The woman is twenty years younger than him and just as smart, if not smarter. Hargrave poached her from the NSA only two years ago.

Burke: "Alpha Four, hang tight. I'm almost there."

More gunfire erupts—a full-on salvo. Hargrave watches the screens, wishing he could see what was happening inside.

LaSalle: "I'm hit!"

Hancock: "Fuck this. We're going in."

Burke: "No! I've got Alpha Four and am bringing him out."

LaSalle, talking through clenched teeth: "Fuck."

Hargrave says, "Alpha Three, sitrep."

Burke, his voice interlaced with steady gunfire: "Alpha Four took a bullet to the leg. But he can walk. Should be out in another minute."

The op's directive was for the team to get in and out without notice—and this has all at once become a major clusterfuck.

Hargrave trades another glance with Salazar. He sees the question on her face, but he doesn't want to commit yet.

The gunfire continues, unabated, muffled voices from the enemy shouting in the background, and then they hear Burke again—"Go, go, go!"—and LaSalle grunting in pain, and then Burke saying that LaSalle is headed out and that he needs to stay back for a minute to lay down suppressive fire.

Hargrave: "Negative, Alpha Three. Get out of there now!"

Burke: "Alpha Four is moving too slow. He needs time."

Mitchell Hargrave shifts on his feet, crossing his arms again, his gaze glued to the monitors.

Again, he feels Salazar's eyes on him.

Again, he knows exactly what she's thinking.

He shakes his head at her, mouths, *Not yet,* and turns his attention back to the screens.

The gunfire has become sporadic, but from the overhead view afforded them from the UAV, they spot a vehicle headed down the road—enemy reinforcements.

Shit, Hargrave thinks. *Shit shit shit shit shit.*

"Alpha Team, you've got tangos coming in from the east."

LaSalle: "I'm almost to the truck."

Hancock: "Alpha Three, what's your location?"

The gunfire increases, a sudden staccato—and then the sound of Burke grunting, his voice clipped and rough.

"I'm hit."

LaSalle: "Shit. I'm headed back."

Burke: "No! I . . . I can make it. I can—"

A single gunshot, close enough to Burke's transmitter that it causes all of them to jump.

Then . . . silence.

On one of the screens, Daniel Burke's vitals flatline.

Hancock: "Control, what's happening? Do Alpha Two and I need to head back in?"

Hargrave stands there staring at the monitors but not seeing them, hearing the echo of gunfire coming from the transmitter in his ear, and at first he isn't aware that Rita Salazar is saying something to him until she shouts his name.

"Mitchell!"

Blinking, he slowly turns his head in her direction. Sees her standing there, her eyes pulsing with intensity.

She nods, just once, and after a beat, Hargrave steps forward and places his hand on Theo's shoulder.

"Reroute the UAV to get a clear shot of the gas line."

In his ear, Hancock says, "Control, what are you doing? We can get to him."

"Negative, Alpha One. You don't have time."

"We do. Give us two minutes."

"Stand down. Alpha Three is dead."

A beat of silence, and then Hancock's voice again.

"Copy, Control."

On the screens, they watch as the rest of the team evacuates in a truck, speeding down an access road.

The enemy's approaching truck spots them and starts in their direction.

Hargrave says, "Theo, lock onto the truck."

Theo guides the UAV through the air thirty thousand feet above the action, places an infrared target on the pickup.

Hargrave says, "Go ahead," and Theo presses a button and within seconds one of the Hellfire missiles obliterates the pickup into flames.

Hargrave feels hollow inside. After all these years, after all the ops his team has gone on, he has never lost anyone.

He feels Rita Salazar's eyes on him. He ignores her as he stands up straight and clears his throat.

"Now the building," he says. "Take it out."

PART I
NO ESCAPE

1

"Sir?"

The gentle voice, muffled and lost behind the blood pounding in my ears. My pulse having quickened. Every muscle, tense.

"Sir, are you ready to board?"

My eyes, scanning the terminal. Spotting a young couple, barely in their thirties, walking hand in hand. A woman in her forties staring down at her phone as she hustled toward her gate. A businessman with glasses, a phone to his ear, talking louder than was socially acceptable and not appearing to care at all, ignoring the annoyed looks people kept throwing him.

"Sir, we need to close the doors."

The tone now edging on exasperated. Especially as everyone else had boarded the 9:50 a.m. flight and I was the lone holdout.

But still I ignored the voice's owner. Scanning the terminal, searching every face. Trying to match any of them up to the men I'd worked with a year ago before walking away from my life.

"Sir!"

The gate agent was standing next to me now. A mixture of

irritation and concern on her face. Then, maybe sensing something was wrong, her eyes softened.

"Is everything all right, sir?"

I had no weapons on me. I couldn't bring any on the plane, not through security, and besides, all the weapons I'd stored in Vegas this past year had since been stripped apart and their pieces scattered so they could never be reassembled.

When I didn't answer, the gate agent took a hesitant step forward. Cleared her throat.

"Sir, if you're not boarding, I need to know right now."

It had only been a minute, but Noah's words still echoed in my ears.

If you get on the plane, it will go down. It'll be shot out of the sky, but it'll be reported as engine failure. Hundreds of people will die.

There was a chance he was lying. A chance that it was all bullshit—that a team hadn't been sent to eliminate me. That the government wouldn't actually shoot a plane loaded with civilians out of the sky just to take me out.

Still, there was a chance he was telling the truth. Like the other men on my team, I had trusted Noah, but only so far. It was true, I had saved his life, and now he told me he was returning the favor. Giving me a heads-up just minutes before I was ready to step onto a plane and disappear forever.

How long do I have? I'd asked, and Noah, after a beat of silence, had answered, *We're already here.*

But so far I hadn't spotted anyone. Not from my old team, at least. Though our team had been trained to blend into our surroundings. To disappear in plain sight. So that we could sneak up behind a target and slit their throats or inject them with a drug that would stop their heart within a matter of seconds.

Beside me, the gate agent shifted on her feet. Glancing at

her counterpart stationed by the door. Then turning back to me, clearing her throat again.

"Sir, are you—"

I started away from the gate without a word. Setting the phone in its cradle. Snatching a pen off the stand and slipping it up the sleeve of my right arm. Still scanning the terminal. Clocking every face, every posture, every stride. Searching for any threat.

"Sir, your bag!"

I closed my eyes, took a deep breath. Turned back and flashed an embarrassed smile.

"Sorry. My mind's all over the place. That was my wife. There's been a death in the family. I won't be going on this flight, I'm afraid."

If the woman wondered why my supposed wife had called the gate phone instead of my mobile, she didn't ask. She played her part beautifully, empathy all at once blooming across her face.

"I'm sorry to hear that, sir. I'm not sure they'll be able to refund your ticket, though."

"Thank you," I said, grabbing my bag as I headed away.

When I was out of sight of the gate agent, I ditched the bag. Not the smartest thing to do in this post-9/11 world—somebody would notice it unattended and call for security, who might panic and send the bomb squad—but I had nothing of importance in the bag and it would only slow me down.

I spotted two cops coming my way, both in Las Vegas Metropolitan Police Department uniforms. They didn't look too vigilant, talking to each other. I caught only a snippet of their conversation—"The vice president didn't do anything wrong, I guarantee it"—and then I was past them, keeping my face tilted down as I scanned the people around me.

A man sipping coffee as he let the moving walkway ease him down the terminal. A woman paging through a magazine as she sat near her gate. An older man on a laptop, pecking away with only his index fingers.

I noted a few people watching the news on their phones. Word had already gotten out that Senator Harold Browne had been taken into custody. As I stepped past one man staring down at his iPhone, I caught a glimpse of the senator being escorted out of the Lucky Star, my old friend Adam Reed beside him.

I'd called Adam only days ago when I was in Los Angeles. Crouched in the quiet darkness of a private estate. Fingers squeezed into a fist. Doing everything I could to ignore that ever-present voice in my head telling me to kill.

Stop thinking of the past. Stay focused on the present. The here and now. Unless you want to get yourself killed.

I headed for the exit. If something were to go down, I didn't want to endanger the civilians here in the terminal.

I flashed on the young family I'd watched getting off a plane only fifteen minutes ago. The young boy who'd tripped and fell and his older brother who'd rushed back to help pick him up. I hadn't spotted the family since, and I didn't want to spot them again, especially if the team made themselves known. The last thing I wanted was for those two brothers to end up in the crossfire.

Shit, what crossfire? All you've got on you is an airline-branded ballpoint pen.

Fair, but I was skilled enough to do severe damage with a ballpoint pen. But so were the men hunting me. And something told me each and every one of them was armed with something more lethal than a black-inked Bic.

I spotted a door off to the side. EMPLOYEES ONLY, a sign on it read. Scanning the crowd around me once more, I vectored for the door, dropping the pen into the palm of my hand to get a solid grip.

Placing my other hand on the door handle, I paused.

Closed my eyes.

Took another deep breath.

Then opened the door and slipped inside and found myself staring at the muzzle of a pistol.

2

"Where is he going?"

In a control room over two thousand miles away, Mitchell Hargrave stared at the monitors along the wall. A half dozen LCD monitors, the size of sixty-inch flat-screen TVs, each showing the hacked security footage in real time from Harry Reid International Airport.

When nobody answered him, Hargrave gazed around the room.

"Well? Where the *fuck* is he going?"

His two techs—Theo and Julian—worked their computers as they tried to stay with Daniel Burke, who had left the gate he'd been waiting at and was headed . . . somewhere.

Standing in the corner was Samuel Chen, deputy director of the CIA, who'd been called in to supervise this op. Sitting in a chair in the other corner, eyes on a tablet, was Hargrave's number two, Rita Salazar.

Both Salazar and Chen looked over at him, but neither said a word.

Hargrave, trying to maintain his cool while gritting his teeth: "Will somebody fucking answer me?"

Theo, hands blurring across his keyboard, said, "We don't know. We're working on it."

"How about who called him? Have we determined that yet?"

Julian had been tasked with that detail. As soon as the female gate agent had handed Burke the phone, Hargrave had stepped forward, feeling his blood run cold.

It had been mere luck they'd managed to track Burke to the airport. Hargrave was still having a hard time believing the man was alive. In fact, at first he refused to believe it until he saw the evidence for himself—the fingerprint provided by the chairman of the Joint Chiefs of Staff. Then, last night, facial and gait recognition had identified Burke in the casino hotel Senator Harold Browne had been abducted from—which was why he'd immediately dispatched the team to Las Vegas. Then, less than an hour ago, Burke had been picked up again by security cameras as he entered Harry Reid International.

From the transmitter snug in his ear, Lucas Hancock spoke. "Control, what's the status?"

Hargrave said, "Alpha One, we're still tracking him through the terminal."

Another voice spoke up, this one belonging to Dennis Rowe. "Where the hell is he going?"

It took everything for Hargrave not to snap back at the operator. They were all used to working in highly tense situations, but this was different. Hunting one of their own . . . only, would Burke be considered one of their own since he'd faked his death a year ago?

Hargrave said, "Alpha Two, maintain your position. Does anyone have eyes on Alpha Three?"

Alpha Three being Noah LaSalle, whose transmitter had

been acting up, his communication going in and out. Hargrave had considered pulling him and sending him back out to the truck where Michael Kincaid was waiting, but there hadn't been any need: the plan right then was to ensure Burke got on the plane to Washington, DC, where he had a forty-minute layover before another plane flew him out of the country.

They wanted Burke on that plane, and now the man had left the gate behind and was headed only God knows where.

Hancock said, "I haven't seen Alpha Three in several minutes. Two, have you seen Three?"

Rowe: "No, Alpha One."

Hargrave asked, "Julian, have you had any luck yet tracing that call?"

The tech shook his head as he typed furiously at his computer.

"No, sir."

"That's fine. We'll figure it out later. Just don't lose him."

So far Theo had tracked Burke through the terminal, flipping over from one view to another to always keep him front and center. The man's eyes darting this way and that, searching for any danger. It wasn't clear if that was just Burke's natural instinct or if somebody had tipped him off.

Christ, of course somebody had tipped him off—that much was obvious to anybody in the room.

Hargrave said, "What's he doing now?"

Theo glanced up at the screens.

"It appears he's headed for a maintenance hallway."

Hargrave said, "What's the exact location? Alphas One and Two, you need to get there *now*."

3

My initial thought was wrong: the muzzle belonged to a silencer, which was attached to a pistol.

An HK VP9 Tactical, to be exact. Dark matte finish. At least ten nine-millimeter rounds in the mag. More than enough to do the trick.

Without any thought I batted the pistol aside, a bullet tearing into the wall near my head with a distinct *pfft*.

Gripping the pen tightly in my hand, the ballpoint ready to pierce flesh, I breathed, "What the fuck, Noah?"

The space here was tight, a utility hallway meant for employees, but right now it was just the two of us. Noah recalibrated his aim, but I grabbed his wrist to hold it in place, our noses now inches apart. He spoke without moving his lips.

"Security camera behind you. We need to make this look good. Punch me in the face."

I didn't need him to tell me twice. Dropping the pen and moving forward, my fist cracked against his jaw. He staggered back, and I stepped into him, grabbing his wrist and wrestling for the pistol.

As we grappled, I kept my face tilted away from the camera above the door.

"How many?"

Noah punched me on the side of the head with his other hand, though it wasn't with much force.

"Four counting myself."

Another punch.

"Who?"

Noah slammed me into the wall, kneed me in the stomach.

"Hancock, Rowe, and a new guy Kincaid."

Bent over, feigning pain, I snapped my head up and clipped the edge of his chin.

"He any good?"

Noah stumbled back, a hand to his face.

"He's a quiet son of a bitch. Has got a darkness in his eyes. A true killer for sure."

"How about back at The Office?"

Noah raised the pistol, and I spun into him, grabbing his wrist again and shoving him into the wall so that our backs were to the camera.

"The same team as before. Along with the deputy director of the CIA."

This last part gave me pause.

"The CIA's in on this?"

Elbowing Noah in the stomach with enough force to keel him over, I yanked the pistol from his grip, sent it skittering across the floor. I started for it, but Noah launched himself at me and we both hit the ground, hard.

Noah flipped me over, punched me in the face.

"Why'd you fake your death?"

"Long story."

"You didn't turn, did you?"

"Hell no."

Noah reached for the pistol. I shoved him into the wall, crawled on top of him, and placed my hands around his throat but didn't squeeze.

"Would they have really shot down the plane?"

"No, but I had to keep you from getting on it."

"Why?"

"The FBI plans to arrest you in DC."

With a strangled grunt, Noah bucked me off. I hit the wall. An elbow to the face, a shot to the groin, and the pistol was only inches away, both of us wrestling and stretching our arms, playing it up for Hargrave and everyone else watching back at The Office.

"Can't Control hear us?"

Noah shook his head as he clawed at my face.

"As soon as we got here, I started messing with my transmitter. It's been going in and out this entire time."

A gasp farther up the hallway. We both paused, looking up to find a janitor staring back at us.

I shouted, "Get the fuck out of here!" and the woman, wide-eyed, screeched and scurried away.

Noah, with blood dripping from his nose, said, "Quick, before the others get here, we need to end this."

His eyes slid toward his left arm.

"Break it."

"You sure?"

"No, but otherwise I won't be able to explain you getting away."

Another punch to the face while we rolled on the ground.

"Thanks, Noah."

"Just do me one favor."

"What's that?"

He clenched his teeth, already preparing for the pain as I grabbed his arm and braced it against my knee.

"Make it clean."

4

Despite the angle, the quality of the camera in the maintenance hallway was shit. Theo had managed to hack into it so they could watch Burke and LaSalle going at it. A series of punches, kicks, and elbow jabs, each man throwing the other into the wall, and then they were on the ground, both trying to reach for LaSalle's pistol.

"Alpha One, Alpha Two, where the *fuck* are you?"

Hancock: "Headed straight there, Control."

Rowe: "What's happening now?"

Hargrave said, "Alpha Three has engaged the target."

The plan had been for Burke to fly straight to DC, where FBI agents would already be waiting to take him into custody. It wasn't Hargrave's first choice, but this was a call made above his head, and after all, he was a good soldier who followed orders.

That was why the team had spread throughout the airport. No need to engage Burke or even get close enough for him to spot one of his old colleagues. The plan had been for him to proceed as if nothing was wrong. The only reason the team was there at all was to ensure he got on the goddamned plane, and if he didn't, to track down and subdue him.

But now everything had fallen apart. One of his men was getting the shit kicked out of him, and he could tell Samuel Chen wasn't happy—hell, Hargrave thought, join the fucking club—and Hargrave knew once this was all over he would get his ass chewed out.

Then again, it wasn't the first time and probably wouldn't be the last. Hargrave was fifty-four years old and had been playing this game most of his life. He knew when to nod and when to salute, and he knew when to keep his mouth shut, and he knew how to run successful missions, which was how he had lasted this long.

But this . . . this was turning into a complete shit show.

On the other monitors, Theo tracked Hancock and Rowe as they converged on the same location. Only they had to move swiftly, as though trying to catch a flight, and not full-out run as they didn't want to draw any undue attention. The last thing they needed was for one of the airport cops to stop them. They'd gotten onto the grounds through a side exit, which was how they'd managed to bring their weapons, because his team never went anywhere without being armed.

Which right now made Hargrave worried they might lose LaSalle because of it.

Suddenly Rita Salazar cried out, breaking him from his trance.

"Jesus Christ!"

Hargrave's eyes snapped up to the screens. Burke was climbing to his feet, his back to the camera, mostly obscuring LaSalle. Hargrave wasn't sure the reason for Salazar's reaction at first until Burke stepped over Alpha Three, and he felt his stomach drop.

Burke had broken the man's arm.

What's more, Burke was right now picking up LaSalle's pistol. Standing up straight. Walking back to LaSalle and turning to him so that his back was once again to the camera.

In Hargrave's ear, he suddenly heard Alpha Three's voice, raked with static.

LaSalle saying, "You're a piece of shit, you know that?"

And Burke, without a word, raised the pistol.

Then the distinct and throaty cough of a suppressed slug being fired.

5

Unscrewing the sound suppressor from the HK's threaded barrel and slipping it into my sport coat pocket, I secured the pistol in my waistband. A second's hesitation and I scooped up the pen from the floor as I continued toward the door.

It had been only a minute since that janitor appeared around the corner, and it wasn't a stretch to think that she'd already contacted security. This area was going to be a circus in a matter of minutes. Maybe seconds.

Stepping back into the terminal, I scanned for Lucas Hancock and Dennis Rowe. Both good men I'd worked with for years. I wouldn't call them friends—I wouldn't even call Noah LaSalle a friend—but they were men I trusted, at least as far as I could trust men who killed others for a living.

What they were, first and foremost, were soldiers who did what they were told, and based on what Noah said, they had been told to ensure I got on my plane. And now that I hadn't? There was no telling what their directive might be.

An airport terminal is always busy in the late morning,

especially in a city like Vegas. People coming and going—businessmen and couples and families, a group of college-aged kids wearing snapbacks—but still I didn't spot Hancock or Rowe.

I started toward the main exit when the heavy pounding of rubber-soled shoes headed my way. A half dozen airport security and three police officers, all of them sprinting.

I turned away to gaze at the drink menu of a nearby kiosk, carefully wiping at my nose and face. Neither of us had been throwing hard punches, but we'd needed to make it look good for the folks back in DC, so it wasn't surprising when my fingers came away with some blood.

Grabbing a handful of napkins, I quickly dabbed my face. Not a lot of blood, but still. I tossed the soiled napkins in a trash can and continued on—and immediately spotted Lucas Hancock.

Early forties, tall, muscular. Dressed in jeans, tennis shoes, and a light jacket that helped conceal his firearm. He was twenty feet away. Our eyes met, and for a moment we didn't do anything but just stare at each other.

Lucas's eyes were hard and flat, his jaw tight.

He mouthed, *You fucking killed Noah.*

I shook my head, then caught movement past Hancock.

Dennis Rowe quickly approaching.

Loud voices rose behind me down the terminal, with someone shouting for an ambulance, and now everybody was looking to see what all the fuss was about, even those hunkered down at the slot machines dotted around the concourse.

Everybody except me and my two old colleagues.

Like Hancock, Rowe had murder in his eyes. He started moving at an angle, positioning himself so that he was on my right, Hancock on my left.

I said, "Fancy seeing you fellas here."

Dennis Rowe growled exactly what Hancock had mouthed at me.

"You fucking killed Noah."

Before I could say anything, Rowe charged forward. The bright lights in the terminal flashed off the knife in his hand. He came at me fast, slicing the blade through the air. I dodged the knife and threw my elbow into the side of his face.

Meanwhile, Hancock had started forward, though he was in no hurry. That's why he'd been assigned as Alpha One. Our leader. Our point man. Always cool under pressure. Always calculating every move, every contingency, so that he didn't make a mistake.

Others nearby noticed the scuffle. A woman shouted. A man, filming the crowd of cops with his phone, spun to start filming us.

Rowe twisted around, slicing the blade again, the edge sharp enough to tear through my sport coat and shirt and meet flesh.

I thought, *Fuck this*, and grabbed for the pistol in my waistband, aimed it skyward, and fired three rounds.

Absolute chaos.

Everyone started screaming and shouting and racing away, diving behind kiosks and slot machines, and all the cops and security down the terminal spun around at the sound.

Hancock had already been reaching for his gun. Like Noah's, it had a sound suppressor attached to the barrel. But in the heat of the moment the cops didn't realize that the three shots that had just rung out were way too loud to have been issued from a silencer.

The pistol now concealed behind my back, I pointed at Lucas Hancock and shouted, "He's got a gun!"

More screams and shouting. Several of the cops hustled forward, drawing their sidearms. Their focus on Hancock and the pistol still in his hand as I'd already dropped the HK into the nearest trash can.

Now pointing at Rowe, I shouted, "And he's got a knife!"

People started running away, and I joined them, glancing over my shoulder as I fled toward the nearest exit.

The last thing I saw before I rounded the corner was Lucas Hancock—Mr. Alpha One himself—raising his arms high as a half dozen cops swarmed in on his location.

6

"He's alive."

Mitchell Hargrave's face snapped up at Theo's words. He'd been standing for most of the op, but after watching Daniel Burke shoot Alpha Three, he'd felt all the energy drain out of him and had plopped down in his chair. The rest of the team heard what had happened, and he knew what they would do next. All of them—at least the two who had known Burke—already feeling betrayed that the man had faked his death. And now knowing that Burke had murdered one of their own?

"What are you talking about?" he asked, rising to his feet.

One of the screens still showed the hallway, though it had been overrun by security and police, making it nearly impossible to see Noah LaSalle's body. But now two of the security officers had stepped away, giving them a clear view of Noah being helped up.

Samuel Chen turned to Hargrave.

"Call your men off."

"What?"

"Your men!" Samuel shouted, pointing at the screens.

Now that the police had shown up, people had stopped to see what was going on. Ever since 9/11, whenever there's heavy police presence in an airport, it always gives people pause. But Hargrave spotted Lucas Hancock and Dennis Rowe, expertly threading through the crowd.

Right toward Daniel Burke.

Within seconds, Rowe surreptitiously pulled a knife from his pocket.

Samuel Chen said, "We need Burke alive."

Watching the screens, wetting lips, Hargrave said, "Alpha One, Alpha Two—stand down."

If either operator heard him, they didn't acknowledge it. Dennis Rowe didn't slow, engaging the target with his knife, and before they all realized it Burke had pulled out a pistol and fired three bullets into the air.

A stampede ensued. People running everywhere, including Daniel Burke, who was doing what he'd been trained to do: becoming one with the crowd, blending in, disappearing. Meanwhile, security and airport police had their weapons drawn and were approaching Alphas One and Two.

Hargrave turned to Rita Salazar.

"Contact whoever you need to contact at the airport. Tell them that those men are undercover and that nothing better happen to them."

Samuel Chen said, "Your team is unsanctioned."

Hargrave wanted to laugh out loud.

"Do you think the fucking police know that?"

Chen's face was expressionless, his eyes dark.

"You've lost the target."

Hargrave gritted his teeth. He shook his head and watched as Hancock and Rowe were forced to the ground and cuffed.

He said, "Alpha Four, do you read me?"

Michael Kincaid's eerily calm voice came through the transmitter in his ear.

"Copy."

"The target is headed toward your location. Do not let him get away."

7

Before I broke Noah's arm, he told me to take the gun with me—to stand over him with my back to the camera and fire off a single round by his head. The reason, he said, was because otherwise it might seem suspect that the one and only Daniel Burke wouldn't outright eliminate someone who he knew was hunting him.

I hadn't thought about it much at the time—only seconds had passed, and I knew other, less friendly operators were headed my way—but I'd agreed and fired a bullet at the floor a few inches from Noah's head.

Now, minutes later, I had become one with the crowd. But the crowd was chaotic, with many people shoving past others, causing some to stumble and fall, while airport staff tried to funnel people in one direction and asked everyone to stay calm.

An old lady with a cane had fallen to the ground, and I paused long enough with another man to help her back to her feet. Then spotted the family from earlier, the husband and wife and two boys: the younger one being carried by the father, the kid crying, his face buried in his father's chest, and it hit me for a second how he would probably remember this fear for the rest of his life.

Then I was outside, streaming through the doors along with everyone else, and the drivers of the cars and taxis caught in the sudden melee looked out in confusion.

Where to now?

I had no transportation. The BMW M3 had been confiscated by the police after I'd left it in the desert a mile away from the Hacienda with Olivia in the trunk. There was the Ford Taurus I'd left in the storage facility where I'd kept the M3 this past year. The thing was a piece of junk, but it still worked, though I no longer had the key to get into the storage unit. Plus, since I'd burned the ID used to purchase that unit, it wasn't like I could plead my case with an employee to grant me access.

I still had an apartment just outside Los Angeles where I'd been staying this past year. A one-bedroom that was crazy expensive but which I'd used as my base of operations between visits to Vegas. I still had a few months left on the lease and could hole up there, though there was no telling whether the people hunting me already knew about the place.

My first impulse was to call Teddy. Ask her just what the fuck was going on. Why she hadn't given me a heads-up.

But not yet. Not now. Not while I was still part of a fleeing crowd that didn't know where to go, only that they had to keep running for their lives.

I started toward a couple of taxis, but other people reached them first, diving into the back seats and shouting at the drivers to go. Only the drivers couldn't get far, not with everyone flooding outside, and the disorder was so mesmerizing—a living sea of frantic bodies— that I didn't notice him approaching until it was almost too late.

Kincaid. I recognized the guy at once. Noah had described

him as a quiet son of a bitch with a darkness in his eyes, a true killer for sure, and that fit the man heading my way to a T.

Unlike everyone else, who was either running away in fear or watching in confusion, this man's expression—his entire demeanor—was ice-cold. Standing at least six feet tall, weighing about 260 pounds, with a buzzed head and dark eyes zeroed in on me.

I was conscious of everyone around us—especially the children—and didn't want anyone to get caught in the crossfire.

Except I'd ditched the VP9 back inside, meaning there would be no crossfire if the man decided to pull a pistol and let loose.

The sky was clear, the morning sun stretching a flurry of shadows. I headed toward the right, trying to separate myself from the crowd.

Kincaid easily followed in my direction.

Maybe, I thought, I could outrun him. Make it to a taxi not caught in the endless flow of fleeing bodies and dart out of there.

But before I knew it Kincaid was on top of me. Despite the man's size, he moved like a breeze. I turned back just in time to see him right behind me.

One of his meaty hands morphed into a vice around my throat.

Shoving me up against the wall with so much force that my feet dangled a few inches above the ground.

I attempted to knee him in the groin, but if I managed to make contact, the man didn't show it. He didn't even flinch. I tried using both hands to pry his iron grip off my neck, but no luck. Then I started swinging with my left hand, smashing my fist against the side of his head, but it barely fazed him.

Those dark eyes, staring right back at me. No emotion at all. A true killer for sure.

But the eyes widened, just a bit, when I drove the tip of the ballpoint pen through his cheek.

His grip loosened enough that I touched the ground again, and I crouched down and planted both feet against the wall to drive myself forward into this unholy monument made of flesh.

Kincaid stumbled, tripped, and fell to the ground.

But like before, he was barely fazed. Slowly sitting up like he was Michael fucking Myers after being thrown out of a second-story window, he glared back at me, the tail end of the pen dangling from the side of his face.

I didn't stick around to watch him pull the pen out. Or stand up. Or try to put his bear trap of a grip around my throat again. I scrambled away. Conscious of all the security cameras stationed everywhere. Knowing that techs back in DC were right now hacking into the security feeds to track my movements.

So I kept my face tilted down and tried not to walk like myself so that gait recognition wouldn't pick me up, and when I spotted a discarded baseball cap on the ground I scooped it up and set it on my head while at the same time slipping the sport coat off and trashing it in the nearest bin, and soon I came across a taxi and climbed into the back, and when the driver asked me what the hell was going on inside the airport, I told him to drive, to drive, to just motherfucking drive.

8

Samuel Chen stepped up next to Hargrave, spoke in a quiet voice.

"May I see you in the hallway?"

Hargrave stared at the screens as his two techs did everything they could to trace where Daniel Burke had gone. They'd watched the scuffle outside between Burke and Kincaid, then watched Burke hurry away after he'd jammed—what was it, a small knife?—into the operator's face, and then . . . *poof*: gone.

He blinked and gazed at the CIA man, then glanced over at Rita Salazar with a phone to her ear, speaking with someone at the airport.

"What is it?" Hargrave said. "Whatever you have to say, you can say it in front of my people."

"Hallway," Samuel Chen repeated, then turned and exited through the only door in the room.

To save face, Hargrave didn't follow immediately, instead crossing his arms as he gazed again at the screens. Five minutes had passed since Burke disappeared, but for somebody like Burke, five minutes was all he needed. Part of his training was to blend into his surroundings, disappear into a crowd, and with the airport still in a frenzy it wasn't surprising the man had managed to ghost so quickly.

The only question was, how long would it take them to pick up his trail again?

Salazar finished her call and approached Hargrave.

"Want me to come with you?"

Still staring at the monitors, Hargrave shook his head.

"No. Keep an eye on the op. What did the head of security say?"

"He's a bit pissed we didn't give him and his people advance warning, but when I reiterated it was for national security purposes, he agreed to play ball. Either way, Alphas One and Two are being taken away for show but will be released soon."

"What about Alpha Three?"

"Same, though they're having a nurse put a splint on his arm first."

Something about this made Hargrave frown—a missing piece he couldn't quite grasp—but he nodded and turned and stepped out into the corridor where Samuel Chen was waiting, thumbing at his phone.

This building was one of a handful of top secret locations throughout DC in which operations were conducted. They were two floors down, and above them was a three-story office complex whose workers had no idea that unsanctioned ops were run out of a dark room several floors below.

Hargrave folded his arms over his chest, injected just the right amount of irritation into his tone.

"What is it?"

Samuel Chen eyed him with disdain. For over a decade now Hargrave and his team had operated independently, without oversight from any official agency. That right there had brought on some resentment, and the only saving grace Hargrave and his team had was that they were always successful with their missions.

Well, except for last year, when they'd lost Daniel Burke and Hargrave had had no choice but to call in a series of drone strikes, because the enemy finding Burke's body would cause even more of a headache than trying to explain how several Hellfire missiles had inadvertently destroyed a building.

Now the deputy director had been brought in because the CIA had claimed a bounty on Daniel Burke's head. For the past year, it hadn't been a problem because the entire world had believed the man was dead. But now that he wasn't, the CIA wanted a scalp.

The CIA officially has no law enforcement function, especially within the United States. So that was where Hargrave and his team came in. They were the ones that veered outside the prewritten lines, doing their work in the shadows so that any and all government agencies could claim total deniability if and when the time came. Many of their missions were so secretive oftentimes the president wasn't even aware.

Samuel Chen said, "You are so fucked."

The vexation in the man's voice surprised Hargrave. Since he'd arrived at the start of this op, Chen hadn't said more than two dozen words.

"Excuse me?"

"You heard me, Mitchell. You and your team had one simple task: ensuring Burke got on the goddamn plane."

"Our task was to ensure Burke returns to DC, and that is still going to happen."

"That remains to be seen. But my boss? He's not happy right now. Neither is the FBI."

Folding his arms, Hargrave took a step toward the man who was two inches shorter than him. Chen held his ground, his dark eyes gazing up at Hargrave. Not cowed in the slightest.

"This is my op," Hargrave said. "And it's over when I say it's over."

"You lost the target."

"We haven't lost shit."

"Two of your men have been injured. One is probably headed to the hospital as we speak."

"Nobody's headed to the hospital," Hargrave said, his voice tight, but then all at once something occurred to him.

Without a word, he turned away from Chen and headed back into the control room.

Salazar was standing behind the two techs, staring at the screens as Theo and Julian continued to search for Daniel Burke with the available security and traffic cams at their disposal.

She said, "We still haven't found the target yet."

Hargrave sensed Samuel Chen stepping into the room behind him. Ignoring the man, his focus now on the screens, he crossed his arms.

"That's fine. I know exactly where he's headed."

9

The taxi dropped me off on the Strip, right across from the Bellagio, where I'd stayed only a week ago under the name Stephen Walker. My seventh time coming to this town with various aliases, searching for a scam I wasn't sure existed—until one morning I woke up in room 247 of the Lucky Star Hotel & Casino with a supposed dead woman in the bathtub.

I headed into the Miracle Mile Shops, which I'd run through last week, being chased by a detective who was now dead. Keeping my face tilted low and ambling with a limp so that gait recognition didn't pick me up on any feeds. I figured by now Hargrave and his crew were hacking into every security camera in Las Vegas, and I didn't want to make it easy for them.

In one of the shops I purchased a fitted Raiders hat; in another shop I grabbed jeans and a hoodie sweatshirt; and in another shop I picked up sneakers and left some of the paper in the right shoe to help with the limp. Then I secured two new burners, because while my iPhone was encrypted and there should be no way for The Office to track it, there was no telling just how much surveillance capabilities had advanced in the past year.

I should have already tossed the phone, but I needed to make a call first, because already I was running through the different possibilities. If Noah was to be believed, I wasn't entirely sure why the FBI wanted to take me into custody, but now that their plan had fallen apart, they would be looking for other ways to get to me.

And the truth was, I had no family. Not anymore. My brother, James, killed himself nearly two years ago after coming to Las Vegas. He'd met a beautiful woman at a nightclub, thought he was having the time of his life, and then the next morning woke up in a hotel room that wasn't his to find that very same woman dead in the bathtub. And what did my brother do? He didn't run, didn't panic. He called hotel security to report what happened because (I'd like to think) deep down he knew he'd done nothing wrong and that everything would be sorted out once it was all said and done.

But the head of hotel security—a guy named Ryan Fisher—had been in on the scam. He'd contacted two police detectives who came to look at the crime scene and convinced my brother that this was something they could overlook . . . only if he were willing to part with his entire life savings.

I'd like to think James refused at first. That he shook his head adamantly and told the detectives he wasn't going to do that. My big brother—who had always been there when I was younger, who stepped between me and our father when our old man was on a tear—being a decent, honorable man.

But the detectives had convinced him he had no other choice, not if he didn't want to spend the rest of his life in prison. So he agreed to give up his life savings, then went back home where he immediately regretted the decision, thinking only about that young woman and how her family would forever wonder who had murdered her.

Around that time, James had fired off his first email, asking me to call him. He'd sent it to my encrypted email, the one I rarely used. In fact, my brother was pretty much the only person in the world who knew the address.

I remember receiving that email. Sensing something was wrong. And then immediately recalling a lunch with him two months prior: a ritzy place near Rittenhouse Square, the two of us sitting near the bar, James ordering the maple plank–roasted salmon. How while my brother had seemed off at first his mood had shifted after the first fifteen minutes, and we had a great time, drinking bottles of Yuengling and telling stories and jokes, and then James went and brought up our father and how he'd been feeling guilty about how we as boys hadn't done anything when our father lumbered up the stairs that night to beat the shit out of us and suffered a massive heart attack, the kind that seized his entire body and felled him like a giant tree.

So I ignored my brother's initial email, just as I'd ignored the second one when he asked again for me to contact him, saying that it was important. Eventually, I figured, I would respond. Tell him that this was an account I rarely checked. After all, I was often traveling. Or at least that's what James believed, not really knowing what I did for work, only that it had something to do with consulting for the government, which was a fancy roundabout way of saying that I worked as an unsanctioned killer.

But then the third email came in. The one laying out what had taken place during his trip to Vegas. James told me he couldn't live with himself for what he finally accepted he'd done. How it wasn't fair to that young woman's family. The knowledge of her death would haunt him forever, so he felt he had no choice but to take his own life.

I'd been on a mission in Hungary at the time, having just completed a task that Mitchell Hargrave assured us would protect our country. Our team had completed the op and we'd boarded a Boeing C-17 Globemaster III headed back to the States. With nothing else to do, I checked my email because part of me was curious if James was going to bother emailing a third time or whether he'd gotten the hint that I still didn't want to talk to him.

And I'd seen what he'd written to me.

What was essentially his suicide note.

As soon as we landed, I flew to Pennsylvania. By then my brother's body had already been found. Someone he worked with at the foundation grew concerned when he had missed several meetings, and when James hadn't answered their calls, they'd stopped by his apartment, thinking maybe he was sick. And when there was no answer, they tracked down the super to let them into the apartment—where they found my brother lying dead on his bed, having downed an entire bottle of sleeping pills.

Now as I exited the mall, the bright sun even higher in the pale-blue sky, the fronds from the palm trees lining the sidewalk shivering in the late-morning breeze, I called Teddy—and got her voicemail.

"Call me as soon as you can."

Rattling off one of the burner's numbers, I disconnected, was ready to remove the iPhone's SIM card and snap it in half before smashing the phone for good measure.

But then I closed my eyes. Took a slow, deep breath.

Whispered, "Shit."

I may no longer have any family, but there was still somebody in my life I cared about. Somebody whom I'd known when I was a boy and whom I hadn't seen in nearly twenty years. Somebody who had told me only a few days ago that she never wanted to see me again.

The Office would be looking for anything that might draw me out of the shadows, and the truth was I'd done it before—when Stephanie Nguyen had been held hostage, I'd come to her aid. I hadn't even hesitated.

Of course, there was a chance Hargrave and his team might not know about Stephanie—and even if they did there was a chance they wouldn't bother touching her—but I doubted it.

Because I'd been trained by these people. I knew exactly how they thought. I knew exactly what they would do when they had no other options.

Dialing her number, I placed the phone to my ear.

10

Stephanie Nguyen was five hours into her eight-hour shift and was already exhausted.

She hadn't been sleeping well, her dreams haunted by Detective Jared Sutton and how he'd so easily slipped into her home that terrible night to take her hostage. How he'd forced her to sit at the kitchen table with a cloth bag draped over her head for what felt like hours. How he'd pressed the barrel of his gun under her chin like it was the most natural thing in the world.

That man—that awful, despicable man—had been killed right in front of her, his body laid out on the kitchen floor like a prop, his blood seeping along the grout lines in the tiles.

She had wanted to call the police, knowing that it was the right thing to do, but Danny had convinced her otherwise. Telling her that contacting the police would only make things worse. Giving her some line about how powerful people were involved and that if she called the police it would bring her to their attention.

At the time, she'd believed him, too overwhelmed by everything that had happened, allowing him to take the man's dead body away and clean up the kitchen, and then that was that. Her house had always felt empty since her ex-fiancé left, and now it felt even emptier—like a black hole, sucking in everything around it.

Stephanie had begun to wonder whether she should take some time off. Maybe stay with her father in Pennsylvania for a few days. Or fly to Hawaii—she hadn't been there since Adrian had proposed, getting down on one knee on that beach in Olowalu as the sun set, that yellowish-red glow shimmering off the ocean. For some reason she'd felt like her relationship with him had spoiled the place, but she shouldn't let something like that hold her back. She should reclaim it, make it her own.

Hell, she could go anywhere—part of her had always wanted to travel the world, feel a bit more adventurous, not so stuck in the rut of everyday life—but she also knew that wasn't going to happen.

Why?

Because Stephanie Nguyen had always played it safe. She never did anything impulsive, never took a chance. Some might say this made her boring while others—like herself—would say it made her practical.

Maybe she should call the police, tell them exactly what happened. How Detective Jared Sutton and a computer hacker named Eugene had broken into her house late Sunday morning. How they'd held her captive so that Danny would be forced to return.

Stephanie would be lying if, while sitting at the kitchen table with that cloth bag over her head, the thought hadn't crossed her mind that maybe Danny wouldn't come back for her. After all, they'd only known each other briefly a long, long time ago. Back when she was in high school, when she was dating James Burke—only then he'd been going by Jimmy.

Jimmy and Danny, brothers who were polar opposites, what with Jimmy being outgoing and kind, and Danny . . . well, Stephanie remembered him being mostly shy. Or maybe that was only around her—she hadn't seen him much outside the home setting, and why would she? Danny was four years younger than Jimmy and in middle school, so of course Stephanie wouldn't have had much interaction with him outside the few times she'd seen him at the house.

And then one night last week Danny showed up out of nowhere as she was leaving work. He'd been shot, had a wound in his back, and asked her to help patch it up. At the time, she had wanted him to go to the ER, had wanted to call the police, but he had convinced her otherwise. Even now, she wasn't sure how he'd managed that. Just like later, when he'd told her about the woman he had tied up in the trunk of his car and how he needed to interrogate her (a woman named Olivia, who had helped mastermind so many horrible, vile things), somehow Danny made her see how it was the only—

"Knock, knock."

The voice was accompanied by a rap of knuckles on the desk, and Stephanie startled, blinking and looking up to find Patrick Casey standing in front of her.

A tall, fit man with short red hair, he was young and handsome and kind. He had asked her out a few months ago, but she'd come up with some excuse to decline and since then he hadn't asked again, probably figuring the ball was now in her court.

"How are you doing, Dr. Nguyen? You look . . . distracted."

A nice word for *tired* or *exhausted*. She'd looked at herself long and hard in the mirror this morning, debating whether the bags under her eyes had gotten worse. Wondering how much longer she could manage to act like nothing was wrong. And then once again hesitantly going downstairs, worried more strangers might be lurking around the corners, and then taking an ultrabright flashlight and shining it all over the kitchen floor, searching for any traces of blood even though she'd searched every day for the past several days.

"Didn't get much sleep last night," Stephanie said because she felt she had to say something.

Patrick Casey was one of the police officers stationed at the hospital. He was nearly a decade younger than her and was handsome enough to get any girl he wanted, but for some reason he always tried flirting with her on those rare occasions she wasn't busy. And, honestly, this wasn't one of those times. She'd just seen a patient who was presenting with abdominal pain—the second time the patient had been in here with the same issue this month—and had been typing up her notes when she drifted, once again thinking about the sudden clap of the gunshot in her kitchen and Detective Sutton's body holding her in place jerking as the bullet tore off the side of his head.

For one crazy, delirious second, she considered asking Patrick if he knew Detective Jared Sutton. She imagined he did. She'd even seen the detective's name pop up on the news, how authorities were looking for him in connection to the place out in the desert called the Hacienda. Abducting women and selling them to the highest bidder. When Stephanie had heard that woman Olivia say that, she'd nearly bitten off her tongue in rage.

Patrick said, "How about some coffee? I can head out to the lobby and get you one. My treat."

Maybe she should go out with Patrick. She hadn't really dated anyone since Adrian broke off their engagement. Which had been, what, two years now? Sure, she'd gone out on a few dates here and there—usually those that were set up by friends, because even now the apps scared her, the idea that somebody would take only a few seconds to glance at her picture on a screen and decide whether to swipe left or right.

"Thanks," she said, meaning it, "but I already had coffee. Don't want to get too much caffeine in my system, you know?"

She smiled, hoping he would smile too. Which he did—a warm smile, a kind smile—and he nodded and said he'd see her around and drifted away, and Stephanie diverted her attention back to her computer, which had been idling long enough for the screen saver to pop up.

Stephanie went to jiggle the mouse to wake the screen when her phone vibrated in her pocket. An incoming call.

She slipped the phone out, wondering who could possibly be calling her, when her heart rocketed up into her throat.

There wasn't any name on the screen because she hadn't bothered saving one, but she recognized the number.

Danny.

What the hell was this?

The last thing she'd told him was that she never wanted to see him again. Even after he'd removed the detective's body, after he'd cleaned up the kitchen, she hadn't said one word to him. Only closed the door behind him and locked it. And then couldn't sleep for the past several nights.

The phone was still vibrating, and without any conscious thought, she tapped the button to cancel it.

For a second or two, the phone was blessedly silent and still. Then it started vibrating again.

Again she declined the call.

She realized she should block the number and even started to do so when her phone vibrated once more, only this time with a series of text messages.

> Stephanie

> Please call me

> Your life is in danger

11

Déjà vu.

That's what it felt like.

Being back at the same hospital where I'd come a week ago, though then it had been by the cover of night after a shoot-out at a nightclub and a high-speed chase which resulted in Allister Martin's Escalade flipping over. I'd stayed in this very same parking garage, slumped low in the M3, feeling the dull burn of a bullet wound in my back as I watched hospital employees coming and going until, finally, I spotted her.

Had my brother not looked up Stephanie Nguyen—his old high school sweetheart—after his divorce, I would never have known she lived and worked in the same city I'd come to in search of my prey.

James had drafted an email to her, noting that he would be visiting Vegas for a few days and asking if she wanted to get together. An innocuous enough request, just one old friend checking in to see if another was free to meet for coffee, but in the end James hadn't sent the email. Why, I had no idea, though

I pictured my brother hunched over his laptop, typing the email out, hovering the cursor over the Send button but then deciding not to pull the trigger. At least not yet. Give it another day or two to think it over and make sure it was the right thing to do.

When Stephanie had asked me how I'd tracked her down, I'd finally told her it was because of James. How James had written her that email, which I later found when I went through his things, as James had left his entire life savings (or what was left of it after his fateful trip to Vegas) to his foundation but had bequeathed the rest of his belongings—all his books and vinyl records and vintage turntable—to me.

I'd found the email and wondered why my brother hadn't sent it, then imagined what might have happened had he clicked Send. How maybe Stephanie would have replied. How maybe they would have gotten together for lunch. How maybe they would have caught up after two decades, both of them nervous at first, feeling awkward, but after a while falling back into that familiar rhythm, like a needle finding its groove.

I don't think anything would have come from their lunch—nothing romantic, at least, besides maybe a hug and peck on the cheek—but maybe they'd promise to stay in touch, exchanging emails every once in a while, even following each other on social media, and when Stephanie visited her father in Pennsylvania she would hit James up and they'd meet again for drinks or dinner, and who knows, maybe that spark that had been there when they were teenagers would light again.

But James hadn't sent the email. He had come to Vegas without telling anyone except me, his little brother, who had bailed on him. James hadn't met with Stephanie, so instead he'd drowned his sorrows along the Strip, spending more money than he probably should have, gambling and ordering expensive meals and drinks, which had caught the eye of the wrong people.

Would James have become a mark had he sent that email and met with Stephanie during his trip?

Impossible to say.

What was possible to say is that had I agreed to go with my brother from the start, he never would have woken up in room 247 of the Lucky Star, and he never would have taken his life.

"Stop it," I whispered, and then gazed around the parking garage to ensure nobody had heard me. Posted up in the stairwell on the third level, the same level where Stephanie had parked her Honda CR-V. Glancing down at my phone every time somebody came up or down the steps, shouldering past me without bothering to wonder what I was doing there.

After speaking with Stephanie—after convincing her that her life was in fact in danger, as the people hunting me would most likely come for her, just as Jared Sutton and Eugene had done only days ago—she finally agreed to meet.

But she said she was in the middle of a shift and couldn't just leave as she was still dealing with patients, though she thought she might be able to wrap up shortly, telling everyone that she wasn't feeling well. So I'd hopped in another taxi and hurried north, having the driver drop me off four blocks away, and I'd meandered for a bit to evade the street cams before entering the parking garage and scaling each level until I'd found the familiar CR-V.

Then I texted her:

I'm here

A few seconds had ticked by before she responded:

OK, leaving soon.

And that had been five minutes ago. Five long minutes that gave Hargrave and his team time to pick up my trail.

I knew the team well, especially the techs, Theo and Julian. They were good. Great, even. The kid who'd called himself the Spider—Eugene—had been a decent hacker, but he came nowhere close to those two.

Nowhere close to Teddy, who I had still yet to hear from.

I was starting to grow impatient, wanting to text her again to ask for an ETA, when my phone buzzed with an incoming call.

Stephanie.

"Where are you?" I asked, and for a second there was complete silence.

Then I heard her unsteady voice, quiet and full of fear.

"Those guys you told me about? I think . . . I think they're already here."

12

Hurrying down the steps, taking them two at a time. Almost barreling into a family as they rounded the corner but managing to twist out of the way at the last second to avoid a collision. The phone to my ear, my grip tight.

"Where are you now?"

Silence again, but only for another second. Her voice, still a shaky whisper.

"I . . . I'm down a hallway."

"Which hallway?"

"I left the ER. Started for an exit. But I . . . I thought I noticed someone following me, so I went in a different direction. And he's still following me."

Sprinting out of the parking garage into the midday sun. Scanning the area for police or anything that looked out of place. Then starting forward toward the hospital's main entrance.

"Where are you?"

Her voice, somehow even quieter.

"I told you, I'm in a hallway."

"*Which* hallway?"

"Heading toward Radiology."

Through the automatic sliding doors, suddenly conscious of the somber atmosphere every hospital contains. Slowing my pace, scanning now for security. Noting the people lined up to check in, to ask questions. My eyes skimming over the signs pointing toward different departments: Cardiology, Neurology, Pediatrics, Oncology.

There—Radiology, to the left.

Vectoring down the hallway, the phone still pressed to my ear. Trying not to draw attention. Aware that I didn't have any weapons on my person but not caring.

"I'm heading to Radiology now. Are you still being followed?"

"Hold on."

Pause.

"Yes, he's still following me."

Her words, spiked with panic.

"Is security around?"

"I don't . . . I don't see anyone."

"Is there a waiting room nearby? Go to it. Sit in the middle of the room."

"Will that . . . will that help?"

Hard to say, but right now I didn't see any other option.

"What does he look like, Stephanie?"

"He . . . he's tall."

"White, Black, Hispanic?"

"He . . . he's white."

I wanted to ask more questions—get a better picture of who was following her, whether I could match that description to Lucas Hancock or Dennis Rowe—but a gurney appeared in front of me, being wheeled around the corner by an orderly, and I almost collided with it.

"Stephanie, where are you now?"

"I just passed Radiology."

The sign coming up said Radiology was down the next hallway on the left.

I sprinted then, not caring who noticed, and rounded the corner.

No sign of Stephanie.

"I'm outside Radiology. Where are you?"

Even more fearful panic in her voice.

"I told you; I passed it. Oh Jesus, he's getting closer. I don't—"

The line went dead.

Rushing forward, glancing at the screen, punching the button to call her back. Straight to voicemail.

Phone still in my hand, I kept moving forward. Glancing back over my shoulder. Deciding how to handle this. If Hancock or Rowe or that large fuck Kincaid were here, they wouldn't be alone.

And I still didn't have a weapon.

Doors along the bright hallway, all of them closed. An exit at the very end.

I spun around, wondering if I'd overshot wherever Stephanie had gone.

That's when I heard a scream.

Muffled and hoarse.

Spinning back around, I raced down the hallway.

Right to the door leading into a stairwell.

Barreling forward without any thought for my own safety, the door banged open to reveal Stephanie standing near the exit door, just past the stairs.

Her shoulders squared to me. Her face, blank. No fear at all in her eyes.

"Stephanie?"

That's when two police officers stepped out from behind the stairs, sidearms already drawn.

Skidding to a halt, I started to backpedal but realized two other officers had materialized in the doorway behind me.

One of the officers by the stairs—a young guy with bright red hair, his name badge reading CASEY—held up a calming hand.

"Whoa there. Slow down, buddy. We don't want any trouble."

None of the officers moved. Their feet planted on the shiny linoleum floor. The barrels of their sidearms dipped low.

I took a step forward, and the same officer shouted.

"That's it—freeze!"

As if choreographed, four sets of department-issued Glocks rose to aim at me. Two ahead, two behind. Each officer standing at least ten feet away. Too much distance to try to rush even one of them, to overpower him and take his weapon.

Officer Casey said, "The lady asked you nicely not to bother her anymore. But you just couldn't help yourself, could you?"

I stared past the cop at Stephanie. Still no expression on her face. Her eyes, dark steel.

I wanted to tell her she had this all wrong. That her life was really in danger. That she was only making things worse.

Officer Casey lifted his chin at me.

"Do us a favor, bud. Get down on your knees and place your hands on the back of your head."

Déjà vu again. Only it had been Detectives Sutton and Ortiz putting me in handcuffs after chasing me from the Bellagio. Two men who had been part of a criminal conspiracy. Not at all like these four officers, who I knew were good men simply doing their job.

For an instant, I realized how I could play this. Lowering myself onto my knees, threading my fingers together on the back of my head. Waiting patiently for the officers to approach. And then, as the one started to clip on the first handcuff, making my move. Twisting and grabbing his wrist. Springing to my feet and yanking him in front of me as a shield. Taking his gun and pressing the barrel against the side of his head. Forcing the other officers to give up their sidearms with the threat that I would kill him. Then grabbing Stephanie and making a run for it.

Or—once again feeling that darkness deep inside me, yearning to kill—shooting all four men in the head as soon as I'd gained possession of one of their Glocks. Four shots. Four easy squeezes of the trigger. Not hesitating once to take four innocent lives.

I blinked and looked past Officer Casey again at Stephanie.

As though reading my thoughts, she slowly shook her head.

All at once something changed. That desire to survive and kill suddenly dissipated. The primal instinct of fight or flight stripped from my DNA.

Without a word I lowered myself onto my knees. Placed my hands on the back of my head. My eyes never once leaving Stephanie as I waited for the officers to move forward and place me under arrest.

13

Staring at the monitors and feeling a tightness in his chest, Mitchell Hargrave said, "Alpha One, the target is coming out now."

Hancock: "With the woman?"

"No," Hargrave said, his jaw tight, "with a bunch of fucking cops."

Earlier, when Hargrave remembered the hacker's interrogation yesterday and how the guy had basically confessed to everything, it had struck him that there was a woman involved who apparently had known Burke's brother when they were kids. Quite a strange coincidence, the woman living in the same city, and Burke had reportedly gone to seek her help after being wounded. Because of this the hacker and a police detective had later broken into her house with the idea that taking her hostage would bring Burke back to them.

Which it had, though everything hadn't gone according to plan because it didn't take long before Burke shot the detective in the head and then overpowered the hacker.

Of course, this wasn't information the hacker had initially

wanted to give up. He had laid out information about several illegal schemes that implicated a US senator—who, from Hargrave's understanding, had just been picked up at some two-star hotel way off the Strip—but when it became apparent the hacker was withholding information, Hargrave had been given the go-ahead to begin enhanced interrogation.

The hacker hadn't lasted two minutes before he started spilling his guts.

So when Burke had initially disappeared on them, Hargrave figured there was a chance he might try to reconnect with this woman.

Hargrave had dispatched the team to the hospital where Dr. Stephanie Nguyen worked after Theo had tracked her location via her mobile phone. Then watched on the hospital's security feed as she received a call.

They followed the woman through the hospital as she tracked down a police officer. That officer used his radio to request backup, and within minutes two squad cars arrived. The doctor made a call and then started down one long hallway after another, the police officers in tow, which was when Hargrave began to feel that tightness in his chest.

Then Alpha Two came over the line, saying they'd spotted the target hurrying into the hospital, and Hargrave told the team to stand by as Theo and Julian would track Burke's movements inside.

Minutes later it became clear what was happening, and Hargrave felt Samuel Chen's eyes on him but ignored the deputy director and watched the monitors.

Now the police were leading Daniel Burke outside, the man's wrists handcuffed behind him. They placed him in the back of one of the patrol cars.

Lucas Hancock's voice came over the radio.

"Control, what's our directive now?"

Hargrave turned to Rita Salazar, lifting his eyebrows. "What do you think?"

Before Salazar could respond, Samuel Chen said, "Stand down."

Feeling his jaw go tight, Hargrave turned to the man. "Excuse me?"

"Let the police do their job. They'll process Burke, keep him in a holding cell, and in less than an hour the FBI will pick him up."

"I thought the idea was keeping the circle tight. Only a handful of agents selected by the FBI director have been briefed on the plan. Now you want to bring in more people?"

"*I* don't want to do anything. You and your team's incompetence have forced my hand."

Hargrave shifted on his feet, squaring his body to the CIA man. Feeling like he did back when he was a kid in Worcester every time he was ready to start a scuffle.

Chen said, "Do you know what your problem is, Mitchell?"

"Tell me, Samuel."

"The lack of oversight has made you and your team sloppy. This wasn't a complicated op. All your team had to do was ensure Burke got on the plane. And yet they somehow managed to screw up that one simple task."

On the monitors, one of the exterior security cameras showed the police officers in the parking lot. A pair of them climbed into a squad car and drove away. The car with Burke in the back still hadn't moved.

Lucas Hancock's voice again.

"Control, what do you want us to do?"

Hargrave held Samuel Chen's gaze for another few seconds but then realized this wasn't a hill he wanted to die on.

Turning back to the monitors, he said, "Alpha Team, stand down."

In an SUV parked across the street from the hospital, the four men inside looked at one another.

Noah's arm had been placed in a splint while Michael Kincaid's cheek wore a conspicuous bandage.

Lucas Hancock prided himself on carrying out successful missions, never losing a man or having anyone get hurt.

That was until last year when the mission in Turkey went off the rails and they'd lost Daniel Burke.

Or *thought* they'd lost the son of a bitch.

Hargrave again: "Alpha One, do you copy?"

Locking eyes with Dennis Rowe, Hancock said, "Copy."

In the back, Noah leaned forward, motioned at his earpiece, and then crossed his finger over his throat.

The rest of the men understood the signal and turned off their transmitters. Which Hancock assumed would drive everyone back at The Office crazy.

Noah said, "This whole thing is bullshit."

Rowe said, "An order is an order."

"But after what that motherfucker pulled? He made us look like fools."

Hancock: "What are you suggesting?"

Noah shook his head, glancing out his window. Something caught his eye, and Hancock traced his gaze and noted a bulky garbage truck rattling down the street.

Noah said, "I have an idea."

14

Two of the cops pulled away in their cruiser, leaving me with Officer Casey and his partner—a muscular Black guy with WILSON etched across his nameplate. The two chatted outside for a minute, deciding what they wanted to do with me or where they should grab lunch, and then Wilson climbed in behind the wheel, Casey sliding into the shotgun seat.

From the radio, a voice squawked a code and noted that there was a robbery in progress at a jewelry store nearby and requested available units in the vicinity.

Wilson waited for other cars to respond, then grabbed the radio and informed dispatch they were headed back to the station with a suspect.

I surveyed the area, gazing past the trees and parked vehicles for any movement. Assuming the team was out there now, watching. Planning their next move.

My first impulse was to stay silent. Not say a word while these two cops drove me to the station. Getting out of the cuffs wasn't going to be a problem—I'd escaped hundreds of handcuffs by dislocating my thumb; after so much practice, it was easy and nearly painless—so the question was the timing.

For whatever reason, I didn't want to hurt these two men. At least not more than I needed to. I figured I would wait until they halted the cruiser and opened the back door, reached in to pull me out. A few jabs to the throat to stun them, nothing more, and then I'd make a run for it. Hope nobody shot me in the back as I fled.

Or maybe I could play this a different way.

"Officers, I believe there's been some misunderstanding."

Neither cop turned in his seat to look at me. Officer Wilson didn't even eye me in the rearview as he steered us toward the nearest exit.

"No misunderstanding at all," Officer Casey said, staring out his window. "You've been harassing Dr. Nguyen. Stalking her, from what she says."

"Is she pressing charges?"

Still staring out his window, not looking at me: "No, but we are."

"Why?"

Now Officer Casey did shift in his seat, hefting my iPhone and the two burners with one hand.

"Because you're clearly up to no good, carrying these around. We gave you the opportunity to explain yourself back at the hospital. You gave us the silent treatment, so we'll see how you feel after some time in a holding cell."

I kept scanning the block, even twisting in my seat to glance out the back. Searching for the Alpha Team.

"Officers, I want to be very clear: some men are hunting me right now, and I worry that the two of you may become collateral damage."

Officer Wilson, sounding amused: "Is that right?"

"This isn't a joke. These men are killers."

Officer Wilson braked at a red light, grinned at his partner.

"Maybe we should've had him committed back at the hospital. Guy sounds nuts."

Gritting my teeth, I realized there was nothing I could say to convince these men otherwise. Then again, would I listen to me if I were in their position? People riding in the back of cop cars undoubtedly tell all kinds of crazy stories.

Still, I kept an eye out. I knew this team. I would recognize them anywhere. Even the new guy, Kincaid, who now had a hole in his cheek thanks to me.

We'd only gone six blocks when a black SUV pulled onto the street ahead of us. The windows tinted, though not entirely dark; through the rear window I could make out one occupant, the driver.

"Officers . . ."

But before I could say anything else, the SUV braked hard, angling to block both lanes.

Cursing, Officer Wilson slammed on the brakes. He threw a cautious glance at his partner, then went to flick on the rack lights.

That was when the garbage truck blasted forward out of nowhere.

Well, not out of nowhere.

From a side street.

Where it had been waiting for the signal.

Despite the short distance, it was traveling at least forty miles per hour—enough momentum to tip the cruiser over as it crashed into the side.

An explosion of glass as the cruiser flipped once and then rested upside down.

The cops were both wearing seat belts, but I hadn't been

granted that luxury. The days-old bullet wound in my back reopened, and there was a sharp pain in my ankle and shoulder.

For a stunned moment, complete silence.

At least, that's how it felt.

Until I realized my ears were ringing. And beyond the ringing, the cruiser's horn bleating nonstop, a low, woeful blare. And that despite wearing a seat belt, Officer Wilson—who had been on the receiving end as the garbage truck smashed into the driver's side—was strangely slumped forward in his seat, upside down. Unresponsive.

Because Officer Casey was saying something to him. Shouting his name. Also upside down as he fumbled for his seat belt.

Seconds had passed. Maybe only two or three. But more than enough time for the Alpha Team to make its move.

"Officer Casey, draw your weapon!"

The cop's head snapped around. I saw a flash of murder in his eyes, but then he seemed to understand my meaning and started scanning the street.

Two men with guns—Lucas Hancock and Dennis Rowe—were headed in our direction. One hundred feet away and closing fast.

Every window in the car had been shattered. Glass fragments everywhere. I scooted forward and kicked at some shards along the passenger-side window before squeezing out feetfirst onto the pavement.

Meanwhile, Officer Casey was radioing in the crash. He'd unbuckled himself and was pushing the door open when several rounds pinged the side of the car.

Casey, now screaming into his radio: "Shots fired! Shots fired!"

Wrists still bound behind my back, I rolled behind a parked van for cover. I cocked my head, listening past the buzzing in my ears. Two distinct pistols, and then a third as Officer Casey returned fire.

The cop scrambled back beside me, peering around the van as he shouted into his radio that there were at least two shooters, maybe three.

"Four," I said.

He wheeled around at me, his eyes narrowed.

"How do you know?"

"Like I already told you, they're hunting me."

More rounds tearing into the side of the van. Vehicles headed down the street screeching to a halt and performing hasty U-turns. People on the sidewalk rushing for cover.

Officer Casey ducked down, glared back at me.

"What the fuck is going on?"

Dislocating my thumb, I slipped my right hand through the cuff and then brought my hands to my front. Popping the thumb back in place, I held out my free hand.

"Give me your gun. I'll take care of this."

Officer Casey stared wide-eyed at the loose handcuff dangling from my left wrist.

"No fucking way."

The cop's radio squawked that reinforcements were five minutes out. Not nearly enough time. We barely had thirty seconds before Hancock and Rowe reached us.

I leaned around the other side of the van, spotted one of the men's reflections on the plate glass window of a storefront. Cautiously moving from one parked car to the next as he advanced.

Now less than forty feet away.

The people on the sidewalk had disappeared. This portion of the street now deserted except for us.

Officer Casey realized we weren't going to make it. That within seconds the two shooters would reach the van. I could see it on his face, the realization that he would soon die. And because the man probably didn't want to go out a coward, he'd decided to make his own fate.

"Casey, don't—"

Taking several deep breaths through his mouth, psyching himself up, the redheaded cop tore around the corner of the van, opening fire, but only managed to squeeze off two rounds before a bullet pierced the side of his head.

He stood motionless for a half second before hitting the ground like a bag of cement.

Face tilted toward me. Blank.

Lucas Hancock shouted, "Hey, Dan! Why don't you come out? We just want to talk."

Staring at the dead cop's face. Running through my options. Knowing I had almost none, at least that would keep me alive.

When Officer Casey fell, his grip on the Glock loosened, the sidearm clattering a few inches away. Not close, but not too far either.

Sirens rose up in the distance. Maybe a mile away. Maybe less. Backup would be here within minutes.

Minutes I didn't have.

Hancock again.

"C'mon, Dan! We just want to catch up."

Okay, fuck this.

Scrambling out from behind the van. Diving forward onto the glass-beaded pavement. Twisting to grab the Glock. Trying to remember how many bullets the cop had fired.

Dropping the mag into my hand. Seeing that there were seven rounds left. Sliding the mag back in place and popping up and placing a bead on Dennis Rowe as he crouched low behind a car.

Squeezing the trigger.

"Shit!" the man shouted as the bullet nicked his arm.

Lucas Hancock leaned out and returned fire, the van's side mirror disintegrating. I ducked behind the cruiser for cover. Glanced over at Officer Casey's dead body, trying to guess which pocket contained the handcuff key.

Hancock shouted, "Seriously, Dan, there must be some misunderstanding. We just want to talk!"

The sirens even closer. Now maybe a minute away.

I realized I had two choices: either try to find the handcuff key or grab my phones.

In the end, the decision was easy.

Rushing forward and squeezing off the rest of the rounds until the slide kicked back, I ducked down and gathered my iPhone and the two burners from the car. I considered prying a spare magazine from Officer Wilson's belt as he still dangled unconscious upside down—but then saw Hancock and Rowe had already fled for the black SUV, which was now peeling away and turning down a side street while ahead, racing toward this location, were flashing lights.

Stuffing the phones into my pants pockets, I secured the spent Glock in my rear waistband, slipped my left hand—the one still wearing the handcuffs—into my hoodie pocket, then started toward an alley only twenty feet away, and did the only thing left for me to do.

I ran.

15

Home.

That's all Stephanie could think about. Leaving the hospital, getting into her sad compact SUV (still another two years of lease payments left), and driving the same eight miles to the same place she'd lived for the past six years.

The house was home because it was where she stayed most of the time. Where she laid her head at night. Where she showered and where she had meals and where, on the rare occasions she had the time, she watched TV or read a book.

But it wasn't *home*.

She wasn't even sure she considered her childhood house home anymore, which was strange because she had lived there almost half her life.

Either way, she couldn't wait to leave work.

But even now as she moved from one patient to the next, asking the usual questions—"Where exactly does it hurt?" "How long have you been having this pain?" "Do you have a family history of this?"—her mind strayed to the phone call.

Danny telling her that her life was in danger and Stephanie, standing stock-still, wanting nothing more than to scream out her frustrations.

When she'd told Danny days ago that she'd never wanted to see him again, she meant it. She'd originally believed that her ex-fiancé was the only man who'd ever ruined her life, bringing her to a city where she knew no one only later to break her heart and leave her, but now Danny had taken the mantle.

She remembered him as a small boy. Just a kid. Shy and quiet, never meeting her eye when they were in the same room. Except one time when she'd arrived at James's house early for a date and he was still in the shower. Little Danny sitting in the living room, reading a book, and after a bout of awkward silence Stephanie asked what he was reading, even though she knew the book well as it had been a favorite of hers in middle school.

Stephanie had always thought her boyfriend's little brother was weird, but he'd lit up when talking about *The Outsiders*. The enthusiasm in his voice was contagious. The brightness in his eyes almost enough to make her smile. But she'd sat there, her face serious, nodding along as Danny told her all about the book—the characters, the plot, how it ended. Then James had come loping down the stairs, his hair still damp, his body smelling like he'd bathed in Old Spice, and he shot his little brother an annoyed look before smiling at Stephanie and asking if she was ready to go.

Where had they gone that night?

Stephanie couldn't remember. Out to a movie, maybe, or mini golf, or maybe bowling. Or maybe none of those things. Maybe they'd gone to a mutual friend's house for a party, or maybe they'd driven around until it got dark enough to sneak down to the end of Crestview Lane to park the car and climb into the back seat and—

"Dr. Nguyen?"

Again, a voice startling her from a daze, only this voice belonged to a nurse.

She blinked, turned around, forced a smile.

"Yes?"

"Patient in bed four is asking when she can be discharged. She said you were going to prescribe something, but I don't see anything on the chart."

Crap.

Stephanie had had that conversation almost an hour ago. She'd meant to put in the order but then Danny had called, and she'd gotten distracted. Listening to a voice she'd hoped never to hear again telling her how he believed her life was in danger. How the people he'd once worked with were now after him, and he worried that these same people—killers, he called them—would come for her just like the detective and hacker.

Stephanie hadn't said anything as she listened to him, and when he was done speaking, waiting for her to say something, she'd simply disconnected the call. Held the phone in her hand for the five seconds it took before it started buzzing again. She'd considered sending the call to voicemail, or blocking the number altogether, but then realized Danny was never going to stop—that this whole thing which had somehow been set into motion without her permission would never stop.

Unless she made it stop.

Which was why, after asking him to come to the hospital to get her, she tracked down Patrick Casey and told him about how an ex-boyfriend had been stalking her and now he was threatening to barge in on her at work and that she was scared.

For a second or two, Patrick had seemed uncertain, wanting to ask more questions, until Stephanie softened her eyes.

"Please," she'd said, making it sound like she was about to cry, and that had sealed the deal.

"Dr. Nguyen?"

Another nurse, calling her name.

Stephanie suppressed a groan as she turned.

"Yes?"

"There's a patient's son out in the hallway asking to speak to you."

"Why isn't he with the patient?"

"He said they had a falling out. That the patient downplays just how critical her conditions are and that he wants to make sure you're aware of what's going on."

"I don't—"

"He says it's urgent," the nurse said, and now Stephanie did let out a small groan of annoyance.

"Fine," she said, and started for the exit leading into the hallway.

She stepped out and looked both ways. A few people coming and going, but nobody waiting to speak to her.

Clenching her teeth, she started to turn away, grabbing her badge to open the ER doors, when she sensed movement coming up behind her.

Before she could do or say anything, she felt the barrel of a pistol dig into the small of her back and heard a voice whisper, "Don't make a sound."

16

Her body stiffening, she turned her head slowly and took me in from the corner of her eye. Stared for a beat, and then twisted around, her nostrils flaring.

Stephanie breathed, "What are you *doing* here?"

I gazed past her down the hallway at the few patients and staff bustling about. Conscious of the security cameras peering down every hallway and The Office's ability to hack into all of them.

"We have to go."

"I'm not going anywhere with you."

"Stephanie."

She glared down at the empty pistol in my hand, still pointed at her. Then gazed up again. Her dark eyes studying my face.

"What happened here?" she asked, tapping her finger to the left side of her own face. I'd already seen my reflection: a few tiny cuts from the shards of glass when the cruiser flipped over.

"Stephanie, we don't have time."

Still with the glare, though something changed in her eyes.

"Where's Patrick?"

"Stephanie, please. The people hunting me will be here any minute. We need to leave."

I moved closer to her, but she stepped away.

"I'm not going anywhere with you."

Looking past her again down the hallway, feeling my jaw tighten. That all-too-familiar rage beginning to pulse.

I pressed the barrel of the Glock into her stomach.

She didn't even blink.

"You're not going to shoot me."

"Who's Patrick?"

"What?"

"Is that Officer Casey? The one with the red hair?"

Her eyes widened, just a bit. Her lips, parting slightly. As though preparing to scream.

"He's dead, Stephanie. We were ambushed a few blocks from here. These people hunting me—they'll stop at nothing. And as I told you, if they need to use you to get to me, they will."

Her face had become stone. Completely unreadable. But when I stepped even closer and nudged her, she didn't jerk away. No resistance whatsoever. As if now she'd become a marionette and me the puppeteer. Leading her down the hallway, still unsure where we were going but only knowing that we needed to leave, and fast.

Down one brightly lit hallway after another, our shoes squeaking off the freshly waxed linoleum, and coming our way a large man in an EMT uniform. Dark-blue dungarees and a gray polo shirt with an ambulance logo on it. His partner had headed to the bathroom while the large EMT dug into his pocket for his wallet as he approached a vending machine.

Slipping the Glock into my waistband, I veered straight into the EMT.

"Whoa!" the guy said.

"Sorry, sorry," I said, bunching up my shoulders in apology.

The EMT glowered at me for a second before noticing Stephanie.

"Hey, Doc. You okay?"

Stephanie shifted her face toward him. Blinked.

"What?"

"Are you okay? Because you look—"

"I'm fine."

Despite her sudden zombielike demeanor, Stephanie had managed to inject some life into her voice.

Blinking again, she gestured at me and said, "I'm escorting this patient to Neurology."

"But why you? Why not one of the nurses?"

"*Excuse me?*"

The tone of a teacher scolding an insolent student.

The EMT looked like he wanted to shrink himself to half his size.

"Sorry, Dr. Nguyen. Didn't mean anything by it."

Stephanie didn't move. She kept watching the EMT until he sheepishly turned away, back to the vending machine. Then she looked at me, and nodded.

We continued down the hallway. Past the other EMT coming out of the bathroom, then around the corner and out the sliding glass doors to the ambulance bay.

I pulled out the keys I'd snagged from the EMT's pocket and directed us toward the one ambulance that shared the logo embroidered on the man's polo shirt.

As though suddenly realizing where we were, Stephanie asked, "What are we doing?"

"Making a getaway," I said, glancing around to make sure nobody noticed as I opened the passenger door for her.

I hurried around the front of the ambulance and climbed up behind the wheel, and now that I was seated, I looked down at the keys and felt my heart drop.

"Shit."

"What's wrong?"

"The other guy must be the driver. None of these keys are for the ignition."

I stared at the dash for a beat, then reached under the wheel and yanked apart the panel.

Stephanie said, "What are you doing?"

Silently, I peered at the wires clustered about until I found the ones I needed, then I used one of the keys to strip the wires.

"Are you *hot-wiring* this thing?"

I didn't answer, playing with the wires, and didn't look up until Stephanie spoke again.

"Hey."

She leaned over and tilted down the sun visor. Caught the keys that fell neatly into her palm.

She gave me a look as she handed me the keys—but then paused when she noticed my left hand, the one with the loose cuff hanging from it and which I'd kept in the hoodie pocket this entire time.

I found the right key and got the engine going. Started to put the truck into gear but then told her to hold on and clambered into the back of the ambulance. Reemerged seconds later with two jackets and baseball caps, both sporting the ambulance company's logo.

I dropped one of the jackets and caps into Stephanie's lap.

"Put those on."

A minute later we'd left the hospital parking lot and were cruising down the street. I purposely went in the opposite direction that the cops had taken me earlier.

Stephanie said, "They're going to report this stolen as soon as possible, you know."

"I know."

"We won't be able to keep driving it long."

"I know."

"So what are we going to do?"

"I'm still working on it. But I need you to do something very important."

"What's that?"

"Call your father. Tell him to leave his house immediately. To leave his phone behind and go someplace isolated."

Stephanie didn't say anything. She sat stock-still, staring out her window. Then, after a minute of complete silence, she said, "Pull over."

"What?"

"Up here in this empty parking lot."

Wary, I flicked the turn signal and steered us into the lot of a building for lease.

"Seriously, you need to call your dad as soon as—"

That's when she started whaling on me. The flat of her palm connecting with the side of my face. Then again. And again. And again.

Tears in her eyes now—tears that she'd managed to hold back this entire time—and she kept slapping me and hitting me, shouting, "I fucking hate you, I fucking hate you, I fucking hate you!"

The onslaught didn't last long. Maybe only fifteen seconds. I stayed motionless the entire time. My eyes open, not flinching once. Until Stephanie wore herself out. Trying to catch her breath, wiping at her face, staring out her window.

"Let's go," she muttered, and I placed the ambulance back in gear.

17

"How are we coming along?" Mitchell Hargrave asked.

Julian sat hunched over a laptop, having separated himself from the other monitors. Right now, Theo was busy running back through all the feeds, trying to ascertain Daniel Burke's location after the shoot-out.

"Almost there," Julian said, his focus glued to the laptop screen.

The door to the room opened and Samuel Chen entered. Hargrave gave him the briefest of glances before turning back to the monitors.

"Alpha One, sitrep."

Hancock: "We returned to the hospital. Any sign of the target yet?"

"Not yet."

Chen asked, "Why are they *back* at the hospital? After what happened, they should get the hell out of the state."

Hargrave shared a look with Rita Salazar before shrugging at Chen.

"After what happened?"

Chen's expression was blank.

"You're joking, right? Your men killed a police officer."

"No, they didn't."

Chen jabbed a finger at the monitors on the wall.

"Are you trying to gaslight me? Because twenty minutes ago I *watched* them do it!"

Hargrave had his arms crossed, trying not to look as restless as he felt. He frowned at Chen, then shifted his gaze back to the monitors.

"Julian, where are we at now?"

"Almost there."

"You said that two minutes ago."

Focus still glued to the laptop, his shoulders slouched forward, the tech said, "We need this to look one hundred percent perfect, right?"

Hargrave didn't bother answering. Of course they needed it to look 100 percent perfect. But with everything that had happened in the past three hours—Christ, had it only been that long?—his patience was waning.

Samuel Chen said, "You need *what* to look one hundred percent perfect?"

Hargrave's first impulse was to ignore the question. He'd already made it clear how he didn't appreciate the CIA sending someone—and the deputy director at that!—to babysit the op. And he also didn't like that after the cop was killed, Chen had muttered a disbelieving curse under his breath and stormed out of the room. Hargrave wanted to know where Chen had gone, whom he may have called, but before he could ask or say anything, Julian sat back from the laptop and stretched his hands over his head.

"Finished!"

Hargrave said, "Excellent. Let's see it."

Julian typed at the laptop, then glanced up at the wall of monitors.

And on the center screen was now a playback recording from one of the traffic cams along the street where the garbage truck had smashed into the police cruiser. They'd already scoured the nearest security feeds—including those controlled by private businesses along the street—and this one showed the most direct view of the action.

They watched the cruiser flip onto its roof. Watched as Daniel Burke first crawled out of the back through the shattered window, then as Officer Patrick Casey stumbled out. Watched as first Burke took cover behind the van, then Casey. Then watched as Casey returned fire until, incredibly, they watched Burke raise a weapon and shoot Casey in the side of the head.

"Jesus Christ!" Samuel Chen said. He turned to glare at Hargrave. "You deepfaked Burke as the shooter?"

Hargrave shrugged as though to say, *Of course we did*. Though he knew on closer inspection—because the police were going to investigate the shit out of this, more so than they would other shootings, as this man had been one of their own—it would be clear the bullet had come from the opposite direction. Julian had managed to make the video work because the feed was rather grainy, a small stroke of luck that made Hargrave believe maybe this entire op wasn't a complete loss yet.

Chen said, "There were witnesses. People saw what happened."

"Nobody saw the cop getting shot."

Theo said, "That's not quite true. As soon as we could, we monitored all the phones and tablets in the square-block radius. Two people were filming out the window of their buildings. They caught what happened, but we've since remotely deleted those files from their devices and the cloud."

"Jesus Christ," Chen said again. Then, to Hargrave: "Do you realize how many laws you and your team have broken in the past twenty minutes?"

Hargrave wanted to tell the man to shut the hell up. To sit down and keep his fucking trap shut and not utter a single word unless spoken to. Instead, he calmly turned to the deputy director.

"This is a matter of national security. You of all people should understand the importance of that."

Chen shifted on his feet, folding his arms and squaring his shoulders at Hargrave.

"Listen here, Mitchell. I know you rose up in the ranks after 9/11, so you seem to think you can play fast and loose with domestic and international laws, but I'm here to tell you those days are over."

Hargrave felt his right hand squeezing into a fist. But before he could say or do anything, the phone hanging on the wall behind them rang.

All at once, Hargrave felt his muscles tense. He'd wondered who Samuel Chen had called when he stepped out into the corridor, and now he had his confirmation.

Rita Salazar was looking at him, a mixture of confusion and worry on her face.

Hargrave nodded, and watched as Salazar approached the phone. Lifted it gingerly from its cradle, placed the phone to her ear.

"Yes?"

Stood motionless for several seconds, listening to whoever was on the other end.

Then, slowly, turned back to Hargrave. Held up the phone, with her palm over the receiver to muffle her words.

"It's the White House."

18

We ditched the ambulance behind a strip mall and walked a half mile up the highway, having left behind the paramedic jackets and hats. I'd also trashed my iPhone in one of the bins along the road and convinced Stephanie to do the same with her phone.

It was almost two o'clock and the sky was still clear except for some hazy clouds hanging on the horizon. Soon we came to a travel plaza teeming with tractor trailers, and Stephanie asked me again what we were doing here.

"For starters, we can't keep driving the ambulance."

"Obviously. But why not . . . you know, steal a car?"

The thought had crossed my mind. But there was no telling how long before the car we stole was reported to the police. And besides, Hargrave and his team would be on the lookout for me behind any steering wheel. I could try to convince Stephanie to drive—they were far less likely to have her face streaming through facial recognition, at least as of right now—but that meant I'd need to ride in the back, and I wasn't sure I could trust Stephanie, especially after what happened during my first visit to the hospital.

"Trust me," I said. "This is our only play."

It may have been our only play, but I didn't like it. Not one bit. I hated being at the mercy of others, especially strangers.

"Here's our pitch. You and I have been dating for three months. Your ex-husband recently found out, and he's threatened to kill us—and what's worse, he's a cop, which is why we can't bring this to the police's attention."

Stephanie said, "Mentioning the police will be a deal-breaker for a lot of these guys."

"True, but I don't see any other way to make this work. Otherwise, it won't present the immediate need to flee town. Plus, I'm offering them cash."

"How much?"

"I've got a thousand dollars on me. I'll offer five hundred at first. Go up if need be. Plus, I can promise more once we get to our destination."

We didn't have any luck with the first three truckers we approached. The first two because they were headed east, and the third because he said he didn't want to take the risk.

A few others wouldn't even talk to us. We'd been ducking through the rows of parked eighteen-wheelers, trying to find the right person, and most never gave us a chance to tell them what was going on, shaking their heads and saying they weren't interested.

Then Stephanie pointed to the woman.

Late fifties, stout, smoking a cigarette as she waddled toward her truck. My first instinct was to skip her, but then I figured what the hell.

"Excuse me? Ma'am?"

The woman paused, turned to look at us. Squinting.

"Yeah?"

I ran through it again, adding even more urgency to

my tone. Glancing all around as I talked, as though worried Stephanie's imaginary ex-husband might show up at any second. Even holding Stephanie's hand as I spoke, as if the two of us were eternally linked—though I could feel Stephanie trying to pull her hand away, not wanting anything to do with the man who had barged back into her life and upturned everything.

When I fell silent, the woman thought about it for a long moment, a heavy frown on her face. She looked like she could be somebody's grandmother. A grandmother who smoked a carton a day and who could probably hold her own when it came to downing shots of bourbon.

"Oh, I don't know," the woman said eventually in her smoker's rasp. "I'm sorry to hear what y'all are goin' through, but I don't think it's wise for me to get involved."

She started to turn away, and I threw a small shrug at Stephanie, who gave me a worried look and then yanked her hand out of my grip.

"*Please*," she said, her voice trembling. "You . . . you don't know how awful he can be. For years he beat me. He knew I couldn't tell anybody—that I wouldn't tell anybody if I knew what was good for me. He told me how he would kill me if I talked to anyone and how since he was a cop, he'd get away with it. And then . . . I managed to leave, I managed to divorce him, and that's a whole other story, but . . . please, please help us."

The woman's eyes softened. She gazed first at Stephanie, then at me, and then sighed heavily.

"Where d'you wanna go again?"

"Los Angeles," I said. "But really, if you could take us as far as the state line, that would be great."

The woman chewed her bottom lip, thinking it over.

"I don't got much room in my cab to fit you both."

"That's okay. We don't want to ride up front anyway. We'll ride in the trailer."

"And how much did you say?"

"Well"—I dug into my pocket, pulled out the cash I'd been waving at the other truckers—"I've got five hundred here. It's yours if you help us. And if need be, we can get you more. I just . . . you know, I'm afraid to use the ATM. At least until we're a bit farther out of this bastard's reach."

The woman glanced at her tractor trailer. Glanced back at us. Still chewing her bottom lip.

Finally, she said, "I guess I can let y'all ride in the trailer. It's gonna be dark back there, and there's nothing I can do 'bout it, but it's somethin'."

"Thank you," I said and grabbed Stephanie's hand again, squeezed it tight.

We started toward the tractor trailer but the woman didn't move. She just stood there, staring back at us.

"Ain't you forgettin' somethin'?"

She held out her small chapped hand. I placed the cash in it, and she took her time counting the bills, even losing track halfway through and restarting. Finally, she seemed satisfied and stuffed the wad into her pocket and nodded.

"All right, then. Let's go."

19

Half of the trailer was filled with pallets of what the woman said were office supplies. Mostly large cardboard boxes stacked up toward the ceiling and wrapped in thick cellophane to keep the pallets from tipping over during transit.

I sat on the dirty metal floor, my back against the side of the trailer, Stephanie sitting across from me.

We'd been on the road now for ten minutes. Based on the sound of the big rig's engine and the speed at which the truck was traveling, we were already on I-15.

I said, "Why don't you try him again?"

Stephanie woke the burner I'd given her, the soft glow from the screen lighting her face.

"I've already texted him. Several times. Telling him to call me. And when I did call him, it went straight to voicemail."

She paused, her eyes growing glassy in the screen's dim light.

"You . . . you don't think that maybe they already—"

"No," I said. "It's way too soon for them to have grabbed him. There's a chance they might not even know about your father yet."

"Then why do you want me to call him?"

"Because I know the way these people think. If they want something bad enough, they'll do whatever it takes to get it. I have no family, no friends. My only connection is to you, and I proved that you mean something to me when I came back because Jared Sutton and that hacker held you hostage."

"Gee, thanks."

"You know what I mean. And now that you're with me, they'll come for anything they view as a vulnerability for you. Which, correct me if I'm wrong, is your father."

Stephanie's burner had fallen back asleep, enveloping us again in darkness. A warm darkness, as there wasn't much insulation in this trailer and already the afternoon sun was turning it into a hot box.

In the dark, Stephanie spoke quietly.

"He was a sweet guy, you know. Patrick, I mean. Always had a smile for me every time I saw him. He would tell me stupid jokes, because he somehow knew I liked stupid jokes. The dumber, the better. He'd asked me out a few months back. I don't know why I turned him down. I was thinking before that maybe it was because I wasn't ready to date again, even though it's been two years, but now I'm wondering if there's something else besides that. Something . . . I haven't been willing to accept."

"Like what?"

"I don't know. I don't know, and it's been driving me crazy. But what's driving me even crazier is how Patrick didn't hesitate when I told him about you. He knew I needed help and he didn't even think twice. He—"

Her voice broke.

"You're cursed, Danny. You know that, don't you? Everything you touch—everyone you get close to—dies."

A heavy silence stretching between the two of us, pushing us miles apart.

I shook my head in the dark.

"That's not true. You're still alive."

I heard Stephanie snort a laugh, and then her burner lit up as she tried to call her father again.

"Voicemail," she mumbled, yawning. Then said, "Dad, it's me. I need you to do me a favor. It's extremely important. Bad people are after me. I'm worried they might come for you to get to me, and I can't contact the police. I'll explain when I can, but I need you to do this for me. When I was eleven, during the summer, do you remember the place we went to? Mom's favorite place in the world? I need you to go there. Right away. Don't tell anyone. Don't pack. Just get in your car and go. Leave your phone behind. Please. I love you."

The burner went dark again, bathing us in black. The swinging doors to the trailer squeaked beside us. There was no way to open those doors from the inside. We were locked in here until the trucker—she hadn't given us her name—let us out. I didn't like it at all, but I also didn't see any other way of leaving the state without The Office potentially tracking us.

Yawning, I asked, "Where did you go when you were eleven?"

Stephanie didn't answer.

I gave it a few seconds, then tried again.

"Hey."

Still nothing.

"Stephanie?"

I pulled the burner phone from my pocket, turned on the flashlight app. Shined it across at Stephanie, who was slumped with her back against the side of the trailer. Her eyes, closed.

"Stephanie?" I said again, though this time my voice was mostly a yawn, and I realized my eyelids were growing heavy.

And that there was another noise around us besides the truck's engine and those massive eighteen wheels traveling over the highway going at least seventy miles per hour.

A quiet, almost silent, hissing.

The sudden, warning shriek of a Klaxon going off in my head, I tried to stand up, bracing myself against the wall. But for whatever reason the muscles in my legs gave out and I fell back down.

The phone slipped from my hand, flipped over, and landed with its screen face down. The flashlight portion illuminating the darkness. But not much, as the light wasn't very strong.

Still, as I looked up toward the ceiling, I saw something there. A tiny opening attached to a metal pipe running the length of the ceiling, with other tiny openings every two feet. And coming down from those openings, I now realized, was some kind of spray.

"Son of a—" I started to say, and then darkness took over and I said nothing at all.

20

Despite having worked in government for over three decades—half of which had been in one top secret capacity or another—Mitchell Hargrave had never been to the White House.

He loathed politicians, and POTUS was the ultimate politician—a person who campaigned day and night, put their blood, sweat, and tears into their political career, all to . . . what, become one of the most powerful people in the world?

Anybody who runs for president is a narcissist, Hargrave's father once told him, and through the years he'd come to realize the old bastard was right.

That isn't to say he wasn't invested in who became president. Hargrave had specific ideologies, just like everyone else, and if it had been up to him, somebody else would be occupying the Oval Office—somebody who more closely aligned with his political leanings, that was for sure.

No, President Jeffrey Wagner was not his ideal president, but the man *was* the president, and Hargrave respected the office even if he didn't respect the man—and when the man called, Hargrave had no choice but to answer.

Granted, President Wagner hadn't called personally. Samuel Chen had alerted his boss about how much of a shit show the op had become, and the CIA director must have alerted the White House, who had called demanding answers, and that's why Mitchell Hargrave was here now, in the building itself, riding an elevator with a White House aide down to the basement.

Hargrave felt his stomach tighten with the realization of where they were headed.

After leaving his phones and personal belongings in a makeshift locker, the aide directed him into the Situation Room.

Officially known as the John F. Kennedy Conference Room, because it had been created in 1961 after the failure of the Bay of Pigs invasion, the conference room and intelligence management center were run by the National Security Council staff. Low ceiling, dark wood paneling, a long dark wooden table, and screens on the walls to communicate with heads of state and to monitor operations all over the world.

Right now, on four of the six flat-panel display televisions, were the director of the FBI, the director of the CIA, the director of the NSA, and the director of National Intelligence.

The only person sitting at the table was Charlie Yates, chairman of the Joint Chiefs of Staff.

Yates said, "You really screwed the pooch on this one, didn't you, Mitchell?"

Hargrave, conscious of the three men and one woman watching from the camera situated at the head of the table, pulled out a chair directly across from Yates and sat down.

"Always a pleasure to see you too, Charlie."

Then, as an afterthought, he offered up a nod at the camera to acknowledge those participating from the safety of their offices.

Yates said, "For somebody who has bungled such an easy op, I would've imagined you'd be less cavalier."

"The op isn't over yet."

"Daniel Burke is in the wind."

"We'll find him."

"We already found him," Yates said. "And you, somehow, managed to let him escape."

Hargrave matched the older man's glare. Yates was ten years older, but Hargrave had known him for a good two decades, and there had been times when the two of them had gotten along well—busting each other's balls like they were good friends—while other times they often butted heads.

Hargrave said, "How did you find him, anyway?"

"Excuse me?"

"Burke. As far as I knew—as far as the rest of my team knew—Burke was killed during an op over a year ago."

Yates glanced briefly toward the wall of screens and shrugged.

"You know what you need to know, Mitchell, and let's leave it at that for right now."

The door opened. Hargrave started to stand but when he saw who had entered it took everything he had not to roll his eyes.

Samuel Chen paused, taking in the room and the faces on the screens. A lot of history had happened here, presidents having overseen covert operations all around the world, some of which were still highly classified and would never be made known to the general public.

After a moment, Chen moved to the other side of the table. He nodded at Yates as he took a seat.

"Hello, Charlie."

"Hello, Samuel. I heard you drew the short straw. But good thing you were in that room. Something tells me none of us would have been updated about this clusterfuck otherwise."

"Christ, Charlie," Hargrave said, "stop with the histrionics. We're all adults here."

"A cop was killed!" Yates snapped. "On your watch. On US soil. By one of your team, no less."

"No."

Yates, raising a bushy eyebrow: "Excuse me?"

"My team didn't kill the cop."

"That's not what I heard."

"Then you heard wrong," Hargrave said, doing everything he could not to look at Chen. "We have video of Burke shooting the cop."

Charlie Yates's shoulders dropped as he sank back into his chair.

"Christ."

"Exactly," Hargrave said. "Burke has escalated things to the point where I don't think we have any further choice in the matter."

"What are you saying?"

"What do you think I'm saying? He needs to be taken off the board for good."

Yates stared for a beat, digesting this, and then shook his head.

"No. That's not the directive. Not with what Burke knows. Not after he—"

That was when the door opened again, and the president of the United States entered.

21

"Don't get up," President Jeffrey Wagner said as everyone in the room started to rise to their feet.

Following the president was Lawrence O'Neal, Wagner's chief of staff. O'Neal was in his late forties, while Wagner was in his midfifties. Tall, trim, and already growing gray, Jeffrey Wagner knew how to command a room.

The president took the chair at the head of the table, his chief of staff taking the chair to his right. Wagner acknowledged the four directors on the screens, thanking them for making the time, and then looked around the table until his commanding gaze settled on Hargrave.

"You're Mitchell Hargrave, I presume."

Hargrave cleared his throat, suddenly feeling nervous.

"Yes, Mr. President."

"So you're the one who runs an ultra top secret kill squad that I didn't even know about until an hour ago. Fantastic."

The president's dry tone hung heavy in the air. His eyes narrowed as he gazed again around the room.

The director of the CIA spoke on the screen.

"Mr. President, as I explained, the reason you were not informed—"

Wagner cut the man off with a wave of his hand.

"Yes, yes. Full deniability and all that crap. Plus, I understand this team was formed under my predecessor, and he didn't even know about it. Not that that makes me feel any better. Now, tell me what the hell is going on."

A brief silence as nobody wanted to begin.

The president leaned forward, folding his hands on the table.

"Lady and gentlemen, I am a busy man. I'm not here to waste your time, so I would appreciate it if you didn't waste mine. As I know you're all well aware, my vice president was recently arrested due to his involvement in a . . . particularly disgusting set of circumstances. Sometimes you think you know people, and other times they pull the wool right over your eyes."

Wagner paused, his gaze flashing on each person's face.

"Despite what the other party and some in the media say, I take my job very seriously. I pore over every page of the PDB—every day—and it disappoints me to learn that although I'm the chief law enforcement officer of this country, everyone in this room and on these screens has deemed it wise to withhold information from me."

Charlie Yates said, "Mr. President, as you just mentioned, the idea was to ensure you have total deniability in case—"

"In case what? That a top secret operator—one that doesn't fall under any purview of the many intelligence agencies this country runs—decided to go rogue and fake his death?"

After another bout of silence, Wagner laughed.

"Oh, and let's not forget that Senator Harold Browne was taken into custody earlier this morning on so many corruption charges it boggles the mind. It's my understanding Harold refuses to talk with law enforcement until, and I quote, 'POTUS gives me a preemptive pardon.' Well, lady and gentlemen, I want to make it clear that man will get nothing from me, just as the vice president will get nothing. And if that means I lose the chance at a second term in the next six weeks, then so be it."

Silence again, a bit lengthier this time. Hargrave was amazed by just how heavy the silence felt in this room. Not even a faint buzzing coming from any of the lights.

President Wagner leaned forward in his seat, his eyes hooded.

"Tell me everything there is to know about this Daniel Burke."

Hargrave glanced across the table at Charlie Yates, whose expression made it clear that he didn't want to take the lead.

Figured, the coward.

Hargrave said, "Burke joined the military right out of high school. He started his career in the infantry and managed to work his way up fast through the ranks and was soon working for JSOC. His commanding officers there saw something special in him, so they pulled him aside for . . . delicate tasks."

The president asked, "What did these officers see in him?"

Another hesitant glance at Yates, and then Hargrave cleared his throat again.

"To put it bluntly, Mr. President, he was a killer."

President Wagner made no reaction.

"Is that supposed to shock me, Mr. Hargrave? I was born at night, but not last night. I know our military trains men and women to do the jobs nobody else can do, not unless they don't want to lose sleep at night. So what else?"

"After a few years in JSOC, I recruited him to be on my team."

"Your team."

"Yes, Mr. President."

"And how many are on your team?"

"Four men. Last year that had included Burke until . . . well, until we believed he had died on a mission."

"This was the mission in Turkey. The one where Hellfire missiles were deployed to destroy a building which nearly caused an international crisis."

"That's right, Mr. President."

"Tell me again—why were those missiles necessary?"

"When it became clear Burke had been killed—or that we believed he had been killed—I thought it best to destroy any evidence of his body. Otherwise, I believed the Turkish government would have used Burke's body to justify starting a war."

"Uh-huh," the president said in a tone that made it clear he didn't like the answer, not one bit. "As for your current team, I understand three of your men were injured today."

"Correct. Burke stabbed one man in the face, broke another man's arm, and grazed another man with a bullet."

"Why?"

The question threw Hargrave.

"Excuse me, sir?"

"Earlier, you said that Daniel Burke was a killer. So why did he stab one man in the face, break another man's arm, and graze a third instead of killing them all?"

"That . . . I cannot answer."

Charlie Yates quickly added, "We have evidence that Burke killed a police officer this morning."

The president's face visibly paled.

"What?"

"Before the Alpha Team could capture him, he was arrested by the police. He managed to escape, and in the process he reportedly shot a police officer to death."

Hargrave didn't care for the added *reportedly*, so he said,

"We have video, Mr. President, if you would like to view the incident."

He could feel Samuel Chen's eyes on him, boring deep.

President Wagner said, "Good God, no. Were any other officers injured?"

Hargrave nodded.

"Another officer who was driving was knocked unconscious during the incident in question. He was taken to the hospital and is in stable condition."

President Wagner was quiet, absorbing this. Then gazed around the room again.

"Do we know why Daniel Burke was in Las Vegas?"

Nobody spoke at first, waiting for someone else to speak. Finally, Yates leaned forward in his seat.

"We're not entirely sure, Mr. President."

"Is that the case? Because I've been briefed on the information provided by the young man who calls himself the Spider. It appears that Daniel Burke's brother had been one of the victims of the scam linked to Senator Browne. Apparently because of this scam the brother committed suicide. And because the brother committed suicide, Daniel Burke went to Las Vegas to find the people responsible and bring them to justice."

The president leaned forward again, his voice going low.

"Now, Daniel Burke may be a killer, but does that sound like the man you've described to me?"

Under the table, Hargrave's leg was bouncing. He reached down, placed his hand on the leg to stop it. Waited a few seconds to see if anyone else would speak.

"Mr. President, it's a bit more complicated than that."

President Wagner glanced at his chief of staff, then sat back in his chair and lifted his hand.

"All right then, Mr. Hargrave. Go ahead. Enlighten me."

"Well, sir, there's a reason that as soon as we learned Burke was alive, we sent a team to Vegas."

"And what is that reason, Mr. Hargrave? Tell me what Daniel Burke has done that forced your team to put together an unsanctioned operation on United States soil."

A furtive glance across the table at Charlie Yates as Hargrave shifted in his seat.

"As I mentioned, it's a bit complicated, sir, so I guess the best thing to do is tell you what nobody else has said thus far about our target."

"Which is?"

"Based on what we now know Daniel Burke did before he faked his death . . . well, Mr. President, pardon my language, but the man is a goddamned traitor."

PART II
NORSEMEN

22

The night is thick and still. The sky, cloudless and salted with more stars than I've ever seen.

Insects in the trees surrounding the building, a natural symphony. A forceful pulse, matching my own.

I stand outside in the dark and smoke a cigarette. A new habit which has become a boring routine at the black site. Sleep, rise, eat, interrogate, eat, sleep. Again and again and again.

After a while, card games become stale, everyone familiar with everyone else's tells.

Behind me, the door creaks open.

Tyler Quinn says, "We've got a new arrival."

I inhale deeply on the cigarette, despite not enjoying it, and then drop the butt to the ground and smash it with my boot.

Without a word, I head back inside.

The site isn't large. Only ten holding cells, about twelve-by-twelve feet. An office, a makeshift rec room, a bathroom, and that's it.

Except, of course, for the room at the very end of the hallway.

My favorite room, though even now I'm loath to admit it to myself. Always careful not to smile when I'm in there during an interrogation, for fear that others might notice.

The killing room.

Tonight it's quiet. At least it will be for the next hour or so. Until we crank up the heavy metal. Don noise-canceling headphones to drown out the nonstop screaming. Trying to break these men one way or another because they're all guilty, and it's our job to learn whatever we can from them to win the war on terror.

Or something like that.

I follow Quinn down the hallway to one of the front rooms. Adam Reed and Julie Davies are already here. Four others are assigned to the black site, working opposite shifts: Gene Clark, Cody Metcalf, Anne Kerberos, and Zach Lambert.

Standing between Adam and Julie is a man with a cloth bag over his head. Wrists and ankles shackled. Adam gripping one arm, Julie the other.

Adam says, "Just came in."

I say, "English-speaking?"

Julie, nodding: "That's what the report says."

Adam asks, "Where should we take him first?"

And I smile and say, "Where do you think?"

The man is marched down the hallway to the killing room. It's not a large room by any means. A metal chair is bolted to the floor. A rusty drain underneath the chair. Because there are times when we need to hose the chair down—the place reeking of shit and piss and blood—and let everything wash away.

Quinn smacks the switch just inside the door. The lights in the ceiling buzz on. Adam and Julie prod the man to the chair, pivot him, and force him to sit down. Adam carefully securing our new guest to the chair with the shackles he's already wearing.

Beside me, Quinn holds up a file that wasn't in his hands

seconds ago. He opens the cover, starts paging through. With every new arrival we get a brief dossier, only the essential information, and later that dossier is burned, no trace left behind.

"Check it out," Quinn says and tilts the file in my direction so I can read our new guest's name.

My heart stops.

This . . . this doesn't make any sense.

The name printed on the page reads JAMES BURKE.

My gaze snaps toward the man in the metal chair. The man sitting there, motionless. Silent. As though knowing exactly what will happen next and already having accepted his fate.

Before I can say anything, Julie pulls the black cloth bag off our new guest's head.

My brother blinks at the harsh glow above him, then gazes around the room. First at Julie, then at Adam, then at Quinn.

Then at me.

"What do you think?" Quinn asks.

I stare at my brother. My mouth suddenly dry. My stomach, tight.

"Hey," Quinn says.

Blinking, I look at him.

"Huh?"

"I said, what should we do with him?"

I look back at my brother. But the person sitting there is no longer James. It's Ryan Fisher, the Lucky Star Hotel & Casino's head of security.

I blink again and it's now Olivia. Gorgeous, deadly, cold-blooded Olivia.

I blink again and it's now Allister Martin. The Englishman with his crystal-blue eyes and crude business acumen.

Another blink, and suddenly it's my brother again.

"Hey," Quinn says. "Did you hear me? I said what should—"

"—we do with him?"

The voice had changed, morphing into one I didn't recognize. A low tenor. Deeper bass.

My head was pounding, and I realized I was standing, though that was because two strong hands were holding me up. My face tilted forward, eyes closed.

Opening my eyes a crack, I saw dirt and grass illuminated by the bright afternoon sun.

A woman's voice said, "Did ya find anythin' useful on him?"

Another male voice said, "You mean besides the empty Glock? We found a burner—the same kind like we found on the woman. Also a bunch of cash. And he's got those handcuffs on one wrist. They look police-issue, just like the Glock."

"Did you find anythin' else on the woman?"

"Nothing else besides the burner. No wallet. No keys. Nada."

The first male voice said, "Nuh-uh, that ain't right. She had a badge."

The woman said, "What kinda badge?"

"Oh yeah," the second man said. "Looks like she's a doctor."

"You don't say?" the woman said thoughtfully. "Well, it don't matter. He'll be here soon."

I lifted my head, just a bit. Enough to take in the two sets of boots on either side of me. Scuffed black leather. Two sets of jeans on meaty legs. The men holding me each weighing at least two hundred fifty pounds.

Standing in front of me, only a few paces away, another pair of boots. I remembered seeing them not too long ago. Back at the travel plaza. The old woman with the raspy voice. Shaking her head when we asked for her help, starting to turn away, wanting nothing to do with us, before reconsidering. Acting as though she was taking pity on our dire situation.

Playing us from the start.

I lifted my head a bit more and noted a farmhouse standing fifty yards away. A large barn with faded white paint beyond it. This area—wherever we were—rural and deserted. Out in the middle of nowhere. Just dirt and grass and distant hills.

"Shit," the woman said. "He's awake."

Before either man could react, I lifted my foot and stomped it on one of the men's boots, attempting to twist out of their grip. Surprise was a factor, but it didn't give me much, both men immediately reinforcing their hold on my arms.

I twisted again, into one of the men this time, and kicked out at the other man, right at his balls. The strike hard enough to force him to loosen his grip, and I freed my arm and punched the man still holding me in the face.

For a beat, I was able to take in my captors. Large men with long beards. Wearing sunglasses and jeans and short-sleeved shirts and leather vests with some logo stitched over the left breast. Behind them, the woman's tractor trailer and two Harley-Davidsons.

Then I heard the woman shout, "Don't shoot him—he's still useful!" and I realized one of the men had pulled a gun.

I watched him bring it up, aiming the barrel straight at my face, so that my focus wasn't on the second man.

Who had slipped off the M4 strapped over his shoulder and slammed the butt of the rifle right into the side of my head.

Cue darkness.

23

Mitchell Hargrave rode the elevator down two flights to the subbasement and strode down the corridor to the room he'd spent most of the day in until he was summoned to the White House.

It was almost eight o'clock here on the East Coast, and he'd already been awake for close to fourteen hours and figured he'd be awake for another fourteen.

In the control room he found Theo and Julian at the computers, Rita Salazar standing behind them, her arms crossed.

Salazar turned when the door opened.

"How'd it go?"

Hargrave didn't want to talk about it. At this point in his life he'd made it a goal to never interact with the president, regardless of party affiliation or ideology. It had become a game in a way, as he'd had contact with pretty much every other high-ranking official in the United States government. There was something about being behind the scenes that he craved, the knowledge that he was almost invisible.

"Better than expected."

"Did you meet with POTUS?"

"I did."

"And?"

"And he's on board, at least for the time being. He definitely wasn't happy to hear that Burke murdered a cop."

"Samuel didn't come back with you?"

"No, thank God." Hargrave tilted his chin at the monitors. "Have you found him yet?"

Salazar shook her head.

"Not yet. We tracked him back to the hospital where he met with the doctor, and they slipped away in an ambulance."

"An *ambulance*? How'd they manage that?"

"It appears they stole it. We tracked them south from there, but they ditched the ambulance behind a strip mall."

"Where'd they go then?"

"They headed down the highway to a truck plaza, where we lost them."

"How? There must be cameras all over the place."

"There are, but they disappeared into the myriad of parked tractor trailers."

"How long ago was this?"

Salazar checked her watch, said, "About three hours ago."

Hargrave felt his stomach drop.

"And no sign of them?"

"None. From what we can guess, they managed to hitch a ride, either in the cabin or in one of the trailers. A good number of those trucks have extended cabins, the kind with a bed in the back, so if need be, they could have hidden back there and any traffic cams wouldn't spot anyone but the driver."

Hargrave, now addressing the techs: "So what have you two been doing this entire time?"

Theo said, "We've been tracking each truck that's left the plaza. They've headed in every direction imaginable."

Julian added, "Except . . ."

Hargrave waited, his arms now folded, one eyebrow raised. "Except?"

"Well, I floated the idea that maybe they didn't hitch a ride at all. Maybe they used the mass of eighteen-wheelers to mess with us and slipped out a different way."

Hargrave felt his teeth grinding against each other; this whole thing had gone sideways so fast he wasn't sure what else to do.

He asked Salazar, "Where's the team?"

"Still in Vegas. They did a sweep of the truck plaza but couldn't find anything. That's why the working theory right now is that they stowed away in one of the trailers."

"How many trucks are you tracking right now?"

Theo said, "Almost two dozen."

Hargrave was quiet, a hand to his face, fingers rubbing at the stubble on his chin. Different shots of traffic cams along different interstates were popping up on the monitors as the techs kept track of each tractor trailer.

"I have a thought," Salazar said. "Why don't we coordinate with highway patrol to pull over the trucks? They do a quick search, confirm the trucks don't have any stowaways, that helps narrow down our leads."

Still watching the monitors, Hargrave shook his head.

"It would make our lives a lot easier, but we can't bring in law enforcement. They'd ask too many questions. If we tried to throw the national security line at them, that would raise even more questions. Plus, by now I'm sure a BOLO has gone out for someone matching Burke's description in the cop's murder. On the off chance a highway patrolman does find Burke and the doctor, what's to say the patrolman doesn't do something stupid, or that Burke manages to overpower him? No, right now let's keep our focus on this."

Something occurred to him, and he frowned.

"Wait. What about the doctor? Do we know if she has her phone on her?"

Salazar said, "She did. We tracked her phone as well, but she tossed it in a trash can right after they ditched the ambulance."

"What about Burke's phone? Any way to triangulate his signal from the airport to the hospital and then the truck plaza?"

Silent, Julian's shoulders dropped.

Hargrave felt ice in his veins as he said, "What's the issue?"

Julian glanced back, shrugged.

"No issue, sir. It's just . . . there's a lot that needs to be done, and right now it's only the two of us. And we haven't gotten any breaks at all. Well, I did get like two minutes to take a piss, but I could sure use a cigarette."

"What are you asking for, Julian?"

"I mean, can't we bring in some more people? You know, to help lighten the load?"

Hargrave wanted to keep the circle as tight as possible, though he couldn't disagree with the man. This op was supposed to be clean and easy. Only a few hours of their time, to ensure Burke got on the plane, and then the FBI would pick him up once he landed. The Alpha Team was there to oversee the op, to make sure Burke did what he was supposed to do. Now, three of his men were injured and somebody on the team—it wasn't clear whether it was Hancock or Rowe—had fucking killed a cop.

Hargrave thought it was time to check in with Alpha One when he felt his personal phone vibrate.

A set of incoming text messages that were the last thing he wanted to see with all the rest of the shit going down today.

> 911

> She needs to c u

> Now

24

Pain.

Dull, throbbing pain.

It was the first thing I noticed when I came to. An ever-present ache radiating from the side of my head where the man had slammed me with the butt of his rifle.

A concussion, for sure, but as I opened my eyes and lifted my head, I realized a concussion was the least of my problems.

One of the men was standing in front of me. Just standing there, arms folded, head tilted to the side. When he saw I was awake, he grinned.

"Well, well, well. Look who's up."

I was standing, though *standing* wasn't quite accurate. I was upright, yes, because my arms were extended above my head, wrists once again bound together by handcuffs. A metal J-hook kept the handcuffs in place. The J-hook was attached to a thick wire that stretched at least forty feet up to the ceiling, where it was attached to a winch.

The man sauntered to a workbench against the wall where

he picked up a controller the size of an old TV remote. A wire fed from the controller to the wall, which fed to another wire that traveled all the way up to the ceiling.

The man pressed a button on the controller. An electric groan emitted from the winch, the wire attached to the J-hook growing taut and then lifting me into the air.

But only a few inches. Just enough so that my feet swayed above the ground. The steel ringlets of the handcuffs tearing into my skin.

Setting the controller aside, the man said, "Don't go nowhere."

We were in the barn. That giant barn door open, late-afternoon sunlight streaming in. A million dust motes floating about like stars. An ancient pull tractor in one corner. An old Chevy pickup in another.

On the workbench where the man had placed the controller, an assembly of tools I recognized from my past life. Hammers. Pliers. Saws. Many of them still crusted with blood from previous uses.

The man headed out the large door, which granted me a view of the lush landscape beyond. Rolling hills and tall grass. A split-rail fence skirting one of the hills for what looked like miles. The sight almost beautiful and serene if not for the fact this man—and whoever else—planned to do me harm.

Wait, no.

Not just me.

Stephanie.

Where the hell was she?

Earlier today I'd dislocated my thumb to escape these handcuffs, but it's a bit more difficult when those handcuffs are attached to a hook that's attached to a wire that's dangling you several inches above the ground.

That isn't to say I didn't give it a try. But gravity was not my friend, and no matter how hard I tried to gain leverage, it wouldn't work.

Scanning the barn again, looking left and right. The J-hook even granting me the ability to turn myself in a circle.

They had me suspended in the middle of the barn. Nothing close to me, at least within reach.

Unless . . .

Shifting my body, trying to build up momentum. Creating a pendulum. It wasn't clear whether the wire would get me close to anything worthwhile, but I had to try. Because there was no telling what these people planned on doing with me—and with Stephanie, wherever she was.

So I kept moving, left and right. Like I was a kid again on the playground swings. A simple motion every child knows. Back and forth. Back and forth. Back and forth.

A minute had passed since the man had exited the barn. Or maybe two minutes. Three. Time having gone a bit fuzzy. The pain still throbbing on the side of my head. The edges of the world blurry.

But I kept swinging. Gaining even more momentum. Trying to stretch my body as far as physics would allow.

Once, the tip of my shoe brushed the edge of the workbench, but that was it. Still, I kept swinging, despite the handcuffs tearing into my wrists. Blood had started trickling down my arms. If I kept going like this, the cuffs might shred the skin right off. But still I kept swinging, and swinging, and swinging.

"The fuck are you doin'?"

The man had returned, along with his friend—the one who'd clocked me with the butt of his M4. He still had the rifle strapped over his shoulder, watching in amusement as I swung limply through the air.

The first man snatched the controller off the workbench, stabbed his thumb at the other button.

A sudden whirling above my head, the winch quickly loosening. I was midswing when the wire went slack and I fell, hard, onto the barn's dirt floor.

Pain again, though this time different. More concrete, somehow.

The man punched another button on the controller, and the whirl came again, the wire growing taut once more and dragging me into the air. Higher this time, my feet now hanging several feet off the ground.

The man with the controller said to the guy with the M4, "You sure this is him?"

The other man had his phone out, peering at the screen and then glancing up at me. After a couple back-and-forths, he nodded.

"Yeah, it's him."

The man with the controller lowered me a bit so that my feet were now only inches from the ground. Somehow, it was worse than when I was several feet in the air.

"We use this contraption here from time to time to string up niggers. And spics. And, well, just about anybody we want. Except we've never used it on a white man. Have we, Mike?"

The other man—Mike—slowly shook his head.

"No, Jim, we have not."

"See, our club hates nigger and spics. But wanna know what we hate even more? Fuckin' cop killers."

Mike strolled forward, holding the phone up for me to see the screen.

The *Las Vegas Sun* website. The headline on the front page read: Cop Killer on the Loose. And under the headline, a picture. It was grainy, but if you looked hard and close enough, the face there looked almost like mine.

"Duncan's gonna be here real soon," Jim said. "He likes to be the first one to test out new merchandise. Even if they are niggers and spics. Not sure we ever got a chink before, but she's real hot, ain't she?"

I said nothing.

Mike slid the strap off his shoulder, set the rifle against the tractor. Took off his leather vest—I spotted NORSEMEN in big letters across the back shoulders of the vest, with the image of a Viking axe stitched underneath—and carefully draped it across the tractor's seat.

"Barb told us about how you're on the run. Is that true? Say, the abusive cop husband—is that the one you killed? Shit"—he pulled the Glock from behind his back, where he'd had it secured in his waistband—"this ain't his, is it? Tell me you didn't execute a cop usin' his own fuckin' gun."

Mike looked disgusted by my silence.

"You did, didn't you, you twisted son of a bitch? Probably emptied the whole mag into the poor bastard, what with it bein' empty and all. Had to reload the thing because, as my daddy always said, an empty gun is a sad gun."

As if to prove he wasn't fibbing, Mike dropped the magazine so I could see the jacketed 9x19mm Parabellum cartridges for only a second before reseating the mag with his palm. He shoved the pistol back into his waistband, glanced at Jim, and then strode forward and slugged me in the stomach.

A burst of pain—bright, sharp pain—but I did everything I could not to react.

Jim said, "Uh-oh. Looks like we got ourselves a tough guy."

Mike stepped back, glaring up at me. Nodded slowly.

"Yeah, Jim. Looks like we do."

"And so remind me, Mike. What is it that we do with tough guys again?"

Mike, a slow smile spreading across his ugly face: "We have ourselves some fun."

Jim set the controller aside and took off his own leather vest, hung it by a hook on the wall. Then he gazed over the various tools spread out on the workbench. His fingers rapping mindlessly against the wood as though making up his mind what he wanted for a snack and not which torture weapon he should use first.

"So," he said, selecting a large knife and turning back to me. "How 'bout we have some fun?"

25

"So you're a doctor, huh?"

Stephanie said nothing. She was lying on a musty bed, her hands bound to the headboard. An old brass headboard that probably looked gold maybe forty years ago.

The trucker sat on a wooden chair by the door. Her arms crossed, her face scrunched up as she examined Stephanie.

"I always wondered what it would be like to be a doctor. I imagine you gotta be real smart, don't ya? Do a lot of school, a lot of studyin'. That was never for me. I did okay in school, but I wasn't book-smart, not like some of my friends."

The woman shrugged like, *What are you gonna do?*

"My boy is a Norseman, just like his daddy. Women like me, we ain't allowed to be members, but we can still help out here and there. What I do is drive that truck, and I drive it good. Sometimes we transport people in the back. I need to use that spray to knock 'em out when they start gettin' real antsy."

Zip ties secured Stephanie to the headboard, the thick plastic biting into her skin.

Earlier, a man had been in the room, leering at her. Stephanie had felt her stomach clench, the look on his face making her want to puke. But then the trucker appeared and told him to beat it, that Jim wanted to see him, and then the woman settled down in the chair and peered at her as though Stephanie was something she'd never seen before.

"He should be here soon, you know. Duncan, I mean. He runs the club. At least the one here on the West Coast. His brother Ike runs the club out east. Both of 'em are real smart. Book-smart *and* street-smart. And Duncan . . . he likes to test out the new girls once they come in. Always gets a first crack at 'em."

The woman saw something on Stephanie's face and grimaced as she waved a hand.

"Don't you go judgin' me, girl. It's a livin'. Got bills to pay just like everyone else. I could tell you what's gonna happen to you—how you're gonna spend the rest of your life—but I imagine you already get the picture, what with you bein' book-smart and all. You ever do drugs? I imagine not, a pretty doctor like you. But I bet some of them doctors do drugs. Prescription stuff like speed, is my guess. You work long shifts, a real stressful job. Need something to keep you goin', don't ya?"

Stephanie said nothing, staring back at this awful woman. Doing everything she could not to burst out into tears.

"They're gonna start you up with somethin'. Heroin is my guess. That's one of the things the club dabbles in. Heroin and meth and crack. And guns. And, well, people. The club does it all. They'll get you hooked on somethin' so strong it becomes your whole life. You won't go a minute without wonderin' when you'll get your next fix. And because of that, you'll do whatever you're told. I get the sense you think you're one of them strong feminist types, that you can fight 'em off, but let me tell you somethin': you ain't shit."

A single tear coursing down the length of her cheek. She quickly blinked, willing any others away. Not wanting the woman to see.

"You might as well cry, girl. It's okay. You'll get used to it. I know I did. Not . . . well, you know. But the guilt. When I first started doin' this—when I brought girls like you to this farmhouse—there were times I couldn't sleep at night. Now . . . well, I sleep fine. Usually because I have myself a gummy before bed. Those always help. But shit, I ain't feel any guilt anymore. Sometimes I wonder what that says about me."

"It says you're a sociopath," Stephanie blurted. She couldn't help herself.

The woman cackled.

"Is that your professional opinion, *Doctor*? Maybe so. Maybe so. But I'm a sociopath who lives in a decent house and has a nice nest egg for when I retire. Tell me, girl: What's it like bein' in love with a cop killer?"

Stephanie didn't reply. She felt more tears trailing down her cheeks, tears she knew she couldn't stop and couldn't hide from the woman.

"That boy"—the trucker tipped her head toward the window, which Stephanie remembered looked out at the barn—"he killed a police officer earlier today. My son saw it on the news. And you . . . you said your ex was a police officer. So tell me—did your man kill him? Is that why you're runnin'? See, I knew you two were up to no good. Made it even easier for me to know it was okay to put you in my trailer. But you thought I wasn't gonna do it at first, didn't you? Ha! This old girl's still got some tricks left in her, yes I do."

Earlier, when Stephanie was alone in this creepy room with the cracked yellow paint and the spiderwebs in the corner, she'd yanked on her bindings as hard as she could. The zip ties were secure, of course, but the old frame didn't seem to be all there. She'd wondered if she yanked on the headboard hard enough, would the whole thing fall apart? At least enough to free one of her hands?

Now she said, "You must be so proud."

Something changed in the old woman's eyes. A flash of anger.

"What's that now?"

"You said your son's a member of this club, right? Somebody who does a lot of horrible things? He really got screwed in your gene pool."

The woman's brow furrowed.

"Shut your mouth."

"Oh, I see. He's a mama's boy, is that it? Is that why you help the club out like this? Because you need to keep an eye on him. What—you still need to wipe his ass too?"

The woman shot to her feet, her face growing flush.

"I said, shut your mouth!"

"Or wait a minute. Are you one of those mothers who like to diddle their sons when they're boys? Some Norma Bates shit?"

"Goddamn you!"

The woman moved toward her, fingers curling into fists, jaw clenched, and Stephanie waited until she was right beside the bed before making her move.

They had only secured her wrists, nothing else. Which meant her legs and feet were free to do whatever they pleased. And they'd allowed her to keep her shoes. The Brooks Glycerin running shoes she wore in the ER because it killed your feet to be standing all day. So as the woman advanced, Stephanie swung over onto her side and kicked out with her right foot, striking the woman in the stomach. The woman bent forward, surprised, and Stephanie kicked out with her left foot, right at the woman's face.

The woman stumbled away, tripping over her feet, and fell

face-first toward the floor—awkwardly, her neck twisting the wrong way.

In the sudden quiet of the farmhouse, Stephanie heard something snap.

The woman lay there on the wooden floor. Her breathing heavy and shallow. Trying to speak but not having the strength or ability to do so.

"Fuck you," Stephanie said, and then she started yanking again on the brass headboard. Not caring how much noise she made. Not worrying that this woman's son might be somewhere in the house and that he could open the door at any second. Forcing herself not to think about the man named Duncan and whoever else might be coming with him to this farmhouse to do God only knew what with her body.

She yanked and yanked and yanked until all at once part of the frame gave way, allowing her enough room to sit up and yank even harder.

Bit by bit, the rest of the frame came loose.

Stephanie got to her feet cautiously, the frame still behind her back, her wrists still secured. But at least she wasn't fastened to the bed anymore. That was a start.

On the floor, the woman kept emitting noises that may have been words. She tried moving her body but something was wrong with her spinal cord, the motor commands from her brain no longer able to issue commands to her limbs.

Part of Stephanie—the good part, the humane part, the part that had become a doctor—wanted to check on the woman, to see what was wrong.

Another part didn't give one shit and allowed her to do what she did next.

Which was to kick the woman in her head, again and again and again.

Then, taking a moment to catch her breath, she knelt, positioning herself so that she could search the woman's pockets. Which was nearly impossible, what with the metal frame, but she managed to make it work.

Though she found nothing of interest besides the woman's keys and phone. No knife. Nothing she could use to shear off the zip ties.

Struggling to stand back up, Stephanie stared down at the woman before kicking her once again, then sidestepped out into the hallway.

Down the hall to the kitchen, trying to keep her balance with the bed frame across her back, and then leaning awkwardly forward so she could start yanking open drawers.

She found a rusted knife, positioned it in her hand so that the tip was pointed toward her wrist with the sharp end against the zip tie, and started sawing.

It took less than a minute before she managed to sever the bindings.

The sound of the brass headboard crashing to the floor was the sweetest thing she'd heard in a long time.

Stephanie stood there then, breathing heavily.

She gazed out the window at the long drive leading up to the farmhouse.

Besides the woman's tractor trailer and two motorcycles, there was nothing.

Then she glanced out at the barn.

Danny.

Stephanie started moving room to room, searching for weapons.

It wasn't until she ventured down into the basement that her eyes grew wide and her breathing hitched in her throat.

She whispered, "Holy shit."

26

Tiny sharp kisses all over my body, Jim hooting and hollering as he poked me with the tip of the knife, laughing and dodging every time I kicked out at him.

But he soon grew bored and returned to the workbench, worked the controller while Mike worked my body, throwing jabs left and right, one after another, like I was a living punching bag. Jim raising me up and down so that my toes almost touched the floor, messing with my head while Mike messed with my internal organs as blow after blow slammed into my abdomen.

At one point Jim stabbed the button so hard the winch in the ceiling whirled wildly, creating so much sudden slack that I fell flat to the ground. At which point Mike started kicking me in the ribs, repeatedly, until he drew his foot back and kicked me once, right across the face. A spray of blood shot out of my mouth, painting the ground, and then Jim worked the controller again, and once more I was lifted into the air, my arms above my head, my torso free to undulate as I attempted to kick out at Mike, who only laughed as he dodged and weaved like we were sparring.

Then Jim said it was his turn and Mike, arming the sweat off his brow, hocked a loogie at me before turning to switch places.

But Mike decided to mess with Jim, playing with the controller so that I kept jerking away every time Jim tried to take a punch, Mike cackling like it was the funniest thing he'd ever seen while Jim's face grew redder and redder, his jaw tight, yelling at Mike to stop fucking around until Mike hoisted me all the way up to the ceiling, my feet dangling helplessly, before he let me drop.

The line went slack as I plummeted. I braced myself, ready to slam into the ground again. But Mike stopped the line at the last second, my arms above my head jerking up so fast it was a wonder I didn't dislocate both shoulders.

"Fuck this," Jim muttered, storming back to the workbench. He grabbed the pliers off the table, shook them in his buddy's face. "Now you let me have some fun before Duncan gets here, got it?"

Mike nodded obligingly and watched as Jim stalked back to the middle of the barn. More dust motes filled the air, swirling in the late-afternoon sunlight. Jim passed through the constellation, the pliers held out to his side.

"Now, what should we tear off first?"

He seemed to be asking the question to himself, but Mike, still standing by the workbench, answered.

"How about his toenails?"

Jim chewed the inside of his lip, thinking it over.

"We could do that. But I'm gonna need help gettin' his shoes off. And holdin' him steady. What with the way he's been kickin' and all. Fuckin' cop killer."

Mike set the controller aside and met his friend in the middle of the barn. He eyed me carefully, taking a few steps forward, and as soon as he was within reach I kicked out at him with one foot, then another. Mike dodged each kick, laughing again, and then bolted forward and bear-hugged my legs to keep them in place.

"Go on, then! Get his shoes off!"

Jim scrambled forward, yanking at one of my shoes, then peeling the sock off. He shifted his body so that he could get better leverage, but still I squirmed as much as possible, flapping my foot and toes and trying to kick out with my other leg.

Because I knew what was coming. I'd done it before. Many times. Back in my past life, when I was a different person. Though maybe I was kidding myself—maybe I was still the same person, just now with better insight.

Before, we typically secured a prisoner to a chair. Their arms and legs bound, each binding so tight they couldn't move a muscle. Which made it so much easier to cut and stab and tear off appendages. Almost too easy. Like child's play.

Part of me—a distant, unfamiliar part—said that this was karma. That after everything I'd done in my past life, all the people I'd tortured, all the people I'd killed, I deserved this.

Another part said, *Fuck that shit*, and I squirmed even more violently, enough so that Mike lost his grip.

Kicking out again with my foot that still wore the shoe, trying to go for one of the men's faces. The shoe's tip grazed the side of Mike's face, and he growled up at me, practically flinging himself forward again to grip my legs and keep them still.

"Come on, fuckin' do it already!"

Jim grabbed my leg, repositioned himself so he had a better grip. Holding my bare foot with one hand, the pliers with another.

"Now, which little piggy do we want to butcher first?"

Mike said, "Do the big toe."

Jim said, "The big toe it is then."

From where I was dangling, I couldn't see the pliers as they clamped onto the toe, but I felt them. The cold, unforgiving weight of the rusted metal. Still trying to squirm, to buck, to do anything to delay the pain that I knew was coming.

And then I felt it—searing white agony as Jim tore the nail right off.

But I didn't make a sound. Not even a grunt. Just stayed where I was dangling in the air, my eyes squeezed tight, holding my breath.

Mike said, "Guess we do got ourselves a tough guy, huh?"

I opened my eyes. Jim held the pliers up, inspecting the bloody nail.

"Maybe we should send 'im to the cop's family. A little bit at a time. But explain to 'em first whose body parts it is. We don't want to freak 'em out."

"I like that idea," Mike said. "Feels like good retribution. What do you think, cop killer?"

That's when we heard it.

Sudden and faint.

Outside, up toward the farmhouse, a woman screaming.

27

Jim turned away, holding the pliers to his side.

"What do you think that was?"

Mike said, "Go check it out."

"Why not you?"

"I got my arms full right now."

"Let him go."

"So that way he can start kickin' and swingin' and makin' a bunch of noise? I don't think so."

"That didn't sound like your mom, did it?"

"No. Now go, hurry!"

Making a face, Jim started toward the door. The pliers still in his hand. The nail still dripping blood, splotching the dirt every couple of feet.

The toe from which that nail had been torn was bleeding too. I couldn't see the toe, but I felt the blood seeping from it. Mike still holding my legs in place but having angled himself so that he didn't get any of the blood on him.

Jim moved over to the tractor, dropped the pliers, and picked up the M4.

Back toward the entrance again, walking slowly, the rifle now held with both hands. Until Mike said, "Get on with it!" and Jim grew some steel in his spine and strode forward quickly, not wanting to look weak in front of his fellow Norseman.

Jim stepped outside and a gunshot rang out.

One shot, that was all, and then Jim hit the ground with a thud. From where I was hanging, I could just see the top of his head and the dark blood starting to pool.

Mike released his hold on my legs and started to head in that direction, reaching for Officer Casey's Glock still tucked into his rear waistband.

But before he could get far, I bucked my hips and stretched out with my feet and wrapped my legs around his neck.

All at once Mike started punching at my legs around his throat, but the more he punched the tighter I squeezed, feeling every muscle in my lower body straining.

Mike jerked left and right, trying to loosen the stranglehold, but I held on. The steel handcuffs tearing into my skin, drawing even more blood.

I stared ahead at the top of Jim's head outside. Only a few seconds had passed, but no other gunshots had sounded, no other movement. I had no idea what had happened but had the faintest notion of who the shooter might be, so it wasn't surprising when Stephanie stepped around the corner, a pistol in both hands.

Stephanie trained the barrel on Mike but hesitated, worried that she might hit me.

I shouted, "Shoot him!"

She advanced another couple of steps, aiming for the man's center mass.

"Shoot him!"

Meanwhile, Mike had stopped punching and prying at my legs. His hand dropped to his rear waistband again, going for the Glock.

As Mike brought the gun up, I unwrapped one of my legs from around his neck and kicked down at his arm, the man squeezing off a shot that tore into the dirt, and at the same time Stephanie recovered her nerve and shot him twice, right in the chest, then kept moving forward, screaming now, squeezing the trigger repeatedly until the slide kicked back.

She stood there then, gazing down at the man, the gun now hanging at her side. Until, after a moment, realizing that we were safe, at least for the time being, her body shuddered and she leaned forward to vomit.

Once the nausea had passed, she wiped at her mouth with the back of her hand and blinked up at me.

I said, "Don't mind me. I'm just hanging around."

She dropped the gun and started forward, now eyeing my bloody toe.

I said, "You'll need to use that controller over on the workbench."

Seconds later both my feet were back on ground. Stephanie rushed over to release the handcuffs from the J-hook.

"Your foot."

"It's fine."

"And God, look at your wrists."

The blood continued to drip down my arms as I staggered toward the workbench. Looking over the tools, trying to find something I could use to free me of the handcuffs. Before the men had hoisted me into the air, they'd tightened each ringlet to the point that dislocating my thumbs wasn't an option this time.

"Can you use those?" Stephanie asked, and I turned to see

her pointing at a pair of bolt cutters hanging on the wall by the Chevy.

A minute later the handcuffs clanged to the dirt floor, and without any thought I pulled Stephanie into an embrace, and as soon as I did, she broke down, sobbing, her face pressed into my shoulder.

"It's okay. It's okay."

"No. No, it's not. I just took a life. *Two* lives."

"You didn't. You saved your life. Yours and mine."

She leaned back, studied my face.

"Is that how you've always justified it?"

I didn't answer her because I didn't have a good response.

"We should get going before others arrive."

"First we need to patch you up. We don't need you bleeding out."

Stephanie started to step away but noticed the expression on my face. Frowned.

"What's wrong?"

I stood motionless, listening carefully.

Stephanie heard it then too, that distant oncoming rumble of thunder.

I nodded toward Jim's body outside as I gathered my sock and shoe and slipped them on.

"Drag him in here. Then close the doors."

"What are you going to do?"

Again, I didn't answer her because I didn't have a good response. All I knew was that we didn't have long. Maybe a minute if we were lucky.

Motorcycles—what sounded like an angry swarm—heading in our direction.

28

Earlier today I'd limped to try to beat gait recognition software, but now I limped for real, a jolt of pain spiking up my leg with every step as I moved as fast as I could to the rear of the farmhouse. Forcing the back door open and hurrying down the hallway, sweeping the reloaded Glock back and forth.

Living room, dining room, bedroom—and it was in the bedroom that I found the old woman trucker, lying on the floor. At first I thought she was dead, but then her body twitched and she emitted a gurgling noise. Trying to say something but not having the power to do it.

I left her there and kept moving, straight to the kitchen. Not sure what I was looking for but knowing there had to be something. Because the guy in charge would arrive within the next minute, along with his underlings, and I wasn't confident I could take them all on by myself. If it were only me, I'd risk it, even with my injuries, but not with Stephanie hiding in the barn.

"Come on, come on, think," I murmured, closing my eyes, trying to see something that wasn't there.

Then an image materialized, a snapshot of memory when I was standing outside with the woman trucker and the two bikers and gazed around the property—the large natural gas tank positioned on the other side of the house.

I did another quick circuit of the first floor, making sure all the windows were closed, and then returned to the kitchen and yanked the stove out from the wall until the pipe snapped and I heard the quiet hiss of air.

Then down the steps to the basement, where Stephanie had told me she'd found a cache of weapons. I was expecting only a handful of guns and rifles, but it was an actual armory. Dozens of automatic rifles, semiautomatic pistols, flash-bang grenades, and other goodies like preloaded magazines all lined up orderly along the wall.

I grabbed an M4, loaded it with a mag while pocketing a spare, then collected a few grenades and hustled up the steps.

Now the growl from the motorcycles was even louder. I paused to peek out the window and saw the dust cloud in their wake. Looked to be at least a half dozen riders, about a quarter mile away.

I placed a few grenades in the kitchen, then hurried to the bedroom.

"You can't move at all, can you?"

The woman's only response was to gurgle.

"Good," I said, pulling the pin on one of the grenades and securing it under her body so her weight kept the safety lever in place.

Heading back outside through the rear door, edging to the end of the house to peek around the corner, I watched the bikers as they stepped off their Harleys.

I pegged Duncan the moment I saw him. A large guy with long gray hair and a long gray beard. The other men unconsciously acquiescing to him like all men do to top dogs.

Duncan took off his sunglasses and said something to the men, then motioned at the house and headed inside.

Three of the men followed him. Two started toward the barn.

Shit.

Leaning against the side of the house to take pressure off my toe, I watched the two men and heard the others as they entered the house, none of them immediately smelling the gas that had been circulating for the past minute.

"Barb! We're home!"

I couldn't wait here any longer, not if I didn't want to get blown up. So as the two men almost reached the barn, I started running. Moving at an angle where I came at the barn from the side. The sun dipping lower and lower toward the horizon.

Behind me, I heard someone from the house shout, "What the fuck? Barb!" and I pictured one of the men, having ventured deeper into the house, stepping into the bedroom to find Barb lying motionless on the floor. The man dropping to his knees and turning the woman over, exposing the grenade and releasing the safety lever. The man's eyes going wide, mouth starting to open to shout at the others, to warn them, when—

Ka-BOOM!

Even though the house was one hundred feet away, the blast was still enough to knock me off my feet.

Ears ringing, a massive fire cloud at my back, I climbed to my feet, snatched the M4 off the ground, and kept moving.

Moments before the explosion the two bikers had opened the barn doors, shouting when they saw the dead bodies inside. I'd told Stephanie to hide and imagined her somewhere in the dusty dark, probably behind the pickup, the rifle in hand. Waiting until the last second before taking any more lives.

I hurried forward, bringing the M4 up, flipping the rifle's

selector switch to Burst as I sighted on the two men running out of the barn at the sound of the explosion.

Two squeezes of the trigger, two three-round bursts, the rounds tearing into each man's chest and sending them to the ground.

I moved steadily, keeping the rifle aimed, as I approached them. Watched as one of the men, only moments from expiring, tried to reach for his gun.

I fired another three-round burst into his face, then into the other guy's face for good measure.

Someone screamed in agony behind me, and I spun around.

One of the bikers had made it out of the house, his entire body ablaze. He stumbled forward and fell to the ground, started rolling back and forth to try to extinguish the flames for what good it would do.

Stepping into the barn, I called, "Stephanie?"

She popped up behind the pickup, rifle in both hands.

"Did you get them all?"

I nodded and started toward the pickup. The thing was at least four decades old. There was no guarantee it would start, but we had to try.

We climbed into the truck. I checked the sun visor, but no keys magically appeared.

Stephanie shrugged when I looked at her.

I got out and hurriedly limped over to the workbench, returned with a flathead screwdriver. Jammed it into the ignition and turned it like a regular key. The engine groaned but then finally caught, the old girl sounding decent for her age.

I slotted the gearshift into Drive and we jerked forward out of the barn, past the two dead men, and straight into the oncoming twilight.

29

Tasha met Hargrave at the door when he let himself into the house. As was her penchant, she didn't look worried so much as irritated.

He asked, "How bad?"

"Bad," she said flatly and motioned for him to follow her.

Which he did, feeling the muscles in his shoulders tighten with all the stress of the day. First Daniel Burke, then the White House, and now . . .

He turned the corner to find his eighty-four-year-old mother in the living room. She was sitting in her favorite easy chair, a urinary bed pad underneath her.

Hargrave paused when he saw her sitting in the chair, staring blankly at the television. An episode of *The Adventures of Ozzie and Harriet* on the screen, his mother's favorite show. She watched it constantly, though on those rare occasions when Hargrave would try to engage his mother in conversation, she couldn't tell him one thing about any of the episodes she'd watched that day.

As Hargrave always thought when he was faced with the reality of what had become of his mother: *Fuck Alzheimer's.*

He turned to Tasha, one of the four women who looked after his mother.

"You said it was an emergency."

"At the time, it was. She kept trying to leave the house. Every time I stopped her, she became violent. Started screaming about bees. Finally, I had no choice but to give her a sedative."

The bees. Hargrave had always heard about them growing up. How you always had to look out for the nasty things. How a single sting could put you in the hospital—or, worse, in the ground.

Only Hargrave wasn't allergic to bees. Not like his mother, who had almost died from a sting when she was young. Something she had never wanted to talk about, a traumatic episode that she didn't want to relive, though he remembered when his mother had watched the movie *My Girl* she'd almost had a mental breakdown when Macaulay Culkin was stung.

Now, there were times when his mother—in her demented brain—believed the bees were back. All at once she was a young girl again, though in Hargrave's mind it wasn't clear if she'd already been stung or if some part of her knew she would be stung very soon.

"I was about to text you again, to tell you not to bother coming. But she only calmed down a few minutes ago, and I knew you were already on your way."

Hargrave's mother still hadn't even noticed him standing in the room. Her gaze fixed on the TV, with Ozzie and Harriet saying something to little Ricky.

Stepping forward, Hargrave smiled down at his mother and sat beside her on the corner of the sofa. Reached out his hand and gently took hers, gave it a slight squeeze.

"Hey, Mom."

Blinking, she slowly shifted her head in his direction. Stared at him with her blank eyes. At first, zero recognition, but then, after a few moments, she smiled weakly.

"Mitchy."

What she'd called him when he was a boy. A nickname he'd liked when he was five years old but had quickly grown to detest, and even though as a kid he told his mother he didn't like that name—he wanted to be called Mitch, just Mitch—she'd sometimes forget and call him that anyway, and it was only much later in life that Hargrave would wonder if the dementia had started to settle in sooner than the doctors believed it had.

"How are you feeling, Mom?"

The smile faded as that lack of recognition entered her eyes again. She gazed at the TV once more, then looked over at Tasha standing in the doorway before slowly leaning toward Hargrave to whisper.

"The bees are back."

"They're not, Mom."

"They're back, and they're going to get me. They're going to *kill* me."

A slight emphasis on the second to last word, though with the sedative already working its way through her system, she didn't have the strength to put too much force into it.

Hargrave motioned at the TV.

"I see you're watching *Ozzie and Harriet*. What's this episode about?"

Redirecting her when she started up was the only way to keep her focused these days.

His mother stared at the TV again, though as Hargrave watched her eyes, he couldn't tell if she was really watching it. After a moment, he realized her gaze was shifting around the room, searching for a dreaded insect that wasn't there.

Tasha stayed in the doorway, watching. Hargrave ignored her, feeling that same anger he did whenever one of the personal care aides was close by, and squeezed his mother's hand again.

"Mom?"

She blinked again and looked at him. Again not even a hint of recognition in her eyes.

Still holding her hand—not wanting to let go—Hargrave leaned forward and kissed her on the cheek. His voice, tender.

"I love you, Mom."

He left her there in the living room, watching a show she'd once loved but probably no longer remembered. Tasha followed him to the door, where he paused as the day's exhaustion nearly knocked him over. He stood motionless, his eyes closed, trying to regroup. Then opened the door and stepped out without saying a word to the caregiver.

This part of Georgetown was always quiet. Tonight the sky was clear, a light breeze rustling the trees along the street. A woman was walking her dog down the redbrick sidewalk, the dog sniffing at every tree along the way. The woman smiling and nodding at Hargrave as though they knew each other, even though they were complete strangers.

This wasn't the life he had always envisioned himself having. Not when he was younger and had a more naïve outlook on life. He'd imagined a wife, kids, maybe a dog or two to race around the backyard. Cookouts on the weekends. Baseball practice in the evenings. Trips to Delaware Beach during the summers.

What's worse was that he'd gotten close once, many years ago. Over two decades by this point. A woman named Sara, with whom he'd believed he was meant to spend the rest of his life. Even his mother had been taken with her, and she'd always had high standards for the girls he dated, wanting only the very best for him.

But, well, sometimes things don't work out, no matter how

hard we try to square that circle, and so instead this was his life now—the life he'd had no choice but to accept.

Climbing into his Mercedes, he called Rita Salazar.

"Any updates?"

"None with the tractor trailers, no. But I've dispatched the team to Los Angeles."

"Why?"

"Because I think I know where Burke is headed next."

30

We abandoned the Chevy in a strip mall in Van Nuys and headed down the sidewalk, passing a liquor store and Chinese place and beauty shop and tattoo parlor. The few palm trees lining the block looking sad and weary painted against the evening sky. The faded light from the streetlamps glinting off the cars as they headed up and down the boulevard, some playing bass so loud I felt it in my bones.

Soon we came to a thrift shop and circulated through the aisles searching for clothes. A few shoppers noted the bruises on my face and the dried blood caked on my clothes but didn't say a thing. I paid for our items with the cash Stephanie had reclaimed from Jim and Mike—along with the burners—and we continued another few blocks before entering a pharmacy.

Stephanie kept her face tilted down, just as I'd instructed her, having already explained about facial and gait recognition. I wasn't sure Hargrave and his team had had a chance to upload Stephanie's facial and gait info into the system, but if they hadn't done so yet, they would soon.

We hadn't spoken much since our escape. The trucker had taken us just over the state line, so it wasn't that far of a drive to reach LA. Stephanie mostly stared out her window. I didn't hear her crying, but sometimes I caught her wiping at her eyes.

Now as we left the pharmacy with two bags of medical supplies and continued down the block—both wearing baseball caps and sunglasses, courtesy of the thrift shop—Stephanie asked where we were going.

"Here," I said as we came to a bus stop.

A handful of people were waiting, most staring down at their phones. Since nowadays it looks strange if you aren't entranced by your phone, I slipped the burner from my pocket and gazed down at the blank screen. Stephanie noted what I was doing and pulled out her burner, doing the same.

Five minutes later the bus arrived. I paid our fare with cash, and we found seats near the back.

Once the doors had groaned shut and the driver pulled away from the curb, Stephanie said, "I hope there's not a bomb on this bus."

Her quiet voice just loud enough for a woman sitting near us to hear. The woman gasped, looking horrified.

Stephanie quickly shook her head and forced a smile.

"It's a joke. A bad joke. But don't you remember that movie? *Speed*?"

The woman gave Stephanie a nasty look like, *Are you out of your mind?* and then shifted in her seat to continue working on her sudoku.

I leaned in and whispered, "Maybe ease off the bomb-on-the-bus jokes."

Stephanie let loose a quiet, desperate laugh.

"I'm sorry. I sometimes say stupid things when I get nervous. But you remember that movie, right?"

"Of course I do."

"Dennis Hopper puts a bomb on the bus that gets triggered when the bus hits fifty miles per hour. And then the bus can't go under that speed or else the bomb blows up."

Stephanie's smile this time didn't look nearly as forced.

"I had such a massive crush on Keanu Reeves. I mean, I guess I still do—the man is gorgeous—but I remember seeing that movie back in middle school and I was just . . . in love. And your brother, when he found out, he *hated* Keanu. Like someday the guy would show up at school and whisk me off my feet."

Stephanie was staring down at her phone now, absently running her thumb over the power button. Outside her window, businesses and restaurants and homes breezed past.

"Maybe he didn't get my voicemail."

"He did."

"But what if he didn't? What if—what if there's something wrong with his phone? What if they . . . you know."

"They wouldn't have gotten a team together to pick him up this quickly."

Cautiously, she turned her face to look at me, her eyes hidden by the sunglasses.

"Are you lying?"

"No."

The old George Costanza trick that it's not a lie if you believe it's not a lie, but despite the confidence in my tone, my heart wasn't in it.

If The Office was on top of things, they would have looked into Stephanie Nguyen immediately, learned everything there was to know about her. Where she went to high school, where she went to college, the reason she'd moved out to Las Vegas. Her engagement and then de-engagement. How the man she was supposed to marry married someone else and now had kids. They'd maybe consider using him as leverage but then realize the only family member Stephanie had left was her widowed father. Living alone in Lanton, Pennsylvania. An easy target for sure.

But would they go to that extreme?

I realized Stephanie was still watching me. I couldn't see her eyes, but I could sense her studying the side of my face.

She said, "Don't do that."

"Don't do what?"

"After everything that's happened today—after everything you've done—don't lie to me."

The bus began to slow for the next stop.

I said, "This is us."

We stepped off the bus and continued down the block. Passing by a Chevron station and Indian restaurant and check-cashing place. Then up another three blocks. Then down an alleyway. Up another four blocks. Down another alleyway. Up another two blocks.

Stephanie kept pace beside me, silent, but I could tell the constant detouring was getting on her nerves.

Then we came to the apartment building, and I told her to wait by the front doors.

"Where are you going?"

"I don't have a key anymore, but there's a way to get inside around back. I'm going to break in, and then I'll come let you in the front. Just stay here and don't attract any attention."

I started away but halted when Stephanie whispered my name.

"Danny."

Slowly, I turned back.

The glow from one of the streetlamps glinted off Stephanie's sunglasses as she gazed up at the building and then back at me.

"What is this place?"

I thought about it for a moment, and then answered the best way I knew how.

"Home."

31

Only it wasn't home.

Not really.

The truth was, I didn't have a home. Hadn't had a home since I was a boy. When I lived with my brother and my mother in those long, weird years after my father's death.

Stephanie said, "Hold still."

Déjà vu again. The two of us stuffed into a tiny bathroom, just like a week ago. Only this was an empty apartment in LA and not Stephanie's house in north Vegas. But the tableau was mostly the same: me sitting on the toilet lid while Stephanie did her best to patch me up.

I had my sock off so that my foot was bare, exposing the bloody mess that was my big toe. Stephanie did what she could to clean it with disinfectant and then bandage it before leaning back and motioning me to stand up.

"I could do all this myself, you know."

"Yes, I'm sure you're an expert at cleaning up the remnants

of torture." Her tone, dry. "Now, stand up and take off your shirt. Let me check on those stitches."

As I rose from the toilet and began to peel off my shirt, I was reminded that I'd never wanted to bring Stephanie into any of this. That I'd approached her in that parking garage after her shift because I'd had no other choice, having been shot at and a bullet fragment stuck in my back, specifically in a place I couldn't reach. That was why I'd gone to seek her help.

Wasn't it?

Stephanie said, "This looks awful."

"Gee, thanks."

"It's not just the scar. Did those men cut you too?"

"A little bit."

"Christ. Here, let me see what I can do."

I stood there as she cleaned each and every place Jim had stabbed me, the wounds stinging when she applied the alcohol. Then she stepped back, inspecting the bullet wound in my back again.

"I told you before it was going to scar, but this... you never got it restitched after last week?"

And where, pray tell, I wanted to ask, would I have gotten the bullet wound restitched?

Staring at the drab bathroom wallpaper, I said, "I don't mind scars."

"I can see that." Her tone now thoughtful. "I wanted to ask you before but didn't feel it was my place. Now, I figure what the hell. How'd you get this nasty scar on your shoulder?"

Slipping the shirt back on, I turned around. Examining the bandages on my wrists. Deciding whether or not to tell her the truth.

"I'm not sure you'll believe me."

Stephanie snorted a laugh as she started cleaning up the discarded medical supplies.

"After everything I've been through today, I'll believe anything."

I glanced at my reflection in the mirror, at the tiny cuts marking my face. Stephanie had done what she could but there wasn't much that could be done. I couldn't quite bandage them all up, though I wondered if maybe it was worth a shot, as that might mess with facial recognition. Then again, bandages on the face would be too conspicuous. As it was, you couldn't see the cuts unless you were standing close to me.

Of course, the bruises from where Mike kicked me were another story.

"I told you about the job I had before, the one I walked away from."

"You mean the whole reason you had to fake your death."

"Yes."

"You actually didn't tell me much at all about the job."

I paused again, considering.

"I was part of an unsanctioned team that operated all over the world. Black op stuff, though we weren't part of any official agency or department. That was by design. If something happened to us, the government would disavow us entirely. Which meant if we got caught by the enemy, we were screwed."

"That sounds terrible. Why would you agree to do that?"

It struck me that this was the first time somebody had voiced the question. When Mitchell Hargrave had approached me about joining the team, I hadn't thought twice.

"I knew I would regret it if I didn't. I wanted to serve my country however I could, and I knew this was vital work."

"Did you like it?"

"At first I did. I believed what we were doing—the missions we were being sent on—was for the good of the United States.

And most of the missions we went on were just that. But a few others . . . I learned after the fact we were essentially cleaning up messes."

"So the scar. Were you shot?"

"No. That's where the tracking device was located."

Stephanie did a double take.

"You're joking."

"I'm afraid not."

"They put a tracking device in you."

"Yes."

"With your permission?"

"More or less."

"What does that mean?"

"It was part of the job description. A way to ensure The Office always knew our location during an op."

"The Office?"

"That's what we called it."

"So they put a tracking device in you."

"Yes."

"And then you, what, sliced open your back to remove it yourself?"

"Basically. After a certain amount of time, it would dissolve, but I had to take it out before then."

"You said after the fact you learned you were essentially cleaning up messes. How?"

"I had a source."

"And this source . . . is this the person you were texting earlier?"

Silent, I brushed past her out into the main living area. Which was sparse to say the least—a single table, folding chair, and a small wide-screen TV sitting on the floor.

Having collected and bagged the discarded supplies,

Stephanie followed me. She stood there for a moment, gazing around, and sighed.

"This has got to be the most depressing apartment I've ever seen."

"Again: gee, thanks. But to be fair, I never intended on coming back here."

"Wait—you actually *lived* here?"

"For the past year, yes. This was where I mostly stayed when I wasn't in Vegas."

"Still . . . didn't you have any furniture?"

"Not really. The lease on this place is up in six months. I was going to leave it as is, but then . . . you know."

"Where were you headed, anyway? At the airport this morning, I mean."

"The UK."

"What's in the UK?"

"Nothing in particular. I'd been through there a few times but never for more than a day. I figured I'd travel the country, then work my way through the rest of Europe. Then maybe Asia."

Stephanie crossed over to the table. She tossed the bag of trash on top and eased herself down onto the folding chair.

"Outside, you called this place home."

"I did."

"I'm sorry, but this is a pretty pathetic place to think of as home."

I shrugged as I leaned back against the kitchen counter.

"I never really had a home. Even as a kid. That was something I realized a few years ago. Because home is supposed to be a safe place. A constant place. But with my father . . . I never felt safe with him around."

"Even after he died?"

"Then, the house just felt . . . different. Empty. Quieter, for sure. But still . . . it didn't feel like home."

"I feel sorry for you."

"I'll say it yet again: gee, thanks."

"I'm serious, Danny. You got dealt a raw hand. You and your brother both. Am I happy you dragged me into this? Of course not. But I'm here, being chased by a team of killers, and all I want to know is how is this going to end."

"I'm not sure."

"That's a shitty answer."

"It's the truth."

"What do they want from you?"

"I don't know."

"Do you think your source would know?"

"Most likely, but she's not talking to me right now."

"Why's that?"

"She says I lied to her."

Stephanie stared up at me.

"Did you?"

"Did I what?"

"Lie to her."

I took a moment to think about it. Shrugged.

"Honestly, I have no idea."

"Fantastic," Stephanie said dryly. She turned away, gave the room another once-over, then grabbed the remote and turned on the TV. "So while my life's now in danger, and probably my dad's life too, you don't even know what you did. But maybe it's on the news."

Stephanie absently surfed through the channels. It was just after eight o'clock and cable news was still wall-to-wall coverage of the vice president and how this impacted the presidential race. Also thrown into the mix was brief footage of Senator Harold

Browne. The smug son of a bitch smiling as he was being led out of the Lucky Star Hotel & Casino, my friend Adam in his FBI jacket right beside him.

Stephanie kept clicking the remote. The Dodger's game zoomed past. Then a rerun of *Friends*. Then a game show. Then some infomercial.

I said, "I have an idea."

She leaned back in the folding chair with a sigh, tossing the remote on the table.

"Regarding what?"

"I don't know what the government wants from me, but I know somebody who might."

32

Adam Reed hated an empty house.

Usually when he came home his son and daughter and wife were there, and it was their combined spirits that he sensed when he passed through the garage door, that spark of life vibrating throughout the entire house that always warmed his heart.

But when he came home and his wife and kids were out, he'd always felt the emptiness deep down inside, as though it were palpable, a living thing that could be poked and prodded and bent out of shape.

The house had been empty now for almost a week. Helen having taken the kids to her parents' house in Arizona after the raid on the place in Pasadena.

The country had become so polarized in the past couple of years that many people believed another civil war might break out at any time. Adam had always thought these people were off their rockers, but in the past few days he'd gotten a taste of what it was like to become a hated target to several million angry citizens.

Somebody had leaked his name. It wasn't quite clear who, but Adam assumed it had to be another agent, someone he'd worked with to keep this country safe but who felt a loyalty to the vice president for whatever reason. His name had been leaked to the press, and suddenly online sleuths were digging up everything they could find on him, including information about his wife and children.

The bombardment of emails was bad enough—a quarter of which called him a nigger—but the nonstop calls were another thing. He'd disconnected the landline, then contacted the phone company to request an unlisted number. Though he knew it wouldn't help much—those who wanted to harass would figure out other ways to harass, and it was because of this he told Helen to take the kids away, at least for a week, though in the back of his mind Adam knew there was a chance his family may never return to this house.

Now, sitting in his leather recliner, the Dodgers game playing silently on the TV, a beer sweating on the coaster beside his chair, Adam stared at his wife on his phone and tried to hide the exhaustion from his face.

"I miss you."

"I miss you too. So do the kids. They keep asking me when we can come home."

Fortunately, their kids were still young. Laura six years old, Malcolm four. Both too young to be exposed to social media. Both still young enough not to fight their parents when they sensed something wasn't right.

Helen said, "I saw you today. I've been watching the videos online. You and that senator coming out of the hotel."

Adam took a slow pull of his beer, swallowed heavily.

"Did I look handsome?"

"You always look handsome."

A brief silence, and Adam wished his wife was here with him now, sitting on his lap, gently caressing his cheek.

The volume of his wife's voice ticked down a notch.

"It's going to get even worse, isn't it? I know this senator isn't as big a deal as the vice president, but there've got to be other politicians involved, right?"

Adam hated lying to his wife—he'd made it a point from the start of their marriage never to do it—so he told her the truth.

"I don't know."

Another silence. A voice said something in the background. Helen looked away from her phone, said, "Okay, I will," and then smiled back at him.

"Dad says hi."

"He doesn't hate me, does he?"

Adam remembered the day he'd asked Helen's father for permission to marry her. Standing in the backyard of their house in Queen Creek, the sky cloudless and the air dry. How the man had shaken his hand a bit too long, studying his face, and then finally said he would grant that permission as long as Adam promised never to do anything to hurt his daughter or future grandchildren.

His wife said, "Of course he doesn't hate you. He understands what kind of pickle this is."

Adam started laughing—he couldn't help himself.

"Pickle. Yeah, that's one way of putting it."

A text notification appeared at the top of the screen. From a number he didn't recognize.

> We need to meet

Helen said, "What's wrong?"

Adam blinked.

"What do you mean?"

"I can tell by your face something just happened. You didn't get another one of those awful emails, did you?"

Another text message from the same number.

> I need your help

Adam said, "Yeah, something like that. Listen, I need to make a call, but I'll text you later. Give the kids a kiss for me."

He could tell by his wife's expression that she was worried. She'd always been worried about him, knowing that his job was dangerous, but in the last week those fears had ramped up exponentially.

"I love you, babe," Helen said, and Adam smiled and said he loved her too, and then their all-too-brief FaceTime session was over and he stared at the two messages from the number he didn't recognize.

It was a Los Angeles area code, but that didn't mean anything.

Adam stared at the screen, his thumbs hovering over the digital keyboard. He closed his eyes, took a deep breath, and typed.

> Who is this?

> Hondo

Adam's sigh was so heavy it was a wonder all the air didn't leak out of him.

He typed back,

> Don't contact me

> Adam, please

> I mean it

> I need your help

> It's a matter of life and death

An exaggeration? Possibly. Though Adam had never known Daniel Burke to exaggerate. Just as he'd never known him to make things up. Which was why he'd felt confident taking the tip to his superiors last week. They'd granted him a team, which had rolled right out to the estate, and even though Dan had told him who would be there, part of Adam had refused to believe it.

Until he'd seen the son of a bitch with his own eyes.

Adam typed,

> Where are you?

> In LA

> This isn't a good idea

> I know

> But I wouldn't ask if I had any other choice

Adam started typing, *Fuck you and never contact me again.* His thumb hovered over the Send button, and for a moment he stared at the words, surprised he'd even written them at all.

It had been unconscious, simply what he was feeling, what was in his gut, but he knew it wasn't the right thing to send.

He deleted the line, then typed again.

> If we meet it needs to be someplace public

> Agreed

> I know the perfect place

Adam stared at the screen. At the words on the screen. At the words that could get him into a lot of trouble.

He knew it would be in his best interest to delete the messages and block the number. Dan might contact him again from a new number, and Adam could just block that too.

But he'd worked with Dan in the past, and he thought of the man as a friend, in that way you view somebody you've spent over a year of your life with in a god-awful situation where you're forced to do god-awful things as a friend.

It had taken years before the nightmares had stopped. Nightmares that he'd never even told Helen about. The only person he'd told was Dan, on those rare occasions they saw each other, and Dan's response was always the same.

I'm happy for you, brother. Because mine have never stopped.

It had been years since then, and Adam had always wondered if the nightmares had ever stopped for Daniel Burke. Admittedly, Adam had been surprised to hear the man even had dreams like that. He'd always been so stoic. So quiet. So . . . dangerous.

Adam remembered what Tyler Quinn had once said about Dan, and it had stayed with him ever since.

The guy's a complete psychopath. I think he gets off on this stuff.

This stuff being what they'd done to prisoners at the black site in the Philippines. Back when Adam was a soldier. Before he was a husband and then a father. Before he became a family man who suddenly had a whole different set of priorities in life.

He should delete the messages, block the number. Or no—screenshot them and email the whole text chain to his superiors. Show them what a good, honest agent he was. A team player.

That's what he should do.

What he kept telling himself to do.

Instead, he found his thumbs typing a single word.

A question.

> Where?

33

Dodgers Stadium.

One of the oldest and most iconic baseball stadiums in the country.

Located in the valley of Chavez Ravine, the ballpark provides views to downtown Los Angeles, the green hills of Elysian Park, and the San Gabriel Mountains, depending on where you're standing.

But at night—like tonight—the only thing that really sticks out are the glittering lights of downtown LA.

Except, of course, for the insanely bright and massive LED bulbs spotlighting the stadium itself. And all the lights in the parking lot surrounding the stadium. And the heavy roar of the crowd inside.

At the top of the seventh inning, the parking lot was still packed. After all, it was the last home game of the season, and if the Dodgers clinched a win tonight, they were headed to the playoffs.

Adam Reed parked near Gate C and walked to the main entrance, where he found a ticket waiting for him under his name.

Through the metal detectors, he entered a sea of blue and white—virtually everyone wearing the team's colors.

His ticket was for a seat in the infield loge box, overlooking left field.

He headed in that direction, past the kiosks, past the kids with their mitts, past the teens wearing snapbacks and playing with their phones, past the men ducking out to grab a last-minute beer or Dodger Dog or take a piss. All the way to the level where the seat was located.

Adam started to head down to the seat when I separated from the crowd, a plastic cup of beer in my hand, and advanced close behind him.

"Keep moving," I said, taking his arm to redirect him.

To his credit, Adam barely flinched. He took a quick furtive glance around the level as we kept moving.

"Where are we going?"

"Just walking. Thanks for coming, by the way."

"Hondo," Adam muttered, shaking his head. "I almost forgot we called you that back at the site. Why did we call you that again?"

"Because during downtime I'd read those old Louis L'Amour paperbacks."

"That's right," Adam said. Then, gazing around the mezzanine: "Shit, I haven't been here in years."

"Still a Cubs fan?"

"Always."

Adam had been born and raised outside of Chicago. Back at the black site he often discussed his love for the Cubs and how, as a young boy, he'd dreamed of joining the team.

That was until high school when he realized he couldn't hit for shit and his fielding wasn't much better.

Adam said, "I wasn't going to bring a weapon, if that's why you picked this place."

Again, living in a post-9/11 world: metal detectors the way of life at all major sporting events and concerts.

"I won't lie and say it didn't cross my mind. But I figured a crowded public spot would be the best place to meet. By the way, I'm glad you're not wearing your Cubs hat."

Like me, Adam wore a royal-blue Dodgers cap. Keeping our heads tilted down so the bills obscured our faces from the myriad of security cameras stationed around the stadium.

Adam said, "I should be angry at you."

"Why?"

"You've ruined my and my family's lives."

I paused, but only for a beat. I'd known Adam was married, that he had kids. And when I'd contacted him last Saturday night, part of me had known there was a chance his family would get swept away in the fallout. That's why, after I'd told him how the vice president was at the VIP party, I also told him he could pass the tip along to another agent who could take the ball. But Adam, always one to do what's right, led the charge.

"Do you want me to apologize?"

"It wouldn't matter if you did. Why are you limping?"

"Partly to avoid gait recognition, partly because I had a little run-in with some bikers earlier today. A gang calling themselves the Norsemen."

Now it was Adam who paused.

"You're joking."

"You've heard of them?"

"Of course I've heard of them. They're white supremacists who dabble in everything from running guns to human trafficking. A pair of brothers run the club: one oversees the West Coast and is stationed somewhere outside LA, the other oversees the East Coast and is stationed somewhere outside Baltimore."

"Yeah, well, the brother overseeing the West Coast has been permanently forced into early retirement."

Adam paused again.

"Did you kill him?"

I said nothing.

Adam asked, "Is this why you wanted to meet?"

I hesitated, still not sure how to continue. Even though I'd been thinking about this for the past hour, ever since I'd messaged him.

"It came to my attention this morning that the FBI planned to arrest me when I got off my plane in DC."

I watched Adam's jaw tighten as he processed this.

"How do you know that?"

"That's what I was told."

"By whom?"

"It doesn't matter."

Adam was faster than I remembered: he snatched out his hand to grab my arm, causing some of the beer to slosh out of my cup. He leaned in, his voice low.

"Yes, it does fucking matter."

The crack of a bat on the field, and the crowd erupted as a white dot soared in the air, headed for center field.

Adam and I turned to watch the play. The ball arcing and coming straight down. The center fielder on the other team racing to the fence, eyes glued on the ball. The man leaping in the air, extending his glove . . . so that the tip just managed to make the catch.

A rumbling chorus of groans tore through the stadium as the opposing team trotted off the field, ending the seventh inning.

As we continued through the crowd on the mezzanine, Adam asked, "How did you know?"

"How did I know what?"

"About that party. About the VP. About all of it."

"It's a long story."

"Do you think I live close by? I busted my ass to get here as soon as possible. To meet with someone who is apparently wanted by the same agency I work for. The least you can do is humor me."

I drank my beer, just like any other fan here at the stadium. Buying myself time.

"Dan."

"Like I told you, it's a long story."

"I was told you had been killed."

"Who told you that?"

"Quinn."

"You stay in touch with him?"

"Off and on. My impression is he checks in on everyone who was at the site."

"He's never checked in on me."

"Well, that's not surprising, is it?"

Another solid crack of the bat. Again we turned to watch. The ball soaring high into the air, straight toward left field. The Dodgers fielder sprinting to meet it. But it was clear within seconds the ball was going over the wall.

A healthy chorus of boos, and Adam shook his head as we continued moving.

"The Dodgers are going to pull it out in the end. They always do."

"So as far as you know, my name hasn't been flagged by your agency?"

"If it has, I haven't heard about it."

"Any chance you could make some inquiries?"

"For what purpose, exactly?"

"Well, the truth is, I'm not sure why they'd want to arrest me."

"You faked your death, Dan."

"That can't be the only reason."

Adam stopped suddenly, grabbing my arm to halt me in place. Turning toward me, his eyes narrowing.

"What else aren't you telling me?"

I took another furtive glance around the mezzanine, scanning everyone's faces just like I'd been doing since I got to the stadium a half hour ago—and then pushed Adam forward.

"Keep moving."

"Why?"

"They're here."

34

"Shit," Mitchell Hargrave said. "The target made Alpha Two."

It was just after midnight on the East Coast and most of the team had been working nonstop for eighteen hours. Theo and Julian still at the computers, Rita Salazar standing with him off to the side, monitoring the screens. That asshole Samuel Chen was still here too, though he kept popping in and out, asking for updates.

When Hargrave didn't hear from Dennis Rowe, he cleared his throat.

"Alpha Two, do you hear me? Pull back."

Rowe: "I don't think he spotted me."

"It doesn't matter. We can monitor the target from here."

It hadn't taken the techs long to hack into the Dodgers Stadium's security feed. As soon as they'd tracked Adam Reed from his home to the ballpark, Julian and Theo did their tech magic to grant them access. So as soon as the FBI agent parked, they were already tracking him. Watching as the man grabbed a ticket at the gate and then continued into the stadium, the game already halfway over. The man alone . . . until he wasn't.

It was Rita who suggested they monitor Adam Reed. She'd been poring over as much intel on Daniel Burke as possible. Most of the reports marked top secret, and even many of those redacted, but she had kept digging until a name made her pause.

She said the name had sounded familiar, but she couldn't put a finger on why until suddenly everything had clicked into place.

Adam Reed was the agent who'd led the charge at the private estate in Pasadena Saturday night—the one that had ensnared the vice president.

Then, just this morning, he'd been on hand to take Senator Harold Browne into custody.

Based on the information gleaned from the hacker who called himself the Spider, the private estate had been connected to the senator in a roundabout way.

Plus, as far as they could tell, Adam Reed had yet to disclose who'd tipped him off about the party in LA—and then later that Harold Browne was in some off-Strip hotel and casino.

And since they'd lost track of Daniel Burke—none of the tractor trailers they'd been monitoring having given them any luck—they had no choice but to keep an eye on Reed.

They'd remotely hacked into his phone and saw that he was FaceTiming with his wife when he received a series of text messages from a burner.

The messages had been vague, which the team figured was the point, Burke probably assuming they were already keeping an eye on the FBI agent.

Which was why when Adam Reed asked where to meet, the response had been puzzling.

The place in town you hate the most.

Then, a note that a ticket would be waiting for him.

Now they watched as Burke and Reed increased their pace through the crowd.

Hargrave felt his fingernails digging into his palms. Goddamn it. His men were much too eager to take Burke down, after what had happened at the airport. And then blocks away from the hospital. And then the fact that he'd managed to disappear somewhere at that truck plaza.

The team wouldn't let the target get away again, and Hargrave worried that one of them was going to do something stupid.

Hargrave asked the techs, "Where are Alphas One and Four?"

Lucas Hancock had also entered the stadium, with Michael Kincaid staying outside, and Noah LaSalle—with his broken arm now in a cast—waiting in the SUV in case they needed to make a quick getaway.

On such short notice his team couldn't smuggle guns into the ballpark, as they had to go through the metal detectors like everyone else, but both men were carrying what were essentially plastic knives. Made of an ABS/nylon/fiberglass composite, the knives were easily passed through metal detectors, and in the hands of men like Lucas Hancock and Dennis Rowe, they were deadly.

"What the hell is he doing?"

Samuel Chen's voice snapped Hargrave to attention. He looked up at the monitors and noted that the target had slowed completely.

Then, after a beat, Daniel Burke turned on his heel and headed back the way he and the FBI agent had come.

Straight toward Alpha Two.

35

Adam paused to glance around the mezzanine, his voice tight and nervous.

"Who's here? What are you talking about?"

I took his arm and kept us moving as I scanned those around us. Adrenaline now coursing through my system. Sizing up every person we passed, deciding whether they posed any threat.

"There's a kill team hunting me."

"A *what*?"

"They came for me back in Vegas earlier today, right when I was about to board my plane. I'm pretty sure I lost them, which means they must have followed you."

"Nobody followed me. I was careful."

"Nobody followed you by car, maybe. But they did, by either drone or traffic cams. Or—what about your phone?"

"I left my phone at home. Which means I won't answer if Helen calls, and she'll start panicking. Goddamn it, Dan. What did you drag me into?"

"You need to leave."

"What about the kill team?"

I slowed my pace, all at once feeling the weight of the beer in my hand.

"I've got an idea."

"God, you know how I always hated when you said that."

"Head for the nearest exit. Now."

Before Adam could say anything else, I turned away from him. Spinning on my heel, performing an exact one-eighty. Now headed back directly from where we came. My eyes locking on Dennis Rowe standing fifty feet away. The man wearing a Dodgers cap that looked too clean, too bright.

I strode straight for my ex-colleague. Dennis leaning against a pillar, staring down at his phone. His lips moving almost imperceptibly as he communicated with Hargrave and the rest of the team.

I figured by now the techs had hacked into the stadium's security system. Access to every camera in the place at their disposal. They'd probably been tracking Adam since he left his house. Because he'd been the one who'd gotten a tip about the VIP party. And those in the know—because I figured Eugene had already spilled his guts—would know I'd gone to that VIP party to save the women who'd been abducted.

It didn't take a genius to put two and two together.

When I was less than thirty feet away, Dennis Rowe finally acknowledged me. His dark eyes shifting up from his phone, his gaze meeting mine. His jaw, going tight.

Dennis held the phone in his left hand, his right hand down at his side. I figured he had a weapon on him. Maybe not a pistol—too difficult to sneak one through the metal detectors, but there were other weapons that could be passed undetected through such a security checkpoint. More weapons than you can probably imagine.

Fifteen feet away now. Moving quick.

Dennis held my gaze as he dropped the phone to his side.

Still trying to play like we didn't know each other. Like we hadn't gone on dozens of ops together over the years. Like we hadn't killed the enemy together.

When I was five feet away from him, I shouted loud enough to be heard over the music and the crowd and the blood now thundering in my ears.

"What the fuck, man? Why'd you grab my girl's ass?"

A few people nearby turned to see who was shouting.

Dennis's glare was pure venom. But still he tilted his head in a sort of shake, a gesture of both annoyance and awe. As if to say, *Well played, Burke.*

Beer still in hand, I stepped back to shout at the crowd, morphing my voice to sound buzzed.

"This asshole sexually assaulted my girlfriend!"

There were still a few people nearby watching, but others had moved on. Nobody caring about a drunken dispute when the Dodgers were so close to making the playoffs.

Okay, fuck this.

"Asshole!" I shouted, throwing my beer in his face, then spun and started in the other direction.

Two security guards were hurrying this way. One of them on a walkie-talkie, saying something I couldn't make out because there was another crack of the bat out on the field and the entire stadium erupted in cheers.

Pausing briefly just like everyone else, turning to look out at the field, hoping the security guards would hustle past without any hesitation.

They did.

I continued on, my pace having quickened, not looking over my shoulder as I headed for the nearest exit.

A vice latched onto my arm, and that familiar voice spoke loud enough for me to hear over the music and crowd.

"Let's not make this any messier than it needs to be."

Hancock. Standing right behind me now. Pressing something sharp into my back.

"The barest amount of pressure will pierce your kidney."

Still staring toward the exit, only one hundred feet away, I said, "Lucas?"

"Yeah."

"You know I didn't kill any cop."

"The cop was an unfortunate accident."

"Whose bullet was it? Yours?"

Silence.

"Thought so."

I jerked around and clamped a hand on Hancock's wrist clasping the knife, holding it in place. Then, gripping the man's wrist while the man gripped my arm, I pivoted Hancock into the nearest pillar with enough force to knock the wind out of him.

His grip loosening on my arm, I brought my elbow up and smashed it repeatedly against his face.

A fountain of blood squirted from his nose. Hancock planted his foot behind my leg and pushed me backward. I tumbled onto the ground, smacking the back of my head against the concrete, and before I knew it he was on top of me, pinning me in place.

"I told you not to make this any messier than it had to be, Dan. You never listen."

With the knife still in hand, Lucas looked as though he might stab me in the throat—but before he could bring the plastic blade down Adam Reed appeared out of nowhere, shoving Hancock from the side, sending him sprawling to the ground.

Adam shouted, "Go!"

I scrambled to my feet, meaning to turn back toward Lucas,

to continue the fight, but Adam stepped between us, shouldering me aside.

"I mean it, Dan. Get out of here!"

I could hear shouts nearby, security and police heading this way.

Sprinting toward the exit, glancing over my shoulder as I went. Lucas back on his feet now, knife held low at his side. Adam stepped forward, threw a punch at Lucas's face. Lucas ducked it and brought up the knife, and they started grappling for it, Adam trying to hold Lucas's hand in place, and as I hit the gate that led outside—where I knew even more police and security might be waiting, not to mention the rest of the team—I turned around to see the tip of the plastic blade slide into Adam's stomach.

Instinctively, I wanted to race back and take that plastic knife away and slit Lucas Hancock's throat.

Instead I watched Adam's face across the distance. His eyes wide and glassy. His lips moving soundlessly, mouthing one word.

Go.

I kept going. Right out of the stadium. Past the people milling about. Scanning every face in the crowd, trying to spot a face I recognized or one that recognized me.

There—fifty feet away, that large son of a bitch, barreling straight toward me. A wide flesh-colored Band-Aid on his cheek where I'd stabbed him with the pen earlier today.

Three security officers and a cop were racing in from the other direction, hurrying toward where Adam Reed now lay.

Because it had worked so well this morning, I shouted it again.

"Gun! He's got a gun!"

Kincaid halted in place. His flat eyes somehow going even flatter.

The cop and one of the security guards peeled away and headed over toward us. I pointed, my voice high and hysterical.

"He's got a gun!"

A woman screamed. People started running. A man just as large as Kincaid, decked out in all Dodgers gear and probably a dozen beers in, decided to play hero. He charged at Kincaid right as the cop and security guard blew past me.

I hurried away, breezing past the palm trees, and headed deeper into the parking lot.

"Dan!"

I whipped my face around.

Noah LaSalle was peeking around a black SUV. His left arm in a cast, waving me over with his other hand.

"Hurry!"

I diverted course. Surveying the lot as I went, searching for any other threats.

I slowed when I was ten feet away.

"What do you want?"

"Let me get you out of here."

"No way."

"Come on, man. Hurry!"

I eyed the SUV. The back windows tinted. As far as I could tell, nobody was hiding inside with a shotgun ready to blast my head off.

I started to back away, shaking my head.

"Wait!" he breathed, stepping around the SUV and aiming a pistol at me. Just like this morning, this one had a sound suppressor threaded on the barrel.

Without another word, he fired off a shot. I heard the bullet zing right by my head.

"Goddamn it," Noah muttered. "You had to break my good arm, didn't you?"

As soon as Noah had fired the shot, I'd dropped down to take cover. Staying low, hurrying around a car, ducking behind another. Listening to the soft scrape of Noah's feet on the pavement as he tracked me.

"I'm sorry about this, Dan. But we honestly thought you were dead. And we figured with you dead you could take the heat."

Sirens rising up in the night, headed this way.

"I tried to make it clean back at the airport. Told you where to find me. You came in faster than I expected. That's how I managed to miss the shot. Told you it was all part of the show, and you fucking believed it."

Still crouched low, moving from one car to the next, then leaning out far enough to see around the bumper.

Noah was two cars away. He was aware that his footsteps made noise and was trying to walk as silently as possible.

"Come on, Dan. Be a team player. Take one for the team. I'll make it quick and painless."

The only thing I had on me was the burner. I slipped it from my pocket, waited for the right moment, and tossed it in the air.

The phone didn't make much noise when it hit one of the cars, only a flat thump, but it was enough for Noah to turn in that direction—and as soon as he did, I sprang up from behind the car and flung myself at him.

We hit the ground hard, Noah landing on his broken arm. The added distraction of the sudden pain made it so I could easily tear the pistol from his grip. Then I was standing back up, aiming the silenced gun at his head.

"What are you talking about? What heat did you think I could take?"

He snarled up at me, his face rippling with painful rage.

"Fuck you!"

More sirens. They would be here within the minute.

Noah said, "Just get it fucking over with."

"I'm not going to kill you, Noah. But that doesn't mean I still want you in play."

I shifted the pistol and squeezed the trigger twice—one round in each kneecap.

Noah's scream reminded me of the men we'd tortured in the killing room. Pure primal agony.

I hurried away, scooping up the burner I'd tossed, threading between the cars to the edge of the parking lot.

Four LAPD squad cars came tearing up the drive, sirens blaring and roof lights blazing, an ambulance in tow.

I kept moving, through the trees, and down a steep slope to a chain-link fence topped with barbed wire.

The four-foot kitchen mat was right where I'd tossed it nearly an hour ago. I picked up the mat and threw it over the barbed wire, then climbed the fence. The mat didn't do the best job—many of the barbs still managed to poke through—but it was good enough for me to make it over the top without tearing too much flesh.

Then I was skidding down the rest of the embankment, swiveling my head back and forth as I scanned the cars parked along the street.

Where the hell was Stephanie?

She'd agreed to wait here until I showed up, unless I called her first. Because in the back of my mind I figured the team would find me and I'd need a quick exit.

I dialed the number to Stephanie's burner.

One, two, three rings, and then an automated message saying the voicemail hadn't been set up yet.

"Goddamn it."

I couldn't blame her for bolting. Not after the day she'd had. Not after everything that had happened in her life since I showed up in that parking garage a week ago.

No matter. I would just have to find another set of wheels. I didn't have much cash on me, but I could manage. First, I needed to—

Headlights flared up the road.

I started in the other direction, wanting to keep my face obscured, my left hand—the one opposite the approaching car—gripping Noah's pistol.

The car slowed as it approached, and from the sound of the raggedy engine I felt the muscles in my shoulders loosening.

Stephanie eased the Chevy Malibu I'd stolen from a used-car lot to a stop.

I didn't bother asking where she'd gone. I tore open the back door and jumped in.

Stephanie twisted in her seat to look at me.

"Is that your blood?"

I glanced down at my shirt. Specks of Lucas Hancock's blood from when I'd busted his nose sprinkled the fabric. I shook my head.

"Drive."

Stephanie put the car in motion, headed for the 101.

"Where to?"

I tipped my head back against the headrest, closed my eyes, tried to slow my heart rate.

"Just drive."

36

Mitchell Hargrave sat forward in his chair, holding his face in his hands.

Around him, he could hear everyone busy working—Theo and Julian once again trying to ascertain where Daniel Burke went while Rita Salazar was making calls, alerting the police and Dodgers Stadium security that Lucas Hancock and Dennis Rowe and Michael Kincaid were working for the US government, hunting down a domestic terrorist.

And then there was Noah LaSalle, who Hargrave realized he should have recalled earlier in the day when Burke broke his arm. Instead, LaSalle had been left behind to operate the SUV and somehow managed to get himself shot in not one knee but two.

He sensed movement beside him. Samuel Chen quietly stepping close and leaning down, his voice a whisper.

"You are so fucked."

Hargrave's eyes snapped open. He pushed himself to his feet, turned and pressed his face so close to Chen's that their noses almost touched.

"What did you say?"

Despite the two inches Hargrave had on Chen, the CIA deputy director didn't blink.

"You heard me. This was supposed to be an easy op. All your team had to do was make sure Burke got on that plane. It's so easy a third grader could have managed it. But somehow you and your boys fucked everything up."

Chen's eyes went wide when Hargrave grabbed his shirt and pushed him straight back against the wall.

"What the fuck is your problem?" Hargrave growled. "We're on the same goddamn team."

"No, we're not. I work for the CIA—a legitimate agency. You work for . . . well, I don't know. I bet you don't even know either."

"I work for the United States government."

Hargrave heard the quiet clearing of a throat and shifted his head far enough to see Rita Salazar standing there, a phone to her ear. Her face a mask of worry, she silently shook her head at him.

All at once he realized where he was standing, what he was doing, and released his hold on Chen, stepping away to give the man space. But still he couldn't bring himself to apologize. Not to this snide son of a bitch who shouldn't even be here.

He asked Salazar, "Any updates?"

Rita thumbed the mute button on her phone.

"I'm making progress. The captain I'm speaking with says he understands, but the problem is the FBI agent Alpha One stabbed."

Hargrave ran a hand over his face.

"Christ. Lucas didn't kill him, did he?"

"Not as of yet. The agent's been rushed to the hospital and is currently in critical condition."

"Then what's the problem?"

"Accountability. After everything that happened and the

strong police response, the captain says somebody needs to be held responsible."

Hargrave felt Samuel Chen's eyes on him, imagined the smirk the man was trying to hold back. He reached out his hand.

"Let me talk to him."

Salazar started to shake her head.

"I'm not sure—"

"Give it to me."

Hesitant, she handed him the phone. Hargrave took it off mute and placed it to his ear, gazing back at the screens.

"This is Mitchell Hargrave. To whom am I speaking?"

"This is Captain James Klein of the Los Angeles Police Department."

"Captain Klein, as my associate was telling you, our team has been tracking a domestic terrorist for the past couple of days. For some reason he ended up at the stadium. Our working theory right now is that it's a potential target."

Silence for a beat, and then the man cleared his throat.

"One of your men critically injured an FBI agent."

"Yes, and I'm sorry to hear that, but did the agent identify himself? Unfortunately, sometimes this happens. An off-duty police officer or soldier sees something going down and tries to intervene without knowing the facts."

"Still," the police captain said. "The man lost a lot of blood. He's in the ICU as we speak. It's still not clear whether he's going to pull through."

"Again, Captain, I'm sorry to hear that, but my current directive is hunting this domestic terrorist. This same man shot and killed a police officer in Las Vegas earlier today."

The silence this time lasted a bit longer.

Finally, the man said, "Tell me again: What agency do you work for?"

"Unfortunately, Captain, that's top secret."

"You do realize, Mr. Hargrave, that sounds like a bunch of BS. For all I know, you could be anyone."

"Fair enough. However, this operation has been signed off by President Wagner himself. We'll have someone from the White House contact you within the next fifteen minutes with confirmation."

Hargrave disconnected the call, tossed the phone back to Salazar, who stood there staring back at him with her mouth hanging open.

He said, "Make it happen. Get Lawrence O'Neal out of bed if that's what it takes. We just need something official from the White House."

Behind him, Samuel Chen coughed out a disbelieving laugh.

"I was wrong before, Mitchell. *Now* you're fucked."

For the next ten minutes, they made calls while the two techs continued to search for Daniel Burke. Salazar managed to get the president's chief of staff on the line. She ran through everything that had happened, and then, when it became clear she was getting pushback, Hargrave got on the phone and explained how this needed to happen ASAP, and if Lawrence didn't want Hargrave driving over to the White House to wake the president and explain how his chief of staff wasn't doing his job, then he needed to make the fucking call.

In the end, Lawrence agreed, just as Hargrave knew he would.

After Salazar called Captain Klein back and explained how he would receive a call from the White House in the next five minutes, she noted that the man with the broken arm who had been shot in both knees would be flying back to DC for further medical care.

Samuel Chen shook his head.

"Domestic terrorist, huh? Not many domestic terrorists out there who would leave a man alive like that and instead only cripple him."

Again, Hargrave ignored the deputy director.

"Julian, Theo—one of you decide who'll take a break first. There's a cot down the hall. Not ideal, I know, but right now I can't afford to bring in anyone else. And Rita—why don't you head home and try to get a few hours of sleep?"

"I can sleep on one of the cots."

"No, you've been here longer than I have. I'll run point until you come back to relieve me. Hopefully we'll have tracked down Burke and have him in custody by then."

37

It was well past 2:00 a.m. on the East Coast when Rita Salazar arrived home to her apartment.

The city streets mostly deserted. The traffic lights cycling through for the half dozen vehicles still out this late at night. In only a few hours every surface street would be clogged with traffic.

Jade had sent her the usual texts, asking how late Rita would be working, whether she should stay up so they could watch Netflix, and then saying she was headed to bed.

Rita quietly let herself into the apartment, set her keys and bag on the table near the door.

She was hungry but couldn't eat, not after the past twenty hours. Her blood pressure still riding high after everything that had happened today. After everything she had inadvertently allowed to let happen.

She noted Jade's bag and keys on the kitchen counter, right next to a cluster of those jar candles she loved so much. Candles smelling of teakwood and sea salt vanilla and cashmere jasmine and almond macaroons and any other ridiculous scent, but Jade loved each and every one of them and so Rita loved them too.

She padded down the hallway and peeked into the bedroom. Jade sprawled out on the bed, her body covered by a single sheet, the box fan in the corner set on low to provide white noise.

Rita closed the door and headed back to the kitchen. Opened the fridge and stared inside. Closed the fridge and found herself gazing at the photos on the door. Selfies she and Jade had taken with their phones and then had developed because they felt it was good in this digital age to have actual photographs of the two of them together—the kind they had when they were kids, those glossy photos that parents would slip into thick, three-ring albums and bring out whenever there was company.

She stood there, staring at the photographs, deciding what to do next. On the drive home all she'd done was think about the burner she had hidden in the trunk—the one she'd retrieved earlier in the day after Mitchell had gone to the White House, telling the two techs that she needed a smoke. A vice she'd picked up in high school and had kept ever since. Not because she liked to smoke but because it often afforded her the excuse to step out in stressful situations.

And today had become the ultimate clusterfuck of stressful situations.

She'd driven all the way home with the burner in the trunk, having only used it briefly during her smoke break, and when she arrived home part of her considered just leaving it there. She'd even started inside and had managed almost twenty paces before turning around and hurrying back.

Now she slid the burner from her pocket.

Life had been so much easier before she was in a relationship. That wasn't to say she didn't love Jade—they'd been together six months now, after meeting on the apps and hitting it off, and within the past two months Jade had moved in—but life had undoubtedly been different before she had a full-time roommate.

Before Jade, Rita had been free to search her apartment periodically to ensure that nobody had placed any bugs in the light fixtures or vents. Now, she still searched the apartment, though she had to do it on the sly when Jade wasn't around, running the countersurveillance detectors over the appliances and outlets and anywhere else someone might leave a listening device.

Paranoid, maybe, but she'd built her career on paranoia.

Naturally, Jade didn't know what she did for a living. But this was DC, so saying that you did contract work for the government was pretty much all you needed to say to keep the conversation moving. Not like Jade, who worked two jobs—one as a barista, another as a yoga instructor. Their schedules typically made it so that they rarely saw each other, which can often play havoc on a relationship. But Rita had always been a lone wolf, so as far as she was concerned it was the perfect setup.

That was one of the main reasons she'd quickly taken to the apps: a simple hookup, nothing more, to get the stress out, to find some release. She'd never once considered she might *fall* for someone she met on the apps—mostly because she'd never been good with relationships. Not even the relationships with her family. Especially after what happened to her little brother when he was seven—her mom and dad growing more distant, not just from each other but also their only remaining child.

Rita powered on the burner and waited for the encrypted phone to find a signal.

And then, as expected, the messages came pouring through.

> What did I lie to you about?
>
> Tell me

Then, hours later:

> You know I didn't kill that cop
>
> This is bullshit

Then, less than an hour ago:

> Noah tried killing me
>
> Twice now
>
> He let it slip—how they thought my being dead would work out in their favor
>
> Are YOU involved in this??

Rita stared at the question. She had no idea what Burke was talking about and didn't care. She'd been wrong about him, she realized. She had thought he was different from the other men on the team. They'd gotten along. Talking to each other like they were close friends and not merely colleagues. Burke letting it slip how sometimes he wasn't sure this was the right job for him. Saying that the ops didn't always feel right.

Around that time Rita had started feeling the same way. Especially as she'd begun working closer and closer with Mitchell.

The man had brought her on only three years ago, plucking her almost out of nowhere from the NSA. Telling her the whole reason he'd chosen her was because she was an analyst who saw things differently than him. Opposing viewpoints were crucial, he said. And besides, he was getting older and wanted someone close by to keep an eye out in case he missed a step.

Curiosity is what did her in, just like that damned cat. She'd always been told to question things, and so she'd started questioning the ops from the start. Never to Mitchell directly—she wasn't a big believer in career suicide—but once the after-action reports had been filed she did her own research, her own digging.

And the more she dug, the deeper she found herself, until the one op in Nepal when it became clear things were not what they seemed.

When she'd let Burke know the truth, he'd almost lost his shit. But he quickly cooled off, saying that he understood the game now. And that there was no getting out of the game. Not for a guy like him. Though—he looked at her after a beat—would she be willing to help him with something important?

She'd always liked a challenge. The more impossible the task, the more alive she felt. She'd already been doing stuff on the side, using the handle *Teddy*. It was what her brother had called her. He had a teddy bear that he adored and called Teddy, and he had a sister that he adored and called her Teddy too. Even after their parents repeatedly told him his sister's name was Rita, he kept calling her Teddy.

Now, Rita sent a message back:

> The only thing I'm involved in is bringing you to justice

She didn't expect an immediate reply, but Burke responded within seconds.

> Bringing me to justice for what?

> You know what. You're a fucking traitor

> TEDDY I DON'T KNOW WHAT YOU'RE TALKING ABOUT

Rita started to type a reply but then deleted it. Stared at the screen, deciding what to do next.

She couldn't bring this to Mitchell's attention. It would put her in too much trouble. Fucking sink her. Forget losing her job and security clearance—she'd end up in prison, right next to Burke, assuming he didn't get himself killed by the team before the FBI took him into custody.

After a minute, Burke sent another flurry of texts.

> There's something else going on here

> You know it too

> Something doesn't add up

> When they thought I was dead they wanted to use my death to blame me for something

> But whatever it is I'm not involved

> I swear to you on my brother

Rita's breath caught in her throat. Burke hadn't talked much about his brother, though she knew he'd killed himself two years ago, that one of the reasons Burke had faked his death was so he could try to figure out what had happened. Like Rita, Burke didn't like to talk about his past. Too many bad memories. Too much pain.

She had agreed to help him, but of course she wasn't going to do it out of the kindness of her heart. She said she'd require money for her services—lots of money, because while she loved her day job, she also wanted to retire comfortably someday.

Burke had agreed without hesitation.

Like the rest of the team, he didn't have much life outside of The Office. So the money that came in he set aside. Even made some strategic investments that paid off nicely.

If Burke was lying, would he invoke his brother like this?

Christ, of course he would!

Rita felt so foolish. She always did the utmost research into everything. Even Jade—when it became clear their relationship was becoming serious, she'd done a complete background check. And not one of those bullshit background checks employers did either—she did a deep dive into every aspect of Jade's life, from when she was in elementary school to the present. Family, friends, past girlfriends and lovers. Where she worked. And, of course, her social media.

Admittedly, Rita hadn't done the same deep dive into Burke, and that was because at that point she'd thought she knew him well enough.

"I thought I heard you out here."

Rita dropped the phone to her side and turned to find Jade standing in the hallway, wiping the sleep from her eyes.

"Another late night, huh? They work you too hard."

Rita managed a smile, though it didn't feel right on her face.

"I'm used to it by now."

Jade crossed over and pulled her into a hug. She started to kiss Rita but leaned back, frowning.

"I don't have morning breath already, do I?"

Rita had slipped the burner into her back pocket when Jade approached, and she hoped that Jade wouldn't feel it, wouldn't ask questions. She hated lying to her girlfriend. Hated it more than anything in the world. Though if she had to, she would lie. She'd say that it was another work phone, nothing more than that. Jade would believe her—Rita knew she would.

Rita tried on another smile, this one feeling much more comfortable. She reached out and took her girlfriend's hand.

"I'm exhausted. Let's go to bed."

38

"Any answer?"

Slumped in the back seat to avoid the traffic cams, I stared at the burner, waiting for Teddy to respond. Several minutes had passed since my last text—the one invoking James—but still nothing.

I set the phone down and stared out the window at the darkness rushing past. A half hour before midnight and we were on Interstate 5, headed north, the two-decade-old Malibu maintaining surprisingly well at seventy miles per hour.

When I didn't answer, Stephanie eyed me again in the rearview.

"Who is this person you're texting, anyway?"

My first impulse was to ignore her. She didn't need to know more than she already did. But then I remembered how much her life had gotten blown up because of me and figured she deserved the truth.

"Her name is Teddy."

"This is the contact you mentioned."

"Yes."

"And so who is she exactly?"

"For lack of a better word, she's a hacker."

"You mean like that kid from last week?"

Eugene. The young guy who looked like a door-to-door Latter-day Saint. Hair neatly combed, thick clear glasses on his face. I'd been surprised by how steady he held a pistol on me when I stepped into Stephanie's kitchen, though later, after I'd killed his partner, his hand had started shaking like a lone tree in a hurricane.

Another thing I'd learned in the killing room: you can try all you want to hide your fear, but eventually it seeps through.

"She's better than that kid. Way better."

"How do you know her?"

I hesitated, split between withholding the truth and telling Stephanie everything.

"I used to work with her."

"Doing what?"

"She . . . she helps oversee the team I was on."

This late at night, traffic was sparse. A handful of vehicles on the highway with us headed north. A handful in the other lane headed south. People lost in their own lives, oblivious to the world around them in one way or another. I envied them.

Stephanie had been maintaining a steady speed, keeping the Malibu five miles over the limit and centered in the lane. But now the car shuddered as her hands convulsed on the steering wheel.

"Are you fucking *kidding* me?"

"Relax. She has as much to lose as I do."

"You just said it yourself: she's overseeing the team sent to kill you. How does she have anything to lose?"

"It's . . . complicated."

Stephanie checked the rearview again, this time looking past me, before flicking the turn signal and easing us to a stop on the side of the highway. She punched the button for the four-ways, unclipped her seat belt, and twisted in her seat to look at me.

"I think it's time you uncomplicate things."

I glanced over my shoulder to peer out the rear window. Headlights of all sizes and shapes, distances apart. Any one of them could be a highway patrol cruiser. The cop could stop to check and see what was wrong. And in doing so, they'd ask to see Stephanie's driver's license, the car's registration, then shine a flashlight at her passenger in the back and notice the blood on my shirt.

"It's a long story."

"Do I look like I care? My entire life is over now because of you. But in the past several hours I've come to realize that you're my only chance of surviving. And something tells me I'm your only chance at surviving too. So we're stuck with each other, for better or worse. And if that's the case, then I want to know everything."

I held her gaze for another beat before glancing out the rear window again. Thought for a moment, and then nodded.

"Her real name is Rita Salazar. Her hacker name is Teddy. Don't ask me why because she never told me."

"Okay, good. That's a start. What else?"

"Stephanie, we can't stay here along the berm like this. Not unless you want to attract the wrong kind of attention."

This made sense to her. Nodding, she killed the four-ways and put the car in gear, got us back on the highway, the twenty-year-old engine clanking to gain speed.

"Where are we going, anyway? You had only told me to drive north."

"We're headed to Wyoming."

"Wyoming?"

Surprise in her voice. She eyed me again in the rearview.

"What's in Wyoming?"

"At this point, our only hope."

39

Hargrave had gotten word that Noah LaSalle had arrived in DC an hour ago and was promptly transported to a secure facility downtown.

On the outside, the building looked like any other office complex in the city. Four stories tall, red brick, dark plate glass windows. And, like the building where he and his team had been stationed for the past twenty-four hours, most of it *was* an office building.

But underneath were several levels, many of which featured rooms that would have fit nicely in a hospital.

Doctors and nurses contracted by the government ran these facilities, treating high-level politicians and alphabet agency personnel when they couldn't go to the hospital for one reason or another. Usually to ensure the media didn't catch wind of someone's failing health, or if someone had a UTI or STD or any other condition that would make great fodder for the Beltway media.

LaSalle was being monitored at a facility five miles south of the current base of operations, and after another arguing match with Samuel Chen, in which Hargrave forced the deputy director to stay behind to keep an eye on things, Hargrave got in his car and drove as carefully as he could, his fingers so tight around the steering wheel it was a wonder he didn't crush the thing like it was made of centuries-old parchment.

Then he was riding an elevator down to the second sublevel and following a nurse to a room at the end of the corridor, where he found Noah LaSalle lying in a hospital bed.

"They gave him a sedative before his flight," the nurse noted as LaSalle appeared to be sleeping. "I'll let the doctor know you're here."

He closed the door behind Hargrave, leaving the two of them alone, the room both modern and plain in the way only government bureaucracies can manage. Besides the bed in the middle of the room and the cluster of machines standing beside it, monitoring LaSalle's vitals, there wasn't much else. Not even a TV. Or a camera in the corner.

LaSalle stirred awake as Hargrave stepped up next to the bed. His arm and both legs had been casted—his arm recasted after his most recent scuffle with Daniel Burke.

"I tried," LaSalle said, his voice distant, and Hargrave gave him a warning shake of his head before slipping an RF detector out of his jacket pocket.

It took him a full minute to sweep the room, including the bed and cluster of machines, and once he was satisfied that nobody had planted a bug, he pulled over a chair and sat down so he was facing the door.

"What the fuck happened?"

LaSalle shook his head slowly, yawning and running a hand over his face.

"Like I said, I tried. I did everything I could."

Hargrave, his eyes roaming over the man's broken body: "Did you?"

"I'd made it sound like I was doing him a favor. Trying to save his life. Got him in that utility hallway and tried to shoot him as soon as he came through. But he . . . he was faster than I anticipated."

"How is that possible? You worked with the man for years. You know all his moves."

"I don't know what to tell you. Burke . . . something about him is different now."

"Different how?"

"I don't know! But he was fast enough to knock the gun aside when I fired. I played it off like it was for show because you and the others were watching."

"He broke your arm."

"Yeah, I told him to."

"What?"

Hargrave's tone, incredulous.

LaSalle said, "I knew he had me. That I'd missed my chance. And I figured I should keep up the pretense that I was on his side. So I just, I don't know, panicked. Told him to break my arm. To make it clean. As, you know, otherwise it wouldn't make sense for him to leave me alive."

"He fired a round at your head."

"I told him to do that too. Right after he broke my arm, something clicked in my head, and I realized there was still a chance. So I told him to make it look like he shot me. Just to create some chaos. But the truth is, I figured if the other guys heard what Burke did, they'd want retribution."

"You thought they'd forgo the op's directive and try to take Burke out themselves."

LaSalle, nodding groggily: "Yeah, that was my plan. My hope."

The doctor entered then, breezing into the room carrying a computer tablet that she swiped and tapped at as she approached the bed.

She gave Hargrave a perfunctory nod, then asked LaSalle, "How are you feeling?"

LaSalle shrugged, yawning again.

"Like shit."

The doctor typed something on the tablet, then dropped it to her side.

"Unfortunately, you're going to feel that way for a while. We've pumped you with several pain medications, but your body has experienced a great deal of trauma in a short amount of time. I'm sorry to say you won't be returning to the field anytime soon."

The doctor asked him if he had any questions, and when LaSalle said he did not, she asked Hargrave the same.

"No, Doctor. Thank you."

She started toward the door, walking backward as she again glanced down at the tablet.

"I'll be here until noon when my replacement takes over. He'll want to check on you when he arrives. Until then, if anything comes up, I'll be around."

Then she was gone. The room silent except for the quiet beeping coming from the machines.

Hargrave gave the machines a cursory glance, noting the various vitals on the screen and the wires feeding down to LaSalle's body.

LaSalle, releasing another breath: "And then I spotted him leaving the stadium. I realized that was my last chance, so I had no choice but to take it."

"Did you tell him anything?"

"Like what?"

Answering a question with a question. A classic deceptive move. Giving yourself time to come up with a lie.

Hargrave shook his head, stepping around to the other side of the bed, so he was now standing with his back to the door.

"Are you sure you didn't tell Burke anything?"

"What . . . what would I've told him?"

Hargrave unbuttoned his shirt with his right hand, watching LaSalle's eyes as the man watched him, brow furrowing.

He whispered, "What are you *doing*?"

After the fourth button, when it became clear LaSalle was transfixed, Hargrave shot out his other hand, the syringe needle piercing the man's neck.

LaSalle's eyes went wide. He reached for the call button and Hargrave slammed his fist against the man's throat, right on his trachea, hard enough to stun him.

Hargrave grabbed the patches off the man's chest, one after another, and quickly applied them to his own. The same with the pulse oximeter on the man's finger. Holding his free hand over LaSalle's mouth so that the man didn't cry out, keeping an eye on the monitors to note any abnormalities.

Later, the doctors would run through all the data, try to see if anything had gone wrong on their end, and there would be a moment where the vitals spiked, though that was expected during a cardiac arrest. Even though that spike would be there for only a second before returning to normal. Hargrave knew some keen-eyed doctor might take notice, and they might even question it, especially after completing a toxicology report. However, the compound Hargrave had just administered was formulated to not show up on any report.

When LaSalle's body started convulsing, Hargrave pulled his hand away and stepped back. Just stood there, watching the man. A man that Hargrave had trusted these past several years, more so than any of the other men on his team. Back when fate had forced him in this direction and he'd needed a member of his team to help him.

Hargrave whispered, "You stupid, stupid fool," and even then he wasn't sure who he was addressing, LaSalle or himself.

He pulled out his phone—not his work or personal phone, but his *other* phone—and fired off a single text message.

Then he continued to watch Noah LaSalle in the final moments of his life.

After the man had taken his last breath and his body went still, Hargrave waited a full five minutes before reapplying the patches and pulse oximeter.

As expected, the machines started screaming, the vitals on the screen flatlining. Nurses would crash in here at any second, the doctor following close behind, but Hargrave had a role to play and that role started now.

He raced to the door, flung it open, and shouted as loud as he could.

"Help! Help! Somebody help!"

40

Rita Salazar couldn't sleep.

Not even after the crazy day she'd had—the constant drip of adrenaline circulating throughout her system.

She was tired, yes, exhausted even, but no matter how long she lay in bed, no matter how much she tossed and turned, no matter how much she willed herself, she couldn't fall asleep.

Beside her, Jade was already snoring quietly. Rita envied her girlfriend, the way she could fall asleep within minutes. No need for any pills or gummies. Her body naturally letting her drift away. Jade had once joked it was because she had zero stress in her life, though sometimes Rita wondered if that was true—if Jade somehow did manage to make it through life without even the barest trace of anxiety.

As she'd done every few minutes for the past four hours, she rolled over and checked the time on her phone.

6:17 a.m.

Mitchell had granted her only a few hours to go home and rest. He expected her to return by eight. Sometimes sleeping pills helped, but she didn't want to be too groggy after only a few hours of sleep—especially with the importance of this op.

Which was why she'd just been lying here this entire time. Either staring at the ceiling or closing her eyes, trying to think of nothing.

But no matter how hard she tried, her mind kept returning to Daniel Burke.

That traitorous son of a bitch.

Rita couldn't believe she'd fallen for his act. She typically prided herself on being able to read people ever since she was a girl and had no choice but to read others to get by. Her parents, her teachers, even the people who came into the home to work with her brother. She had to know when to smile, when to frown, when to avoid others at all costs.

I swear to you on my brother.

The words kept haunting her. Kept drilling their way deep inside the corners of her mind. Those words, echoing as though in a dream, despite the fact she'd only read them on her burner.

Burke's brother hadn't been a lie. There was no way to fake that. She'd even looked him up, saw not only the pictures online but also all the work he'd done for abused kids. Maybe that was one of the reasons she'd agreed to help Burke when he'd told her that his brother took his life and how he suspected it had something to do with his trip to Vegas.

He'd never shown her the email his brother sent, but he had described it. How James Burke had detailed his vacation. About what happened to him there. About the guilt that had continued to build, like a pressure cooker pushed to its limit, and how he'd felt helpless and desperate and only had one way to release it all.

Still, that didn't explain the evidence presented to her yesterday. The evidence that Mitchell had shared with the team, explaining why the FBI and CIA wanted Burke so badly.

She couldn't believe she'd been so naïve. So foolish.

And yet . . .

I swear to you on my brother.

She tilted her head to ensure Jade was still fast asleep, then quietly slipped out of bed and headed to the living room and her makeshift office.

One of the drawers in her desk had a false bottom. That was where she kept her laptop. Her *secret* laptop, the one that she'd built from scratch.

Her gateway onto the internet beyond the everyday internet everyone was familiar with.

Rita sat at the makeshift desk in the corner of the living room by the light of the work lamp. Her iMac took up a good portion of the desk, its screen dark, showing her reflection as she booted up the laptop and then went through all the security measures she'd become so accustomed to—the various proxies and VPNs and everything else, making herself essentially invisible with no way to trace her location or identity.

Months back she'd installed an advanced rootkit on the system at work. More as a challenge than anything else. To see how secure the United States government's security infrastructure truly was.

Turned out not to be that secure, at least when the fox was already inside the henhouse.

She'd installed the software in a way it wouldn't be traced back to her if it were found, but days had passed, and those days had become weeks and those weeks had become months, and now Rita sat here in her mostly dark living room, crouched over a laptop that she kept secreted away because Jade did not know anything about her hacker life and never would, no matter how serious their relationship became.

With the rootkit she could access the entire network without being detected. At least, so far she hadn't been detected, though she also knew there was a chance alarms wouldn't sound immediately, as the government hired many bright cybersecurity experts and one of them might have sniffed out the rootkit and was just waiting for the moment she logged on so that they could track her location.

Though, again, with all the various proxies and VPNs she had running, it would take hours before they realized she was in DC, and even then it wouldn't bring the heat to her doorstep.

First order of business: digging into the evidence Mitchell had presented to the team. Various wire transactions to offshore bank accounts in Burke's name. A few hundred thousand dollars here and there. All the wires having originated from Russia.

Mitchell noted a year ago it had come to the CIA's attention that somebody on the team was selling secrets to the Russians. But before they could determine who it was, Daniel Burke had died on that op in Turkey—and not too long after that, they'd found evidence of those wire transfers.

Her fingers quietly tapped the keys, the mouse pad clicking every few seconds as she tore through the system. Going beyond the available evidence. Diving deeper into areas that she didn't have access to, at least when it came to her security clearance.

Access, for instance, that only Mitchell Hargrave had.

It didn't take her long at all to find it.

Evidence of another overseas transaction. Three million dollars wired from Sberbank in Russia to a bank in the Cayman Islands.

Three million dollars.

To an account in the Caymans.

Under her name.

Rita felt a spike of adrenaline, every muscle growing tight as she stared at the laptop screen.

She whispered, "What the motherfuck?"

Movement behind her. She sensed it before her eyes flicked to the dormant iMac on the desk, its blank screen showing her reflection—and, off to the side, Jade's.

She slammed the laptop screen down with so much force she was afraid she might have cracked it. Already running through the various excuses in her head. What she would tell Jade about this laptop, maybe explain that she'd brought it home from work.

"Hey," she said, adding a burst of enthusiasm in her tone, trying not to sound too startled.

She started to turn toward her girlfriend when she saw something in Jade's hand, a syringe, the fine needle glinting in the soft light thrown from the work lamp—the needle that was right this instant being thrust toward Rita's neck.

Swiveling in her chair, she managed to grab hold of Jade's wrist right as the needle was only inches away from puncturing her skin.

For half a second, Rita had time to glance up, to look into Jade's face—and didn't recognize it at all.

The face was the same as it had always been, the same face that had attracted her from the start, which she had come to love, but there was something different about it now, especially in the eyes—they had become darker, flatter, predacious.

Jade punched her in the stomach and Rita, feeling all the air rush out of her, hit the carpet hard. She tried to sit up but Jade was suddenly there, a knee on her chest, holding her in place as the needle tip was again on a downward arc toward her neck.

"Stay still," said a voice that belonged to her girlfriend but which didn't sound anything like her. Gone now was the familiar, easy midwestern twang. Replaced now by . . . was that a Russian accent?

Struggling, reaching, doing everything she could, Rita's fingers grazed her laptop on the desktop: a little, just a little, and then ... she grasped the corner and managed to bring it around, slamming it straight into the side of Jade's head.

The hit had little momentum, but it was hard enough to knock Jade off balance.

Rita sat up, and as Jade turned back to her, Rita swung the laptop again, putting all her strength into it, everything she had, so that this time when the computer slammed into the side of Jade's face, Rita knew she'd shattered the screen for good.

Jade hit the carpet, the syringe tumbling from her hand. Rita watched, not sure what to do at first—stunned motionless—and then all at once scrambled on her knees for the syringe.

She'd barely made it a few feet when a hand grabbed her ankle and yanked her back.

Rita hit the carpet hard, almost smashing her face. She managed to flip herself over just as she felt Jade on her again, crawling up the length of her body, driving her knee into her chest.

She felt Jade's hands—those soft, smooth, lovely hands—wrapping around her throat.

"Shh," said the woman in that Russian accent. "It will all be over soon."

Rita kicked and flailed her arms, reaching up with one hand and pushing it against the woman's face as though that might somehow magically get her to move away.

Her vision, beginning to darken. What little oxygen she had left almost gone.

Until, all at once, her other hand, which had been groping around the carpet this entire time, made contact with the fallen syringe.

Her fingers curling around the plastic, she swung her arm up—the needle stabbing the woman right in her neck.

Rita's thumb, squeezing the plunger.

The woman's eyes—the ones that Rita no longer recognized—grew wide. Her hands around Rita's throat loosening as her body began to shake, then convulse.

Rita pushed her off and the woman fell to the carpet beside her, flapping around like a fish out of water, until . . . her entire body went still.

Her eyes—those dark, flat eyes—staring up at nothing.

Rita quickly sat up. Feeling first at her throat, gently prodding at every place it hurt, before scrambling to her feet.

Staring down at the woman who wasn't really Jade—or, no, the woman who was Jade but who wasn't the woman Rita had thought she was.

Call the police.

That was her first impulse. But it was the impulse of a civilian, not someone in her line of work, who dealt with terrorists and spies every day.

Who only minutes ago learned that a foreign bank account in her name contained three million dollars.

Money that had been wired there by a Russian bank.

Even before she flipped open the lid, she knew the laptop screen had been shattered. Which made this computer she'd built from scratch—the one she'd always used as Teddy—now worthless.

Leave.

Her second impulse. Pack her things and get the fuck out of there. Or, shit, there was no telling if others might be coming. No time to pack her things—just get the fuck out.

But first, she had to check on something. That curiosity wouldn't have it any other way.

She found Jade's phone in the bedroom, resting on the wireless charger on the nightstand where she always kept it while she slept.

Rita tried opening the phone, but of course it was locked.

Breezing back into the living room, standing over the woman's dead body, Rita aimed the screen at her face.

Yep—that did the trick.

The first thing she saw was an encrypted messaging app.

A Washington, DC, number she didn't recognize had texted only five minutes ago.

> Do it now

No other texts from this number, though Rita suspected that was because they'd been deleted.

Whoever the fuck this woman was, she was a professional and wouldn't have left any evidence behind.

Rita stared at the screen, biting her lip. Deciding what to do next.

Screw it, she thought, then typed one word and pressed Send.

> Done

Should she take this phone with her? Yes, she might as well. After first popping out the SIM card, of course.

As for her phone, she would need to leave it behind. Not the burner, though. That one was coming with her.

Now what?

No time for packing. No time for gathering any valuables.

Well, except for the photo album of her brother.

She'd take that along, for sure.

And the laptop—she might be able to salvage some parts later. For now, she needed to disappear.

That was the first thing she had to do.

Well, no.

The first thing she had to do was ensure she *could* disappear.

On the iMac, she enabled many of the programs she'd had hidden there for emergencies, though *this* particular emergency had never crossed her mind.

She paused briefly, gazing down at the body of the woman she'd fallen in love with. A woman she'd randomly met on the apps—but which she now understood had been no chance encounter. Whoever had been targeting her had her in their sights for over a year, establishing a well-documented dossier that knew every detail about her life.

Within two minutes, she'd accessed the apartment building's security system and shut off all cameras—as well as all traffic cams within a four-mile radius.

Then she wiped the computer and reset it to factory settings, took one last look around the apartment, and started for the door.

But paused when her eyes lighted on the jar candles on the kitchen counter.

And like that, she realized what she needed to do next.

ACKNOWLEDGMENTS

Writing a novel is never an easy feat; publishing one is an even more monumental task. My deepest gratitude and thanks to my agent, Tess Callero; to Michael Signorelli for his always insightful editorial feedback; to Josh Stanton, Josie Woodbridge, Rachel Sanders, Rebecca Malzahn, Brianna Jones, Alenka Linaschke, Kathryn Zentgraf, Candice Roditi, Bryan Barney, and everyone else at Blackstone; to Edoardo Ballerini for being the best in the business; to John Cashman and Adam Perry for the early reads; to Tina Brown for the late-night fact-checks; to the bookstagrammers and other reviewers who championed the first book in the series; to librarians everywhere for everything they do every day; and, as always, to Holly.

Chen waited a beat for dramatic effect.

"So what do you say? Are you that person?"

Across the table in the interview room of a top secret max security prison with no official name, Olivia Ramirez leaned forward and stubbed out her cigarette in the empty paper cup. She stared down at the table for a long moment, then lifted her eyes to him. A slow, calculated smile spreading across her face.

"When do I start?"

the doctor disappeared. I've sent people down there searching everywhere, but so far no luck. My guess is they left the continent. Probably hitched a ride on some cargo ship headed out of Buenos Aires."

Chen yawned—he couldn't help himself—and leaned back in his chair.

"So, as you know, President Wagner lost the election—by only five points, which was closer than many people predicted after all the shit that went down. The new president is an opportunist, for sure. Not even a full month had passed after being sworn in and he was already striking deals with the Saudis."

Chen smiled to himself again.

"I was let go from my official position, of course. But that's not surprising—new president, new cabinet. Fortunately, before President Wagner left office, he took my suggestion and approved a task force. He allowed it to be set up much the same way as Mitchell Hargrave's team—zero oversight, unlimited budget. I get to pick who's on my team, which is why I'm here today meeting with you."

He leaned forward and started paging through the file in front of him.

"From what I understand, you are brilliant—practically a genius. And you're loyal too, based on the fact that the entire time you've been here you haven't said one word. Not even in court. Some even think you're mute, but I know that's not the case, is it?"

Another cloud of cigarette smoke came toward his face, but this time Chen didn't wave it away.

"Look, I'm going to cut to the chase. I'm offering you an opportunity to get out of here. I need somebody like you on my team. Somebody who's loyal. Somebody who's brilliant. But most of all, somebody who loathes Daniel Burke and will do whatever it takes to see him dead."

CODA

"It's been almost six months now. Six long months and still no sign of Daniel Burke or Rita Salazar."

Samuel Chen shook his head, releasing a sigh.

"Actually, no—I shouldn't say *no sign*. We did eventually track Burke's movements. It seems he and Dr. Stephanie Nguyen headed down to South America—along with the good doctor's father. Entering the United States isn't easy, but leaving? No sweat at all."

A cloud of cigarette smoke drifted toward his face. Chen waved it away with his hand.

"Apparently Dr. Nguyen's father had cancer. He only had months to live. It didn't make sense to me at first why Burke would agree to take him out of the country, but I imagine it was at the request of Dr. Nguyen. It's almost sweet, when you think about it."

Chen smiled to himself, shook his head again.

"Anyway, it appears they worked their way all the way down to Argentina. After Mr. Nguyen passed away, Burke and

"What . . . what kind of life is that?"

I took a moment to think about it, to contemplate a sincere, honest answer, and then went with the first thing that came to mind.

"An exciting one."

Stephanie didn't say anything for a full minute—the longest minute of my life.

Finally, she nodded.

"Okay. Against my better judgment, I'll come with you."

She paused again. Looking down at her feet. Looking back up.

"But only under one condition."

"No. You don't get to speak. You don't get to say anything. Not after you've destroyed my life. Not after you got Patrick killed."

I said nothing.

"I'll go to the police. The FBI. The CIA. Whatever agency there is that will listen to me and understand I had nothing to do with any of this. They'll believe me. They'll help."

But her tone betrayed the fact she didn't believe these words. I could even see it in her face, a dawning realization that no matter who she spoke with, no matter how much she pleaded and begged, nobody could help her.

I said, "And then what? Go back to Vegas? Go back to the job you hate?"

"Screw you. I don't hate my job."

"Maybe not, but you never answered my question."

"What question?"

"The one I asked you two weeks ago when we were in your kitchen having breakfast. I asked if you were happy. You never answered me, so answer me now. You may love your job—you may be great at it—but are you happy?"

Stephanie said nothing.

"Come with me."

"What?"

"Come with me."

"Where?"

"I don't know. Somewhere out of the country. Like Teddy, we can't stay here anymore."

"You're crazy."

"Maybe. But maybe not."

"We . . . we would be fugitives."

"Yes."

"For the rest of our lives."

"Yes."

me this was fun while it lasted, but now it looked like the fun was over, so he split."

"Without even a goodbye."

I shook my head in disappointment, then shrugged.

"Yeah, okay, that sounds about right."

Teddy said, "You do know who you should be apologizing to, don't you?" and lifted her chin in Stephanie's direction.

I nodded.

"What are you going to do now?"

"I have no clue. But I can't stick around here, that's for sure. What about you?"

I glanced again at Stephanie, still standing with her arms crossed.

"No idea. But we'll figure something out."

———

Teddy didn't stick around much longer. Not when it was clear there was nothing else that could be done.

We watched her drive out of the factory, a small cloud of dust rising in her wake, and then I turned to Stephanie. Braced myself as I took a deep breath.

"I'm sorry."

She said nothing.

"For everything. For walking back into your life, getting you involved. I shouldn't have done it."

No reply. At least, not at first. After several long, tortuous seconds, she looked away, tried to steady her breath, and then redirected her glare straight at me.

"My life is over now. Because of you."

I opened my mouth to say something and she shook her head once, as sudden and decisive as a scythe.

Teddy waited at the factory until we'd arrived.

"Mitchell was dead?"

"Yes."

"Did you kill him?"

"No."

"Daniel."

"I didn't, Teddy. Why would I do that after everything we did today? The whole purpose was to get that laptop—that proof—to give to POTUS."

"And Mitchell didn't have a laptop."

"Not on him, no. I imagine whoever killed him took it."

"Sergei," Teddy said. "Or whoever the fuck has been calling themselves Sergei all this time."

I checked on Stephanie, who stood leaning against the car with her arms crossed, her face a mask of emotion.

I turned back to Teddy.

"I'm sorry."

"For what?"

"Everything. Had I not asked you to help me two years ago, this wouldn't have—"

"Save it, Daniel. This shit would have happened regardless. Mitchell was in too deep. He'd just granted himself some extra time by blaming you after he believed you were dead. He still needed someone else to take the fall. The more I think about it, the more I realize the whole reason he'd brought me on in the first place was to one day pin this all on me."

A heavy silence except for a bird somewhere near the ceiling flapping about.

Something occurred to me, and I asked, "Where's Quinn?"

"He left about fifteen minutes before you got here. Said something about his boss having called about a job. He told

80

I had Stephanie drop me three blocks away and then kept my head down as I headed for the parking garage where Mitchell Hargrave told me to meet him.

I drew my gun and held it low as I climbed the steps to the top.

The level was empty. The afternoon sun shining bright in the sky. It was so bright I had to lift my hand to visor the glare, scanning the level for the man who had once been my boss.

As soon as I spotted him lying on the ground several yards away, my grip on the pistol tightened.

I hurried forward, staying low as I surveyed the nearby buildings for a sniper.

I crouched next to Hargrave.

There was no need to check for a pulse.

Someone had shot him in the forehead.

And the laptop—if there ever had been a laptop—was gone.

"What about that woman who was with Burke—the doctor from Las Vegas?"

"She seems to have disappeared as well."

"Does she have any family?"

"She has a father who lives in Lanton, Pennsylvania, but he seems to have gone missing too."

"I don't like this, Mr. Chen. Not one bit."

"Neither do I, Mr. President."

"I appreciate your meeting with me today on such short notice."

"Of course, sir."

"Now, I have several meetings I must attend before I head back out on the campaign trail. If you'll excuse me."

"Certainly, Mr. President. But before I go, I . . ."

"Yes?"

"Well, sir, I don't like the idea of Burke and Salazar being out there. Every intelligence agency has been put on high alert to keep an eye out for them, but . . ."

"Say it, Mr. Chen."

"I feel additional resources may be warranted."

"Such as?"

"I never believed Mitchell Hargrave's Alpha Team was wise. The idea of zero oversight with a team so lethal . . . it can be dangerous, as we've seen."

"I agree, Mr. Chen."

"Still . . . a task force dedicated to hunting Burke and Salazar and other traitors like them may be something worth considering."

"Perhaps. Now, Mr. Chen, I really must head to my next meeting. Thank you again."

"Anytime, Mr. President."

"Oh, and Mr. Chen? Regarding a task force . . . I'll think about it."

it always ends up stalled thanks to red tape and petty interparty bickering. But a team like yours—imagine the power one can have to run ops all over the world in secret, the way markets can be manipulated for financial gain. Sure, we can have the country's best interest at heart, but we can also change the world the way we want it and don't have to worry about poll numbers and fundraising and all that tedious shit."

Mitchell Hargrave's face growing paler and paler. His lips moving but producing no words.

"I have a very good feeling I'll be put in charge of running your team—or what's left of your team. By now, Lucas and Dennis and your precious tech Julian should be dead. Michael Kincaid's been working for me this entire time. The same with Theo. I'll fight to keep them on the team. And then I'll add a few more, handpicked especially by me. Such as Lawrence O'Neal, who I also have in my pocket."

Hargrave's eyes starting to lose focus, his face dipping down.

"Don't worry about your mother, Mitchell. I'll make sure she's taken care of. Truly. I'm sorry to have placed her in that position, but she didn't know any better, did she? If only the rest of us could be so blissfully naïve."

Samuel Chen standing back up, raising the silenced pistol at Hargrave's head.

"Goodbye, Mitchell."

The slightest pressure on a trigger—all it takes to end someone's life.

"So right now we don't know the whereabouts of Daniel Burke or Rita Salazar."

"No, Mr. President."

Samuel Chen pocketing the phone with a chuckle.

"You've got to love technology. All these years you believed you were speaking to an actual Russian, when it was just an AI program."

Hargrave staring up at him, trying to speak but not having the strength.

"You managed to hit the jackpot, didn't you, Mitchell? You found a way to circumvent the law to create a tier one team with zero oversight and an unlimited budget. When I first learned of your Alpha Team, I couldn't believe it. Not that a team like yours couldn't exist, but that the agency heads allowed it to exist."

Chen shaking his head.

"Believe it or not, Mitchell, I've come to respect the hell out of you. There's a reason you've lasted this long. You're quick on your feet. The walls were closing in, and as soon as you believed Daniel Burke was dead, you managed to place all the blame on him. Kudos. Honestly."

Smiling again.

"You've been in the game so long you know how to keep a clean nose. It took a while to figure out the best way to squeeze you. And there she was, your mother, right there all along."

Tapping the laptop again thoughtfully.

"Let me ease your conscience, Mitchell. None of the secrets you sold ever went to Russia or any enemy country. Hell, I had access to all the same intelligence. None of it was new to me. But I needed you compromised for this to work. And it did work, didn't it?"

Hargrave blinking up at him, his breathing shallow.

"It wasn't cheap to hire everyone involved. But I know a few billionaires who like the idea of working outside the law. You see, Mitchell, whenever something needs to happen through Congress,

Crouching down, tapping the sound suppressor against the laptop.

"It's all in here, isn't it? The evidence of all your sins. Everything Sergei asked you to give him to keep your mother safe."

A slow smile spreading across Chen's face at Hargrave's expression.

"That's right, Mitchell. I know all about Sergei."

Holding up a phone with his other hand, tapping the screen. A voice issuing from the tiny speakers, the low and heavy Russian accent familiar.

"Because I am *Sergei*."

"Tell me, Mr. Chen. What's this I hear about Mitchell Hargrave's mother?"

"Apparently there was a shoot-out at her doctor's office."

"My God. Any casualties?"

"No civilian casualties, no. Several fatalities, but they were individuals involved in the shooting."

"Do we know who these individuals were?"

"We're still trying to determine that, sir."

"How is Mrs. Hargrave doing now? From what I understand, she was shot."

"She's doing as well as can be under the circumstances."

"I also understand she has severe Alzheimer's."

"That's correct."

"What will happen to her?"

"Well, Mr. President, there doesn't appear to be any next of kin. I was hoping, with your permission, to put her in a home that will take good care of her."

"Absolutely. That poor woman shouldn't have to suffer because her son was a traitor to this country."

"Did you tell anyone about this, Mr. President?"

"I did not. In the past two weeks, what with my vice president and Senator Browne, not to mention my ex–chief of staff, I've realized I no longer know who I can trust."

"He lied to you."

"Yes, Mr. Chen. I think that's clear by now. He and Rita Salazar sowed chaos yesterday so they could track down the remaining team members and eliminate them."

"Did Burke say how he planned to prove his innocence?"

"He said he would bring me evidence of the real traitor."

"Did he say who the real traitor was?"

"He did not, but I suspected he meant Mitchell Hargrave."

"What did Burke want in return?"

"A pardon. For him and Rita Salazar. I was willing to do it too—if the evidence was solid. I *needed* it to be solid."

"Sir?"

"Because as much as I try to act otherwise the truth is I want to be reelected. That's all that matters in politics—being reelected. And, well, I needed something substantial to show the American people."

"So you believed exposing Mitchell Hargrave as the traitor would be the win you needed."

"Well, it was a thought. But Daniel Burke was already one step ahead of me, wasn't he? The entire time he meant to take out the rest of the team, including Mitchell Hargrave."

Hargrave on the ground, his back against the hard brick wall, staring up at Samuel Chen.

Samuel Chen lowering the pistol and stepping forward, saying, "I told you to ask yourself who else you could trust on your team."

Lucas Hancock hearing the explosion in his ear. Looking first to Michael Kincaid to ensure he'd heard the same before shouting for Chen and Theo to respond. Then, hearing only silence, looking to Michael Kincaid again and seeing the barrel of the man's pistol aimed right at his face. Feeling the jolt of adrenaline as he reached for his own weapon—and then nothing at all.

"Who is the man who survived?"

"His name is Michael Kincaid. He joined Hargrave's team after Burke faked his death."

"He was brought over from the CIA?"

"Yes, Mr. President. I sent him myself once we'd begun to suspect Hargrave and the rest of his team were compromised."

"A spy."

"Yes, sir."

"And he was there when Daniel Burke fired on them."

"That's right, Mr. President. Burke shot Lucas Hancock in the face. As for Michael Kincaid, he took a bullet to the leg."

"What's his condition?"

"Stable, sir. The same with the tech who survived the explosion."

"What's his name again?"

"Theo Wilson, sir. He's currently in critical condition, but the doctors believe he should make it."

"He pulled the wool over my eyes."

"I'm sorry, sir?"

"Daniel Burke. He contacted me the other night. Said that he was innocent. That he was going to prove his innocence."

The two techs sitting in the dark room, staring at their screens.

Theo getting up to grab a coffee, stepping past Dennis Rowe in his wheelchair.

Rowe watching the monitors, believing Hancock and Kincaid had flown to Boston in search of Daniel Burke.

Theo pulling a sound-suppressed HK45 Compact Tactical from behind his back and shooting first Dennis and then Julian in the back of their heads.

Communicating with Hancock and Kincaid for a few minutes, then shutting off the cameras in the corridor and then walking down to the stairwell, pulling out a trigger device linked to a half dozen demolition bombs spread throughout the subbasement and basement and first floor.

Holding the device for just a beat, taking a deep breath, and then pressing the trigger.

"Do we know what caused the explosion?"

"Right now we're still trying to ascertain what may have happened. The investigators on-site have found what they believe is a piece from a suitcase bomb."

"What do you think happened?"

"Well, Mr. President, I think Burke and Salazar determined the team's location. Somehow they managed to sneak several bombs into the building and detonated them when they felt the time was right."

"For what purpose?"

"Tying up loose ends."

"And so the other two members of the team—"

"Yes, Mr. President. They were attacked too."

Hargrave, grunting as he stumbled back. Both hands pressed against the bullet wound weeping blood from his stomach. Numbness already beginning to tingle throughout his body. His face starting to pale. Wide eyes shifting up to take in his shooter.

"Tell me again how you determined Mitchell Hargrave was also a traitor."

"The CIA has been keeping tabs on The Office since the beginning. We'd been noticing some . . . let's say, irregularities. When I initiated an official investigation a year ago, it was around the time Daniel Burke faked his death. Hargrave put all the blame on him."

"You believe they were working together."

"Correct. I believe Burke faked his death to work behind the scenes for Hargrave."

"So what about Las Vegas?"

"I'm sorry?"

"I've read the transcript of the interrogation of the young man who calls himself the Spider. How Daniel Burke reportedly went to Las Vegas to bring justice against the people who deceived his brother."

"As you know, Mr. President, Daniel Burke killed a police officer in Las Vegas after he was taken into custody. He also murdered Ambassador Greenham."

"What is Rita Salazar's role in all of this?"

"We believe Hargrave and Salazar were selling secrets to the Russians."

"Who is left from Mitchell Hargrave's team?"

"Well, Mr. President, as you know, the control center was destroyed in an explosion."

79

"Let me get this straight, Mr. Chen. You're telling me all the chaos in this city yesterday was the work of Daniel Burke."

"Yes, Mr. President. Daniel Burke and Rita Salazar."

"And you have no idea where they are."

"No."

"You say Daniel Burke killed Mitchell Hargrave."

"Yes."

"Why?"

"From what we can ascertain, Burke believed Hargrave had betrayed him, now that we have evidence Mitchell Hargrave was in fact also a traitor."

"So Daniel Burke shot him."

"That's correct."

"Right there on top of that parking garage."

"That's where Mitchell Hargrave's body was found, yes."

PART V
LOOSE ENDS

"Finally," he said, laptop gripped with one hand at his side as he started to turn around. "I never thought you'd get here. My flight leaves in—"

He heard the *pfft* from the silencer a millisecond after he watched the burst from the muzzle, the .45 ACP round penetrating the side of his stomach and exiting through his back.

The laptop fell as he instinctively pressed his hands against the bullet wound.

A bee, he thought erratically. *I've been stung by a bee.*

face the music, own up to what he'd done and spend the rest of his life in prison.

Maybe if he were a better man, he would do that.

Then again, if he were a better man, he never would have found himself in this position in the first place—his back against the wall with his mother's life at risk.

Hargrave still wasn't sure how he would keep his mother safe once the truth was revealed. She had obviously done nothing wrong—she had dementia, for Christ's sake!—but with him gone out of the country, who would be there to advocate for her?

It hurt his heart to think she might end up in some decrepit nursing home where the residents spent all day in dirty diapers and staff rarely checked on them.

What's worse, she would have no idea what was happening, no sense as to why she was there or what had happened to her son.

Hargrave had already messaged Burke his location, telling him that he would hand off the laptop, and Burke had responded that he was on his way.

That was now, what, ten minutes ago?

Burke should be here any minute.

Hargrave would turn over evidence of all his crimes, which would be turned over to the government he had once so proudly served—but not before he could get on a plane out of the country.

He'd already purchased a ticket. His flight left in an hour. As soon as Burke arrived, Hargrave would head straight to Dulles. No luggage. No carry-on. Not even a toothbrush. He'd land in a foreign country and start from scratch.

Standing there on the top of the parking garage, listening to all those distant sirens and bleating horns, his ears had become attuned to the world crumbling around him that he easily heard the soft scrape of footsteps behind him.

Nurses whisked the patient away so that doctors could immediately begin the process of removing the bullet and patching her up.

All this time the patient kept moaning, saying the name *Mitchy* again and again and again.

When nurses came to speak to the woman who'd brought the patient in, to learn more—such as the patient's name—nobody could find her anywhere.

Mitchell Hargrave stood on the top level of the parking garage and listened to a world gone mad.

Sirens and car horns still filled the air, but not nearly as many as an hour ago.

He'd retrieved the laptop but didn't take his Mercedes—knowing that it was registered in his name and that very soon every law enforcement agency in the country would be looking for him.

So he left the car behind and started walking, doing his best to evade the traffic cams and any other surveillance that might pick him up—even conscious of the satellites right then potentially monitoring the area.

He'd gotten a text message from Daniel Burke that they'd dropped his mother off at the hospital.

It wasn't an ideal scenario—he'd wanted to have her transported two states away, where he had already set up a room for her at a nursing facility that would take exceptional care of her for her remaining days—but in retrospect, it felt like the right amount of karma that his mother would get shot for his sins.

He'd taken his passport with him this morning. Never once had he thought he'd have to flee the country a common traitor, but what other choice did he have? Sure, he could stay and

Quinn checked his watch. Almost noon.

"I don't have my passport with me."

"You won't need it. You and the rest of the team will be flying private. Where are you, anyway? I figured you'd be home relaxing."

"I'm in DC."

A throaty chuckle.

"No shit? I've been watching the news. Looks to be complete anarchy. Nobody seems to know what's going on. You don't have anything to do with that, do you?"

Quinn knew the question was asked in jest, but when he said nothing his boss's chuckle faded and there was an uneasy silence.

His boss said, all business now, "I'll have a jet pick you up at Manassas Regional Airport in two hours."

Then the man clicked off and Quinn found himself standing in the middle of the deserted factory, stuck in a cocoon of silence.

As much as he wanted to return home and see Tango and Cash, he knew they were just as happy hanging out on the ranch with his neighbor's dogs.

Quinn would miss them, but that was okay—the truth was he missed the work even more.

The new patient came into the emergency department at ten minutes before twelve.

Brought in by a woman shouting that the patient had been shot, which wasn't surprising to hear based on the activity happening now all over the city, including reports of gunfire.

The way the woman spoke to staff, explaining what had happened and giving the specific location of the gunshot wound, it was clear she had medical training.

"I believe so. Thanks again for all your help, Cyrus."

"Anytime. Will I be seeing you around?"

Teddy wasn't sure how to answer that. The truth was, she didn't know what the future had in store for her—even if what was on Mitchell Hargrave's laptop proved she and Daniel Burke were innocent, she wasn't sure she could continue working for the government. Even if she'd done nothing wrong, the stink was already on her. Nobody would look at her the same way again, and in truth, she was fine with that: because moving forward she knew she didn't want to be Rita Salazar anymore.

"Maybe, Cyrus. Maybe."

And gently patting him on the arm, she left the hacker den and disappeared down the hallway.

———

When Tyler Quinn returned to base, his phone buzzed with an incoming call.

His boss.

"Enjoying your time off, Tyler?"

"It has its moments."

"Ready to jump back into the fire?"

Quinn hesitated. He wanted to see how this Hail Mary op played out. Wanted to maybe get to know Stephanie Nguyen a bit better. Wanted to return home and spend time with his dogs.

But he knew that if he declined, his boss would just go down the list to assign someone else, and once you started declining jobs word would begin to spread, and he couldn't have that.

"Where's the job?"

"Madagascar."

"When?"

"I need you on a plane tonight."

78

Teddy had listened to everything—the car chase, the Norsemen arriving at the industrial park, the shoot-out—and as Daniel and Stephanie sped to the nearest hospital, she stepped forward and cleared her throat.

"Shut it down."

The four hackers all paused to look back at her. Two quizzical expressions, one bored, one angry.

"Come on," said the woman with the piercings. "We were just starting to have fun!"

Teddy said, "Fun's over. I've transferred the agreed-upon amounts to each of your cryptocurrency accounts."

The woman with the piercings mumbled something under her breath but started closing out the windows, just as the rest of the hackers did.

Teddy turned to Cyrus, who hadn't moved from his spot by the door. Despite the man being blind, he seemed to know she was facing him and smiled.

"You accomplish what you set out to do?"

"She's been shot, you bastard!"

"Yes, and we'll get her to a hospital. But the clock is ticking, and the more those seconds tick by, the more I'm starting to remember how much I don't trust you."

"Danny!" Stephanie again. "We don't have time for this. We need to go now!"

"Where's the laptop?"

"In the parking lot where this all started. The laptop's secured in the trunk of my car."

"Danny! She needs to get to the hospital *right now*!"

Hands raised to his sides, Hargrave started backing away, out through the garage door.

I aimed my gun at him.

"Where the fuck are you going?"

"The hospital isn't on the way. So you take her. I'll make it back to my car. I'll text you a location and meet you there to hand over the laptop."

"The hell you will."

"Danny!" Stephanie slapped the roof of the car to get my attention. "She is *dying*!"

I took my eyes off Hargrave for only a second, noting the panic in Stephanie's face, and when I looked back, the son of a bitch was gone.

Stephanie's expression behind the wheel a half second before I heard the gunfire and watched the car's headlights shatter.

Drawing my pistol, I lunged through the open door, not sure how many were waiting outside—and spotted only Ike Cooper straddling his bike, the big man bleeding in several places, his face pale, the Glock in his hand shaking as his body grew weaker and weaker.

He said, "You brother-murdering piece of—" but that was as far as he got before I put a bullet between his eyes.

As the biker's body dropped to the ground, I panned the muzzle around the rest of the industrial park, searching for any other threat.

"Danny!"

Stephanie was out of the car, leaning into the back. Saying something to Hargrave who was now shouting.

"Mom? Mom, look at me. Look at me!"

Hurrying forward, I noted the bullet hole in the windshield and felt my stomach drop as I looked inside to find Hargrave's mother shot in her upper chest.

"Mitchy . . ." The woman's voice, faint. "Mitchy . . ."

"It's okay, Mom. You'll be okay."

"The bees . . . I think one stung me."

Stephanie crawled into the back seat, doing her best to examine the old woman. Telling Hargrave to focus, to apply pressure to the wound.

I said, "No."

Stephanie's face whipped around to look at me.

"What do you mean, *no*?"

"You ride in the back and apply pressure. I'll drive. As for Mitch, he has a laptop to retrieve."

Hargrave said through clenched teeth, "You son of a—"

"We had a deal, Mitch. Your mother for the laptop."

Stephanie stood there, gun steady in her grip, aiming for center mass.

I held up my hands.

"It's me!"

The gun lowered, inch by inch.

"Where's Hargrave and his mother?"

"They're already in the car."

Stephanie started to turn away but then wheeled back, the pistol rising swiftly, a single gunshot echoing in the tight space as I heard the metal door screeching open behind me.

I turned to find the merc in the doorway, half his face torn away by Stephanie's bullet.

Turning back to her, I said, "Quinn was right. You are a natural."

She said, "Let's go," and turned away, heading deeper into the building.

I followed her to the car I'd stashed here earlier this morning. Hargrave and his mother were already in the back.

Stephanie said, "The key's in the ignition," as she headed for the passenger side.

"You drive."

"What?"

Her tone making it clear she didn't want to be anywhere near a steering wheel after the past fifteen minutes.

"At least drive it outside once I open this door."

A heavy chain hung loose by the garage door, which faced the opposite side of the courtyard. I waited until Stephanie had the engine going before I started pulling down on the chain to lift the door, pausing when the door was open only a few feet to duck down and see if there was any trouble outside.

Then I kept tugging on the chain as the door continued to rise, the late-morning sun filtering in, and I was aware of

The distance between the bikers and the Russians about fifty feet. The distance between the Russians and us about the same.

One of the mercs said, "Who the fuck are you?"

To which Ike Cooper said, "Who the fuck are you?"

To which I shouted, "They're with me, Ike!"

The mercs and caregivers glanced at me, confused.

I shouted, "I may have been the one who killed your brother, but they were with me when I did it!"

Even across the expanse of nearly one hundred feet, I could see the rage burning in Ike Cooper's face.

"You motherfucking piece of shit!"

Later, it would be impossible to determine who'd fired the first round—one of the bikers or one of the mercs—but within seconds the courtyard had become a kill zone, a flurry of bullets whizzing every which way, blood squirting and bodies hitting the ground.

By then, Hargrave and his mother had reached the metal door. Hargrave had yanked it open and ushered his mother inside, Stephanie only a few feet behind.

When the salvo started, I had to dive behind the car for cover, leaning against the front tire. Waiting for a lull in the gunfire before popping up to ensure the coast was clear and sprinting for the door. Casting a glance around the courtyard and taking in all the dead and wounded bodies, bikers and mercs and caregivers alike, though one of the mercs had taken cover, not a scratch on him.

The merc noticed me making my escape and fired several bursts in my direction, bits of brick splintering from the wall as I ducked low and bolted through the open door, slamming it shut behind me.

Damp musty darkness inside. It took a few seconds for my eyes to adjust.

77

The steady rumble of an oncoming storm.

The mufflers and exhaust pipes of over two dozen Harleys loud enough to rattle the dirty windows in the buildings around us.

Discreet wasn't in the Norsemen's vocabulary. Not when they wanted to make a big, bold entrance. And as the biker gang poured around the corner—each wearing sunglasses and leather vests with the gang's logo prominently displayed—the mercs and caregivers spun to take in the new arrivals.

I glanced at Stephanie and Hargrave, nodded at them, and lifted my chin toward the metal door only a few yards away.

Arm still around his mother, trying to keep her calm and quiet, Hargrave began to lead her in that direction.

Stephanie started to sidestep that way too.

One by one the bikes' engines quieted, men of all sizes straddling their six-hundred-plus-pound motorcycles as they drew an assortment of weapons—pistols, shotguns, rifles, even a machete.

"What's your game, Burke?"

"No game. Do you see that door right over there? We're going to go straight through it. But first . . ."

I turned as the SUV screeched around the corner and came to a sudden halt.

All four doors opened, the two Russian caregivers climbing out with the remaining mercs. Five men, two women. Seven in total. All heavily armed.

Under his breath, Hargrave said, "Burke . . ."

"Don't worry, Mitch. They're not going to shoot. They need you alive."

"I'm not so sure about that anymore."

"Besides . . ."

I paused for only a beat, hearing something in the distance besides that endless chorus of sirens, and smiled.

"You wanted to know what plan B was? Here it comes."

"Teddy," I said, "any word back?"

"None. Want me to resend?"

I thought about it for a moment, then shook my head.

"No. Leave it as it is."

I spotted a few cop cars streaking by here and there, units being dispatched all over the city, and even a few fire trucks roared past, lights and sirens blazing.

"Turn here on the left."

Stephanie yanked the wheel, the car fishtailing. Her foot flat against the gas pedal, she continued to swerve in and out of traffic until I directed her to another side street that led into an industrial park, much like the deserted factory back near Baltimore.

Hargrave had gotten his mother to quiet down, though when I checked on her she still looked scared to death.

Ducking his head to survey the area, Hargrave said, "Where are we?"

I didn't answer. Just grabbed another fresh mag to have it in place in case I needed it as I directed Stephanie to make another turn—leading us into a dead end.

Stephanie halted the car right in front of the weather-beaten, paint-flecked wall.

I opened my door.

"Let's go."

Hargrave said, "Burke, what the hell is going on?"

Tall brick walls surrounding us on three sides, the space here maybe two hundred feet across. A couple of empty dumpsters, trash scattered here and there.

I opened Hargrave's door and told him to get out.

He glared up at me, then shifted to say something to his mother before stepping out. He gazed around the area again and narrowed his eyes at me.

"Just wait," I said calmly, still staring past him at the building—and as soon as the merc and two caregivers rushed outside, one of the Ford Expeditions came screeching around the corner and halted long enough to load up the three of them.

I shouted at Stephanie to drive, and she slammed on the gas again, the car's four-cylinder engine screaming in protest as we jolted forward.

Still twisted in my seat, making sure the SUV was following, I said, "Teddy, send the message."

Teddy's voice in my ear: "Will do."

We were approaching an intersection, the light red, and Stephanie's first instinct—just like anyone's—was to slow down.

"Keep going!"

"What?"

"Go around these other cars."

"But both lanes are blocked. I can't—"

"The oncoming lane, Stephanie!"

Grimacing, her fingers white against the steering wheel, she jerked us into the oncoming lane, feathering the brake as we entered the intersection and then smashing her foot against the gas again, cars swerving out of the way.

Quinn's voice in my ear: "You headed to the second location?"

"Yes."

"Need me for anything else?"

"No. Head back to base."

"Copy."

Teddy and her hacker crew had created gridlock throughout the city except in this area, and now they controlled the traffic lights, ensuring we had all greens as Stephanie tore down one street after another, handling the car better than I expected. Aggressively maneuvering around slower-moving vehicles, even leaning on the horn when she needed to.

backward, aiming the muzzle down the hallway, waiting for any movement, while behind me Hargrave pushed his mother through the glass doors and shouted at me to hurry.

I'd just started to turn around when I caught movement from the corner of my eye. Not one of the caregivers but a man decked out in tactical gear—not police or HRT or any law enforcement agency, but a merc.

The man had his assault rifle raised and let loose, a torrent of bullets raking the air above me as I hit the ground for cover.

Rolling over, taking an extra beat to steady my aim, I squeezed off three rounds.

One connected with the man's ankle, sending him to the ground.

The second merc charged around the corner, the two remaining caregivers in his wake.

I was aware of tires screeching outside, Stephanie behind the wheel, Hargrave flinging open the back door and helping his mother inside. I fired off a few more shots before vectoring straight for the passenger-side door.

Stephanie had already taken off her seat belt, meaning to get out so I could take her place, but I jumped into the shotgun seat and smacked the dash.

"Drive!"

After a millisecond of hesitation Stephanie stamped her foot on the gas, the car jerking forward as she steered it straight for the nearest exit.

I dropped the mag, checked to see how many rounds were left, then twisted around in my seat to look past Hargrave with his arm around his mother.

"Slow down."

As Stephanie lifted her foot off the gas pedal, Hargrave shouted, "What are you doing? We need to go!"

Slamming the door shut, I shouted at Hargrave to keep moving, his mother with tears in her eyes asking if the bees were coming.

I moved backward down the hallway, my pistol aimed for any movement. Then we turned a corner and I spun around to keep up.

Hargrave was still grimacing in pain, wanting to apply pressure to where he'd been shot. I noticed a subcompact SIG in his hand, its slide kicked back.

"I panicked," he said, gritting his teeth through the pain. "I saw them coming and opened fire. Foolish of me. Maybe they wouldn't have returned fire had I not—"

I shouldered him aside when I spotted a collapsed wheelchair leaning against the wall. Yanking it open, I wheeled it around and pushed it toward Hargrave.

"Here."

Hargrave flung the spent pistol away, grabbing the wheelchair and saying, "Mom, I need you to sit down in this, okay?" while his mother continued to cry and I kept my focus on the end of the hallway, my gun gripped with two hands to keep it steady, so that when one of the Russians peeked around the corner I fired a round at her head, bits of plaster flying everywhere.

"Go, go, go, go!"

Hargrave took off running, pushing his mother as fast as he could.

I continued to move backward, squeezing off a few rounds here and there as suppressive fire, until we'd turned yet another corner and a set of exit doors stood straight ahead, the late-morning sunlight illuminating the textured glass.

I swapped out magazines as we moved, pulling back the slide to chamber a new round. Hearing Teddy in my ear telling me that Stephanie was almost there. Continuing to move

76

I drew my gun as I hurried up the hallway, my head on a swivel, Teddy in my ear directing me every step of the way, and right before I reached the door I heard gunfire on the other side, a sporadic staccato and then even more gunshots erupted, people screaming and running for cover.

The door burst open and Mitchell Hargrave was there, pain on his face as he carry-dragged his mother, the woman hysterical as she kept shouting, "What is it, Mitchy? What's happening? What's happening?"

I noted the blood on Hargrave's shoulder as I pushed past him and returned fire down the hall, a bullet striking one of the Russians in the throat and sending her to the floor.

A burst of rounds tore into the wall near my head, one of the women having taken cover in a room fifty feet away, the other woman peeking around the corner, returning fire.

In my ear, I heard Quinn's voice tell me two mercs were headed inside and decided I didn't have enough firepower to stick around and see what happened next.

Teddy telling Mitchell Hargrave which direction to run and then Dan's voice saying he was almost there—and he caught movement from one of the men in the parking lot, peeking around a Tesla.

Quinn almost squeezed the trigger, knowing he could easily put a bullet right through the man's face, but instead scanned the parking lot again.

Meanwhile, the men he had shot were busy crawling away, none of their comrades attempting to pull them out of the line of fire.

So not only were they highly paid, but they were also spineless fucks who had no honor.

Good to know.

The driver of the Expedition whose tire he'd shot out had still driven the vehicle a bit farther before he jumped out and took cover behind a tree.

Sirens in the distance, though he'd been hearing sirens for the past thirty minutes, Teddy having worked her magic to keep law enforcement away.

The other SUV, unfortunately, had moved to a position that was out of his range of fire. He realized a few of the men were moving that way, staying low behind the cars, while two others backtracked to the building's entrance.

Quinn had a split second to fire off a round at one of the men before they entered the building.

His bullet missed, the sidewalk spitting up concrete.

He said, "Dan, you've got two mercs headed inside."

In Quinn's earpiece, a sudden bout of gunfire answered.

any passengers—were civilians. Either waiting to pick up passengers or drop them off.

Still, Quinn felt it in his gut—these were killers hired to perform a task and were excellent at what they did.

So it wasn't surprising when he heard one of the caregivers in his earpiece start speaking—telling the others to alert Sergei of the deception and to send in the teams outside—that the doors of each SUV sprang open and men began to spill out.

Wearing body armor and chest rigs and carrying Knight's Armament SR-16s in the middle of the day confirmed that these men were highly paid and didn't give a single fuck about discretion or not harming civilians.

Which made it all the more easy for him to start picking them off, one by one.

Tracking the men through his scope, finger caressing the trigger, his breathing calm and steady, he first sighted on the men's heads but then reminded himself this wasn't a combat zone and was instead United States soil and shifted his aim.

Like he'd done back in Chicago, he sent a .300 Winchester Magnum round straight through one man's knee, then another man's knee, before the others realized they were under attack.

As soon as he'd taken out the first man, the drivers put the Expeditions in gear and started maneuvering out of the parking lot.

As the other men had taken cover—and were no doubt trying to pinpoint his location to return fire—Quinn shifted his aim toward one of the SUVs.

Following the vehicle with his scope, finger again caressing the trigger, another slow breath in and out, and then half a second after his rifle jerked, the SUV's rear tire exploded.

The few civilians outside had since fled, hiding behind cars or ducking back inside.

Quinn scanned the area again, ignoring the voices in his ear—

rest of the team, and heard every awful word said by the woman to Hargrave's mother.

Then she heard what sounded like Hargrave stabbing the woman with something—instantly Teddy flashed on the syringe Jade had tried to attack her with—and suddenly the doctor appeared from another room, stepped across the hallway, and opened the door.

Teddy said to the hacker overseeing the doctor's office, "Show me an exit for them, now!"

Which was how, as soon as Mitchell Hargrave had left the room and was leading his mother down the hallway—and as the three other women rushed past the receptionist—Teddy viewed a real-time layout of the building and which hallways were unobstructed.

"Mitchell, it's Rita. At the end of the hallway, turn left, then turn right at the end of the next hallway. After that, go straight to the exit at the end."

Teddy ignored the chaos on the other monitors and kept her focus on this one screen—watching Hargrave hitch his mother up onto his hip with one arm as he hurried to the end of the hallway while the three remaining Russian agents raced to catch up.

Tyler Quinn had positioned himself on the roof of a building four blocks away. From this vantage point, he had a clear view of the parking lot in front of the doctor's office except for some tree cover near the eastern end, which slightly obscured one of the two SUVs that may or may not contain backup.

So far, nobody had gotten out of either vehicle.

There was a chance the drivers of each vehicle—as well as

75

In the dark of Cyrus's hacker den, among the myriad of motherboards, monitors, and other computer parts, Teddy stood behind the four hackers she'd hired to create upheaval all over Washington, DC.

She'd created a makeshift control center, rigging several of the hackers' computers to some of the larger wide-screen monitors so that she could keep an eye on things and help direct the rest of the team.

A transmitter in her ear, just as there was in everyone else's—even Mitchell Hargrave's.

While three of the other hackers were busy triggering bank alarms and creating gridlock all over the city, another had hacked into the security feed at the doctor's office. So Teddy had watched everything this entire time, except when Hargrave and his mother and one of the faux caregivers were taken back to a room that had no cameras inside, at which point they lost visual.

But she was linked in with Hargrave's transmitter, like the

Tasha knew it too—this particular cocktail was purportedly Russian-made—and her eyes went wide as she dropped the phone and reached for the pistol holstered to her ankle beneath the baggy scrubs.

Hargrave kneed her in the face, sending her sprawling to the floor—where her body started jerking as the seizure took hold.

Hargrave crouched, yanked the subcompact pistol from the ankle holster, and had just started to rise when there was a knock at the door.

"Well, Mrs. Hargrave, I hear you—"

Dr. Peters paused midstride. Wide, bespectacled eyes first registering the gun clutched in Hargrave's hand and then the woman seizing on the floor before shifting back to the gun.

Hargrave said, "I'm going to need you to move out of the way, Doc."

Dr. Peters silently side-shuffled as Hargrave grabbed his mother's hand, helped her stand, and led her toward the door, the doctor's panic-stricken eyes tracking him the whole time.

Hargrave leaned out, surveyed the hallway, and coaxed his mother to follow him.

"Daniel?"

"Yeah, I heard."

"Have you figured out plan B yet?"

"No, but I have some advice for you."

Sudden raised voices out in the waiting room at the end of the hallway. Hargrave paused long enough to glance back the way they'd come—and watched as one of the caregivers tore open the door.

"Which is?"

"Run."

"She is so certain the bees are coming to get her. Who is to say she is wrong?"

"Knock it off."

"Oh look"—the woman's Russian accent really starting to bleed through—"somebody found his balls."

"Mitchy?" His mother's frail voice, floating up behind him. "Mitchy, I'm scared."

Glaring back at Tasha, he started to turn away, saying, "It's okay, Mom, there are no bees," and it hit him a second too late that he'd shifted to the left, showing the woman a good view of his ear and the transmitter nestled there.

Before he could spin back in the other direction, Tasha said, "What is that?"

Calm breath in, calm breath out.

Slowly, Hargrave turned back to the woman.

"What is what?"

"In your ear."

"I don't have anything in my ear."

"Yes, you do."

She pulled out her phone, dialed a preset number.

Hand slipping into his pocket, Hargrave said, "What are you doing?"

Tasha's flat, cold eyes pinned him in place as she spoke into the phone.

"The son of a bitch is playing us. Alert Sergei. Alert the teams outside. Tell them to—"

Her eyes tracked the syringe arcing through the air a half second before Hargrave buried the needle into the side of her neck.

Unlike with Noah LaSalle, he felt a stab of satisfaction as he depressed the plunger with his thumb, administering two hundred cc's of a compound that would cause the woman's heart to seize in a matter of seconds.

A nurse led them down a long hallway to a room, giving the clipboard Tasha handed her a cursory glance before typing briefly at the computer. She asked them why Mrs. Hargrave was being seen today, checked his mother's temperature and blood pressure, and then announced the doctor would see them in a few minutes before breezing out of the room.

Hargrave, sitting next to his mother, watched Tasha as she examined the medical diagrams on the walls.

After a minute, her back to him, Tasha said, "I bet you hope she dies soon."

Hargrave said nothing.

Tasha turned and grinned at him.

"It won't change anything when she does. Sergei and the rest of us will still be in your life. You will never be rid of us."

In Hargrave's ear, Daniel Burke said, "Sure sounds like nobody hugged this chick when she was a kid."

Tasha took a step forward.

"What is so funny?"

"I'm sorry?"

"You are trying not to smile."

"It's this whole situation. The paranoia you all have. It's comical."

Tasha stared at him for a long moment, then turned to look down at his mother.

"The bees are coming, Mrs. Hargrave. They will be here very soon. They are coming just—for—you."

Burke: "Yeah, this chick is a complete psycho."

Hargrave didn't realize his fingers had curled into fists until he'd shot up from his chair and stepped between Tasha and his mother.

"Stop it."

An amused look on the woman's face.

along with Theo. Hargrave had left to take his mother to a medical appointment. As for Burke and Salazar, it was believed they were also in the area—and working in coordination with Hargrave.

Hancock's first instinct was to demand to see this new intel for himself. He'd even started to do so when Chen offered to show him once the op had been completed and Hargrave, Burke, and Salazar were all taken into custody. Hancock had heard the disappointment in the man's voice, how he'd been fooled just like the rest of them, and it had given Hancock the resolve to push through and see this to the end.

They were now on the top level of a parking garage in Georgetown, waiting for Theo to give them directions. The building Hargrave had reportedly taken his mother to for her appointment was only two blocks away. Burke and Salazar could be anywhere.

They had the car's windows cracked to let in some fresh air, which made it even easier to hear the sirens screaming all around them.

Hancock said, "Control, we're hearing sirens nearby."

Theo said, "Copy, Alpha One. There appears to be some glitch all over the city."

"What kind of glitch?"

"Traffic lights keep acting up. They're almost all red, creating gridlock. Several bank and fire alarms have gone off. However, right now it's unclear if any robberies or fires are actually in progress."

Hancock shared a glance with Kincaid. He felt his jaw tighten as he gritted his teeth.

"It's Burke."

Chen: "We don't know that for a fact, Alpha One."

"No, but I feel it in my bones. It's Burke. Mark my words. This time the son of a bitch isn't getting away."

at his mother, hoping to ease the worried look in her eyes, and gently patted her hand.

In his ear—Hargrave had purposely sat so that the ear with the transmitter was out of view from the four women—Daniel Burke spoke quietly.

"Thought you'd appreciate a quick sitrep. That Ford Expedition hasn't moved since it arrived. Nobody's gotten out yet. Another Expedition pulled in. Nobody's gotten out of that one either. My guess, both vehicles contain four mercs each. And I still haven't come up with a solid plan B yet. Other than that, everything looks peachy."

Lucas Hancock never liked going into an op without sufficient intel in place.

He wanted to view maps, building layouts, satellite imagery, anything he could get his hands on to ensure his mission was successful.

Hancock hadn't liked the idea of flying to Boston last-minute—it hadn't worked out well for them back in Chicago—and he especially didn't like the call he'd received from the CIA deputy director.

According to Samuel Chen, the intel that Burke had been spotted in Boston was false.

What's worse, Chen suspected Hargrave had tasked Julian to manipulate the data to make it appear as though Daniel Burke was caught on camera in Boston's North Station.

There was even suspicion that Dennis Rowe might somehow be involved, so both he and Julian had been detained by officers while Hancock and Kincaid had been sent to Georgetown. Samuel Chen noted he would oversee the op at the control center

"I can help you here."

Tasha said, "They're with us."

The receptionist checking them in produced a low whistle.

"My, my. You must be very popular, Mrs. Hargrave, traveling around with an entourage like this."

Tasha tried on a smile that surprisingly fit her face.

"We all provide round-the-clock care for Mrs. Hargrave. We are quite invested in her well-being."

"I can see that," the receptionist said. "However, due to space limitations, Dr. Peters allows no more than two additional people in the room at any time. Typically that includes only family or powers of attorney, but in this case he'll understand the need for one of Mrs. Hargrave's caregivers to be in attendance."

For a split second, Hargrave considered asking that only he accompany his mother back to see Dr. Peters. But he knew what kind of trouble that would bring as Sergei and these four women were already on high alert.

In the end, it was decided Tasha would accompany his mother, and she could pass along any pertinent information to her colleagues.

The receptionist asked if there were any medical or medication changes. When Hargrave said there were not, the woman handed him a clipboard anyway and asked that he fill it out while they waited for the nurse to call them back.

As they sat down—Hargrave's mother between him and Tasha, the other caregivers picking chairs nearby—he handed the clipboard to Tasha.

She shot him a look filled with pure poison, and he merely smiled.

"This is your job, isn't it?"

Tasha grudgingly accepted the clipboard. Hargrave smiled

74

Dr. Peters's office was located on the first floor.

The waiting room had a handful of people spread throughout, some filling out forms and others staring at their phones, nobody paying any attention to the TV in the corner featuring some inane morning talk show.

The woman who checked them in smiled brightly at his mother.

"Hello, Mrs. Hargrave. How are you this morning?"

For a moment his mother didn't answer, gazing all around the room as if she'd never been here before, and then she leaned forward to whisper.

"I'm scared."

"Oh no. What are you scared about?"

"The bees."

"Oh, Mrs. Hargrave," said the receptionist, who had heard all about the bees before, "you've got nothing to worry about. There aren't any bees here. This is a safe space."

One of the other receptionists waved to the three caregivers lingering near the door.

"Who were you talking to?"

"Not that it's any of your business, but I am in the middle of a workday, and my work is highly confidential."

"You don't have to be here."

"The hell I don't. She's my mother."

Tasha's eyes were flat and cold.

"And she is our responsibility."

Then, as though remembering that they were out in public and not hidden away from the rest of the world in Hargrave's home, the caregiver's face lit up with a smile, her tone becoming almost singsong.

"Okay, now, Mrs. Hargrave. It's time for you to see the doctor."

Tasha helped his mother out, showing a gentleness Hargrave hadn't thought she possessed. As Victoria pulled away to park the car, Tasha directed his mother toward the automatic glass doors, pointing at Hargrave.

"Look who's here!"

His mother paused long enough to gaze up at him. She stared for a beat too long, not recognizing him, until something changed in her eyes.

"Mitchy!"

"Hi, Mom."

"What are you doing here?"

"I'm here to see you. You and the doctor. You're here to see Dr. Peters. Do you remember Dr. Peters?"

It was clear she didn't, but still she tried to act like she did, a frozen smile on her face.

"Come on, Mom," Hargrave said, gently taking her arm, and as he led her inside he briefly caught the reflection off the glass doors and saw not just Tasha following him but the three other caregivers as well, coalescing behind them like a trio of wraiths.

telling you the truth. But I am telling you the truth: save my mother, and I will give you the laptop."

Hargrave continued to scan the area, now searching for Burke, when he spotted a black sedan turn the corner at the intersection and enter the parking lot.

"This is them."

Hargrave could see three people in the sedan: Victoria driving while Tasha sat in the back with his mother.

A few seconds later, another black sedan turned into the parking lot: Rebecca and Gwendolyn.

This will work, Hargrave thought, and started it as a chant in his head: *This will work. This will work. This will work.*

Then Hargrave heard Daniel Burke's voice in his ear—"Check your six"—and he very calmly and inconspicuously glanced toward the other end of the parking lot.

An SUV slowly rolled in. Windows tinted, so it was impossible to see who was inside, but Hargrave could make out the driver, and even from this distance and the slight glare coming off the windshield, he sensed in his bones who occupied the vehicle.

Mercenaries.

The phone still to his ear, he said, "I think we have tangos in the black Ford Expedition."

Burke: "Mm-hmm."

"Was your plan to pick off the caregivers here in the parking lot?"

"That was plan A."

"What's plan B?"

"I'll let you know once I come up with it."

Victoria eased the sedan to a halt right underneath the pavilion. Hargrave dropped the phone back into his pocket as he started forward to get the door—but Tasha opened it herself, throwing him a heated glare.

him, sunglasses on her face and a dark baseball cap on her head, and Hargrave stared after her, momentarily speechless, before he realized there was now something in the palm of his hand.

A tiny black case, about half the size of a container of dental floss.

He knew exactly what it was and surreptitiously popped the lid and slipped the transmitter out and secured it in his ear.

Grabbing his phone and placing it to his other ear for show, he said, "Daniel?"

The voice through the transmitter was crisp and clear.

"Howdy, boss."

"Was that the infamous Stephanie Nguyen who just happened to walk past me?"

"It was."

"Impressive. Do you have anything to do with all the sirens I'm hearing?"

"No comment."

"I see. Where are you now?"

"Nearby. Nice Mercedes, by the way."

"Thank you. But it's not in there, you know."

"What's not in there?"

"The laptop. In case you decided to break into the car once I entered this building with my mother and her captors."

"The thought never even crossed my mind."

"It's stored in a secure location. As soon as my mother is safe, I'll hand it over."

"I realized something this morning, Mitch. Something I don't much care for."

"What's that?"

"This whole plan hinges on trust. And right now, I don't think either side trusts the other very much."

"Fair enough. I don't expect you to trust me. And I don't expect you to believe me when I give you my word that I'm and while it had that feature, Hargrave had picked this particular model because it contained GPS tracking capabilities.

His mother seldom left the house, but there were still times Hargrave would absently check the app to ensure she was still there, both comforted and dismayed by the fact his mother was a prisoner without even knowing it.

Now he watched the blinking red dot head to this location, only three miles away. Depending on traffic, they would arrive early.

The morning sky was robin's-egg blue, a cluster of white puffy clouds gathering on the horizon beyond the trees. A slight breeze in the air, which he knew could affect a bullet's trajectory depending on how far away the sniper was positioned, though based on how the sniper had taken out Dennis Rowe back in Chicago, Hargrave felt confident the man knew what he was doing.

What if they don't show up?

It was something Hargrave had been thinking about all morning. That Burke and Salazar had decided not to follow through on the agreement. Maybe because they didn't trust Hargrave to follow through on his end. If that were the case, Hargrave couldn't say he'd blame them much. Even now he wasn't sure whether he could trust himself.

Checking the app again—that blinking red dot inching closer and closer—he shoved the phone back into his pocket and started for the entrance.

He stepped up under the pavilion as a few people came and went—an old man being pushed in a wheelchair, a woman leaning heavily on a rollator walker as her daughter walked slowly beside her—and he had started to survey the parking lot again when somebody bumped into him.

"Sorry, so sorry," mumbled a woman as she started past

73

Hargrave's mother was scheduled to arrive at ten fifteen, exactly fifteen minutes before her appointment, so he parked his Mercedes in front of Georgetown Geriatrics & Palliative Primary Care just before ten o'clock.

A four-story redbrick building that also included offices for the Heart & Vascular Institute, Ambulatory Care, Radiation Oncology Center, and several other providers.

He exited the car, surveying the parked vehicles, buildings, and trees.

A chorus of sirens in the distance—more than usual—but otherwise nothing looked out of place.

Then again, why should it?

He figured Burke's sniper had set up a nest somewhere close by. Far enough to pick off the caregivers once they arrived. And any other surprises Sergei decided to throw their way.

Hargrave checked an app on his phone, one linked to the personal emergency response system his mother wore around her neck. The caregivers believed the device was to detect falls,

"Goodbye, Mitchell."
And then the man was gone.

They were on the Gulfstream again, taxiing for takeoff, when the rear-mounted engines started to subside their roar outside.

Lucas Hancock and Michael Kincaid, sitting in leather seats across from each other, shared a puzzled glance.

Hancock rose and started toward the front of the plane. He'd only taken a few steps before one of the pilots emerged from the cockpit.

"Change of plans."

"What are you talking about?"

"Just got a call from the deputy director of the CIA. Somehow he managed to get through to me directly."

The pilot held out his phone.

"He said he needs to talk to you."

"That's a mistake."

"Oh really? And tell me why that is, Mitchell."

"The whole point of this op was to keep things quiet. If you bring in HRT operators, that's going to raise a lot of eyebrows."

This time Samuel Chen laughed out loud.

"My God. You are delusional, aren't you? But I get it, Mitchell. You're a sad old man who's stuck in his ways. You can't move past the fact that Daniel Burke has made a fool out of you."

"I've got POTUS on my side."

"Do you? And how exactly are you going to get ahold of him? Your only contact was Lawrence O'Neal, and he's since been excommunicated."

Hargrave was silent as he thought about it. He needed this op to continue—at least for the next several hours. It was now almost seven and his mother's appointment was at ten thirty. If Burke and Salazar and their sniper friend and whoever else was involved came through, then his mother would be safe, and Hargrave would be on a plane out of the country.

Hargrave asked, "Are you headed in?"

"Am I headed in for what? Your sad excuse of an op? No, I have actual work that needs to be done today. Daniel Burke isn't the only threat this country faces."

Hargrave opened his mouth, meaning to tell Samuel Chen how he needed him at The Office today to oversee the op because his mother had a doctor's appointment, but realized just how ridiculous that would sound.

Swallowing, he tried his best to inject some heat into his tone.

"Coordinate HRT. Get the whole Boston Police Department in on the action for all I care. But my men are flying in and there's nothing you can do about it."

A beat of silence on the other end, cold and calculating.

station. Julian says he did the same thing an hour ago—that that's how they picked up his location."

On one of the monitors a man ambled through a train station. The man was not Daniel Burke, but thanks to the ever-evolving deepfake technology, Julian had performed a master class–level of deception that had easily deceived a man who'd once worked closely with the target.

Hargrave said, "So what don't you get?"

"Burke knows what it takes to stay off the grid. Yet, for whatever reason, he purposely walked through that train station back in Chicago to bring the team out there. And now it looks like he's doing it again."

Hargrave stood with his arms folded, watching the monitors of various spots around Boston.

"Sometimes there is no easy answer, Dennis. Daniel Burke is a traitor—he's gone so far off the reservation there's no telling what's going through his head."

Hargrave's work phone buzzed. Samuel Chen. He excused himself and stepped into the corridor to take the call.

Chen said, "I got your message. Do we know yet why Burke's in Boston?"

"No, but I'm sending the team there as we speak."

"What team?"

"Hancock and Kincaid."

The CIA deputy director snorted in disbelief.

"After the past several days and everything Daniel Burke has managed to do, you honestly think Lucas Hancock and Michael Kincaid can take care of this? Absolutely not."

"I thought you'd said our fates are now linked."

"They are, which is why I'm done humoring you and your team. I'll coordinate with the FBI to get an HRT unit mobilized."

72

Hargrave was again surprised to find Dennis Rowe in the control room.

The man was sitting in his wheelchair in the middle of the room, his casted leg raised, watching the monitors.

Hargrave hesitated for a moment before closing the door and striding over to stand next to him.

"You should be at home resting."

"I can't rest while Burke is still out there. If I can't be in the field, then this is where I belong."

"How'd you hear about this anyway?"

"Lucas called. Said him and Kincaid were flying to Boston. I imagine they're at the airfield now."

Hargrave checked his watch.

"They should be departing any minute."

Rowe shifted in his wheelchair, grimacing at the pain in his leg.

"I still don't get it, though."

"What?"

"Back in Chicago, why Burke walked through that train

I couldn't hear. Quinn threw me a glance before he set the mag aside and started helping her put on the vest.

In my pocket, the burner vibrated.

A text message from Teddy.

> Ready when you are

The girl with the piercings said, "So what do you want us to do?"

Teddy glanced at Cyrus, who stood silently by the door, and then smiled at the group.

"Create chaos."

"Are you sure you can do this?"

Hesitantly, Stephanie nodded. She tried to put on a brave face, but I could still see the fear hidden behind her eyes.

"It's okay if you can't. We can still make it work another way."

Stephanie gazed past me at Quinn by the panel van, loading his gear. He went about his work without acknowledging us, though with the quiet of the factory, it was likely he could hear every word.

"I'll be fine."

"Stephanie—"

"I said I'll be fine, Daniel."

No more childhood nicknames from the girl I'd known when I was a kid. Ever since last evening, when we'd stood on the roof staring out at the setting sun and I'd told her about the killing room, her mood toward me had shifted. Not that it had ever been openly bubbly, but I'd felt like she could tolerate my presence. Now, her level of disgust toward me was at a critical high.

"Do you need help with your vest?"

"No."

She shouldered past me and headed straight for the panel van. Quinn paused loading the mag of his sniper rifle as she approached. She held out her vest, said something low enough mother's, or so her mother had claimed. Instead, she realized she no longer had to hide behind that façade and could now be the person she was always meant to be.

"Teddy"—Cyrus's voice ticked up in talk show–announcer fashion—"here are your bandits."

Four faces swiveled in her direction. All of them young—no more than twenty-five, tops—and staring at her with tired, bored eyes.

"These are the best of the best," Cyrus said. "And they know how to keep their traps shut."

"And," said an attractive young woman with short pink hair and an array of piercings all over her face, "we like to get paid for our time."

Teddy stood there, taking in the crew, the one she'd requested from Cyrus last night after the news from Mitchell Hargrave about Sergei bringing in reinforcements. Daniel felt confident he could provide makeshift boots on the ground, while another problem presented itself.

"Okay, listen up. Cyrus says he trusts you and I trust Cyrus, which is why I'm standing here. Yes, you will be paid—very handsomely. In fact, from what I understand, Cyrus already told you how much I'm offering."

A round of nods circled the group.

"The job I'm asking you to do is relatively simple, but it doesn't come without potential risks."

Another guy with bleach-blond hair and thick glasses chugged on an energy drink as he raised his hand like they were in grade school.

"What kind of risks are we talking?"

"Prison time. Ten years, maybe twenty."

If this was meant to scare off any of the hackers, they barely blinked.

71

At six o'clock that Tuesday morning—as the sun was beginning to rise in the hazy sky, the quiet city beginning to stir—Teddy trampled down the concrete steps to the narrow alleyway and hurried to the metal door.

When she knocked, she expected a few minutes to pass before Cyrus answered, but the man opened it almost immediately, gazing out with his sunglasses.

"About time."

She stepped through the doorway and waited for Cyrus to close and lock the metal door.

"I told you I'd be here at six."

Cyrus started down the hallway, the tips of his fingers grazing the wall as he moved.

"I know. Just figured you'd be early on a day like today. After all, you're the one who called them all together."

As she followed Cyrus to the hacker den, it occurred to her that she was no longer thinking of herself by her actual name—the one she'd been born with, her first name a favorite of her

"Mitchy," his mother said as he came to stand beside her bed, reaching out for his hand.

Once again Hargrave was astounded by how frail his mother had become, as though he could disintegrate her bones by simply squeezing her hand. This woman who had always been there when he was young to feed him and bathe him and patch him up. This woman who was his mother and who he loved unconditionally—the whole reason why he had fallen into this bottomless pit of despair in the first place.

"I'm here, Mom."

"Mitchy"—her voice as fragile as a dead leaf—"I'm scared."

Had his mother seen the guns? Did she know who these so-called caregivers really were?

"The bees, Mitchy. They're close by. I can hear them."

Hargrave gave his mother's hand a slight squeeze, enough to let her know he was right there with her. Because suddenly he realized this may be the last time he saw her like this, just the two of them alone.

Glancing back toward the open door, he leaned forward and gently kissed her forehead. Then whispered into her ear.

"It's okay, Mom. The bees aren't going to get you. Nobody is going to get you. You might never see me again, but you'll be safe. I . . . I promise."

The women made no reply.

"I still plan to be at the appointment later this morning."

Again, nothing.

Hargrave continued down the hallway to his mother's bedroom. The door was partly open, and he knuckled it the rest of the way to peek inside.

Like the other night—like all the nights he'd looked in on his mother while she slept—there was an instant where she appeared dead and he felt that sudden surge of relief start to wash over him.

Knowing that his mother couldn't possibly be enjoying her life now that the dementia had staked claim and started to invade the rest of her body.

Then wondering whether that was true, whether there was still part of her—this woman who had birthed him and raised him and loved him for who he was—that was still in there, wanting to live as many days as she could.

Hargrave hated to think about those times when he'd contemplated putting her out of her misery—partly because he didn't know for sure she was in misery and partly because it made him sick to remember all those times he thought about bringing in a syringe with the special compound and injecting her with it.

It wouldn't be a pleasant death, but it would be quick, and what's more, it would appear natural to everyone who cared—a medical examiner if it came to that but more importantly to Sergei.

And then, suddenly, Hargrave would no longer have that boot on his neck, pinning him in place.

"Mitchy?"

His mother's soft voice, speaking to him like a ghost as he started to turn away.

Gazing down the hall to ensure the women weren't nearby, he stepped into the room. The hallway light intruded, causing his mother's eyes to glow like two crystals in a dark cave.

He couldn't say anything to the women downstairs. They would only look at him with their cold stare. Maybe ask what he was so worried about—did he have something to hide?

And so he'd gone to bed, just like any ordinary night, but unlike any ordinary night, he couldn't sleep.

Staring at the ceiling and the shadows as the trees outside his window played off the streetlamp. Listening to the occasional car driving past. Listening to the familiar rhythm of his heart tap-tapping away in his head.

When his work phone buzzed, he opened his eyes and checked the clock on the nightstand and saw he'd been out for nearly two hours.

Julian calling, with the update Hargrave knew the man would give.

"Sir, we've got an alert on the target."

Sitting up, wiping the snail's trail of drool from his mouth, trying not to sound as exhausted as he felt.

"Where?"

"Boston."

A quick shower and shave and then he dressed and hurried down the stairs to find the two women assembling their gear at the dining room table.

The sight stopped him—the array of pistols and bullets and body armor—and he couldn't help but laugh out loud.

"Being a bit paranoid, don't you think?"

The women paused cleaning and loading their weapons. Menacingly silent.

Hargrave said, "I need to head into work. Something's come up."

70

Somebody had snapped the thread.

One of the women holding his mother captive, more than likely.

Hargrave had noticed it late last night after his call from Sergei. He'd gone upstairs to hide in the sanctity of his office—one of the few places in his home these awful women had never set foot—when he happened to see the thread was no longer in its place across the door.

An old-school spy trick, sure, but Hargrave was an old-school guy. Plus, the thread had done its job all this time.

And now it'd been snapped.

Meaning someone had been in his office while he was away.

He'd entered cautiously, examining each foot of space with the utmost care. Inventorying the items on his desk and the bookcases and shelves. Trying to spot anything out of place.

Taking a countersurveillance device from his desk, he swept the office, from floor to ceiling and back again, searching for any listening or video device, but after an exhaustive search, he came up with nothing.

"What?"

The biker who'd spat out his tooth shook his head.

"Only one of the guys attacked us. The other just stood there and watched."

"One man," Ike said, his tone still flat. "One man did this to the two of you."

Again, the bikers shared another glance.

The second one said, "There was four of us. The other two had to go to the hospital."

Ike's fingers had gone white around the textured grip of the pistol in his hand.

"Who the fuck was this guy?"

"We don't know."

The biker who'd spat out his tooth pulled a black disposable phone from his pocket.

"But he tossed this at us before he left. He . . . he told us to give it to you."

Ike stared at the burner in the biker's hand. Suddenly feeling like he was five years old again and cowering beneath those fireworks blasting rainbows in the dark sky above his head.

"What am I supposed to do with that?"

"He said he'll call you tomorrow to let you know where you can find him. So that he can finish things."

Ike kept staring at the phone, still not wanting to take it. Carefully, he flicked his gaze up at the two bikers.

"So he can finish what?"

Both men glanced at each other again, and it suddenly became clear neither wanted to answer.

"Goddamn it"—fire in Ike's voice now—"tell me what he said."

The second biker swallowed hard.

"He said he's the one who killed Duncan. And that you're next."

had called the West Coast home for the past decade or so, ever since they'd expanded their territory, but this was where his little brother had been born and raised and by God this was where he would be laid to rest.

The body would come in tomorrow. Every Norseman available on the East Coast planned to attend the funeral—the only ones not coming were those on the clock, because despite how important family was, business was even more important. You couldn't slow down for even a day while building an empire.

As much as Ike hated his father, who'd been dead for nearly two decades, he figured the old man would approve.

A heavy banging at the front door, loud enough to make Shelley jump.

Ike grabbed his gun off the table and hurried over to the door, peeking through the curtain before yanking the door open.

Two of his men stumbled inside, their faces so beaten he could barely recognize them except for their bloodstained vests.

"The fuck happened to you?"

One of his men started to speak but then moved his jaw around and reached up to catch the tooth he spat out.

"We got jumped."

"By who?"

The other man shook his head, grimacing in pain.

"Never seen 'em before."

"Don't tell me they were niggers."

The second man shook his head again.

"Nah, they was white. Two of 'em."

The first man said, "We'd parked our bikes and were headed in to get somethin' to eat when these guys came out of nowhere."

Ike asked, "And these guys did this to you?"

The two bikers shared a hesitant glance.

Ike's voice, already tense with fury, went flat.

puddle soaking the carpet, and Shelley, eyeing him carefully as she kept her distance, started toward the kitchen.

"I'll clean it up."

"You better clean it up, you fucking bitch."

Shelley returned with a roll of paper towels. Before she could crouch down to start mopping up the mess, Ike grabbed her arm.

He both hated and loved the flicker of fear in her eyes as he felt her body stiffen.

"Hey. Look. I . . . I'm sorry."

Only a weak man ever apologized—another one of his father's idioms—but over the past couple of years he'd begun to understand the value in that five-letter word. Especially when he felt it deep down inside, like he did now.

Looking down at the carpet, her body trembling ever so slightly, Shelley swallowed.

"It's fine."

"No, it's not fine. I shouldn't have snapped. But my brother . . . I can't believe he's gone."

Slowly, so very slowly, she shifted her head to look at him. Those deep brown eyes staring back into his.

"I know. That's what I was sayin' earlier. That I'm sorry he's gone."

"You've been saying sorry since it's happened."

"Because I *am* sorry. He was your little brother. Nobody should ever have to lose a little brother. Especially like that."

Ike squeezed his eyes shut. Images of the farmhouse flashed by, those taken by the men who'd arrived later to find the entire structure in flames.

And Duncan—his baby brother—a charred mess on the front lawn.

After much thought it'd been decided to have his brother's body brought back East to be buried here. Sure, Duncan

July picnic, a cacophony of sudden booms, little Ike screaming in fear after every explosion above his head, his father's drunk friends laughing at him, making him the butt of their jokes, and so his father—already a half dozen beers in, if not more—grabbed him by the arm and shouted at him to stop crying, shaking him so hard he dislocated Ike's shoulder.

They were in the living room, the old clock on the mantel showing almost eight o'clock, and like his old man Ike had developed a taste for beer. Nothing could whet his thirst the way an ice-cold beer did, and so far tonight he'd had . . . what was this now, his eighth?

"Hey."

Shelley rising from her spot in the easy chair beside him. Sauntering toward him in that special way she had about her, those thirty-six-year-old hips swaying back and forth, that blessed muscle memory kicking in from her dancing days. Placing a hand on his shoulder to get his attention before easing down onto his lap and hooking an arm around his neck.

"I'm sorry, you know."

Ike took another pull on his beer and set it aside on the table next to the chair—but the can tipped over, rolled to the edge, and fell to the floor.

"Goddamn it!"

Shelley was already in motion before he could fling her off him, lithely rotating herself on his lap and standing up and stepping far enough away in case he tried to smack her.

Ike wasn't proud of the times he hit Shelley, but she understood that sometimes he had no choice. And after the past several days, ever since he'd gotten word about what had happened in California . . . well, he'd needed to vent his rage, which explained the new bruise on the side of Shelley's face.

"Christ!" Ike shouted, staring down at the can and the

69

Real men didn't cry.

That's what Ike Cooper's old man always said, what he'd told Ike and his little brother Duncan every time they sniffled with tears.

Ike understood now that he was forty-seven, but at the time he was only six—Duncan four—and the menace in their father's voice demanding they not cry often made it so that they couldn't help but burst into tears.

Their mother wasn't much better, always staying to herself in the kitchen, either smoking and drinking and cooking or cooking and drinking and smoking, and whenever the boys hurt themselves playing outside or scuffed their knees, she would always heave this world-weary sigh as though she was forever cursed to tend to these boys she treated as strangers but who were in reality her sons.

"Whatcha thinkin' about?"

Shelley's voice snapped him from his reverie. Flashes of Ike when he was five years old and the fireworks at the Fourth of

I found Quinn in the back of the panel van dozing and tapped his foot to wake him.

"Let's go pick up food."

Yawning and wiping the sleep from his eyes, he said, "You can't do that without me?"

"I can, but on the way we need to make a detour."

He clocked something in my tone and frowned.

"What kind of detour?"

"The kind that's going to help us recruit an army of our own."

"No big *deal*?" Her tone, incredulous. "Are you being serious right now?"

I said nothing.

"So what did Tyler do?"

"He tried to get me to stop. Tried talking the others out of going so far when it was clear the detainees didn't know anything. And a few did—they started backing off. But the more they backed off, the more I doubled down. And Quinn . . . we got into it a couple of times. One time we even came to blows. Since I had seniority over him, I reported him to one of our superiors, making up some phony reason to try to railroad him. I was trying to get him court-martialed."

"Jesus."

"Yeah, it wasn't my finest moment. But at the time I honestly believed Quinn was obstructing my work. That if I only kept doing what I was doing, I could get the intel needed to stop the war. Or some bullshit like that."

"So that's why Tyler said the next time he saw you he'd kill you."

"Yeah."

"But he didn't kill you. Only punched you in the face."

"That's because Quinn's a good guy. Always has been."

"You knew he would help us, even after what you'd done to him."

I listened to the constant stream of traffic on the highway, the few cars speeding up and down the street below. Then the heavy rumbling of motorcycles as three bikers breezed past.

Even from this distance and with the sunlight fading, the familiar patch on the back of their leather vests caught my eye.

Feeling my toe start to pulse with pain, I nodded slowly.

"Yeah. I knew he would help."

"I started going off-book. A little bit here and there. Testing the waters, I guess you could say. Just to see what I could get away with. To see whether everyone else at the black site could keep their mouths shut. And then when I realized they were on board, I started escalating things. And when that didn't cause anyone to blink, I escalated things further until . . ."

I dropped my face, released a heavy sigh. Feeling that familiar rage deep inside screaming at me to keep my mouth shut. Sensing that if I kept going Stephanie would never look at me the same way again.

"I'm assuming you're familiar with the boiling frog theory. That if you put a frog in a pot of water and slowly turn up the heat, it will stay there until it's cooked to death. But if you put a frog in boiling water, it'll jump right out. That's essentially what happened at the black site. We were all frogs—or the people I worked with were frogs—and little by little I started turning up the heat. So that when Quinn finally joined us, the whole place was about ready to boil over."

"He didn't approve of the torture."

"It wasn't that he didn't approve of it. I don't think he cared one way or another if we tortured the enemy. But when we put prisoners in the killing room and started working on them, Quinn knew almost right away whether they were telling the truth. But I didn't care. I just kept . . . doing what I always did."

"Did you say *the killing room*?"

Closing my eyes again, I nodded.

"That's what we called it. What *I* called it. Because . . . look, do you really want me to tell you this stuff? Because I will. But I want you to understand I'm not the same guy I was then."

"You tortured a man back in Vegas. The one who ran security for the Lucky Star."

"I only waterboarded him a little. It was no big deal."

studied her face. The contours of her cheeks, the slope of her nose. The faintest traces of crow's-feet at the corners of her eyes.

She was beautiful and I wanted to tell her but knew that I couldn't, that not only was the timing wrong but that this was something I could never tell her, not now or in the future, because that wasn't the sort of relationship we would ever have, no matter how much I hoped otherwise.

"I told you about the black site I was stationed at in the Philippines. Prisoners who came to us were the worst of the worst. Our job was to interrogate them for any information they could provide to help us in our fight against the war on terror."

I shifted away from Stephanie, staring out now at the fading sun.

"*Enhanced interrogation* is what they called it. A cleaner, more sanitized term than *torture*. But torture was what it was. I say this now like it's obvious, and I guess at the time I knew it too, but I didn't care. I was told to do a job, so I did the job. I believed it was for the common good. I was helping to save the country. All that."

I shook my head.

"Men who were paid a lot of money by the military came up with certain enhanced interrogation techniques we were instructed to follow. And we did follow them—the loud heavy metal, forcing detainees to stand up for hours on end, refusing them water. But . . . after a while we started doing other things. More extreme things."

"Like what?"

"You don't want to know. Trust me. But these enhanced interrogation techniques we were told to follow weren't doing the trick. So we decided to ratchet things up."

A beat of silence as I closed my eyes.

"*I* decided to ratchet things up."

Stephanie's voice softened.

"What did you do, Danny?"

studying for my medical exams. But Teddy had some cigarettes on her, so I bummed a few."

Stephanie pulled out another cigarette, cupped her hand to light it, and blew a stream of smoke from the corner of her mouth.

"If all goes well, by this time tomorrow we'll all have our lives back."

It took me a moment to realize she was echoing what I'd said earlier.

Slowly, she turned to look at me. Her face awash in that near-twilight glow. Her eyes, flat.

"You believe it, don't you? That if we manage to do this—if we save this man's mother, if we get the evidence from him that proves you and Rita are innocent—that . . . what, everyone lives happily ever after?"

I said nothing.

"Maybe Rita gets her job back or does something else in the government. And you—your plan was to leave the country, so I'm guessing that's what you'll do, go to Europe or wherever. And Tyler will go back home to his dogs. But what about me? How am I going to explain things to my coworkers? They're never going to treat me like they did before. God, Patrick is *dead* because of me. Because of you."

Again I said nothing.

"You need to tell me. You need to tell me right now. What's the issue between you and Tyler? Why do you dislike each other so much?"

"Stephanie—"

"No, Danny, I need to know. I won't be able to sleep tonight if I don't. Hell, I'm so wired I doubt I'll be able to sleep anyway. But Tyler won't tell me, which means it falls on you. So tell me, Danny. *Tell me.*"

In the reddish-orange wash of that oncoming twilight, I

with only two of these women. Not four and possibly more. For all we know, this Sergei is building an army."

"Maybe so, but I like a challenge. What about you, Dan?"

I nodded, conscious of Stephanie's posture, her expression.

"Yeah. Tell Hargrave nothing has changed. The plan is still on."

Later, as the sun started to set, igniting the sky in a brilliant reddish-orange, I stepped out onto the roof to find Stephanie standing at the edge, smoking a cigarette.

"There you are."

She turned slightly at my voice but didn't look at me, instead focusing again on the fading sun being slowly swallowed by the horizon.

A healthy wind blew through, whipping away the wisps of smoke from the cigarette. Traffic out on the highway a quarter mile away and a few cars on the street below.

"Teddy told me she thought she saw you coming up here. It's best if you stay inside. You'd be surprised how good some of these spy satellites are nowadays."

Stephanie said nothing, made no move or acknowledgment. Just kept standing there, staring out at the horizon.

Stepping up next to her, I peered down at the weeds poking through cracked asphalt and the trash littering the tall grass by the chain-link fence. We were nearly ten stories up with no guardrail bordering the edge.

"I didn't know you smoked."

At first I thought she would continue to ignore me, but she took another drag, enough to burn the rest of the cigarette, and then flicked the butt over the side.

"I haven't smoked since college, back when I stayed up late

68

"Shit."

"What's wrong?"

"Well, there's good news and bad news."

Teddy glanced up at the three of us who had converged once Jade's phone had started dinging with the incoming text messages from Hargrave.

"The good news is Mitchell secured an appointment for his mother tomorrow at 10:30 a.m."

"What's the bad news?"

"Sergei thinks Mitchell is up to something, especially after the other night. Mitchell says all four caregivers will escort his mother to the appointment, and they're likely to be heavily armed and wearing body armor under their uniforms. And there may or may not be other assets around as backup."

"Christ," Quinn said, rubbing a hand over his face. "Well, nobody ever said this was going to be easy."

"No," Teddy said, "but we also thought we'd be dealing

"I understand your mother has a doctor's appointment tomorrow."

"Yes. As you know, her health is poor."

"This right after your alarm system went off the other night."

"As I told your girls, I had nothing to do with that. Honestly, I think you're going overboard by adding an extra girl per shift."

"*Overboard*? You haven't seen anything yet. I don't trust you, Mitchell. You're a traitor to your country."

Hargrave bit his tongue, wanting to shout that he was a traitor because of Sergei, but he tamped the urge down and let the man continue.

"I don't know if you're up to something but I'm not taking any chances. All four caregivers will escort your mother to her appointment tomorrow. And I might even have others there for backup just in case."

"Others? What are you talking about?"

The man's hearty laugh was enough to make Hargrave's skin crawl.

"You didn't think the four women who look after your mother are the only ones under my employ, did you, Mitchell? I have a countless number of assets at my disposal. And if you try anything stupid, they won't hesitate at all to kill your mother."

their true selves to peek through and daring Hargrave to do anything about it.

Hargrave held up his hands in an *I don't know what to tell you* gesture.

"Look, all I know is I got a call from the doctor's office telling me they wanted to see her tomorrow morning. I asked why and they said they needed to perform a series of tests. Check her online portal if you don't believe me."

As Gwendolyn retrieved the iPad they used to log in to his mother's portal, he drifted over to the doorway and peered into the living room. His mother sitting again in her chair with a bed pad beneath her, watching yet another episode of *Ozzie and Harriet*.

Hargrave wanted to go to her, crouch down, take her hand in his and smile and ask her how she was doing.

He wanted to wrap his fingers around her throat and put her out of her misery.

He wanted to take the nine-millimeter SIG hidden in the safe upstairs and blow his brains out.

A disapproving noise issued from the back of Gwendolyn's throat as she showed the tablet screen to Rebecca.

Rebecca said, "I will notify Sergei."

Hargrave watched his mother for another minute before turning away and heading for the stairs.

Thinking, *You go ahead and notify Sergei.*

Thinking, *You tell him to kiss my ass.*

———

Sergei called him less than ten minutes later, the man's Russian accent heavy and thick.

"What are you up to, Mitchell?"

"Excuse me?"

In the background, he heard a muffled voice say something. Dr. Peters answered at length, then cleared his throat and came back on the line.

"I'll squeeze her in, but I can't promise I'll know how to help her. You might want to reconsider hospice."

Hospice had been floated a year ago to focus on his mother's palliative care and to keep her comfortable in the home because there was no telling how long she had left. But by then Sergei had already taken over his life—and, by extension, his mother's life—with those damned women who weren't trained caregivers and did the bare minimum to look after his mother.

Not for the first time Hargrave wondered what the blessed relief would feel like once his mother did finally pass away, how Sergei would no longer have any control over him—though he also wondered if his mother's passing would change anything, because he was already in so deep he could barely see the blue of the sky from the bottom of his hole.

"Yes, Doctor. I'll think about it."

"Let me hand you back to my nurse. She'll find a spot in my schedule. I'll see you tomorrow."

When he told Gwendolyn about the doctor's appointment tomorrow at 10:30 a.m., fury flashed in her eyes.

"Why doctor's appointment? Your mother is fine."

Rebecca had been lingering in the hallway when Hargrave broke the news to Gwendolyn and stormed around the corner.

"Your mother *is* fine. No reason to see the doctor."

Both women now spoke with slight Russian accents. When they wanted to, they spoke flawless English, but this was their way of showing dominance over him in his home—allowing because his focus is currently on other things. Regardless, we need to work together to see this through. Do you understand?"

Hargrave nodded, feeling a single bead of sweat start to crawl down the back of his neck.

"Completely."

On the drive back to Georgetown, Hargrave dialed Dr. Peters, and after being put on hold for nearly ten minutes, his mother's doctor picked up.

"Mitchell! So sorry for the wait. I was with a patient. I'm told there's an emergency with your mother."

"There is. I need to bring her in tomorrow."

"I'm sorry, Mitchell, but I'm booked out for the next few weeks."

"I need you to squeeze her in, Dr. Peters. It's important."

A beat of silence as the doctor thought it over.

"What's going on with her, exactly? Depending on what it is, you might want to take her to urgent care or even the ER."

"It's her dementia. It's gotten even worse in the past week. If I take her to urgent care or the ER, they won't do anything. But you've been her doctor for the past five years. You know her medical history. And besides, she's always happy when she sees you, even when I don't think she knows who you are."

It wasn't lost on Hargrave that he masterminded and orchestrated highly covert and top secret missions all over the world, that he had a direct line to the president of the United States if he ever needed it, that with only a few phone calls he could have any major government resource at his disposal—but now here he sat in traffic like every other asshole in the city, hoping and praying that this man took pity on him.

"I was barely gone two hours. You were here. What's the issue?"

"The issue is I had Julian and Theo try to track you using your phone's location. They said you had disappeared, like you'd gone off the grid."

Daniel Burke had used a Faraday bag to conceal his phones while they scooted around the city in that panel van—which Hargrave only learned about right before they dropped him off. The bag was designed to prevent electromagnetic signals from being sent or received. It had been a smart thing for Burke to do, but now Hargrave wasn't sure how to explain it.

"I don't know what to tell you. My phones were on. If there was an issue with the signal, take that up with AT&T."

Samuel Chen continued to stand there, his forehead slightly bunched, studying Hargrave. A second ticked by, then another second. Finally the man nodded.

"I'm sorry to hear about your mother. But despite what's happening at home, I need you to focus on the task at hand, which is apprehending Daniel Burke and Rita Salazar."

"And the sniper."

"Yes, and the sniper, whoever the hell that may be. Speaking of which, what did Daniel Burke mean the other night?"

"I beg your pardon?"

"'I know what you've done, and I'm going to prove it.' That's what Burke said after he asked Lucas Hancock if you were listening."

"I have no idea, Samuel. The man is a traitor. I wouldn't believe anything he says."

Chen glanced around the corridor to ensure they were alone and then took a half step closer, lowering his voice.

"As I told you the other day, Mitchell, our fates are now linked. I may not approve of this team you've put together, but so far POTUS seems to be on board, though I imagine that's

67

Toward the end of the afternoon, when Hargrave was preparing to leave, Samuel Chen pulled him aside in the corridor and asked what was going on.

Hargrave tried to play it cool, suddenly feeling like he did whenever his mother caught him in a lie when he was a child.

"Excuse me?"

"You left the building this morning. Nobody could find you. You said you were getting coffee and then you never returned."

Hargrave willed his face and eyes to betray nothing as he held the CIA deputy director's stare.

"My mother isn't doing well."

It was slight, almost imperceptible, but that stern, take-no-shit expression riding the man's face cracked.

"What's wrong with her?"

"Not that it's any of your business, but she has Alzheimer's. One of her caregivers texted that she was trying to leave the house. So I hurried home to help calm her down."

"And you didn't think to notify anyone?"

"I don't love it either, but it's a good deal. Hargrave said he'll help us if we agree."

"Help us how?"

"For starters, he'll send the team away. So at least that'll put Hancock and Kincaid out of the area. As for the personal care aides, he said they've become spooked after your break-in attempt the other night. Now two caregivers are working each shift. Each of them is armed. Personally, I don't think they present much of a challenge, but the issue is they won't let Hargrave's mother out of their sight. Any whiff that something's off, they might just kill her for the hell of it."

"We need to get her out of that house."

"Agreed. Hargrave said he'll contact his mother's doctor and schedule an emergency appointment. The caregivers will drive her. Hargrave will meet them there. He said that's our best window."

Teddy bit her lip again, thinking it over. Her gaze skipping around at Stephanie and Quinn and me as she made up her mind.

"Seems easy. A bit too easy. Only a few caregivers against the four of us? If need be, Quinn can pick them off as soon as they get out of the car."

She turned to him.

"Right?"

Quinn shrugged.

"I'm not so sure this whole Hail Mary play you guys are running is going to work, but I don't have any problem putting some Russian sleeper agents out of commission if need be."

Teddy took another moment to think it over, and then nodded.

"All right. Let's do it."

"Good," I said. "Shoot Hargrave a message. Tell him we're in and he should set up the appointment. If all goes well, by this time tomorrow we'll all have our lives back."

"What communication has Mitchell had with him?"

"Only a few quick calls over the years. Never any face-to-face."

"And these top secret documents he stole?"

"Mitch said the first one was hardly top secret, at least in his eyes. It was information that was already widely known. So he didn't think it was a risk to national security to copy the files and give them to Sergei."

"Was he paid?"

"Not then, no. That came later when the asks started to escalate. By that point Hargrave knew he needed to bring someone in on the team to help him. He said he'd even briefly considered approaching me."

"But in the end he approached Noah."

"Yes."

"And then killed him."

"He admitted to that too. He said he was desperate and felt Noah had become a liability."

"It sounds like you're defending him."

"The hell I am. I'm only telling you what he told us."

"Who else is involved? I'm guessing he needed one of the tech's help to pull all this off. Especially with setting up the offshore bank accounts in our names."

"Julian."

Teddy gritted her teeth, shaking her head.

"Goddamn it. I should have known."

"Hargrave said if we can save his mother, he'll give us the laptop, which we can then give to POTUS."

"And then he'll turn himself in?"

"No. He asks that we give him an hour's head start so he can flee the country."

"Fuck that. That piece of shit deserves to rot in prison for the rest of his life."

description. So he'd broken things off and hadn't had a real relationship since.

But Hargrave said he knew the enemy was always out there, ready to test barriers. He could never be sure that the woman smiling at him in the grocery store produce section was a civilian who thought him attractive or some foreign agent trying to weave their way into his life.

The same with practically everyone else he encountered on a daily basis—the barista at the coffee shop, the woman walking her sheltie down the block, even the mechanic at the garage who changed his Mercedes's oil and rotated the tires.

They could all be spies waiting to get close to him or normal everyday people going about their normal everyday lives and ultimately none of it mattered because this was the life he had chosen and he wouldn't have it any other way.

"He said his mother was diagnosed with early-onset Alzheimer's seven years ago. That over the years it became worse and worse. That his mother had once made him promise to never put her in a home, so he'd hired live-in caregivers. He said the personal care agency he'd chosen had been somehow infiltrated, and before he knew it, each of the four caregivers hired to look after his mother was a Russian agent—at which point a man named Sergei made contact."

"He didn't think to alert the FBI?"

"He considered it. Had even considered sending in the Alpha Team. But how was he going to explain it to them? By that point the threat had already been made clear: try anything funny and his mother was dead."

"So who's this Sergei?"

"Hargrave doesn't know. He thinks he's a cutout for the SVR or GRU. Either way, Sergei's the handler for the women who look after his mother."

"Yes. But only if we save his mother."

"And you believe him?"

"I didn't, not at first. I figured whatever he was telling me was bullshit. But he sounded sincere. He looked sincere. And when we dropped him off, I asked him again if everything he'd told me was true. He said it was. And Quinn was watching his face."

"Uh-huh," Teddy said, not sounding convinced. "And what exactly does Quinn watching his face mean again?"

"Quinn can tell just by looking at somebody whether they're lying."

Teddy, rolling her eyes: "Give me a break."

So I nodded to Quinn, who told Teddy that it was true. That it was even the reason why as soon as he arrived at the black site in the Philippines he knew not to trust me.

My face snapped up when he said this, but he wasn't looking my way. I felt Stephanie's eyes on me, heavy and intense, but I didn't acknowledge her.

"Okay," Teddy said hesitantly, "say I believe you. Say I believe Mitchell is telling the truth. We save his mother and he gives us the laptop, and then what? He's actually willing to go to prison?"

The story Hargrave had told was pretty straightforward: when you worked in espionage, you essentially gave up all semblance of a normal life.

He'd noted that he had almost gotten married once, a long time ago. He hadn't gone into specifics but said that she'd been the love of his life and that ultimately he'd broken things off because he knew it wouldn't work out. They might get married, might have kids, but even at a young age Mitchell Hargrave knew his duty was to serve his country, which meant his wife and kids and even a dog or cat would come second. And besides, he hated the idea of lying to the woman he loved, keeping secrets from her, even though he knew that was part of the job

66

"Hold up," Teddy said. "Say that again?"

We were standing in the damp, decrepit remains of the fabricated metal factory. The panel van parked nearby as well as the SUV we'd driven from Chicago and Teddy's Honda Civic—which she had also stolen from a rental lot.

It was midafternoon and the sun was riding high in the sky, trying to fight past the grease-streaked windows along the top of the factory wall. A few of them were cracked and shattered in places, shafts of bright sunlight shining through.

"Hargrave said he'll give us the laptop. He said it's in a safe on the second floor of his home. He said that even if you'd managed to break into the house, there was no way you'd break into the safe."

Teddy stood there, biting her lower lip.

"He's just going to give us the laptop."

"Yes."

"The one with copies of all the top secret documents he's stolen and sold over the past three years."

"But clearly, you didn't."

"Clearly."

A lengthy silence, and then Hargrave sighed.

"All right. Maybe we can help each other after all. If you and Rita are trying to clear your names, I'm happy to oblige. But only under one condition."

"I'm not sure you're in any position to be making demands, but what's your condition?"

"Save my mother."

"Drop the act, Mitch. I know all about what he was doing to those kids in Nepal. And how you'd sent us there to clean up the mess."

He stared back at me, trying to read my face.

"I'm going to assume Lucas never told you the truth, which means it had to have come from Rita."

"Way to catch up, asshole."

"Who cares, though? Greenham left the country. All the evidence was taken away from the people planning to use it to extort the United States. Win-win."

"Win-win?"

I didn't realize I'd picked up the stun gun again until I saw the flash of fear in the man's eyes.

"The guy raped a bunch of kids and didn't even get a slap on the wrist. He went home and lived his life like nothing had happened. Meanwhile, those kids . . ."

I stared down at the stun gun, feeling its heft in my hand. Remembered using a similar device back in the killing room. The screams of men when I tased their testicles. The overwhelming and ungodly stench when they uncontrollably shit themselves.

"There was a series of abandoned tunnels under that building in Turkey. It was something Rita had alerted me to right before the op. After Noah had headed out and I killed the three men shooting at us, I used my knife to tear out the tracking device in my shoulder."

Hargrave nodded slowly, seeing it all now in his head.

"And you knew we couldn't just leave you behind. The op was too sensitive. We would destroy the building to hide your body."

"That's right. And a minute before those Hellfire missiles rained down on the building, I was already in those tunnels. I almost didn't make it far enough before a wall of fire came screaming my way. For a second, I thought I really was going to die."

"Noah sort of let the game slip back in Los Angeles, right when he was trying to kill me the second time. Said that everyone thought I was dead, and my being dead meant I could take the heat. But he didn't tell me what heat that was. My guess? More than a year ago the government realized somebody on the team was rotten. The walls were closing in. And then I died—or at least you thought I did—and suddenly you had your scapegoat."

"How did you do it, anyway?"

"What?"

"Fake your death."

The light turned green, and Quinn put us back into motion, checking the side mirrors every few seconds to keep an eye out for a tail.

"For a couple of months I'd been looking to get out."

"Because of your brother?"

I shouldn't have been surprised he knew about James, but still it caught me off guard.

"That was one reason, yes."

"I would have given you time off if you'd asked for it."

"How generous of you. But the truth is, Mitch, I knew I was going to need a lot of time off. And the Alpha Team . . . well, it's not a job that you can walk away from, is it? You're either in or you're out, and if you're out, that means you're six feet under."

Hargrave said nothing.

"And besides, I'd gotten sick and tired of the work, especially after learning our ops weren't always aboveboard."

"What does that mean?"

"Let's take Richard Greenham, for example."

"You mean the man you killed?"

"I didn't kill him, but I wasn't sad to watch him die."

"What about Richard Greenham?"

I nodded.

"She's keeping an eye on the place. Keeping an eye on the women holding your mother hostage."

This time his eyes gave the whole game away. A mixture of surprise and fear and relief, all rolled into one.

I said, "Let me run through what I think's going on here, and you can tell me if I'm wrong."

I leaned back, resting my shoulders against the panel van's vibrating wall.

"A couple of years ago—maybe four, five years—you got caught up in something you never expected to get caught up in. I don't think you set out to sell highly classified secrets, but something happened to force your hand. My guess is after the enemy realized trying to turn you wasn't going to work, they focused on the next best thing—threatening the only family member you have left."

Hargrave said nothing.

"On the outside, the women looking after your mother appear like any other in-home caregivers. But how many personal care aides carry sound-suppressed semiautomatic pistols and speak Russian?"

Again, that mixture of surprise and fear and relief flashing through his eyes.

"Rita was the one who set off the alarm, wasn't she?"

Silent, I nodded.

"Stupid girl. She's made things even worse."

"How so, Mitch? I'm being serious when I say I'm here to help you."

"Why would you want to help me?"

"Because right now I think the only way we're both going to survive this is to help each other."

The panel van slowed for another red light.

"She wanted to be. But I worried she might try to kill you."

"I'm surprised you're not here to kill me."

"Who says I'm not?"

The panel van slowed at a red light. Diesel engine idling as cars passed through the intersection and people crossed from one block to the next, and I watched Hargrave's eyes and saw everything he was thinking.

"I wouldn't do anything stupid if I were you. Not unless you want to get another taste of this."

Holding up the stun gun and wagging it in front of his face.

Enough muscle function had started to return that he managed to grimace.

"What do you want?"

"To help you."

"To help *me*? What the hell are you talking about?"

The light turned green and the panel van darted forward with the rest of the traffic, Quinn easing from one lane to the next.

"Let's put all our cards on the table, Mitch. I know you're the traitor."

An adamant shake of the head, the man's jaw going tight.

"Absolutely not. *You're* the traitor. You and Rita Salazar."

I sat across from him on a box, the stun gun in hand. I thought about how good it felt to tase him and how I wanted to do it again.

Instead, I set the stun gun aside. Held up my empty hands.

"No more intimidation tactics, all right? You know my history. You know what I used to do. And you probably know I'd love nothing more than to get you into some dark room with a drain in the floor."

Something changed in his eyes—not a softening so much as a flicker of worry.

"Is Rita really waiting outside my home?"

65

I waited until we'd cruised out of the parking garage and started a circuit of the city streets—Quinn behind the wheel wearing aviator sunglasses and a plain black ball cap and leather gloves—before leaning forward and ripping the bag off Mitchell Hargrave's head.

He sat on the floor of the panel van, his back against the wall, knees pushed up to his chest. Not struggling whatsoever as his body attempted to regain control of his muscle function.

"Hello, Mitch. Long time, no see."

He blinked, seemingly not at all surprised to find me sitting across from him, then cut his eyes toward Quinn.

"Who's that?"

"A figment of your imagination."

"Is he your sniper from Chicago?"

"My sniper, my personal driver—he can do it all. A true Renaissance man. But we're not here to talk about him. We're here to talk about you."

"You're working with Rita on this, aren't you? I'm surprised she's not here."

> Hey asshole. I'm parked outside your house. If you don't get here in 30 minutes, I'll kill your mother.

Hargrave considered returning to the control room, giving his team some excuse why he needed to duck out, but instead he went directly for the elevator, rode it up to the ground floor, and then hurried out to the parking garage. His mind so focused on Rita Salazar and the threat to his mother that as he burst out of the stairwell he didn't notice someone hurry up behind him until it was too late.

He felt the bite of the metal barbs on his neck a split second before fifty thousand volts of electricity instantaneously overwhelmed his central nervous system.

Hargrave lost all muscle control, falling hard to the ground—but he could hear the screeching of tires as a panel van tore around the corner and felt the plastic of flex-cuffs tightening around his wrists and then a cloth bag pulled over his head before strong hands grabbed him and threw him into the back of the van.

When Hargrave didn't respond to Chen's comment, the deputy director turned back to Theo.

"Any luck finding Salazar?"

Theo shook his head.

"None. Like Burke, she's in the wind."

"And is more than likely helping him," Dennis Rowe added, wincing at the pain in his leg.

Lucas Hancock looked like he wanted to punch the wall as he muttered, "I fucking hate traitors."

"We all do," Hargrave said, trying to regain control of his team. "And we're going to find them."

"Are you?" Samuel Chen sounded amused. "You've said that several times already regarding Daniel Burke."

"Yes, and every time we found him, didn't we?"

"You did. And then Burke went and killed a former US ambassador."

Hargrave traded a surreptitious glance with Lucas Hancock, the only one from the Alpha Team who had known the true purpose of the op in Nepal two years ago. And Hancock knew when to keep his mouth shut. Hargrave couldn't imagine he'd told Burke what Richard Greenham had done. Which meant it had to have come from Rita Salazar.

In his pocket, the disposable phone he used to communicate with Sergei vibrated. An incoming text message.

"I'm going to go get some coffee. Does anyone want anything?"

Before any of the men could answer, Hargrave strode straight out of the room. He headed down the corridor to the restroom and yanked the phone from his pocket.

It wasn't Sergei who had texted, but Jade—or, rather, someone using Jade's phone.

Lucas Hancock said, "How did this asshole disappear?"

A rhetorical question because Daniel Burke had had the same training as the rest of the team—they all knew how to blend into a crowd, how to lay low off the grid.

"As I mentioned already," Hargrave said, "he's got help. From whom, we don't know. Unless . . . Julian, Theo?"

Theo swiveled in his chair, cracking his knuckles loud enough the pops echoed in the tight space.

"Still nothing. The security cameras in those apartment buildings across the highway from the museum—where we suspect the sniper was located—were taken offline."

"Just like the security cameras in Rita Salazar's apartment building," Samuel Chen said, his eyes on Hargrave.

Yes—Salazar. They'd received confirmation it wasn't her body in the apartment. Which meant it most likely belonged to Jade. *Most likely* because the body had yet to be identified, and if Jade was in fact a Russian sleeper agent, then it was doubtful there would be any medical or dental records on file anywhere in the country that would help determine her identity.

Which Hargrave knew presented a potential problem. What if somehow the medical examiners *were* able to identify Jade—and could link her to Russia? That would create even more questions, though maybe it might work out, as the three million dollars wired to the offshore account Hargrave had set up a year ago in Salazar's name had come from that same country.

If that info came to light, the narrative would be straightforward: the Russians had paid Rita Salazar for highly top secret intelligence, then sent an agent to eliminate her—only Salazar had managed to escape.

The other night, when Hargrave had been alerted that the body wasn't Salazar's, he'd sent a message to Sergei asking for guidance but had yet to hear anything back.

He was surprised to find his whole team—or what was left of his team—in the room.

Theo and Julian at the computers as always, while Lucas Hancock and Michael Kincaid stood with their arms crossed watching the monitors.

Dennis Rowe was here too, sitting in a wheelchair with a cast on his leg.

And worst of all, that prick Samuel Chen stood right in the middle of the action, the man trying to make it look like he belonged.

Hargrave ignored the CIA deputy director and nodded a greeting at his men.

"Dennis, you should still be at the medical bay."

Rowe made a dismissive noise through his nose as he shook his head.

"Not while that son of a bitch is still out there."

Hancock and Kincaid had been banged up in the public transit bus crash back in Chicago, though their bruises and scrapes were nothing compared to what Rowe had sustained.

Once again, the police had placed the two men under arrest, and once again, Hargrave was forced to have the White House chief of staff intervene to claim that the men were working on POTUS's behalf.

Hargrave knew he could drink from that well only so many times before it dried up and hoped he wouldn't have to do it again.

Mostly because Lawrence O'Neal had been shitcanned. The reports from the news said that he'd rendered his resignation at the president's request, which raised alarm bells all over the political spectrum as it was far from normal for a president to fire one of his closest advisers only weeks before an election.

White House in Turmoil, one headline declared, and based on the past week, that was putting it mildly.

64

Monday morning, bright and early, Hargrave drove over the Key Bridge into Virginia and followed the traffic to Arlington.

After the events of the past couple of days, it was decided to move The Office's location. Another seemingly random building hosting insurance companies and law offices with a subbasement used to oversee covert operations all over the world.

He parked in the garage, took the stairs to the ground floor, and entered the building with a badge. If any of the employees saw him, they'd assume he worked somewhere in the building. They might not even notice if he lingered in the lobby so that he caught an empty elevator. If someone came in right as the doors started to shut, Hargrave would make a show of trying to stop the doors, but of course he wouldn't stop them. Then he'd turn to the left, facing what appeared to be a regular mirror, and would wave his badge over a particular spot, and like that, the elevator would descend to the subbasement.

A quiet corridor save for Hargrave's footsteps as he strode to a room several doors down.

with her arms crossed and her face streaked with tears, and when she reached us she went straight for the back door.

"Let's go," she mumbled, yanking the door open and climbing inside.

Quinn and I shared a look, and then Mr. Nguyen approached, smiling weakly.

"Gentlemen. I'm trusting you to take good care of my little girl. She says you're all in a lot of trouble and that's why I'm hiding out here. I can't say I understand or like it, but she seems to think you'll get everything sorted out."

He was looking at me now, his gaze soul-piercing.

I said, "I hope so, sir."

Mr. Nguyen gazed at the back of the SUV, as though he could see through the tinted glass.

"My daughter has always thought there's an answer for everything. That if she encounters a problem, she can diagnose and treat it. But sometimes life doesn't give us that option, does it?"

He let the question hang there for a beat, and nodded.

"I'll leave you to it. But before I go, can I get your word on something, Mr. Burke?"

"What's that?"

My dumb voice, cracking on those two words.

Stephanie's father said, "Give me your word that nothing will happen to my daughter. Can you do that?"

Sensing Quinn watching me from the corner of my eye, I nodded.

"Yes, sir."

He held out his hand.

"Promise?"

I stared at the hand for a moment before grabbing it and giving it a solid shake.

"Promise."

"The whole reason he's hiding out here is because he's leverage for Stephanie. And she's leverage for you. Which makes me suspect—since your brother's gone—that your parents are gone too."

My first impulse was to say nothing. There was no reason Quinn needed to know anything more about my life than he already did. But for whatever reason, part of me felt I owed him something, so I nodded.

"Yeah, they're gone. My dad when I was a kid and my mom soon after I graduated high school. How about your mom?"

Because I already knew his dad had taken his own life after being falsely accused of selling secrets to the enemy.

Quinn removed his sunglasses, cleaned them using the hem of his shirt, then slid them back on his face. Didn't say anything for several long seconds until, finally, he grunted.

"She's fine. As fine as you can be after suffering several strokes. The last one nearly crippled her. I set her up in a real nice facility outside Des Moines. Under a different name too—well, at least a different last name. No way anyone would ever be able to track her down."

"Do you ever see her?"

"I visit as much as I can. Probably not nearly as much as I should, but she's getting top-notch care and likes the staff and residents there, so she's happy. Tell me something."

"What?"

"If my dad hadn't been set up as an enemy of the state for stealing military secrets, would you have come to me looking for help?"

When I said nothing, didn't even look at him, Quinn nodded.

"Thought so."

For the next several minutes we stood in silence, listening to the birdsong in the trees. As Stephanie and her father neared, I realized Stephanie was walking a few paces ahead of her dad

"I don't mean after your run-in at the airport. I mean before—back when this Hargrave guy didn't even know you were still alive."

"I told you that too—I'd gotten a bullet fragment in my back. It was in a place I couldn't reach."

"Bullshit."

Arms crossed, I shifted to square my body to his.

"Say that again?"

"You heard me. No matter where that fragment was in your back, you could have gotten it out yourself."

I stared at him, debating what to say, before realizing there was nothing to say.

Shaking my head, I turned away from him.

Quinn said, "You want to know what I think? I think part of you wanted to see her. If you had wanted to patch up that wound yourself, you would've done it, plain and simple."

Still staring out at the lake, I said nothing. Thinking about that night just over a week ago. Pulling Olivia from the wreckage of the Escalade and binding her arms and feet and slapping duct tape over her mouth and easing her into the trunk of my car. Injecting her with ketamine to knock her out, then slamming the trunk shut and staring out over the dark desert and feeling that dull burn in my back.

And what had been my first and only thought?

Stephanie Nguyen.

The idea of patching up the bullet wound myself hadn't even crossed my mind. Because maybe part of me wanted an excuse to see her. To see if she even remembered me.

Quinn said, "So your folks are dead, huh?"

"What?"

He lifted his chin toward the lake. Stephanie and her father were now headed back.

63

I looked up as I slipped the burner into my pocket and shifted my weight against the SUV.

"Teddy found a place outside Baltimore we can use for our base of operations."

"What's that," Quinn said, "about an hour from DC?"

"Give or take. Apparently, there's an old run-down factory that's been sitting empty for the past year. Teddy's been hiding out there."

Across the lake, Stephanie's voice echoed.

"*What?*"

Our faces snapped in that direction, and I found myself stepping forward as though ready to race to her—even swim straight across the lake if need be—but I forced myself to stay put.

Quinn said, "You're in love with her, aren't you?"

"Excuse me?"

"Why is she involved in this, anyway?"

"I told you—I was worried Hargrave and the team would use her as leverage."

Her voice was so soft it almost got lost in the breeze pushing through the trees.

"You could," her father said. "But you won't."

On the lake, that lone goose began flapping its wings in earnest as it took flight. Skimming over the water and rising into the air. Their angle on the riverbank so that it appeared the bird was flying straight toward the sun—either to end its life, or to make it anew.

My plan was to fly out and surprise you. You'd always told me to come visit anyway. Even said that I might like it out there for some ungodly reason."

Despite herself, she smiled.

"It's not as bad as people think."

"Nevertheless, I planned to spend the rest of my time with you. Not in the house where I lived with your mother and watched her die. That . . . that didn't sound fun to me."

"It's cancer, Dad. It's not *supposed* to be fun."

"I'm sorry you had to find out this way. Though . . . I suppose there isn't any good way for me to have broken the news. Especially now that you're mixed up in . . . whatever you're mixed up in."

She shook her head.

"Forget all that. I'm not leaving your side. Not even for a second."

"Oh, Stephanie. You said it yourself that this is important. I'm not going anywhere. The people who own that cabin aren't coming by anytime soon. I can stay here for weeks if need be. Sleeping in my car hasn't been pleasant, but I've gotten used to it. It's sort of like camping."

"You've always hated camping."

"I know. But as you grow older, you start appreciating the stuff you never liked before."

She gazed across the lake again, at the SUV. She knew Danny didn't need her in this whole mess. That she would only slow him and Tyler down. That, if anything, her presence was a burden.

But was that true?

She wasn't sure—because deep down in her gut she felt she needed to be there with them to see this through to the end.

"I could stay with you."

"The doctors have given me less than six months."

"*What?*"

Her sudden voice, spiked with emotion, traveled across the lake and echoed off the trees.

For the first time in the past several minutes she remembered they weren't alone and gazed across the lake, surprised that they'd already walked so far, and spotted the SUV parked on the other side, Danny and Tyler leaning against it as they waited.

"Dad, what are you *talking* about?"

"Oh, honey. You know how it is."

"No, Dad, I do not *know how it is*. What do you mean the doctors have given you less than six months?"

"I've been feeling weak for a while now. I cut myself a few weeks ago, a stupid paper cut, and it just . . . wasn't healing. You know how I dislike seeing doctors. They always tell me something's wrong, so in my foolish head, I've always believed that if I don't see them, then I'll be fine."

He fell silent, staring out at that lone goose.

"It's cancer. Not the same cancer as your mother's, but . . . it's advanced. The doctors said I could maybe extend things another year with treatment, but . . . I don't have the will to do that."

"The hell you don't. You're going to do everything the doctors tell you to do. In fact, who are these doctors? We'll call them right now. We'll—"

She didn't realize she'd started crying until her father reached out with his thumb to wipe the tears from her cheek.

"I've lived a good life, Stephanie. A good, long life. I'm tired now, and I miss your mother. And I can't wait to see her again."

"But . . . but . . . but . . ."

Another weak, strained smile.

"Don't think I wasn't going to tell you. I've been cleaning up the house. Giving things away. Getting all my affairs in order.

"I think I'll move back home when this is all over. Spend more time with you. I . . . I need to get away from Vegas for a bit."

Something changed in his face, his eyes all at once guarded. He looked away and swallowed, giving himself time to decide what to say.

She placed a hand on his arm, halting him.

"Dad?"

His face was tilted away from her, showing only his profile, and she could tell he was debating how to move forward.

"Dad, what is it?"

Smiling at her now, tears brimming his eyes.

"I'd love to spend more time with you, honey. You're my favorite person in the world. And I'm sorry to hear you haven't enjoyed living in Vegas. Every time we spoke, you made it sound like everything was going well."

"Of course I'd make it sound like that. I was scared, Dad. After Adrian broke off our engagement, I didn't know who to talk to. Mom was gone and I was alone, and part of me wanted to leave Vegas and move back home, but another part felt that's what a weak person would do, and Mom had always told me I needed to be strong."

"You are strong, honey."

"I don't feel strong. And for the past couple of years, I've been in a rut. Adrian already found another woman, got married, has kids, and what do I have? My job. My work. That's it. No friends. I've put my entire focus on my career, and for what?"

She paused, sensing there was something else her father wasn't telling her. Something big.

"What aren't you telling me, Dad?"

He looked away from her again. His lips moving soundlessly as he tried out different sentences and phrases. Until finally he nodded, having come to a decision, and turned back to her.

"I miss her so much."

"I know, honey. I do too. Now tell me: Who are those men back there? You mentioned them, but who are they really?"

"One of them, Tyler, I only met the other day. He used to be in the military, like Danny."

"And Danny is James Burke's brother."

"Yes."

"And how are you involved with them again?"

"Let's just say I got in some trouble. Nothing of my doing, but now I'm caught up and not sure how I'm going to get myself out."

"You said men were hunting you."

"They're not hunting *me* so much as they're hunting Danny."

"Why?"

"It's . . . complicated."

"Stephanie." That stern father tone she'd always detested as a girl. "Are you listening to yourself? If you're in trouble, let me help you. We can go to the police. We can tell them—"

"No, Dad. This whole thing . . . it's much too big. The police can't help. Trust me, I already tried that, and it didn't end well."

He saw something in her face he didn't like, the alarm in his expression deepening.

"I don't want you in any danger."

She coughed out a desperate laugh, gazing again at that lone goose on the water.

"It's too late for that."

"I can't help you if you don't tell me what's wrong."

"I'm not looking for your help, Dad. I only want to make sure you're safe."

"Stephanie"—that tone again—"it's a father's job to make sure his daughter is safe, not the other way around."

She smiled at him.

Stephanie didn't know what to say—because she honestly didn't know the answer—so she said nothing.

"I almost didn't think it was real. Your voicemail, I mean. It *sounded* like you, but what you were saying . . . it all sounded so crazy."

A Canadian goose floated in the water, halfway across the lake. All by itself. The sun slanted in the sky, painting the bird's shadow on the still surface.

Where, Stephanie wondered, were all the other geese?

Maybe they'd already headed south for the winter and this bird had been left behind.

An outcast, feeling even more lost in a world that never felt like home.

"Hey," her father said softly. "What are you thinking about?"

She steeled herself, trying to steady her voice.

"I thought . . ."

"Yes?"

"I thought something bad had happened to you."

"I'm not surprised, based on the message you left. I hate to say it took me a while to know what you meant. That this was the place your mother said she loved most in the world. You know, Stephanie, she didn't like this place at all. Your mother had never been on board when we purchased the cabin, but when we brought you here the first time as a little girl, you loved it. I think we drove in early in the morning when the sun was rising and shining off the lake, and you said it was like a fairy tale."

"Mom hated this place?"

"*Hate* is a strong word, but it certainly wasn't her favorite. The only reason she said it was her favorite place is because, well, it was yours."

She felt an onslaught of tears threatening and did everything she could to hold them back.

62

They walked together along the gravel drive, beside the grass that hadn't been mowed in nearly a month, being careful to circumvent the scattered goose shit. Silver Lake to their right, the late-morning sun gleaming off its surface.

Her father said, "I was so worried about you."

"I tried calling. Several times."

"I saw you called. I tried calling you back but got your voicemail. As for the other number you called from . . . I don't answer unknown numbers. Do you remember Jean Bergman, from across the street? She was scammed out of several thousand dollars by someone she believed was calling from the IRS. So I've been extra careful not to answer any numbers I don't recognize. I may be getting up there in age, but I still have some smarts left."

He offered up a smile, though it was weak and strained.

"I'm sorry, Dad."

"Nothing to be sorry about. I'm just glad you're safe. You *are* safe, aren't you?"

"Stephanie."

Whether or not she heard me, it was impossible to say, just as it wasn't clear whether she cared if I said anything at all.

Down the porch steps, edging around the side of the cabin, leaning into the windows to try to peek inside. Her body moving frantically, hands trembling with fear, her voice growing hoarse as she kept calling, "Dad? Dad? Dad?"

And then she disappeared around the back of the cabin, and I heard her sudden intake of breath—and without any conscious thought I sprinted forward, wishing I'd brought my pistol from the SUV, imagining Lucas Hancock and that big fuck Kincaid positioned there, somehow having already known about this location and making it here before us.

I noted the tire tracks in the unkempt grass a half second before I rounded the corner and saw the Toyota parked under a tree. The driver's door opening and an older man climbing out, grimacing at his arthritic knees. His arms going wide as Stephanie flung herself into him, sobbing now, her muffled voice against his chest as she said, "You're here. You're here. You're here."

Do you think Stephanie is ever going to forgive you?

Shut. Up.

Do you think she could ever look you in the face again and not see the monster you truly are?

SHUT UP!

"What?" Stephanie asked, pausing to glance back at me. "Did you say something?"

Swallowing, I shook my head.

She frowned, then continued on. Walking faster now. As though the memories were starting to crystallize. Her focus now on the left side of the gravel drive, at the various cabins interspersed between the trees. A few, I noted, had some cars parked beside them while other cabins appeared empty, with a single chain blocking the entrance to discourage anyone from trespassing.

All at once Stephanie's pace quickened. She hopped over one of the chains and hurried down the drive toward a cabin. A squirrel nearby pausing in that all-too-familiar wild animal fear before scampering up a tree.

I hopped the chain and raced to keep up with her.

The cabin appeared empty, like it had been closed up since summer, but that didn't dissuade Stephanie as she raced up the porch steps and cupped her hands to peer inside the front door, then tried the doorknob.

Locked.

She moved down the porch, trying to see through the windows blocked by drawn curtains.

"Stephanie."

Ignoring me, she returned to the door. She tried the knob again. Then banged her fist against the windowpane. Even kicked her foot against the bottom of the door.

"Dad? Dad, are you in there?"

Quinn shifted behind the wheel to look at me.

I looked at him.

We stared at each other for a beat, neither one of us saying a word, and then I nodded and climbed out.

The morning air was crisp, just like it had been back in Wyoming. The sky mostly clear except for some clouds clustered on the horizon. The murmur of insects in the tall grass and birds in the trees.

I circled the SUV. Moving cautiously. Not wanting to spook Stephanie. Who had shifted from her position of leaning forward to standing straight up again. A hand to her face, visoring the late-morning sun as she cast her gaze all about the lake.

She spoke to me without turning around.

"I'll recognize the cabin when I see it."

But her tone betrayed the fact she wasn't sure this was the case. As she said, it had been over twenty years. Her parents had sold the cabin. Maybe the new owners had since renovated. Maybe—

Abruptly, Stephanie started walking, veering toward the left of the fork. Swiveling her head back and forth, creating her very own situational awareness. Trying to spot something that might help reignite those memories.

I looked back at Quinn in the SUV, shrugged, and started after Stephanie. Staying at least twenty steps behind.

What if he isn't here? a voice in my head asked. *What if he never made it because Hargrave sent a team just like you feared he might?*

Shut up.

What if all this time Hargrave has been keeping him in some subbasement someplace, locked in a dark room, waiting for the right time to use him as leverage?

Shut up.

trails, but my mother always said this was her favorite place in the world."

The gravel drive forked off as we approached the lake. A decent-sized lake, at least a mile around, the late-morning sun sparking off its calm, even surface.

Quinn eased the SUV to a halt and eyed Stephanie again in the rearview.

"Which way?"

Stephanie leaned forward, looking left and right. Her lips pursed as she tried to surface the memories.

"I . . . I don't know. It's been over twenty years. The older I became, the less my parents brought me here. I don't think they even came here without me. I remember my dad remarking once how they'd made a terrible investment. I guess some friend had talked them into buying the cabin from him. We rarely made it up here to make it worth it. But . . ."

Her voice trailing off, she shook her head.

"Again, it was my mother's favorite place in the world. And because she loved it so much, so did my dad."

She turned to me, her eyes brimming with anger.

"This would be a whole lot easier if I could call him. For all I know, he never got my message. Or maybe he did and didn't know what I was talking about. Maybe . . . maybe these people found him and he's—"

"He's not."

She stared at me. Anxious.

"How can you say that? You don't know. You don't know anything!"

She flung her door open with so much force I was surprised it didn't fly off its hinges, Incredible Hulk–style. She slammed the door behind her and then bent forward, hands on her knees, face leveled at the gravel drive.

61

"This the place?"

Quinn glanced at Stephanie in the rearview as he slowed the SUV. We coasted along, the entrance to Silver Lake Park looming ahead.

Staring out her window, Stephanie nodded soundlessly.

"What is this place again?" I asked.

We'd been on the road for over ten hours. Stephanie only remembered the campground's name but not the exact address. The name was all Quinn needed, and once he looked it up and noted the area in which it sat—north central Pennsylvania, in the middle of nowhere—Stephanie had nodded and said that was the spot and then hadn't spoken since.

Now Stephanie shifted anxiously in her seat as she peered out her window at the passing trees and the scattered cabins around the lake.

"My family used to own a cabin here. We would drive up from Lanton during the summers and spend a week or two. There wasn't much to do besides canoeing and walking the

A blow to his gut—that's how it felt. After everything Lawrence O'Neal had done for this man, all the endless days and long weekends, seldom seeing his wife and children, and now *this*?

"You're making a mistake, Mr. President."

POTUS flicked his hand at the door as he sat back in his chair.

"You may leave."

"We're less than six weeks away from Election Day. You still haven't made it clear whether Andrew is staying on as VP. The public is already starting to question your judgment. And now you want to fire your chief of staff?"

President Wagner's gaze stayed steady with his.

"I said: you—may—leave."

Lawrence felt that vein on his forehead throbbing in concert with his rage. He wanted to shout. Wanted to laugh. Wanted to cry. Wanted to jump across that iconic desk, wrap his hands around POTUS's throat, and shake some sense into the man.

Instead, he turned away and headed for the door. Let himself out of the room without even a backward glance.

He navigated the White House hallways on autopilot, ignoring the nods and *good morning*s from the staffers he passed, and soon found himself back in his car. The morning sun glinted off the windshield, and he noted a fresh splat of bird shit near one corner, which seemed like a fitting cherry on top of this turd sundae.

Before he started the car, before he returned home and tried to explain to his wife what had happened, Lawrence opened the glove box and extracted the burner he had hidden there.

Lawrence powered it on and stared at the screen, deciding whether to call or text.

In the end, he fired off a simple message.

> We may have a problem.

Wagner said, "He was raping children."

Lawrence made no reply.

"You knew about this."

Again, he stayed silent.

"And you did nothing."

Lawrence started to open his mouth but the president lifted a finger, freezing him in place.

"Actually, no—you didn't do *nothing*. You helped cover it up."

Lawrence didn't think he had the strength to speak—all the energy suddenly zapped from his body—but after a moment he managed to find the words.

"Believe it or not, Mr. President, I did it for you."

"Don't!"

Jaw clenched, face flushed, Wagner shot a finger at Lawrence as though it were a dagger.

"Don't you *dare* say it was for me! Not after what that man did!"

"Plausible deniability, Mr. President. It's part of my unwritten job description. My role is to help support you but also protect you. What do you think would have happened had word gotten out that someone you appointed ambassador—a close friend of yours—was raping children in another country? What do you think the news media would have made of it, not to mention your political enemies? You weren't even halfway through your first term. Think about how many people would have been calling for your resignation."

Little by little, the reality of the situation had begun to set in. Or so it appeared based on POTUS's expression. The predictable righteous indignation having started to fizzle.

Lawrence expected him to sink down into his chair, defeated, but instead the president pierced him again with a glare.

"I expect your resignation on my desk first thing tomorrow morning."

President Wagner was giving him a new look. Thoughtful and measuring at the same time.

"Remind me again, Lawrence. Why was Rich's time as ambassador cut so short?"

"If I remember correctly, Mr. President, his wife was sick with cancer. They had started treatment while in Nepal but decided to—"

"Cut the shit."

Lawrence jerked as if he'd been slapped. The president had never spoken to him like this before, especially not within the sanctity of this office.

His tone, cautious: "Mr. President?"

"Tell me the real reason Rich left Nepal."

Lawrence could feel the steady heartbeat thump in the vein on his forehead and hoped it wasn't pulsing enough for the president to see. Sometimes his wife joked about that vein, telling Lawrence if he wasn't careful he might have an aneurysm.

"I'm not sure what you want me to say, Mr. President. Barbara Greenham was sick. They weren't sure the doctors in Nepal could treat her, and Richard didn't want to be away from her during treatment, so—"

POTUS's fist striking the Resolute desk was enough to cause him to jump.

"I told you to cut the shit, and I meant it. I want the goddamned truth!"

The air in the Oval Office had taken on a strange quality. It was as though Lawrence could suddenly see each individual particle floating around him.

Swallowing, he said, "It sounds like you already know the truth."

The president's fist was still clenched in front of him. His heavy gaze a longbow, having arrowed Lawrence in place.

updates, though he had no idea when the most recent update occurred.

"Last night he was spotted in Chicago. Is that why you called me in here? Honestly, I was hoping you'd decided what to do about Andrew. You know how I feel about keeping him on the ticket. And now that we're less than six weeks away from the election—"

"Richard Greenham was killed last night."

Lawrence nodded solemnly.

"Yes, Mr. President. It's a terrible shame. It appears Daniel Burke murdered him."

"Why?"

"I'm sorry?"

"Why would Daniel Burke murder Rich? I've been trying to wrap my head around it."

"I don't know what to tell you, Mr. President. After the past several days, it appears Burke has graduated from traitor to domestic terrorist."

President Wagner leaned back in his chair, his elbows on the armrests, steepling his fingers. Staring across the desk at Lawrence so intently it felt as though he was trying to look through him.

"Mr. President, what is it?"

"I was just thinking about Rich. I hadn't seen him in several years. We used to be so close. Had gone to parties at college in our younger days. Had almost been caught drinking when we were freshmen. And do you know what Rich did? He let the campus police catch him so I could get away. That's the kind of loyal friend he was."

Again, Lawrence wasn't sure what to say. After nearly four years he still hadn't gotten used to standing in this room. Knowing all the presidents who had come before and all the presidents who would come after, the individual power each of them held.

60

At five minutes past nine o'clock that Sunday morning, White House Chief of Staff Lawrence O'Neal entered the Oval Office to find President Jeffrey Wagner behind the Resolute desk.

During the week, the president always wore a shirt, tie, and jacket while in the Oval Office, but during the weekend he typically wore slacks and a polo shirt. Today was no different, POTUS in a navy-blue polo as he reviewed papers at the desk, looking up briefly as Lawrence strolled in and motioning him forward.

"Thanks for coming in, Lawrence."

"You're the boss, Mr. President."

"I am, aren't I?"

Wagner's tone was thoughtful as he said this, reviewing one last page. He closed the file, set it aside, and looked up at his chief of staff.

"Any updates on this Daniel Burke situation?"

Lawrence paused, deciding how to answer. He knew Samuel Chen from the CIA had been providing the president periodic

PART IV
HAIL MARY

"A pistol, Daniel. With a sound suppressor. And as soon as the alarm went off, the caregiver got on her phone. I was outside and could briefly make out what she was saying. She . . . she was speaking Russian."

"That probably wasn't a good idea."

"Nope."

"So now what?"

I didn't have an answer for him—I was suddenly out of answers—so I gestured toward the lot and the parked SUV.

"Let's get back on the road."

Quinn had just started the engine when the burner buzzed. For a second I thought it might be Wagner, but no.

"Teddy, I've got you on speakerphone. Tell us something good."

A brief silence before Teddy asked, "How long before you think you can make it here?"

I looked at Quinn, who had already keyed in the route to DC on his phone.

He said, "If we drive straight through, maybe eleven hours."

Stephanie made a noise in the back of her throat, shifting in her seat to look out her window.

"We need to make a stop on the way," I said, "so probably more like fourteen hours. Why? Did you have any luck on your end? Because I probably could have had better luck on mine."

"Your conversation with POTUS didn't go well?"

"It could have gone better. They've confirmed the body in your apartment isn't yours, by the way. So if they hadn't started looking for you already, they're doing so now."

Teddy was silent for a moment.

"I think we're in more trouble than we first thought."

"What do you mean?"

"There's something else going on here. Something bigger."

"How so?"

"When I tripped the alarm to get Hargrave's mother and her caregiver out of the house, I saw the caregiver draw a pistol."

"What?"

for your buddy's transgressions? He was raping children, for Christ's sake."

Silence again. I thought maybe the man had hung up. I glanced at the burner's screen but saw we were still connected.

President Jeffrey Wagner said, "What are you talking about?"

"I'm talking about Richard Greenham. The guy you've known since college. The guy who helped with your fundraising when you were starting out. Your very close friend. And how while he was the ambassador to Nepal he was raping children."

"You're lying."

"Oh, please. Weren't you just the one talking about truth and lies and all that bullshit? You covered up for your friend and now you're acting like you had no idea what was happening. You brought him home early!"

"I did no such thing. Barbara was sick and it was decided—"

"My team was sent in there because one of the generals was blackmailing him."

"Mr. Burke, I have no idea what you're talking about."

"Then it looks like you've got more than one snake in your house. If I were you, Mr. President, I'd be careful, because otherwise you might get bit."

Teeth gritted, I severed the call. Then just stood there and stared off into the night, feeling the rocket jet fuel adrenaline still coursing through my body. After several long seconds, once I'd had time to gather myself, I turned to find Quinn and Stephanie still standing by the picnic table. Watching me.

As I approached them, I shot off a message to Teddy that I'd spoken to POTUS and asked for an update on her end.

Quinn asked, "How'd it go?"

"It could have gone better."

"It sounded like you lost your cool there near the end."

"Yep."

traitor. Irrefutable evidence that clears both your and Rita Salazar's names. What do you expect me to do?"

"I expect you to do the right thing."

"And what is that, exactly?"

Again I said nothing.

The silence stretched—five seconds, ten—and then President Jeffrey Wagner released a breath.

"I may be making a grave error in judgment, but I am willing to see this evidence if you can find it."

"That's all I ask, Mr. President."

"Now, tell me something else. How did you obtain this number?"

"Richard Greenham."

"Rich?" His tone, incredulous. "Rich gave you this number?"

"Not willingly, no."

Jeffrey Wagner was silent.

"You haven't heard yet, have you?"

"I haven't heard what?"

"Richard Greenham is dead. He was shot to death."

The president's voice ticked down a notch.

"Did you shoot him?"

"No, but it's probably going to be blamed on me."

"If you didn't shoot him, who did?"

"His wife."

"You're lying. Barbara would never do such a thing."

"I can see why you would think that. She seemed like a nice, quiet woman. But when she learned the truth about her husband, she couldn't help herself."

Now Wagner issued an irritated sigh.

"I should have known better. The deal is off, Mr. Burke. It turns out you are a snake, after all."

"You want to talk about snakes? How about covering up

mine. But sometimes things happen for a reason. We get put in situations that only we can handle. Of course, sometimes those situations are much larger than us—much larger than any of us. Situations that should be impossible to navigate, and yet . . . sometimes we make them work."

Jeffrey Wagner sighed.

"Like you, Mr. Burke, I like to trust my gut. And something in my gut tells me to believe you. But at the same time something in my brain tells me you're a snake."

"I'm not a snake, Mr. President. But I am a snake hunter."

"And this snake you're hunting—is it close to me?"

"Very."

More silence as the man processed this.

"Tell me, Mr. Burke. Are you working with Rita Salazar to capture this snake?"

I wasn't sure what to say, so I said nothing.

"Until yesterday I wasn't aware of Mitchell Hargrave or his team, but since then I've been briefed by the CIA deputy director about ongoing events. He told me Ms. Salazar had been found dead in her apartment. And that it had been discovered she had three million dollars in an offshore account. Just as I understand you had money in an offshore account as well."

"That's not my account."

"And yet there's evidence to the contrary. But even if there is evidence, does that make it the truth?"

I said nothing.

"But then only a few hours ago I received word that the charred body found in Rita Salazar's apartment did not in fact belong to Ms. Salazar."

Still, I said nothing.

"Tell me, Mr. Burke. Say you bring me evidence of the real

had a run-in with one of your ex–team members outside Dodgers Stadium the other night."

"I did."

"And you shot him in both knees instead of killing him outright."

"Yes."

"I'm curious: Why? After all, from what I understand, you are adept at taking lives."

"I have killed people in the past, Mr. President. That's true. Though I would say most of those times had been at the direction of the United States government."

Jeffrey Wagner said nothing.

"I'll be honest, Mr. President. I'm surprised you called me back. And that you're not trying to trace this call."

"Who says I'm not?"

"I know you're not. I feel it in my gut."

"So this traitor," the president said. "Who is it?"

"I'm afraid I can't tell you at the moment."

Silence.

"Not that I don't want to tell you. I could easily give you a name. But giving you a name wouldn't mean much, would it?"

"You're trying to establish evidence."

"Yes."

"Irrefutable evidence."

"Yes."

"So that way there's no denying the truth."

"Yes."

"And in this instance," the president said, "the truth is the actual truth and not a lie we want to accept."

Another beat of silence.

"Can I tell you a secret, Mr. Burke? I never wanted to become president. As a young man it was never a dream of were headed east. I told Quinn to pull off at the next rest area and then I dialed the number from Richard Greenham's contacts and listened to it ring several times before going to voicemail.

"This is Jeff. Leave me a message."

Again, like anybody else's outgoing voicemail prompt. Not a man who had access to the country's nuclear codes.

The burner buzzed again. Same number as before. Not one with a DC area code but a Raleigh, North Carolina, area code, which was where Wagner called home.

The night sky was clear above us. A heavy breeze rustling the tops of the trees around the picnic tables behind the rest area. Traffic sporadic out on the highway.

I turned away from Stephanie and Quinn and placed the phone to my ear.

"Hello?"

Silence. At least for a few seconds. And then the sound of the man clearing his throat.

"I don't typically make it a point to communicate directly with enemies of the state."

"I'm not an enemy of the state."

"So you say."

"It's the truth."

"The truth."

The man chuckled quietly and then fell silent. I let the silence stretch, waiting for him to speak next. *Needing* him to speak next.

"We all want the truth, don't we? Or at least that's what we tell ourselves. But most times we are just as happy being told whatever it is we want to hear, even if it's a lie. And then, eventually, those lies become the truth."

I pictured him shaking his head.

"Tell me something, Mr. Burke. It's my understanding you

59

Five minutes after sending that second text message, the burner vibrated with an incoming call.

I looked up at Quinn and Stephanie.

"It's him."

The phone vibrated again and again.

Quinn said, "Answer it."

I held up a finger as I stared down at the phone in my hand, feeling it vibrate two more times before going still.

Quinn's voice took on an edge.

"What kind of game are you playing?"

"I'm curious to see how desperate he is."

"For what?"

"The truth."

It was just after nine o'clock here, which meant it was just after ten o'clock in DC. We'd managed to get out of Chicago in one piece, Quinn driving a midsize SUV we'd jacked from another rental lot. I'd sent Teddy a message telling her the op hadn't gone as planned but that we had gotten POTUS's number and

His mobile phone dinged.

Sighing again, he picked up the phone. The same number that had tried calling him minutes ago had sent him a text.

> President Wagner, please call. It's a matter of national security

The use of his official title told Wagner everything he needed to know—whoever this was, they were neither family nor friend.

Janice said, "What's wrong? Why are you gritting your teeth like that?"

Wagner shook his head in frustration. Now he'd need to get a new number. It had happened before, years ago. Some reporter had managed to get their grubby hands on his personal cell number, and even to this day Wagner didn't know who had given it up.

He'd have to be even more careful this time. Only actual *close* family and friends.

Then the phone dinged again—and Jeffrey Wagner felt the earth drop out from under him.

> This is Daniel Burke. I know who your traitor is

Iran might attack Afghanistan, his gut had told him to put off any sort of preemptive counterstrike—which had been a blessing, as he learned the next day the intelligence had been faulty.

A hundred other examples, all just as extreme, and he liked to believe he had made the right choice each and every one of those times, or at least most of those times.

But this was an election year—the goshdarned election was only weeks away!—and Wagner knew dropping Andrew from the ticket, especially as he'd picked the man as his running mate nearly five years ago, would only hurt him with a wide swath of voters who adored the vice president and believed he was a victim in this whole mess.

Conversely, another swath was demanding for Wagner to oust him ASAP—and put him in jail for good measure.

Damned if you do, damned if you don't.

He had never much cared which way the penny fell because he always trusted his gut, but now his gut wasn't sure which way to go.

"Jeffrey."

His wife set the tablet aside, shifted her body on the sofa to give him a better look.

"Did you hear me?"

"I heard you."

"And?"

"And what?"

"Have you made a decision?"

His mouth started to open, that awful, dreaded hesitation overcoming him. When he was a boy, he'd always had trouble making decisions, until one day his father grabbed him by the arm and gave him a quick shake, telling him that people didn't respect wafflers and that right now he was a waffler, and did he want to be a waffler all his life?

Now his days were planned down to the minute, his every move communicated from one Secret Service agent to the next, and if he departed the White House for some undisclosed trip, then a reporter would be whisked away with him, in case something newsworthy happened, so the Fourth Estate had eyes and ears on the ground (or in the air) to report history.

"Andrew again?" Janice asked from the other side of the sofa, looking up from her tablet. She often liked to play puzzle games during the evening while the TV silently bounced light all over the dim room.

Wagner shrugged as he set the phone aside. It was almost ten o'clock and he would head to bed in less than an hour. Before his day started, he always tried to get up early to work out—cardio on the elliptical or treadmill. At fifty-four years old, he knew a job like this was awful for stress. There was a reason his hair had already gone gray.

"Probably," he said with a sigh. "I've made it clear to his chief of staff I don't want any contact with him, but he's been trying to get ahold of me any way he can."

He'd already had this conversation with his wife, after he'd had a day to process what happened once he learned about his vice president's arrest along with the rest of the country. He'd received a message from Andrew that it was all lies, just the usual fake news. But Wagner had seen the FBI reports for himself. The whole thing made him sick to his stomach, and he couldn't decide what he hated more: that Andrew had fooled him into believing he was a good man or the position he'd put Wagner in.

As though reading his thoughts, his wife said, "You need to decide soon, you know. It's already been a week. Quite frankly, you may have already missed your window."

Jeffrey Wagner typically prided himself on always knowing the right course of action. When he'd received troubling intel that

58

President Jeffrey Wagner didn't recognize the number.

He dropped the call, just as he'd dropped the few others which had come in over the past several days from different numbers.

There had been a time when presidents like him wouldn't be allowed to have their own personal cell phones, due to security risks and such, but over the years decorum had changed and the rules that hadn't been rules previously but had been more like unspoken guidelines had gotten to the point where Wagner was expected to have his own phone.

Granted, he didn't take it with him into the Oval Office, or even much of the White House. No, he only kept it in the residence, and it was for the few times he wanted to chat with close friends and family who he rarely saw.

Gone were the days when he could go golfing without the Secret Service sweeping the entire course. Gone were the days when he and Janice could decide to hop in the car and see a movie, or get a bite to eat, or just drive aimlessly around town.

"You order a ride?"

I glanced up and down the street to ensure the coast was clear, and nodded.

"Yeah, we ordered a ride."

The driver paused an extra beat to take in our lavish attire, then said, "You know you're supposed to wait in one spot, right?"

I stepped off the curb, opened the rear door, waited for Stephanie to climb in first.

"Sorry about that. Been a crazy night."

"Tell me about it," the driver murmured, shaking his head. He glanced back to make sure we were settled in before putting the car in gear. "Heard there was a shooting over at the Field Museum."

"No shit?"

"Yeah, man. Crazy times."

As the driver pulled away from the curb to take us three miles south, where we would walk several blocks before securing another rideshare to take us another two miles, where we would eventually meet up with Quinn, I heard Stephanie's quiet gasp beside me and looked over.

Her eyes wide, she mouthed, *Sorry*, then shifted her gaze down to Richard Greenham's iPhone.

Whose screen was now forever locked.

I felt Stephanie's eyes on me as I made a hard turn onto a side street.

"You're fucking insane! That bus was coming right at us!"

Eyeing the rearview again, I turned onto another side street.

"I knew we would make it in time."

"Bullshit. We could've died. *I* could've died."

All at once I hit the brakes, the sedan rocking in place.

"What are we doing here?" Stephanie asked, peering out her window. Then, glancing down at the iPhone: "And why do I have to keep this screen from locking?"

I cut the engine as I slipped my own phone from my pocket.

"I want to call Wagner from that phone. He's more likely to answer that way. And at this point there's no way to change the passcode."

I opened my door.

"Come on—let's go."

She stepped out too, looking around the area.

"But what are we *doing* here?"

In the distance, sirens. Maybe the same sirens that had been chasing us. Maybe another set.

I tapped a few times at my own phone and motioned for us to keep moving.

"Keep your head down. I doubt they've accessed the entire city's traffic cam system, but better safe than sorry."

We headed down one block, then up another. Past row houses and tiny fenced-in yards with long grass and tall lamps planted along the sidewalk that stretched over the street like helping hands.

A few people sat outside on their stoops, watching us soundlessly. A dog in one of the fenced-in yards started barking.

Then a fire-truck-red Honda pulled up to the curb. The driver's window purred down.

the median, swerved back into the regular lane, right into the side of the cruiser, forcing it up onto the sidewalk and into the side of a building.

For the next five minutes we continued deeper into the city, taking hard turns here and there, swerving around more traffic, and sometimes even bouncing up onto the sidewalk when the lanes were blocked, the sedan's shocks taking a beating, sideswiping a few parked cars, and all the while Hancock and Kincaid managed to keep pace.

"Danny?"

I heard the uncertainty in Stephanie's voice, the fear that we weren't going to make it out of this in one piece, especially now that three more police cruisers had joined the chase—and that was when I spotted the public transit bus headed toward the approaching intersection.

The bus had a green light, but instead of easing off the gas I stomped my foot on the pedal.

As the sound of the engine's RPMs increased, Stephanie braced herself and started shouting, "Danny? Danny! What are you doing?"

The timing, I knew, was everything.

A few seconds too fast and the SUV might make it.

A few seconds too slow and we might get pancaked.

Fortunately, the timing was just right—we flew through the intersection mere milliseconds before the bus came barreling through, and the SUV, probably figuring they had the engine power to make it in time, tried to stick with us but the bus smashed into its back end, sending the SUV into a fishtail that nearly flipped it over.

The bus's tires screeched as its driver slammed on the brakes, blocking the intersection so that none of the police cruisers trailing us could make it through.

I gave it a beat to think about it, veering from one lane to the next, bypassing the slower-moving traffic and running straight through another red light.

"Rendezvous is still on. It just might take us longer to meet you there."

"Are you sure you don't need help?"

Another glance at the rearview. The SUV was even closer now, almost on our bumper. The police cruiser directly behind it, lights blazing and siren screaming, and it was a solid bet it had already called for backup.

Glancing at Stephanie, I saw the iPhone's screen in her hand start to darken.

"Stephanie, the phone!"

She jerked, startled, and quickly tapped the screen to keep it awake.

"Sorry."

Another intersection was fast approaching, the road ahead split by a median strip, the kind with a concrete divider, and an idea came to me, one of those terrible ideas that seems brilliant at the same time it feels suicidal.

Starting to drift again into the left lane, tapping the brakes as though to make a sudden left-hand turn, and when the SUV had mirrored the movement and was only feet away from the rear bumper, I shifted the wheel again and took us straight into the oncoming lane.

Cars speeding toward us, drivers honking and flashing their high beams, weaving out of the way as we tore forward, going now fifty miles per hour.

The cruiser, however, had been far enough back that the driver didn't make the same mistake as the SUV and continued along in the regular lane.

I threw a glance at the two cops, and then once we'd passed

Those flashing lights had almost reached us. Four police cruisers, two ambulances. And directly ahead was a red light, with that always unhelpful NO TURN ON RED sign posted on the pole. There was no telling how many seconds before the light turned green, but I couldn't wait, not with Hancock and Kincaid behind us. And if I pulled out in front of the police? Maybe none of them would even notice, not after having received a report of shots fired at the museum. They might assume we were innocent civilians trying to flee another mass shooting.

No time to waste—right as the police braked hard to swerve around the corner, I pulled out into the intersection, making the right, opening up the space for Quinn to take a shot.

In our ears, the quiet burst of a round fired through a sound suppressor, and then Quinn's frustrated voice.

"Shit."

"What's wrong?"

"I overcorrected. Missed the rear tire. Took out the bumper instead."

I checked the rearview again. The SUV was even closer now, less than one hundred feet—and directly behind it, a lone police cruiser that had separated from the pack.

Quinn said, "The angle isn't ideal for another try. I risk hitting the cop."

"Don't worry about it. Head out."

"What about you guys?"

Good question. One I wasn't quite prepared to answer as I swerved into the left turn lane. The light here also a bright red but I jerked the steering wheel anyway, goosing the gas to bump us past the oncoming traffic, a pickup nearly clipping us and tacking out of the way at the last second.

"My plan right now is to lose them in the city."

"So no rendezvous?"

57

The sedan had only four cylinders, but still it rocketed forward with enough thrust to push us back in our seats.

One hand on the wheel, swerving us out onto the street and back toward Lake Shore Drive, I tossed Stephanie the phone and said, "Whatever you do, don't let the screen lock."

She stared down at the phone, looked back up at me.

"What?"

Eyes now on the buildings across the highway, trying to spot him in his sniper's nest: "Quinn! The SUV behind me—can you take out the tires?"

In my earpiece, just like in Stephanie's, Quinn's calm, cool voice replied.

"Copy."

I checked the rearview. The SUV was maybe fifty yards back. It had at least two more cylinders and would catch up in no time.

And Quinn was stationed directly across the highway. We were likely blocking his shot, which meant we needed to move out of the way, and fast.

wide, before she glanced at the rearview and then hurriedly undid her seat belt and started to crawl over.

Tapping the iPhone's screen again to keep it awake, I raced around to the driver's side, dove in behind the wheel, and stomped my foot on the gas.

I dropped the thumb, and—nothing happened.

"Huh," I said, looking at my pistol hand. "Let me try that again."

But before I could aim, a .300 Winchester Magnum round traveling at over three thousand feet per second tore through Dennis's knee. He went down in a cry of agony, and I rushed forward, wrestling the Glock from his grip.

Headlights splashed us as a sedan raced forward, Stephanie screeching to a stop only feet away.

"I'm sorry, Dennis. But I did give you a chance."

"Fuck you, Dan," he spat. "You fucking traitor."

As I headed for the car, I said, "The timing could've been a bit better."

In my ear, Quinn said, "What do you want from me? I made the shot, didn't I?"

I gazed at the buildings across the highway. Quinn had set up on one of the rooftops, monitoring the area through a scope this entire time with his upgraded Mk 13 Mod 7 sniper rifle. So if I did encounter any trouble, he would be in position to provide cover.

Those sirens were even closer. I could see the flashing lights coming up Lake Shore Drive, less than a mile away.

Quinn said, "Did you get it?"

Opening the car door, I nodded.

"I got it."

"Meet you at the rendezvous point?"

I started to say yes when I heard screeching tires and a heavy engine tearing around the corner. Watched as a black SUV sped this way. Lucas Hancock riding shotgun, the big son of a bitch Kincaid behind the wheel.

Slamming the door shut, I shouted at Stephanie to get into the passenger seat. She stared at me for a half second, her eyes and shoving past panicked bodies until I burst through the doors into the night.

Just as Lucas Hancock had been waiting at the bottom of the steps on the other side of the building, Dennis Rowe was waiting here. Only while Lucas hadn't drawn his weapon, Dennis held a Glock 17 at his side—and raised the muzzle at me as I skidded to a halt.

"As much as I want to shoot you, Dan, I want you to pay for what you did, so put your gun down—slowly."

Sirens in the distance. Police and ambulances. They would be here any minute.

Like on the other side of the building, I scanned the area, the trees and parked cars, then nodded as I knelt and placed the nine-millimeter on the ground.

"The phone too."

The iPhone's screen started to darken, and I tapped it again to keep it awake.

"Sorry, can't do that."

"Don't make me shoot you, Dan."

"I'm not making you do anything, Dennis. In fact, I'm going to give you a choice. One of the most important choices in your life. Walk away."

"And if I don't?"

"Then you won't walk again for a while."

The man shook his head.

"What happened to you, Dan? You used to be a good soldier."

"Last chance, Dennis."

I raised my right hand, formed a gun with my forefinger and thumb, and pointed it at his leg.

"Walk away right now or get a bullet in your knee."

"You're insane."

"Wrong place, wrong time."

"Lucky for you, it looks like he's going to pull through. Otherwise, I probably wouldn't have any other choice but to kill you."

Lucas, a grin spreading across his face: "I'd love to see you try."

"Can Mitchell hear us?"

Silently, Lucas nodded.

"Good. Then Mitchell, just so we're clear: I know what you've done, and I'm going to prove it."

I caught just the hint of confusion in Lucas's face before I spun around and sprinted back up the steps. A heavy, panicked murmur had fallen over the hall as everyone was still trying to piece together what had happened, but as I stepped through the revolving doors, a hushed silence fell as almost everyone turned to look at me.

It was easy to tell who the one-percenters were and who was their hired help, so when the first bodyguard stepped forward, I was already hurrying over and reached him before he could draw his gun. Grabbing his arm, snapping his elbow, and pushing him up against the wall as I wrestled the nine-millimeter from his hand, then smacked him across the face with the pistol to stun him long enough to keep moving.

Another bodyguard appeared, weapon drawn. He lifted his gun to aim at me, but I didn't give him the chance—firing a round at his knee, then rushing forward to kick the gun from his hand as he hit the floor.

Complete chaos—women screaming and men shouting as they ran for cover, wine glasses shattering and tables and chairs tipping over in the stampede.

I raced through the hall to the south entrance, the bodyguard's pistol in hand, waving it around to clear a path as I shouted at everyone to move, bounding over discarded chairs on rent. The world knew the president of the United States as Jeffrey Wagner, but to Richard Greenham he was simply Jeff.

As I returned to the museum's main level, I memorized the number in case something happened to the phone, then kept it in my hand as I scanned the crowd.

Word had spread that something had happened downstairs—sound of the gunshots had probably even made their way up here. The string quartet had quieted, and more than a dozen people were looking straight at me, probably sensing, just like Richard Greenham, that I didn't belong here.

I headed for the north exit, shouldering past a few men who tried to step in my way and ignoring the questions about who I was and what was happening. Straight for the glass revolving doors, pushing through and starting down the steps—where I spotted Lucas Hancock standing on the sidewalk below.

I halted at once, conscious of the empty revolver digging into my back. Staring down at Lucas, who stared up at me.

"Lucas."

"Dan."

"You do realize this whole thing is one big misunderstanding, don't you?"

"The only thing I understand is that you're a fucking traitor."

Situational awareness kicked in as I scanned the area for the rest of the team. Conscious of the night sky clear above us and the sound of the traffic out on Lake Shore Drive and the lights of the city beyond the trees and the antennae at the top of Willis Tower flashing white.

"You know, Lucas, I never took you for a cop killer."

His eyes, hardening.

"You're the one who killed the cop."

"We both know that's not true. Just like we both know you're the one who stabbed that FBI agent."

Greenham having exhausted all five rounds. I gently took it from her grip.

"If you want to blame his death on me, be my guest. But you did fire the gun. Which means there's gunshot residue on your hands. So before the police show up, you might want to do something about that."

Out in the hallway, the oncoming clatter of footsteps pounding down the stairs.

I checked the phone again, tapped the screen to keep it awake, and stepped past her, slipping the empty revolver into my rear waistband.

Two men almost collided with me as they hurried down the steps. One of them held me in place while the other looked back and forth between me and the bathroom.

I tried to play it cool and step past the man holding me, but his grip tightened on my arm.

I looked at him, said, "You're going to want to let go," and when the man didn't, I stomped on the toe of his ultra-shiny Louboutin loafer and then headbutted him before hurrying up the steps.

Checking on the phone again to make sure the screen hadn't locked, I scrolled through contacts. A few other men hurried down the steps, and I transformed into a frantic mess, shouting that I thought he was dead and that someone needed to call an ambulance, and then I was past the men before they could think twice.

There it was—right near the end of the contacts list: WAGNER, JEFF.

Sometimes it's hard to fathom that presidents and heads of state are basically ordinary men and women, or at least they'd once been before being elected or appointed. People with family and friends who grew up with them, who saw them at their worst, maybe even loaned them money when they were short

56

My first impulse was to hop over Richard Greenham's body and bolt straight for the door, but then I remembered why I'd come here in the first place and knelt down, digging into the pocket Richard had touched when I asked him to call the president.

I pulled out an iPhone, attempted to open the screen, but of course it wouldn't unlock without some form of identification, either a code or Face ID. Greenham was already dead—the front of his body a savage wasteland of blood and guts—so getting him to cough up his six-digit code wasn't an option. His face, however . . .

I aimed the screen at his face, gave it a beat, thanking a god I'd never really believed in that Barbara hadn't aimed high.

It worked. The screen opened and I sprang up, turning toward the door—where the woman was still standing.

Tears in her eyes, mixing with her mascara. The gun in her hands again, aimed straight at me.

Stepping forward cautiously, I reached out my free hand and placed it on the revolver, which I knew was empty, Barbara

"Richard, tell me the truth. Did you—"

Richard sprang forward, grabbing for the gun. I knew he was going to do it, based on how he'd positioned his body. He'd had enough of this bullshit and had begun to realize he was losing his wife from his side of the ledger, and he couldn't have that.

But Barbara—either spooked by the sudden movement or having already come to accept the terrible truth—squeezed the trigger.

BANG!

The gunshot echoed in the tight space, and Barbara Greenham, staring at her husband with wide eyes, maybe amazed that she'd actually fired the revolver at all, squeezed the trigger again, and again, and again.

"You disgusting piece of shit!"

She plugged one last round into his chest and then staggered away, tears now streaming down her face, sobbing as her back hit the wall. Shaking her head, muttering quietly to herself as she stared down at her husband on the floor.

Then, as if a switch had just been flipped, something changed in her eyes. A realization. An understanding.

A plan.

Her gaze flicked up to meet mine, and I saw something there I didn't like.

Helpless, I watched as she stepped to the door. Heaved it open. And screamed as loud as she could.

"Somebody please help! A man just shot my husband!"

"What is he talking about, Richard?"

"I have no idea, dear. He's a liar. Just give me the—"

"I can't say how many children, Mrs. Greenham, because I don't know the exact number, but while in Nepal one of the generals there provided your husband with numerous children, all of whom he violated."

Richard Greenham's shoulders had slumped. His head hanging low. Whatever fight he'd had in him had suddenly evaporated.

"Barbara"—his voice now a quiet plea—"don't listen to him. Please."

I continued, squaring my body to the woman in case I needed to dive out of the way if she—or her husband, snatching the gun from her—squeezed off a shot.

"The general blackmailed your husband. So that he could do whatever he pleased with the US's permission. Or so he believed at the time. Word got back to those in the government, and my team was sent in to eliminate the general and his men and to secure all the videos and photos taken of your husband and those children."

The gun had started shaking in Barbara's hands again. Rage and anger circulating through her body. Her voice, a tiny volcano of words.

"Is . . . is this true?"

Richard Greenham looked up at his wife. Slowly, painfully, he shook his head.

"Of course not, dear. Like I told you, he's a liar. He'll say anything to get what he wants."

"You know your husband, Mrs. Greenham. So you tell me—is he telling you the truth right now?"

Barbara Greenham's eyes shifted again to her husband, and with her eyes, the revolver swung that way too. Leveled right at his stomach.

Greenham said, "He's a liar, Barbara. Don't listen to him. Just give me the gun."

The man was less than ten feet away from his wife now. Moving slowly so as not to spook her.

"Tell her what you did, Richard. Tell her the truth."

Swallowing, her eyes skipping between me and her husband, Barbara said, "What truth, Richard? What is he talking about?"

"Nothing, honey. He's a madman. Completely off his rocker."

"Did you ever wonder why your husband's time as ambassador to Nepal was cut so short? Why he was recalled after not even two years of service?"

Those nervous eyes, ping-ponging between the two of us.

"I . . . I had gotten sick. A touch of cancer. They were able to treat it there, but Richard said it would be better for us to return to the States. He said our healthcare system is so much more advanced."

"An unfortunate coincidence, Mrs. Greenham. He used your medical condition as cover."

"Cover . . . cover for what?"

"He was raping children."

Incredibly, the gun in her hands wasn't shaking as much anymore. There was still a slight tremor, but her grip had become almost steady compared to when she first picked up the revolver. Her eyes had also gained a new type of focus. Maybe even clarity.

The panic in Richard Greenham's voice ticked up.

"He's a liar, Barbara. I'm begging you, please. Don't listen to him. Give me the gun."

He started to take another step closer but halted when his wife swung the revolver in his direction. Not entirely on purpose, no—more that she was directing her focus on him, and so the barrel of the revolver moved as well.

"Look what he did to Jimmy! He said he wanted to do the same to me! Shoot him!"

Despite the gun shaking in the woman's hands, her eyes were somehow calm. Measured. She stared at me as though not sure whether I existed, whether this was real life. Only minutes ago she had been in the main hall with all the rest of her elegant and sophisticated friends, enjoying the string quartet and the drinks and the overall super-super-wealthy vibe, and now here she was with her fingers squeezing the synthetic grip of a .38 Special, forced to make a decision.

As the saying goes, sometimes life comes at you fast.

Barbara was standing only twenty feet away. Not an unreasonable distance when preparing to shoot someone. Even if she had never fired a gun before, there was a good chance she would hit me. Pure dumb luck.

The bathroom wasn't large enough for me to try to make a break for it. Only one way in, one way out. And Barbara was more or less blocking the door—with a gun in her hands.

Turning to Greenham, I said, "Does she know?"

All this time the man had continued yelling at his wife, urging her to shoot me. Now he paused long enough to look at me with wide, panicked eyes. Eyes that told me everything I needed to know.

Her voice unsteady, Barbara asked, "Do I . . . do I know what?"

Hesitantly, Greenham started toward his wife.

"Don't listen to him. He's a monster, Barbara. If you don't want to shoot him, give me the gun. I'll shoot him."

"About Nepal," I said. "What your husband did there."

"My husband? He—he—he was an ambassador to Nepal. Still has the honorary title, in fact."

A touch of pride in her otherwise nervous voice. The revolver still gripped by her two small hands. Shaking.

55

"Shoot him, Barbara!"

Sudden command in Richard Greenham's voice. He jabbed his finger toward me, as though the woman wasn't sure who he wanted her to shoot.

"He—he—he's trying to mug me! He has a gun!"

Calmly, I turned to the woman. Held up my empty hands to show her I wasn't a threat.

"As you can see, Mrs. Greenham, I don't have a gun. And I'm not trying to mug your husband."

"He's lying! He's a liar! Shoot him!"

Barbara was still gripping the gun with both hands. She was a small woman, thin and petite. Her nails stylishly manicured. Her hair swept up in an exquisite style that probably cost a few thousand dollars before tonight's event. She wasn't a woman who knew how to handle a firearm, but that didn't mean she was going to let her guard down.

Greenham continued shouting.

to Nepal—and who had now become a statue, only his nostrils moving as he quickly breathed in and out—I smiled.

"Seriously, Richard. Let's not make this messy."

"Wh—wh—what do you want?"

"I told you what I want. Put me in touch with the president."

His gaze shifting down to his unconscious bodyguard and then back up to me, the man started to nod, started to reach for his pocket—where, presumably, he kept his phone—when all at once the door opened again.

"Dear? Are you in here? I checked the other bathroom and—"

The woman stopped dead as soon as she saw the tableau: her husband standing stock-still, his face pale; a stranger looming over him, with her husband's bodyguard on the floor leaking a steady stream of blood from his face.

Then her wide eyes shifted to the revolver on the floor, only a few feet away. She stared for only a beat, and then lurched forward, sweeping the gun up and aiming it with two shaking hands.

Right at me.

I turned back to Greenham.

"I'm losing my patience, Richard. I need you to put me in touch with Wagner right now."

Greenham's eyes bugged out a bit, disbelieving that I hadn't been cowed by the mere sight of a gun. He looked to Jimmy, who this time motioned with the revolver. His voice, a low growl.

"Seriously, motherfucker. Let's not make this messy."

I didn't even bother glancing at the man. I kept my focus on Greenham. Silent.

Jimmy said, "All right, that's it," and started forward, raising the gun, but as he stepped toward me, I pivoted and batted the revolver away—the piece skipping across the tiled floor back toward the door—and then threw a jab straight at the bodyguard's throat.

Not too hard—I didn't want to fracture his windpipe—but hard enough to momentarily disable the man and to send a message that this interloper wasn't fucking around.

Greenham's eyes were even wider now. He took a step back. The balled-up paper towels falling from his hand.

Jimmy was gasping for air, but he wasn't down for the count. He issued a strangled grunt as he charged forward.

I turned back to him, and like a matador, I waited for the right moment to step aside and then cupped the back of his linebacker head and accelerated his momentum directly into the wall, his forehead slamming against it hard enough to create a dent.

But Jimmy was a big guy, and it usually takes more than one strike to knock out someone of his heft and build. So as he was still standing I grabbed a handful of his hair, yanked his head back, and smashed his face once, twice, three times into the wall.

A starburst of blood as his nose erupted, and he muttered something unintelligible before falling flat to the floor, unconscious.

Turning back to the man who had once been the ambassador

he'd headed to the second level, I would have needed to hurry up there before he left.

Taking a step forward, I said, "I need you to put me in touch with your buddy Jeffrey Wagner."

Those eyes found me in the mirror again. This time, incredulous.

"Friend, I don't know you, but even if I did, I wouldn't put you in touch with my fucking gardener, let alone Jeffrey Wagner."

Another step forward.

"But you have a direct line to him, don't you."

Saying it as a statement, not a question.

Richard Greenham paused. The irritation on his face slowly morphing into suspicion.

"Who are you?"

"I'm the guy who helped cover up your misdeeds."

"Excuse me?"

"I know what happened in Nepal, Richard. What you did to those kids."

This time, he turned his entire body in my direction, giving me a better view of his front. Stephanie had really done a number on him. Almost his entire shirt soaked with red.

Keeping his gaze steady with mine, he shouted, "Jimmy!"

The door opened, and a guy who might as well have been a professional wrestler stepped through. Bunched, angry eyes first looking at Greenham, then zeroing in on me.

"Jimmy, it appears we have an interloper. Please see him out of the building. With extreme prejudice."

The man crouched and drew a small stainless steel revolver from his ankle holster. Held it low at his side, right by his leg. Watching me, he tilted his head toward the door.

"Come on, buddy. Let's go."

54

For a moment, the man didn't move. Just stood there with his back to me, staring at himself in the mirror.

Then, slowly, he tilted his face in my direction. His eyes narrowing.

"Do I know you?"

Millionaires and billionaires—they're in a class of their own. I might have managed to snag a fancy tux, but it clearly wasn't as fancy as any of the others here at this event. Then again, maybe the man could smell it on me, the fact that I didn't belong here.

I said, "I need you to do me a favor."

Richard Greenham made a face, grabbed some paper towels, wetted them, and started dabbing at the red stain on his shirt—courtesy of Stephanie Nguyen.

I'd figured he wouldn't go for the bathrooms on the main floor, which meant he would either go up to the second level or down to the lower level. I'd taken a chance and posted up in the bathroom here, though if Stephanie had alerted me that anyone was in any of the stalls, then strode straight for the sinks and thrust his hands under the sensor to activate the water.

Richard didn't notice the feet that stepped into view as they came off the toilet or hear the stall door as it swung open. But he heard the voice, deep and low and as sudden as a gunshot.

"Hello, Richard. Nice to finally make your acquaintance."

"Quite all right, dear," he managed, realizing everyone was still watching, waiting to see what he would do next. "Accidents happen."

He chuckled to himself, smiling at the watching crowd, catching the eye of his friend Nick across the room chatting the ear off some billionaire, and without any hesitation he turned on his heel.

As he breezed past his driver-cum-bodyguard, who had posted himself off to the side near one of those gracious columns, keeping an eye on the crowd, Richard mumbled, "Come with me."

His bodyguard followed without a word as Richard headed for the stairs to the lower level.

"Give me your shirt."

"Sir?"

Not looking at the man as he hurriedly clomped down the steps: "Did I stutter?"

Jimmy paused, maybe considering the question. He was a larger man than Richard, and taller too, standing at least an extra four inches, and he had an additional fifty pounds on him, so the shirt was going to be big, maybe too big.

"Actually, never mind. Just wait out here in case I need anything."

He was starting to think the stain might be a stroke of good luck. If he played his cards right, he could warm up the room, put everyone in his corner, and thus in Nick's corner. In fact, when he gave his little speech before presenting Nick, he could even make a joke out of it. A moment of levity right before he and Nick asked the crowd to fork over a good chunk of their cash, either as official or—wink wink, nudge nudge—dark money donations.

He stepped into the bathroom, ducked briefly to see if

Crossing into his line of vision, headed to the other side of the hall, carrying a glass of wine, when suddenly she pivoted to turn back around and bam, just like that, the wine splashed all over him.

"Oh my God!"

The woman's horrified voice echoed throughout the hall.

Like a record scratch, everybody paused their conversations so they could all turn to see what had happened.

A familiar rage churned deep inside him—the kind that had no qualms about shouting at waiters and waitresses and concierges when the mood struck him just right—but this woman, whoever she was, was here for a reason, and that was because she'd been invited to contribute to the campaign of his good friend, who honest-to-God believed he could get more votes than the current governor, a bumbling fool who had been doing a shitty job thus far but at least had the electorate on his side.

One or two seconds had passed—maybe more—and he found his gaze snagging on his wife. A frozen smile on her face, her beautiful green eyes pleading with him not to do anything rash.

"I'm so sorry," said the woman who'd bumped into him, grabbing a napkin off one of the nearby tables and trying to dab up the mess for all the good it would do.

Richard had no idea who this woman was—he'd never seen her before, this stunning Asian woman in a sleek black dress—but he wanted to berate her in front of everyone here, just to prove a point.

But no—of course he couldn't do that. Not now. Not ever. Good God, did he want to get himself canceled? It seemed that no matter how much money you had these days, it was never enough to save you from the woke mob.

"There he is!" said a voice behind him, accompanied by a hand clamping his shoulder—and Richard blinked from his daze and smiled and nodded at the man as he tried to remember his name.

Nearly five minutes passed as he listened to the man drone on about one thing or another when the name finally came to him—Cormac—and Richard remembered that he ran some private equity firm and was probably worth close to thirty million, which to Richard, who himself was worth more than one hundred million, wasn't very impressive at all.

As he continued to smile and nod, he spotted Barbara at the other end of the hall, also trapped in conversation.

"Excuse me, I need to check on something," he said, cutting Cormac off midsentence, and he detached himself from the man and started toward his wife, smiling and raising his drink to anyone who caught his eye.

The dinner was being hosted in the Stanley Field Hall, named after the nephew of the museum's founding benefactor, Marshall Field. Gleaming white marble, seventy-five-foot vaulted ceilings, and gracious columns surrounded them—plus the fossil-filled marble floors and the pair of African elephants and the hanging gardens and the prehistoric flying creature whose name kept escaping him.

As he continued through the crowd of men and women here to hobnob with others on their same socioeconomic level and then—hopefully—later write insanely large checks that would help put Nick over the finish line, Richard reminded himself that he hadn't attended any VIP parties in quite a while so there was no way any law enforcement agency would—

His gaze was focused on his wife, who was now twenty feet away, his thoughts wrapped up in that ever-present fear he'd one day be arrested, that he didn't notice the woman until it was too late.

53

Richard Greenham didn't want to be here.

He typically loved these types of black-tie functions—the swankier the location, the better—but after everything went down last week in LA he just wanted to get away, out of the country, preferably someplace that didn't have any extradition agreements with the United States.

But Nicholas Johnston was an old friend—plus, Nick's wife was close with Barbara—and he had already promised to host this dinner, as Nick seemed to believe he had a reasonable shot at being elected the next governor. And of course Barbara had ties to the Field Museum and wanted to throw money at it every chance she got, so when putting together an exclusive event that gathered all the major donors in the state, it made the most sense to have it here.

Still, Richard had convinced Barbara they should take some time away afterward, as it had been months since they'd gone on a trip. His dear wife never needed an excuse to travel, so they were scheduled to leave later that night, heading straight to the airport and hopping on a flight for Europe.

"So . . . what are you going to do?"

"Improvise."

As I pulled into the parking lot to find an open space, Stephanie looked at me.

"Do . . . you think those guys are here yet?"

The Alpha Team.

"Probably. I walked through that train station more than eight hours ago. I imagine they would have boarded a plane within a half hour of the cameras picking me up."

"What . . . what if they find us?"

"They won't."

"But what if they do?"

"Then we'll deal with them."

"*We?*"

I shut off the car, then opened my door and tilted my head toward the museum.

"Let's go cause some trouble."

Quinn lifted his hands and gestured at the house.

"Does it look like I need money to you?"

"You might get hurt. Might get killed. Or worse, might get arrested."

He shrugged wordlessly as he pulled his phone from his pocket.

"Who are you calling?"

"My neighbor. Gonna have him keep an eye on Tango and Cash while I'm gone. But you heard the woman on the phone—we need to hurry. And before we go, I need to grab some of my gear. Something tells me we're going to need it."

―――

The Field Museum is one of the largest natural history museums in the world.

Located right near the lakefront alongside the Shedd Aquarium and the Adler Planetarium, the Field Museum—what with its neoclassical architecture design—attracts up to two million visitors annually, or so I'd read online during the flight to absorb as much information about the building as possible.

I'd downloaded and memorized maps of the museum's layout, watched YouTube videos of people touring the place, trying to pick out any potential areas where I could lure Richard Greenham.

Turning off Lake Shore Drive, we did one pass of the south entrance, where all the guests were exiting their fancy chauffeured vehicles and climbing the steps to the main doors, and I muttered, "Shit."

Stephanie glanced over her shoulder as we drove past.

"What's wrong?"

"They've set up metal detectors inside the doors. No way I can take my gun."

"So that's why we drove all that way to see Tyler. You knew he would help, despite how he feels about you."

I wasn't sure how to answer, so I said nothing at all. I dug the two transmitters from my pocket, each tiny enough to fit snugly in a person's ear. With Stephanie's hair, it was certain nobody would notice, and unless someone was standing right next to me and peering into my ear, they wouldn't notice either.

I handed Stephanie one of the transmitters, and she watched as I placed mine in my ear before doing the same in hers.

"Quinn, can you hear me?"

A beat of silence, and then Quinn's voice came through crystal clear.

"I can hear you."

I glanced at Stephanie, who nodded that she'd heard his voice too.

"We'll be there soon. Are you in position?"

"Copy."

"Good. Just do me a favor. If things get out of hand, try not to shoot me."

"I'm coming with you."

Quinn said it as soon as we'd disconnected with Teddy. It would take over an hour to get to the airfield where the private jet was meeting us, which meant we needed to leave now.

I started to shake my head.

"Quinn, I can't ask you to—"

"Save it, Dan. You know how I feel about traitors. And the fact that one's operating right now in a top secret capacity—very close to POTUS, no less—isn't something I can let stand."

"To be clear," I said evenly, "you're not getting paid for any of this."

I didn't realize I was staring at Stephanie until she sensed my gaze and looked up.

Frowning, she mouthed, What?

I said, "Teddy, while you're dipping into your savings, we're going to need something else."

"What's that?"

"A dress for the occasion and a tuxedo."

I shrugged at Stephanie's horrified expression.

"When in Rome."

Twilight.

We drove up Lake Shore Drive in silence. The only sound the stolen sedan's tires skimming the highway as we maintained a five-mile-above-the-posted-limit speed.

Staring out her window at Lake Michigan, Stephanie said, "Will you finally tell me?"

"Tell you what?"

"Why you and Tyler dislike each other so much."

"It's . . . complicated."

She shifted in her seat to look at me.

"So uncomplicate it."

"It's a long story, Stephanie. We don't have the time right now."

"If Tyler hates you so much, why is he helping us?"

I glanced at her, and even in the dark of this crappy car she was breathtaking.

"That's a long story too, but the gist is his old man was once accused of selling government secrets. It turned out somebody else—a fellow officer—had set him up, but by the time that all came out, his father's entire reputation and career were ruined."

I could feel Stephanie's eyes on me, studying my face.

I gestured at the door, beyond which lay a sleazy parking lot in a sleazy part of town. Parked right outside was the sedan I'd jacked from a rental lot.

"Come on. Let's get out of here before either of us catches HPV."

"Let me get this straight," I said, my hands now braced against the kitchen island as I stared at the phone. "The team that's currently hunting me—and, as far as I know, also trying to kill me—you want me to notify them of my location."

"Yes."

"And why would I do that again?"

"Because I need Mitchell's focus elsewhere. So far, you've gone off the grid, so kudos to you. But because you're off the grid, the team has been most likely recalled to DC. Even if they haven't been yet, it doesn't matter. The fact is, I need Mitchell focused on the chase, which means he'll be back at The Office, which means—"

"He won't be home. Got it."

"If there's any evidence Mitchell is involved in this, it'll be at his house."

"And so, what, you plan to break in like some run-of-the-mill cat burglar?"

"Something like that. Mitchell lives with his mom, who has round-the-clock in-home care. Getting them out of the house won't be easy, but I'll come up with something."

"Fine. So we fly to Chicago. I somehow make myself known to the team that I'm there. Then what?"

"I can get you into the function. That won't be a problem. But once you're there, you'll need to figure out a way to get Greenham alone. Because something tells me that confronting him in front of the rest of the one percent won't go over great."

"What's that?"

"I need you to make it so that The Office knows you're in town."

When Stephanie stepped out of the bathroom, I felt my breath catch in my throat.

"So . . . what do you think?"

I stared. I couldn't help it. I stared because she looked flat-out gorgeous. The black dress certainly helped, but so did the heels, makeup, and whatever she had done with her hair.

She squinted, trying to read my expression.

"It's too much, isn't it?"

Slowly, I shook my head. Still at a loss for words. Until, after a moment, I managed to swallow.

"You look . . ."

Don't say beautiful. Don't say beautiful. Don't say beautiful.

". . . beautiful."

Even from across the short expanse of the sleazy motel room, I could see Stephanie blush.

"Thank you. You don't look so bad yourself."

I stood a bit straighter, smoothing the creases from the tuxedo I'd put on while she was in the bathroom. I dropped my voice so it was low and deep.

"The name's Burke. Daniel Burke."

Stephanie smiled with her lips but not her eyes. In those dark eyes I saw trepidation and fear.

"I'm scared."

"I know. So am I."

She tilted her head, studying me.

"No, you're not. You love this stuff."

private function at the Field Museum for a friend of theirs. A guy running for governor."

"Must be nice," Quinn mumbled.

Teddy continued as if she hadn't heard.

"The election is a few weeks away. This is a last push to squeeze money from super-rich donors. So everyone invited will be heavy hitters. And because they're heavy hitters, many of them will have their own security details on-site."

I stood with my arms crossed, thinking it over.

"What if we got there beforehand? To Chicago, I mean. Confront Greenham before he and his wife even leave the house."

"It's possible. But the man has a full-time bodyguard. And the house has a state-of-the-art panic room. Even if you managed to break into the house and overpower the bodyguard, there's a chance Richard and his wife might make it to the panic room in time, at which point they'll just hide out in there until the cops show up."

"So what are you suggesting? I confront Greenham at this private function instead?"

"Yes. Only I don't recommend traveling to Chicago by car. It'll take way too long to get there."

I glanced up at the others.

"What are you talking about, Teddy?"

"I'm talking about digging into my crypto savings to make this work. I'll charter a private jet to fly you to Chicago."

For a moment, I was speechless.

"That . . . that's very generous of you."

A soft chuckle emitted through the speaker, and then her voice took on an edge.

"Oh, I'm not doing it out of the kindness of my heart. I need you to do something for me when you get there. Something you aren't going to like."

"I haven't even seen the floor in there yet and am already grossed out."

I checked my watch.

"We don't have much time."

"I know."

"If you can't do this, it's okay. We'll figure something else out."

"I know you're only saying that. Without me, the plan falls apart."

I shrugged.

"You're right. The fate of the republic lies on your shoulders."

She shot me an unamused look before grabbing the dress I held and starting for the bathroom. But before she opened the door, she paused to look back at me.

"Are you sure this will work?"

"Positive."

"How can you be so sure?"

Another shrug.

"I saw it in a movie once."

———

It had taken less than an hour before Teddy called back and confirmed Richard Greenham's location.

"He and his wife live in Chicago, in the Gold Coast Historic District. The freaking house costs fifteen million dollars. And as of right now they're currently at home. That's the good news."

We were standing in Quinn's kitchen again, the burner on speakerphone sitting on the granite island.

I asked, "What's the bad news?"

"Time is limited. Richard and his wife are flying out of the country late Saturday night. But before that, they're hosting a

52

"Are you sure you can do this?"

Stephanie closed her eyes, sucked in a deep breath. Slowly turned to face me as she let the breath out.

"I think so," she said, and while she tried to sprinkle in some confidence, her tone betrayed just how scared she was.

"Relax. Everything is going to be okay. Your part is simple. As soon as you're done, head straight for the car."

To say the motel room was disgusting was putting it mildly. The quality was what you'd expect when paying by the hour. A sleazy room with a sleazy bed run by a sleazy guy behind a sleazy check-in counter. But the motel took cash and had an old-school security system that ran on physical tapes, and the sleazy guy was the kind who excelled at keeping his mouth shut and looking the other way, so this was the best spot on short notice for what we needed to do.

Stephanie's gaze skipped around the mildew-scented room, at the lumpy bed and scuffed table and cheap TV, then at the bathroom. The corners of her eyes crinkling as she grimaced.

The phone buzzing in his pocket woke him. Not the burner, but his work phone.

Bright sunlight filtered through the windows.

He blinked against the brilliant glare as he rolled over and dug the phone from his pocket. First saw the time—11:06 a.m.—and then who was calling.

Samuel Chen.

Shit, he'd been out much longer than anticipated. Chen was probably calling to ask where the hell he was so that Hargrave could come and relieve him.

Only Chen told him something much more surprising.

"We found Burke."

Hargrave shot up in bed, the phone to his ear.

"How?"

"Gait recognition picked him up at a train station. Though, as far as we can tell, he didn't take a train in or out."

"Where is he?"

"Chicago."

He'd met his fair share and always declined whenever a photo opportunity arose. Because to him all that stuff was bluster, and the only thing that truly mattered was, well . . .

Family.

That's all the photographs showed: Hargrave through various stages of life with his parents. Some of only his parents. Back when his father was alive and well and the damned dementia hadn't sunk its claw into his mother's brain.

Hargrave thought about what the fire chief had said earlier. A controlled burn. That's what he'd love to do with his life right now. Set various fires to wall him off from all the shit that didn't matter. Or no—all the shit he'd gotten himself mixed up in and which he'd begun to realize there was no escaping.

Or, hell, just set fire to the whole goddamned thing.

Turn it all to ashes.

And then, if all went well, he could rise from those ashes.

Hargrave opened the closet door to reveal a combination lock safe. Inside, along with various keepsakes of his parents, his passport, and some bonds, was a laptop. An air-gapped laptop, meaning it had never been connected to the internet or any network. The laptop contained a copy of every secret that had been stolen and sold over the years. A treasure trove of corruption that would sink him if it ever got out.

Why he kept the laptop, he wasn't quite sure, only that he knew someday it might come in handy.

Flicking off the lights, he shut the door, replaced the thread, and continued to his bedroom.

He felt like he should brush his teeth, maybe take a shower, but before he could he'd fallen on top of the mattress and was out within seconds.

———

Returning to the living room, he looked again at the caregiver.

"When was the last time her diaper was checked?"

Victoria set the book down with an irritated sigh. She said nothing. Just stared at him.

Hargrave said, "I thought I smelled something when I looked in on her."

"And so what do you want me to do? Wake her up?"

Hargrave felt his jaw clench.

"When she does wake up, make sure she's changed as soon as possible."

The nurse set the book aside, folded her arms, and performed a quick *I Dream of Jeannie* head nod.

"Your wish is my command, Master."

His fingers tightening into a fist, he turned away and started for the stairs. Trudged all the way to the top, with each step draining more and more energy out of him. He knew he would fall asleep instantly once he fell into bed, especially with how long he'd been awake. Endless cups of coffee throughout the day only get you so far.

Samuel Chen was keeping an eye on things while Hargrave went home to rest. He didn't like the deputy director being there, though having him involved might work out in the end. Place some blame on the CIA if anything went really off the rails.

He stopped by what had once been his mother's bedroom but which was now his office. He checked the thread he'd left on the doorframe to see if anyone had opened it while he was out.

The thread was still in place.

Still, he flipped on the light and gazed around the room. At his desk and filing cabinets and the framed photographs on the wall. Unlike many in his profession, he didn't display pictures of himself with various politicians and military generals.

51

His mother was already asleep when he arrived home. Victoria, another one of the personal care aides who looked after his mother, sat on the couch in the living room reading a book.

"How was she?" Hargrave asked as he set his keys on the table.

Victoria glanced up, stared at him for a beat, and then shifted her gaze back down at the book.

"Fine," she said absently.

Hargrave ground his molars as he headed down the hallway to his mother's bedroom. The room had once been his home office, but when the osteoarthritis grew worse and it became even more difficult for her to make it up the stairs, they decided to forgo installing a stair glide and kept her on the first floor.

He peeked in on her lying in a hospital bed. Her eyes closed, her lips slightly parted. Completely motionless.

For an instant, he thought she was dead and felt a wave of relief wash over him.

But no—there her chest went, rising and falling ever so slightly, and that familiar sense of dread started to creep back in.

"The Office."

"No," Hancock said. "First we go see Noah."

Under bright, artificial lights, nothing ever looks real.

Noah LaSalle's body was no exception.

One of the medical examiners had pulled it out from a refrigerated slot in the wall. Like opening a drawer in your kitchen to grab a spoon. It almost felt disrespectful to a man who had faithfully served his country for the better part of two decades—well, maybe less faithfully the past few years—but this was what happened to all bodies that came to the facility: stripped naked and laid out on a steel tray so that men and women could cut them apart.

The medical examiner had exited the room to give Hargrave and the other men a moment. Hargrave stood off to the side to let the team have a closer look. Rowe on one side, Kincaid on the other, with Hancock standing at the base of the tray.

The three men stood stock-still for a complete minute. Not one of them saying a word. Not one of them looking away from their fallen comrade.

Then, slowly, Hancock turned to face him.

"Mark my words. The next time we see Burke, he's fucking dead."

And Hargrave, maintaining his solemn expression, had only one thought.

Perfect.

Hargrave started toward the SUV but paused when Lucas grabbed his arm.

"I'm not a cop killer. My men aren't cop killers."

Hargrave said nothing.

"But so far one cop has been killed, and now an FBI agent might die. And for what? This whole fucking thing has gone sideways."

Hargrave hadn't gotten an exact answer earlier, but now he knew: Lucas was the one who pulled the trigger that killed the police officer back in Vegas. As much as the man tried to hide it, Hargrave could see the guilt festering behind his eyes.

"And now Noah's dead too?" Hancock, shaking his head. "You might want to take me off this op, because otherwise, if I see Burke again . . ."

He let it hang there, the silence filling in the fact this man wanted Burke's head on a spike. Which was good. Exactly how Hargrave wanted the man—all the men—to feel, especially since he'd had no choice but to take Noah off the board.

As far as Hargrave knew, none of these three men were bent. Not like LaSalle. When this whole thing had first started—when he'd gotten tangled up with Sergei and had no choice but to do as he was told—he wasn't sure which one of his men he could trust to help him. Briefly, he'd considered Daniel Burke, but it was Noah he ended up approaching. The man was a good soldier, but he was an even better opportunist, and when he understood what kind of money was at stake, it didn't take him long at all to agree to play ball.

They reached the SUV. The men loaded their rucksacks and then started to pile into the back while Hargrave headed toward the passenger-side door.

Hancock grabbed his arm again to stay him.

"Where are we headed?"

Since then, there had been no contact. No reason there should be any contact. That was the way this whole operation worked. For the longest time he'd had no direct line of communication with the woman posing as Salazar's girlfriend. He was only given her number recently when it became clear Burke was still alive and they needed to start wrapping up this whole melodrama as soon as possible.

The late-September night was surprisingly cool and calm, a consolation from the nasty storm they'd had earlier in the day.

He waited until the jet had halted and its cabin entry door with stairs began to open to start forward and meet his team—or what was left of his team.

Somewhere on this base were two Boeing VC-25s, military versions of the Boeing 747 airliner modified for presidential transport. When POTUS was on board, the plane became Air Force One, but when the president disembarked, it was like any other plane.

Funny how status always made all the difference.

Three men descended the stairs, one after another. Lucas Hancock leading Dennis Rowe and Michael Kincaid. Hargrave noted the patch on Kincaid's face where Burke had stabbed him outside Harry Reid International.

The men trudged forward carrying rucksacks filled with their gear, as though they'd just returned from war overseas and hadn't been twiddling their thumbs in California waiting for Julian and Theo to track down their prey.

The first thing Lucas Hancock said to him: "Is the FBI agent going to live?"

Silent, Hargrave motioned to the SUV. Rowe and Kincaid started that way while Hancock lingered.

"Well?"

"Last I heard, he was in critical condition."

50

Hargrave watched as the Gulfstream G500 touched down at Andrews Air Force Base at just past eleven o'clock that Friday night.

He stood outside the SUV he'd taken from the control room in DC. A half-hour drive if the traffic was cooperating, but DC becomes a ghost town at night and so he and the driver made it to the airfield in no time.

As the private jet taxied, its Pratt & Whitney PW814GA turbofan engines still rumbling, Hargrave checked his phone. More out of reflex than anything else. Though, after slipping the phone back into his pocket, he realized he was waiting to hear from the medical examiner. To get confirmation that the body found in the scorched apartment did indeed belong to Rita Salazar.

He thought about the burner in his other pocket. The phone he hated carrying but which he could never be without, not with Sergei's foot on his neck.

Do it now, he'd messaged right after killing Noah LaSalle, and then fifteen minutes later he'd gotten the one-word response: *Done*.

ops behind the scenes for over a decade with zero accountability—don't you think that'll grant us a lot of leeway? My guess is we'll get immediate pardons."

Quinn barked out another laugh, shaking his head.

"You both sound so fucking delusional. I mean, don't get me wrong, I get it. I can't imagine being in your shoes. But say you found this evidence. Say it was irrefutable. What then? Are you just going to traipse up to the White House gates and ask to speak to Wagner? Or email him, maybe? I'm sure we can figure out his direct email address. Something like thepresident@whitehouse.gov. It doesn't matter how much evidence you find, because there's no way in hell you'll ever be able to contact the man directly. And even if you do, who says he'll believe anything you say?"

I was barely listening. Instead, I was thinking about a mission two years ago. An op whose purpose I only later learned had been a complete lie.

"I might know a way to contact POTUS directly."

My voice was so quiet, so hesitant, I wasn't even sure it was my own until I realized both Quinn and Stephanie were watching me.

"What," Quinn said, "you have his personal cell phone number?"

Slowly, I shook my head.

"I don't. But I know somebody who does."

"Yeah," I said. "Me neither. But the question is, what can we do about it? Right now we have no evidence that Hargrave is involved in any of this. Even if we found that evidence, who would we give it to? All the major agency heads believe we're traitors, so anything we brought to them would be outright dismissed."

Silence for a moment.

"There is somebody who might be able to help," Teddy said. "I mean, it's a long shot, but if we collected enough compelling evidence and got it to him, he might believe us."

"Who?"

"POTUS."

Quinn barked out a laugh.

"Are you kidding me? What's that idiot going to do?"

I ignored him.

"The problem, Teddy, is that the president isn't even aware of The Office. He knows nothing about the Alpha Team. You know this. It was designed that way so that if anything happened, he would have—"

"He does know about the team now. Yesterday Mitchell was called to the White House. Apparently, Mitchell and Yates and the agency heads met with POTUS in the Situation Room. Mitchell said they briefed him on the op, at which point he learned about the program."

"Christ," I said. "I can't imagine he took it well."

"Mitchell didn't tell me much, but he did say the president was on board."

"Regardless, even if we gathered enough solid evidence to show President Wagner that Hargrave is behind all of this, what can he do?"

"Think about it," Teddy said. "If we're right and Mitchell is the actual traitor—a man who has been running top secret my location, so I ghosted. But before I did, I read how Noah had passed away last night. He'd had some sort of seizure which caused his heart to stop."

Teddy was quiet for a beat, and then continued.

"The thing is? When I stabbed Jade—or whoever she was—with that syringe, it caused her to have a seizure too. And then . . . she was dead."

"What about the rest of the team?" I asked. "Do we know their location?"

"As of last night, they were still in LA, waiting until we'd picked up your trail. I imagine they've probably been called back home by now."

"Which means the team wasn't in DC last night when Noah had his seizure."

"No."

"But Hargrave was."

"That's right. My guess? Noah was in on selling the intel with Mitchell. They had blamed it on you, but when it became clear you were alive, the FBI planned to take you into custody to give you to the CIA."

"That's why Noah tried taking me out. The whole bullshit story would have fallen apart."

"Exactly. And now Mitchell is tying up loose ends—first getting rid of Noah, and then trying to get rid of me."

I glanced up again at Quinn and Stephanie. Thought for a beat, and then frowned down at the phone.

"Teddy, why didn't you run? You had a head start. They thought you were dead. They might *still* think you're dead."

"Don't get me wrong, I considered it. But I . . . I don't want to run for the rest of my life."

Another glance at Stephanie. She stood staring down at the island, her face stoic, lost in thought.

I flashed on Adam falling to the ground, blood all over his stomach. His lips moving soundlessly, telling me to go.

"You don't happen to know if he's still alive, do you?"

"Last I heard, he was in critical condition, but that's all I know."

"Any way you can get an update for me?"

She coughed out a half laugh.

"I'm not sure that's the most pressing matter right now."

"He's my friend, Teddy. I need to know how he's doing."

"Okay. I'll see what I can find."

"Thank you. But now what do we do? You're burned. I'm most definitely burned. Stephanie . . . what did the team make of her?"

"They know she's involved, but only because you'd gone to the hospital to see her after the disappearing act you pulled at the airport."

"So they don't believe she's an accomplice?"

"At the time, no. But now . . . it's hard to say. Why?"

"Because she's not involved in any of this."

"At this point, Daniel, it doesn't matter. Too much shit has happened. As far as The Office is concerned, she's in this now too."

I checked on Stephanie. She stood with her arms crossed, quiet.

Tango and Cash lay on the floor in the living room, watching us expectantly. They could sense the tension.

Teddy said, "There's something else too."

"What's that?"

"Noah LaSalle is dead."

"How do you know?"

"I managed to piece together parts of my laptop. I still had the rootkit installed back at The Office and tried to access the network again. Somebody there caught on and tried to track

"Why the FBI and not the CIA?"

"Because technically the CIA isn't supposed to conduct clandestine operations on US soil."

"Why do you say *technically*?"

"Why do you think? The CIA does a lot of shit they're not supposed to do."

To the phone, I said, "Teddy, when did you learn about this?"

"I only learned about it a few days ago, along with the rest of the team."

"What about Hargrave?"

"I imagine he knew about it right from the start. He told the team he'd conducted an internal investigation with the CIA's help and determined you were the one selling the intel. But since you were dead, there was nothing that could be done about it, so they decided not to bring it to the team's attention."

I felt Quinn's gaze on me, heavy and sharp. I glanced up at him as I spoke again.

"Teddy, you know I had nothing to do with that."

"I do now, yes. I'm sorry I doubted you. I . . ."

"What?"

"Well, I was pissed off at you. I felt betrayed. I wanted to catch you just as much as the rest of the team did. And so after we lost you in Vegas, I went back through your files. I realized that you'd once worked with Adam Reed. And, seeing as he was the lead agent on both the raid at the VIP party and the one who took Senator Browne into custody Thursday morning, it didn't take a rocket scientist to make the connection."

"So you figured I'd reach out to Adam."

"I thought it was a possibility, yes. We determined his location and kept an eye on him. And when he left his house last night, we tracked him to Dodgers Stadium and got the team there in no time."

my confrontation with the senator, after he'd passed out from what I'd put in his whisky, after I'd transported him up to the Lucky Star Hotel & Casino and put him in room 247, after I'd contacted Adam to let him know where the FBI could find the son of a bitch, the people who believed I was dead had come for me.

I shook my head, scattering the memory, and frowned at the phone.

"Teddy, you still haven't told me why the FBI wants to take me into custody. What did I allegedly do?"

"Just over a year ago, it came to the CIA's attention that some of the team's missions were compromised."

"Compromised how?"

"Top secret intel stolen and sold to enemy countries—all linked to Alpha Team ops."

"What kind of top secret intel?"

"Foreign intelligence assessments concerning North Korea, China, and Iran, just to name a few countries. Plus, intel about US nuclear programs."

"How was this determined?"

"I don't know for sure. Most likely HUMINT or SIGINT. But one way or another, the CIA had determined somebody on the Alpha Team was selling secrets."

Stephanie cocked her eyebrow at the acronyms, so I spelled them out for her.

"HUMINT stands for human intelligence, while SIGINT stands for signals intelligence."

"Human intelligence makes sense to me," Stephanie said, "but what's signals intelligence?"

Quinn said, "Electronic transmissions collected by planes, ships, satellites. It's primarily conducted by the NSA. HUMINT is primarily conducted by the CIA, at least outside the country. Inside, it's the FBI."

Teddy said, "I'd always thought the same thing too. But who else could it be?"

Quinn crossed his arms, shifting on his feet.

"If they had evidence that you'd had three million dollars wired to an offshore account, why sit on it? You said the records went back how many months?"

"The transaction occurred six months ago. But this investigation appeared relatively new. Not even a few days old."

I leaned forward, bracing my hands against the granite island, my gaze heavy on the burner under the bright lights.

"Exactly how many days old?"

"Six."

"You mean—"

"Yes," Teddy said. "Right after Senator Harold Browne sent your fingerprint to Charlie Yates."

I was silent as I processed this. Remembered sitting with the old senator in his hotel room after his debate. Asking how he'd figured out my identity and the man telling me how Detective Jared Sutton had given him a fingerprint which he'd then sent to Charlie Yates, the chairman of the Joint Chiefs of Staff, who was quite interested in knowing where Browne had acquired the print. I imagined there had been an emergency meeting between Yates and the heads of the DNI, CIA, FBI, and NSA, those in the upper echelon who were aware of The Office's existence, and it had fallen on Yates's shoulders to get more information, knowing that this whole thing needed to be handled delicately.

The old senator's voice, echoing in my head: *You should have stayed dead, son. Probably could've had yourself a nice life living in the shadows. But coming here to Vegas, doing what you did, the people who believed you were dead now know you aren't. And . . . do you think they're just going to let that stand?*

Clearly the answer was no. Less than twenty-four hours after

Quinn and Stephanie stood on the other side of the kitchen island. Teddy had been hesitant to say much when I told her they were present, saying she didn't even know Quinn, but when I vouched for him she finally told us what happened.

"Teddy, you said this woman spoke to you in a Russian accent."

"She did. Or at least that's what it sounded like. Eastern European, for sure."

"How did you meet again?"

"On the apps. But I've always been careful with the info I provide."

"Still, somebody was able to figure it out."

Another beat of silence, followed by a heavy sigh.

"God, I'm so stupid. I was in love with her. And she was playing me from the very start. And now . . . now she's dead."

And I was the one who killed her was the unspoken part, though I could hear the emotion in her voice, even over the thousands of miles and the signal bouncing off towers and satellites.

"What else did you determine when you hacked into the system?"

"The only thing I found was records of the offshore account in my name."

"The one with the three million dollars wired from Russia."

"Yeah. From what I could tell, it looked like they were building an investigation against me."

"Who?" Quinn asked, the first time he'd spoken since Teddy started in on her story.

"My guess is Mitchell."

When Quinn shot me a questioning look, I filled in the rest.

"Mitchell Hargrave. He's the one in charge of The Office. He's old-school. Highly intelligent. And, as far as I could always tell, one hundred percent loyal to the country."

49

"You don't know who she really was?"

A beat of silence as Teddy thought about the question, though maybe it was because there was a delay.

I flashed on when I was a kid and asked my mom how the phone worked—how my voice traveled all the way to another state almost instantaneously. My mom, a twinkle in her eye, had told me about the telephone wires and tried to explain how it worked, though at the time I was five years old and couldn't understand much of it, but I loved hearing the enthusiasm in her voice and wished it was there all the time and not just when my father wasn't around.

Teddy's voice finally came back through the speakerphone.

"I thought I did. I did a background check when we first met. And then, before she moved in, I did another one just to be safe. I'm talking about a deep background check, Daniel. Like, all the way back to her childhood. I even saw her transcript from elementary school. Whoever she was, her cover was beyond solid."

"I'm sorry."

My words halted him in place. His back still to me, silent.

"I never had a chance to tell you that. Truth is, I never *wanted* to tell you that."

Slowly, Quinn turned to face me. His expression, flat.

"You had me tossed from the site."

"Yes."

"You nearly had me court-martialed."

Silent, I nodded.

"And for what, Dan? Because I called you out on your bullshit? Because I did what I could to stop you from killing men who didn't deserve to die?"

I closed my eyes. Saw the killing room again, vivid as the first day I'd entered it. The gray cinder block walls. The metal chair in the center. The drain in the floor. The ghost of a smile on my face as I began to imagine all the different possibilities.

"Believe it or not, I'm a different person than I was then."

"It wasn't that long ago, Dan. It hasn't even been a decade."

"People change."

Quinn thought about it.

"Sure. People change. But I'm not so sure people like you do."

"People like me. And what am I exactly?"

"Don't play stupid, Dan. You know exactly who and what you are. You're a killer."

"And you're not?"

"I'm a soldier. There's a difference."

Still holding his gaze, slowly shaking my head: "Not in our world there isn't."

In my hand, the burner buzzed.

A text from Teddy.

> We need to talk

One of the dogs looked up at me, and I swear the expression bordered on *Is that supposed to be funny?*

Tough crowd.

I pulled the burner from my pocket, powered it on. Still nothing from Teddy, not since late last night when I'd invoked my brother. I remembered riding in the back of the car, staring at the screen, first typing out *I swear on my brother's life* and then deleting it because I felt it was too much. But Teddy knew how important James was to me—I'd walked away from my old life in part because of him, after all—so I figured it was the best way for her to understand how serious I was.

Staring down at the screen, I considered sending another message but figured there was no point. If Teddy wanted to contact me, she would. Besides, there was also a chance she couldn't contact me even if she wanted to, stuck in some control room with a half dozen monitors showcasing a variety of security and satellite footage. I knew the team's tactics, exactly how they hunted. I could stay ahead of them for a while, but I wasn't sure how long I could keep this up.

Both dogs suddenly sat a bit taller. I glanced up and saw Quinn jogging back to the house.

"There you are," he said as he stepped inside. He patted both dogs on the head and started toward the basement stairs. Held up a finger at me. "Be right back."

He returned with an M4A1 and three magazines.

"Your girl's a natural. At least with a pistol. I'm curious to see how she handles full auto."

Grinning, he started back toward the patio door but paused.

"So you two aren't together or anything, right?"

When I said nothing, he shrugged.

"I'm always on the lookout for the next Mrs. Quinn."

He started back toward the door.

Stepping out in the hallway, scanning for any danger. Moving stealthily forward, as quiet as could be. Hearing that constant crackle of gunfire until . . . all at once it stopped.

Silence.

Except, no—a quiet whine from downstairs. The dogs.

If the team had tracked us here and was making an attack, it was hard to imagine the dogs wouldn't be barking their heads off.

I found them sitting by the rear patio door. Both twisted their heads to look at me before redirecting their attention back outside.

I stepped up next to them and saw Quinn and Stephanie out back, where Quinn had created a shooting range.

Stephanie wore protective earmuffs and glasses, standing in a classic Weaver stance. Gripping the pistol with two hands, her feet shoulder-width apart, her one leg slightly behind the other, her shooting arm extended toward the paper target ten yards away while her non-shooting arm was bent and placed in front of her body to provide additional support.

Tango and Cash seemed to be enjoying the show, both panting with their ears perked.

"Gentlemen," I said, and the dogs glanced up at me briefly before gazing back outside.

Stephanie had exhausted the mag. Instead of changing it out for her, Quinn walked her through the process, handing her a fresh one. I was surprised to see her handle the pistol like a pro: slotting in the magazine, pulling back the slide to chamber a round, and then firing again at the target.

Many of the shots were wide, but a few struck close to center mass.

I glanced again at the dogs.

"I bet you both want to be out there too. But it's probably best you aren't. You know, you can't fetch bullets."

48

The distant pop of gunfire shook me awake.

Eyes snapping open, I shot up in bed, reaching for my pistol—only there was no pistol, and it took me an extra second to gather my bearings and remember where I was.

Quinn's house. Out in the middle of nowhere. Miles and miles away from the closest neighbor.

That steady *pop pop pop* continued, somewhere outside.

I set my feet on the floor and started to rise, but a wave of dizziness forced me back down. Sitting still for a moment, trying to regain balance, before finally standing and starting toward the door.

I'd already showered and dressed and had laid back on the bed for only a few minutes. A glance at my watch confirmed that I'd been out for almost an hour.

Pop pop pop.

Had Hargrave and the rest of the team somehow tracked me here? Was Quinn right now trying to fend them off as they advanced up the hill?

"You looked pretty confident with that gun earlier."

"Did I? I didn't feel confident. In fact, I felt scared out of my mind."

"Your stance was a bit off, what with how you were standing on the hill like that. Had you shot at me, you probably would have fallen over due to the kickback."

He noted something in her face, and frowned.

"What's wrong?"

"Nothing. It's just—"

her grip tight on the gun as she fired at the biker's chest, again and again and again

"—not long after my fiancé and I broke up, I'd gone out and bought myself a gun. I figured I should at least know how to use it. But I . . . I don't feel confident with guns still."

Quinn gestured toward the house with the tennis ball, both dogs' eyes tracking it intently.

"I've got a shooting range out back. You up for some target practice?"

waited until it was arcing through the air before releasing Tango to go after it.

"I'm like a human lie detector. I can tell whenever someone is lying."

"Bullshit."

"It's true. It's all about reading your opponent. Not just looking for some tell or facial tic, but everything—posture, expression, eyes, even nose. Honestly, that's how I made most of my money when I was starting out. Being a PMC pays well, but do you think it pays well enough for me to own two hundred acres with this view?"

"So where did you get most of your money?"

"Poker. Not to be too conceited, but I could've gone pro."

"Why didn't you?"

Quinn bent to pick up the ball again. She noted that despite how drenched in the dogs' slobber it had become, it didn't bother him.

"Truth is," he said, "I like doing the work I do. There's a challenge to it. Poker . . . there isn't as much challenge, at least for me. It got boring."

"Why do you hate Danny?"

Again, Quinn was in the process of throwing the ball. He paused, considering the question, and then chucked the ball high in the air.

"*Hate* is a strong word. And besides, that's not for me to say."

"I disagree."

"Ask Dan if you want to know."

"He won't tell me. And right now my life is more or less in his hands. And yours. So at the very least, I'd like to know what the issue is between the two of you."

Cash trotted back with the ball, tail wagging. Quinn scooped it up, then glanced at both dogs now sitting side by side, waiting patiently. He turned back to Stephanie.

"Fortunately, they've never needed to yet. But if that day comes, at least I know they've got my back."

Again he threw the ball, and again one of his dogs chased after it while the other sat at attention, waiting patiently.

Quinn said, "So you knew Dan when he was a kid, huh?"

Something about the tone she didn't like, but she couldn't put her finger on why.

"Yes."

"What was he like? I've always wondered about something."

"What's that?"

"Well, you tell me. What kind of kid was he?"

"I don't know. He was quiet whenever I was around. Shy."

Thinking, *And I'm pretty sure it's because he'd had a crush on me.*

"I can see quiet," Quinn said. "Not shy. But then again, he was, what, in middle school when you knew him."

"What kind of kid were you?"

She hadn't meant the question to sound so aggressive, but there it was. Quinn paused only briefly to glance at her.

"I guess I was quiet too. Moving from army base to army base can make it difficult to make friends. I eventually got to a place where I didn't even bother trying because I knew my dad could get papers and ship out the next week."

"Earlier, you'd asked Danny if he was a traitor."

"That I did."

"Then you told him you believed him when he said he wasn't. How . . . how can you be so certain?"

Quinn was in the process of drawing back his arm to throw the tennis ball but now paused. Slowly turned to look at her.

"I'm not sure you'll believe it."

"Try me."

He thought for a moment, and then threw the ball and

be isolating. Maybe if we'd had a kid, she wouldn't have felt so lonely all the time, but I think part of us both knew a baby wasn't going to solve anything, so we never really tried."

Cash had returned with the ball, dropping it at Quinn's feet. Quinn patted the dog's head and Cash went to sit next to Tango, who watched closely as Quinn held up the ball and moved it all around, then when he chucked it up into the sky. That German word again, and Tango tore away, flinging up dirt and grass in his wake.

Stephanie said, "Why do you live out in the middle of nowhere?"

Quinn placed his hands on his hips as he gazed toward the distant snowcapped mountains.

"That view, for one. I've always loved the Rockies. Ever since I was a kid and watched old westerns. I don't mind the city, but something about living out here in the middle of nowhere just feels right to me."

"So when you work, you're gone for months at a time?"

"Give or take. Some jobs last longer than others. Like a recent job had me in Jakarta for three weeks. So I wasn't gone long, but the detail was intense, especially as there was an attempt on the client's life. It paid extremely well, though."

Tango had returned, dropping the ball at Quinn's feet.

Stephanie said, "But what about the dogs? Who looks after them?"

"They stay with a neighbor who lives on a ranch a few miles away. The neighbor has dogs of his own, and my boys love going over there to spend time. They're like puppies when they play with those dogs."

"Puppies that will tear somebody's throat out when given the right command."

Quinn shrugged as he bent to pick up the ball.

again, and on the drive he'd been drifting in and out. The truth was, she was exhausted herself, but she was wired too.

Quinn rose to his feet as he drained the rest of his beer.

"So what do you say? Wanna play fetch?"

The tennis ball soared through the air, a tiny green speck in all that dark blue.

Tango sat at attention, gaze tracking the ball as it reached its apex. Then Quinn said something in German and the dog burst forward, running faster than any dog she'd ever seen. All four legs pumping as it gracefully tore across the field. The tennis ball hit the ground, bounced high, and Tango leaped up and caught the ball in the air.

Quinn clapped his hands and praised Tango as the dog hurried back. Tango dropped the tennis ball at Quinn's feet, then sat beside Cash, who'd continued to sit at attention this entire time.

"Watch," Quinn said to the dog.

Cash's dark eyes tracked the ball as Quinn moved it all around, and then he drew back his arm and threw it high in the air, and right as the ball hit its zenith, he again said something in German and Cash tore forward.

As they watched the dog, Quinn said, "I was married once. Briefly."

Stephanie said nothing. She was trying to take in the stunning view. Breathe in the cool, crisp air. Doing everything she could not to remind herself how much her life had fallen apart.

"I guess it's cliché to say, but she was the love of my life. I imagined having kids with her, growing old together, all that. But . . . it can be hard to maintain a relationship with my work. Away for months at a time. Especially living out here. It can pause, and before she realized it she had looped back to that side street, pulling up right as Danny had come down the embankment.

When she headed down the stairs she found Tyler Quinn sitting in the living room, his feet propped up on a glass coffee table, nursing a beer. Tango and Cash lay on the floor near him. As she entered the living room, the dogs sat at attention, their dark eyes zeroed in on her. Their tails imperceptibly twitching. Until Quinn said something in German and the dogs trotted forward, tails now wagging furiously.

Stephanie bent to pet them both, then glanced up at her host. "Where's Danny?"

The man grinned as he took another pull on the beer.

"I gotta say, I've never heard anyone call him that before."

She shrugged as she wandered through the living room. Noting the books on the shelves, many of which specialized in military history. An old record player. A bonsai tree.

It took her a moment before something clicked, and then she cast her gaze around the house once more before turning to Quinn.

"How long has it been since you split with your wife?"

Amusement in his eyes, but he said nothing.

"Or long-term girlfriend," Stephanie said. "Because I'm assuming these are her clothes. And based on the decor, this place doesn't look like a total bachelor pad."

Quinn stared at her for a beat, considering, and then tipped his head to the side.

"I was going to take the dogs outside to throw the ball around if you'd like to join me."

"Maybe. But first, where's Danny?"

"*Danny* laid down for a bit. Guess the pain meds I gave him were a bit too strong."

Not surprising. She'd done her best to clean his wounds

47

After stepping out of the shower and toweling off, Stephanie found a set of clothes waiting for her on the bed.

Faded jeans about her size and a plaid button-down shirt and socks. No underwear, which she figured was for the best because she wasn't sure she would wear a stranger's underwear, and besides, finding another woman's underwear in a house that so far appeared only to contain a man and his two dogs would be totally creepy.

As she changed she thought about the past twenty-four hours, especially those long minutes outside Dodgers Stadium, parked on that side street, debating running straight to the police. She had even started to, looking up the closest station on her phone, figuring that once she got there and explained everything, the officers could help.

How, she wasn't sure, but she wanted—*needed*—to get her old life back.

Which was when a quiet voice in her head had asked, *What's so special about your old life anyway?*

The fact she hadn't had an immediate answer had given her

Chen made a show of looking at his watch.

"And how many hours has it been so far?"

When Hargrave said nothing, Chen nodded.

"I thought so. If I were you, I'd recall the team. Even if one of your techs managed to pick up the trail within the next ten minutes, I'm not so sure I'd feel comfortable with them going after Burke. Not anymore."

Hargrave found himself mirroring the man's posture, crossing his arms and slightly hunching his shoulders. He turned slowly, arching an eyebrow.

"What are you saying?"

"I'm saying what should be obvious to you by now, Mitchell. First, one of your people was dirty, and now it turns out another was too. If I were you, I'd ask myself how much I trust anyone else on this team."

Chen shrugged, still staring at the screens.

"Anyway, there is certainly the possibility that Ms. Salazar is in fact dead. Then again, nobody has yet managed to track down her girlfriend."

"You think the body belongs to the girlfriend."

"Maybe. Maybe not. Until the medical examiner digs in, we won't know for sure. But they've already secured Ms. Salazar's dental records. We'll know the truth soon."

"Suppose it is the girlfriend. That means Rita killed her. It means she set fire to the apartment to cover it up. Why would she do that?"

Chen gave him another look, this one asking, *Are you an idiot?*

"Why else would she do that? To get a head start, of course. But don't worry—I've already alerted people in the agency. They've added her name to a no-fly list. They've also uploaded her profile so that facial and gait recognition will pick her up if she enters any airport in the country. By the way, I'm sorry again about your operator. He went through a hell of a day with everything that happened to him. It's no wonder his heart gave out the way it did. How old was he again?"

"Thirty-six."

"Thirty-six and had a fatal heart attack. Well, stranger things have happened."

Again, Hargrave wasn't sure how to interpret the man's tone. Was he messing with him?

"A medical examiner will get to his body too," Hargrave said, as though it put the matter to rest. He knew that the compound he'd injected LaSalle with would go undetected. Besides, the man's system had already been pumped with a slew of medications.

Chen asked, "What's the status of your team now?"

"They're still in LA. Julian here is trying to pick up the trail."

Hargrave said, "What are you trying to say?"

Giving him a tired look, Chen crossed his arms as he turned back to the screens.

"I understand your reluctance, Mitchell. You learned one of your men was bent, but that was a year ago, and as far as you knew until yesterday, he was dead. Now you learn another one of your people is also bent."

Talking about Salazar in the present tense, as though Chen knew for certain she wasn't dead.

Besides the two men, there was only one tech at the computers. Julian still running through the security feed at Dodgers Stadium and a one-mile radius, trying to ascertain where Burke had gone. Theo was down in one of the rooms getting some rest so that he could return in two hours to relieve Julian.

Hargrave dropped his voice, as though he didn't want Julian to overhear him.

"I was the one who brought her on. She was my responsibility, and it turns out she was a rat this entire time."

Chen shook his head.

"Not necessarily. I imagine that happened later. Circumstances beyond her control but which had been orchestrated by the enemy. It happens all the time. Or, well, the enemy comes at our people all the time. Normal people see somebody on the street, they think they're another normal person. And maybe they are. But sometimes they're not. Sometimes they're spies sent to infiltrate our lives, to get to know us, to wait until our defenses come down, and then strike."

Hargrave realized he was holding his breath. He let it out silently. Was Chen letting on that he knew something about him? Hargrave had been so careful these past couple of years. Doubly careful. *Triply* careful. Always minding what he said, what he did. Who he was around.

46

The evidence was irrefutable. Plain as day. Plain as, well, the information currently displayed on one of the half dozen screens in the control room.

Hargrave stood beside Samuel Chen. His arms crossed, his jaw tight. He hadn't said anything since Julian placed the financials on the screen a minute ago, and he wouldn't say anything until Chen spoke first.

He kept thinking: *Don't appear too eager. Just let things play out naturally.*

Finally, Chen shifted to look at him.

"It's a bit convenient, don't you think?"

It took everything Hargrave had not to allow the panic to flash in his eyes.

"What is?"

"Daniel Burke shows up on the radar after a year, and as soon as a team is sent to hunt him down, Rita Salazar dies in a fire."

"Are you?"

"Am I what?"

"An enemy of the state. A fucking traitor."

I held Quinn's gaze as I shook my head.

"No."

Quinn stared at me for another beat before he nodded and rose from his stool, taking his plate to the sink.

"I know you're not. That's why I didn't kill you earlier. But look, I'm not sure what you want from me. I'm a hired gun, plain and simple. And you . . . you don't strike me as somebody with much money."

"I have enough."

"Yeah, but what exactly would you hire me to do? Help you go up against the entire US government? No thanks. I may have issues with the government, but I'm not out of my mind."

"At the very least, can we stay here for a few hours to recharge?"

"You can stay as long as you want. And that's mostly because Tango and Cash seem to like your girl."

"I'm not his girl," Stephanie said at the same time I said, "She's not my girl."

Quinn looked at us both, did a terrible job of hiding his grin, and shrugged.

"Honestly, I don't care. I'm between jobs right now, so I'm trying to take it easy for a few days. If you want to stay, stay. If you want to go, go. Doesn't matter to me. But just do me one favor."

"What?"

"When this team tracks you down again—because they will—and assuming they don't kill you outright, don't tell anyone where I live. In fact, leave my name out of it entirely."

from the scam broke into my house. He and this guy who barely looked like he was out of high school, some computer geek. They held me hostage so that Danny would help them escape the country."

Quinn tossed the dogs a few more pieces of chicken, then turned back to us, leaning against the counter. Leveling his gaze at me.

"And did you?"

"Did I what?"

"Help them leave the country."

"No. One of them—the detective—I killed. The hacker I gave up to the feds."

"Interesting," Quinn said, then turned back to the stove and started to plate the chicken and rice. "So then what happened?"

I told him about Senator Harold Browne, meeting him in his hotel room along the Strip after his debate, the conversation we had. How yesterday morning I'd sat across the highway and watched as the FBI walked the old man out of the Lucky Star Hotel & Casino.

"I saw that on the news," Quinn said. "I thought I'd spotted Adam there. So you threw him a bone, huh? That and the VP—he's either become very popular within the Bureau or a pariah."

I didn't want to think about Adam again, whether his wife had become a widow, so I told Quinn about going to the airport, the call I'd received before boarding, and everything that had led up to now.

By then we'd started eating.

Quinn took a pull of his beer, watching me closely.

"So," he said. "The team you used to work with is now hunting you because, as far as Uncle Sam is concerned, you're an enemy of the state."

"That about gets to the heart of it, yes."

had drifted over and sat beside me at the counter, not speaking once, until at one point Quinn turned back and pointed at her.

"How do you play into this whole thing again?"

Stephanie opened her mouth, but based on her uncertain expression, I decided to answer for her.

"She used to date my brother back in high school."

"This is the brother who killed himself."

"Yes."

"Your only brother."

"Yes."

"And . . . how again does she play into this whole thing?"

So I told him about the shoot-out at the Firefly, how in the ensuing madness I'd gotten part of a bullet stuck in my back, so I'd sought out Stephanie's help—and how she'd agreed to give me that help.

Stephanie made a noise then, a slight grumble in the back of her throat. Quinn turned away from grilling the chicken and cocked an eyebrow.

I shrugged.

"She regrets the decision."

Stephanie murmured, "That's putting it mildly."

So I told the rest: how I'd interrogated Olivia in Stephanie's kitchen, and how Olivia told me about the Hacienda and the VIP parties, and how I'd gone out to the desert and saved those girls and then drove out to Los Angeles where I managed to sneak onto the property of the private estate and then happened to see—

"Shut the front door," Quinn said as he took the rice off the stove to sit. "*You're* the reason the VP got nabbed?"

Earlier, Quinn had offered us water or beer. I didn't want to say anything, so I sipped at my bottle of water.

Stephanie said, "During that time, one of the detectives

"Why would I?"

Again, I said nothing.

Quinn said, "I never touched base with you, but that doesn't mean I didn't check up on you, just as I'm guessing you checked up on me. Even if you did black op work, you as Daniel Burke still existed. Your social security number, your file with the government, everything. So when that file closed, it was a pretty safe assumption to make that you had died."

"Well, as you can see, I'm still very much alive."

"Unfortunately. So, national security, huh?"

"Yes."

Quinn nodded, thinking it over. He set the Beretta on the counter and then turned to the fridge.

"It's coming up on lunchtime. I was about to grill some chicken. It's the dogs' favorite. How about I cook, you tell me what's going on, and if by the time the food is ready you haven't convinced me, then I'll kill you both and bury your bodies in the garden out back."

I sensed Stephanie's eyes on me, worried. I tipped my head in her direction.

"She doesn't know you're joking."

"Who says I'm joking?"

"All right," I said, pulling out a stool and sitting down at the counter. "You want to know what's going on? Here it is."

The story didn't take long to recount. Not when you were sticking to the basic facts. Once I got talking, Quinn had started making lunch. He rarely glanced my way, if at all, focusing instead on the task at hand, occasionally tossing bits of chicken to the two dogs who sat with rapt attention as he cooked. Stephanie

track me down. Because my fucking employer doesn't even know where I live."

The dogs, sensing a shift in the air, had stopped wagging their tails. They weren't growling again but standing at attention, waiting for the magic word to release them to attack.

Stephanie had left Noah's gun in the car. Even if she had it, it was doubtful she would try to pull it again, now that she'd seen how vicious and well-trained the dogs could be.

"If it makes you feel any better," I said, holding Quinn's gaze, "it wasn't easy."

After a beat, Quinn lowered the pistol.

"I bet it wasn't."

"Since when do you make bets?"

"Fair point. I love to gamble, but making bets is a sucker's game."

"I saw Adam recently."

"Oh yeah? How's he doing?"

I pictured my old friend back at Dodgers Stadium. Eyes wide and glassy. His stomach dark with blood from where Lucas Hancock had stabbed him.

I wished there was some way to check up on him, make sure he had pulled through, but with Teddy no longer in my corner, I had zero resources.

"He said you told him I was dead."

"That I did."

"How did you know?"

Quinn shrugged.

"I don't know what work you did for the government, exactly, but from what I could tell it was some black op stuff. Am I right?"

I said nothing.

"Anyway, I touch base periodically with everyone from the site."

"You've never touched base with me."

Quinn gave it a beat, and grinned.

"Of course, I wouldn't do that."

He barked out something else in German, and the two dogs sat at attention just like they had been sitting. Then Quinn said something else much less hostile-sounding and the two dogs skittered forward, tongues lolling and tails wagging.

Stephanie was still leaning against me, trembling, but hesitantly leaned down and outstretched her hand for the dogs to smell her. Then, when the dogs' tails kept going a mile a minute, she petted their heads and scratched them behind the ears.

The dogs loved it.

I looked at Quinn.

"You don't have to be a dick."

He shrugged as he set the sniper rifle aside, still grinning. "After what you pulled, I figured it was only fair."

"Sensors along the road?"

"Of course. The road out there doesn't lead anywhere else but to my place. If you keep going, it'll eventually dead-end. So whenever anyone turns down this way, an alarm is triggered."

Quinn shrugged off the ghillie suit and draped it on a hook by the door, then motioned for us to enter deeper into the house.

"As you can see, the kitchen is over there, and through there is the dining room, and through there is the living room. In the back of the house is the room I use for my gym. Upstairs are three bedrooms, and downstairs is the basement, though it's mostly full of my gear."

"You build this place yourself?"

"Built, no. Helped designed, yes."

"For whatever reason, I never pictured you moving to Wyoming."

"Yeah, about that," Quinn said, turning and aiming a Beretta M9 at my face. "I'd love to know how you managed to

45

It turned out Tyler Quinn didn't live in a shack.

Far from it.

Hidden behind the trees was a modern two-story house with clean lines that didn't seem to fit in with the other, more traditional houses we'd passed on the way here.

Two German shepherds were sitting at attention when we entered. Their black eyes zeroed in on Stephanie and me, but they didn't bark or growl or make any movement.

Quinn said, "This is Tango and Cash. They're brothers. Got them when they were puppies and trained them myself. Here, watch."

Quinn barked out something in German—it was too quick for me to catch—and instantly the two dogs started growling, the hair on their backs standing on end, their dark eyes full of menace.

"Now, if I give them the signal, they'll tear forward and rip you apart limb by limb."

Stephanie slowly stepped close to me, so much so I could feel her body trembling.

"Feel free to plug in anywhere," Cyrus said, gesturing at the room he had built but could no longer see.

Rita said, "I smashed my laptop."

"Well, damn."

"At least, the screen is smashed. I think I can salvage the rest. With the right parts."

Cyrus let loose a meaty laugh as he again gestured around the room.

"If it exists, I've got it. Only there isn't much rhyme or reason to the mess. At least, that's what I've been told."

Rita gazed around the giant room, overwhelmed not just by the scope and magnitude of this entire operation but also by the kindness this man was showing her.

"Thank you, Cyrus."

"My pleasure. Glad you finally stopped by. I only hope you're okay."

She was conscious of the burner in her pocket. Had considered texting Daniel Burke at least a dozen times, and each time decided to put it off. Because first she needed more information. More answers. More . . . something.

"Yeah," she said quietly. "Me too."

She'd hooked up with Cyrus over a decade ago, in that way hackers hook up with other hackers. She was aware of Cyrus just as he was aware of her. It's a community in a way, though at the same time it's not. At least, it's not if you also work for the United States government and are tasked with top secret missions all over the world, in which case you need to keep your identity extra secret.

But when Cyrus had started going blind, he told her about his sanctuary and offered her an invitation if she ever needed it. The sanctuary being a hacker's den, where hackers of all stripes could come to get off the grid.

Cyrus had a line directly to the dark web, and while he didn't dabble with much of it himself, he didn't begrudge those who did.

Except when it came to child porn or human or animal trafficking of any kind—he didn't put up with that and made it clear he would burn anyone who dabbled in that shit.

Rita had never been to the den, but Cyrus had given her directions in case she ever wanted to visit. Which had been, what, three years ago now? Yeah, around the time Hargrave had brought her on at The Office. She hadn't even been certain Cyrus was still alive, let alone still at this location, but now he was leading her down a long narrow hall to a large room.

It looked like a giant computer had vomited all over the place. Motherboards and CPUs and GPUs and keyboards and wires everywhere, but there were a few stations set up where people could plug in.

Already two others were hunched over these stations, a woman and a man. Both in their early twenties, both in faded hoodies with a clutter of Red Bull cans strewn about, the woman sucking on a vape pen. Each of them wearing headphones and merely flickering their eyes toward her as means of acknowledging her presence before focusing again on their screens.

cardboard box. Rita wanting to help the woman somehow but knowing she shouldn't stop, that she couldn't. Powering on to the end and then crossing the street to another alley.

Cracked concrete steps leading down beneath the building. Dirty water already starting to pool below, the rusted sewer grate clogged with trash. Rita splashed through to the steel door at the end and banged her fist hard against it.

It took a minute before the door opened a crack, and a gruff voice said, "Who is it?"

"Teddy."

"What do you want?"

"Sanctuary."

The door opened far enough to see the man standing there. Large, bald, with sunglasses on his face and a myriad of tattoos sleeving both arms.

"Haven't seen you in a while."

Technically, the man hadn't seen anything in a while. He'd gone blind several years back. Something hereditary that he had only learned about when he started losing his vision. Rita remembered him telling her how he wished he'd known ahead of time, as that way he would have done things differently in his life. Which Rita also figured was bullshit—people said that all the time and she always figured they would do exactly what they had done before.

Retrospection was a fool's game.

"Been busy, Cyrus. Mind if I come in?"

The steel door creaked as it opened wider.

"Sure thing. But you're not the only fucker on the network. You'll need to be a good girl and share."

She was fine with burning the rest of her things—that was all just *stuff*—but these were photos taken back before everything was digitized and forever stored on social media.

So she'd left everything behind—her apartment, her things, her car, her entire life.

Her first instinct had been to flee for the airport. She'd taken her passport with her. Whoever had sent Jade—her heart still ached to think of the betrayal—had done so behind the scenes. In other words, it wasn't sanctioned, at least by the US government, which meant there was no reason to think she was on any no-fly lists. She could book a flight, board a plane, and be in another country within hours.

Except . . .

The three million dollars in that offshore account. The one under her name which wasn't hers.

Somebody was setting her up, which meant once that information came to light, her name would be automatically flagged in the system. For all she knew that information had already come to light—maybe the hit was sanctioned after all. If she went to the airport and managed to get on a plane, the pilots might delay takeoff until agents boarded to escort her off.

Another rumble in the sky above her, what sounded like a strike. She flashed on memories of when she was a girl and making her little brother giggle. A storm raging outside as she mimed throwing a bowling ball down the lane and then acting as if she were one of the pins, being struck and toppling over. Remembering the brightness in her brother's eyes when he cackled with laughter, momentarily forgetting the scary storm.

Up another block and then down an alleyway. Past dumpsters, a broken shopping cart, a homeless woman under a heavy

44

The angels in heaven were bowling.

That was what her father had told her when she was a girl, frightened as most children are of nasty storms. The kind with sheets of rain battering the earth, heavy wind scraping the windows, slashes of lightning igniting the night sky.

Her brother was terrified of storms too. Terrified of everything, really. Something about his brain not having properly developed. Something Rita would come to understand much later in life, though at the time, a child herself, she didn't know any better.

It was late Friday afternoon, the sky dark and the rain heavy. Rumbles of thunder in the distance, though so far she hadn't seen any lightning.

Then again, she'd been mostly moving about with her face tilted down. Wrapped in a cheap parka she'd grabbed at a thrift shop, one that at least did the job and kept her somewhat dry as she hustled down one block after another. Armed only with her burner, Jade's phone, and the remains of her laptop—and the old photographs of her brother.

"A matter of national security, huh?"

"That's right."

Quinn was less than ten feet away now. He paused to shout, "Relax, lady, I'm putting it down!" and gingerly set the rifle on the ground. Then took a few more steps forward and spoke so quietly he might as well have been speaking to himself.

"So that way I can do this."

And drew back his arm and smashed his fist against my face.

So it wasn't surprising when Tyler Quinn rose out of the tall grass, his body draped in a sniper's ghillie suit. A Remington M40 sniper rifle aimed at me.

Apparently there were some state-of-the-art security features on this property. Probably closer to the highway. An alert that gave Quinn enough time to suit up and get into position before our car even crested the ridge.

"Hello, Tyler."

Quinn said nothing, keeping the rifle aimed for center mass. The wind rippling the edges of the ghillie suit.

Behind me, the Malibu's groaning engine roared, tires kicking up gravel as it rocketed forward.

My hands still raised, I turned to watch as Stephanie veered the car toward me before screeching to a halt and jumping out with Noah's pistol in her hands.

Stephanie didn't speak. Didn't make a sound. She just stood there, aiming the gun straight at Quinn.

Who, after a beat, grinned as he lowered the rifle.

He asked me, "She your partner?"

"No."

"Girlfriend?"

"No."

"Life coach?"

I said nothing.

Keeping the M40 held low at his side and ignoring the gun trained on him, Quinn started forward, narrowing the distance between us.

"You remember what I told you the last time we saw each other, right?"

"Yes."

"And yet you decided to come here anyway."

"I did."

"Are you nuts? Somebody just tried to kill us!"

"It was a warning shot."

"Yeah? Well, warning received."

Still scanning the trees, I turned my head to look at her. Saw the fear in her eyes and tried to convey with the calmness in mine that everything was all right.

"Keep going."

Swallowing, she put the car back in gear and lifted her feet off the brake. The engine groaning again as we continued up the drive, the car at a crawl now as Stephanie was too spooked to go any faster than five miles per hour.

Twenty seconds later, my side mirror disappeared in a burst of debris.

"Uh-uh, nope," Stephanie said, slamming on the brakes again and slotting the gear shift into Reverse. "After everything we've survived already, I'm not dying like this so you can play chicken with some psychopath."

Before she could put the car in motion, I opened my door and stepped out.

"Danny, what are you *doing*?"

I raised my hands and started up the drive. Slowly. One step after another. Clearing my throat so that my voice would project over the wind.

"Quinn, I need your help! I wouldn't have come here if I had any other choice!"

I could hear the engine behind me. Stephanie kept the car running but hadn't headed back toward the gate.

"This is serious, Quinn! Potentially a matter of national security!"

The line of trees stood a quarter mile away. But as I advanced up the drive, I veered to the right. Straight into the field. Right toward where I'd spotted the muzzle flash from the second shot.

Approaching the gate, I kept scanning for trip wires, but it looked like any old gate. Not brand-new, but newish. Though the elements had done what they always did to metal like this. They didn't use the term *weatherworn* for no reason.

A simple latch unlocked the gate. Meaning that when you wanted to go through, you had to get out of your car and open the gate, then get back in your car and drive through, then get out again and close and latch the gate.

I wasn't sure why, but I'd imagined Quinn having a much more state-of-the-art setup.

"Danny?"

Stephanie calling out the window put me into motion. Striding forward, pausing again to scan the fence, and then lifting the latch.

The gate produced a metal screech, but that was it. I held it open long enough for Stephanie to motor through, then closed the gate and reengaged the latch.

Then I stood there, staring up the hill. At the blue grama shivering in the wind. I had no idea what type of house Quinn lived in, only that this was where he lived. For all I knew, it was a shack.

"Go slowly," I said to Stephanie as I slid into the passenger seat.

The drive was about a mile to the tree line. Stephanie kept the car moving at about ten miles per hour. The front windows down, letting in the wind and the groan of the engine and the crunch of gravel on the drive—and then, a split second after Stephanie's side mirror exploded, the echo of a gunshot.

Stephanie screamed as she smashed the brake pedal with both feet. Her eyes wide, she went to throw the car into Reverse.

I reached over and held her hand in place.

"Keep going."

"Not when I knew him. He's always hated the government, but he's a pure capitalist, through and through."

"What does he do for a living?"

"He's a contractor."

"You mean he works on houses?"

A ghost of a smile touched the corner of my lips as I continued to scan for any cameras—and any potential booby traps.

"He's a private military contractor. International organizations often hire men and women like him to keep principals safe when they're out of the country."

"How do you know all this? I thought you said you haven't seen this guy for years."

While I'd told Stephanie a lot, I hadn't told her everything. She didn't need to know how lonely I'd become in the past year. My only interactions with Teddy via encrypted chat and with retail employees at the store or gas station. And of course those I interacted with during my various trips to Vegas. So on that downtime I'd started to wonder about the people I once knew, especially at the black site. I'd continued to suppress the memories of what I'd done in the killing room, but I wondered what had become of the men and women I'd worked with, how their lives had turned out since our time there, so I had looked them up.

A few were easier to track down than others. Like with Adam Reed—he'd always talked about joining the FBI, so it wasn't surprising to find that he hadn't only become an agent but had also managed to rise through the ranks at such a fast clip.

Tyler Quinn was the only one who had seemingly disappeared, and it had taken me much longer to track him down.

I climbed out of the car and felt the wind against my face as it crossed the miles and miles of prairies. The air out here smelling different than in LA. Fresher. Purer.

43

"This is it?"

Skepticism in Stephanie's tone. Minutes earlier she'd turned off the main highway and drove the rugged road for several miles, following a wire fence, until we came to a gate. Beyond the gate, a dirt drive flanked by tall grass—what looked like blue grama—led up a hill toward a cluster of trees.

No mailbox. Nothing to give the actual address.

Still in the back, having sat up straight in my seat since we'd gotten off the highway, I nodded as I scanned the area.

"Yeah, this is it."

Massive clouds continued to drift across the deep-blue sky, blotting out the bright sun.

I hadn't spotted any cameras on the way in—and none were propped up near the gate—but I hadn't expected to see any. Quinn was too careful, too meticulous.

Stephanie said, "Is this guy . . . I don't know how to say it. You know, is he one of those off-the-grid militia types?"

The deputy director glanced around again, and then leaned forward, dropping his voice even lower.

"I made an executive decision, and now our fates are linked. If you and your team don't pull this off, then I'll be railroaded along with the rest of you. I don't like what you did with Burke and that cop yesterday, but I get the reason why. Just do me a favor: play it straight moving forward."

"Sure thing," Hargrave said and thumbed the fob to unlock the doors.

Then he was behind the wheel and started the engine and let it idle for a moment as he felt his phone vibrating—not his burner, which he used to communicate with Sergei, or his personal, which he used to communicate with the in-home caregivers, but his work phone.

Julian. Hargrave put it on speakerphone and asked what he wanted.

The tech said, "I dug around, as you requested."

Despite the hollowness Hargrave felt in his chest, he did everything he could to suppress a smile.

"You mean about Rita's finances? What did you find?"

"Umm . . . well, it's best you get back here so you can see for yourself."

Hargrave shot Chen a worried look, really playing it up.

"Julian, what are you saying? Is it bad?"

Silence for a beat, and then he could hear the hesitant nod in the tech's voice.

"It is, sir. Very bad."

They followed the fire chief back down to the ground floor. On the way, police detectives passed them. The fire chief asked Hargrave and Chen if they needed anything else, and when both men said no, he led the detectives up to the fourth floor to view the body.

Hargrave and Chen stepped outside into the late morning. The sky overcast, the app on his phone calling for rain. Several fire trucks idling about, as well as some police cars and an ambulance. Scores of residents outside too, waiting to be let back in, while others in the neighborhood stood across the street to watch the action.

Samuel Chen said, "I'm sorry for your loss."

Hargrave blinked, surprised by the sincerity in the man's tone. "What's that?"

"First, one of your operators, and now Ms. Salazar."

Earlier, when Rita hadn't returned to The Office and there was no answer to the repeated calls, he'd told his team he would head over to check on her. But before he left, news came over the line that there had been a fire in Rita's apartment building, and Chen had insisted on accompanying him.

Now Hargrave studied the man's face for a beat and said, "Can I ask you a question?"

"Certainly."

"Back at the White House, with POTUS and the others—why didn't you say anything about my team deepfaking Burke as the shooter?"

Chen paused as they reached the car, glancing around as though to ensure nobody was close enough to hear them. He turned to Hargrave, his voice quiet.

"I'd be lying if I said I hadn't planned on throwing you under the bus. But the truth is we need Burke brought in—and you and your team are the only ones who know him. You yourself trained him, and your men worked with him closely, so I figure right now you and your team are the best chance we have."

"Time will tell. It always does. Now, gentlemen, I've humored your request. I'm sorry about your employee, but we must head out now."

Hargrave gazed again at the body on the floor. Burned beyond recognition. Identification would be completed, though it would take some time.

Killing Noah LaSalle had been an unfortunate but necessary outcome. The man had served his purpose and was well trusted, but he'd gotten sloppy. He'd denied saying anything to Burke, but Hargrave had seen the truth in the man's eyes, so he needed to go.

He'd messaged Jade to eliminate Rita, though the plan had been for Jade to use the same compound that Hargrave had used to inject LaSalle. A chemical cocktail that would stop Rita's heart in a matter of seconds.

Setting fire to the apartment hadn't been part of the plan, though in truth, Hargrave wasn't always privy to Sergei's plans.

Still . . .

"Chief, I have a question."

Hargrave pointed at the small camera posted at the end of the hallway, right above the stairwell door.

"Has anyone reviewed the security footage?"

Despite the mask, Hargrave could tell the man was grinning.

"Was wondering when you were going to ask that. Because, see, that's the strange part. All the security footage in this building? It was knocked out for about an hour. From what I'm told, the same with the traffic cams in at least a two-mile radius."

Hargrave felt the hairs on the back of his neck stand on end. He'd have to follow up with Sergei, see if the man had masterminded the security blackout to help Jade avoid detection.

Because otherwise he was starting to have a bad feeling about this whole thing.

he'd managed to go most of his life being vigilant, keeping an eye out for the enemy. And then, one day, the enemy caught him in their trap—and he hadn't had the guts or courage to chew his leg off to free himself.

Now, Hargrave was aware of Samuel Chen asking a question, jolting him back to the present.

"As far as you know she doesn't have any roommates, does she?"

The fire chief stood with his hands on his hips, his dark eyes roaming the blackened apartment.

"I should ask you the same thing. We've asked the landlord, who said people had seen the deceased with a woman on occasion, but if that woman was living here, she hadn't been added to the lease. Still, it is quite curious, isn't it?"

"What is?"

"Well, fires like these don't often start from a couple candles. Or even an electrical fire."

"How do you mean?"

"You ever heard of a controlled burn? Where they start fires to maintain the health of a forest?"

"This isn't a forest."

"No," the fire chief agreed, slowly shaking his head. "No, it is not. But if you look in the bedroom there, and even the bathroom? Every room in this apartment has about the same extent of damage."

"Meaning?"

"Meaning it's as if the fire originated in every room."

A brief silence as the three men watched the others working. Fire investigators taking pictures and measurements. Because it was now suddenly obvious what the fire chief was saying.

"You mean arson," Hargrave said.

The fire chief shrugged.

long after that, Daniel Burke had gotten himself killed—or at least so they'd believed at the time—and all at once Hargrave saw an opportunity to point the hounds in a new direction.

Marking Burke as the traitor had been a no-brainer, especially as the man had no family or friends, nobody who would have to deal with the fallout. And besides, the government wanted to keep a tight lid on things, as it was never good PR to let it slip that they had a rat inside the house. With Burke out of the picture—and Hargrave having manipulated records to prove that Burke had indeed stolen secrets and had even profited by selling them—there wasn't much else that needed to be done.

Except, as the months wore on, Sergei had begun to demand even more top secret intel. And Hargrave, already with his back against the wall, had no choice but to comply. Though he'd also made a request, because he realized the time would soon come to throw Rita Salazar to the wolves.

That was how Jade entered the picture.

Rita had never once mentioned her girlfriend to Hargrave—she'd never even hinted that she was a lesbian—but Hargrave had gotten updates from time to time, alerting him when the occasional dates had escalated into something serious, until it got to the point they'd moved in together.

Hargrave hadn't liked this development, worrying that Jade had gotten much too close, but it was explained to him how this was the next natural step: if Jade had refused to move in when Rita proposed it, then that might cause strain on their relationship and they needed to keep Jade close, just in case.

Just in case.

Having the money wired from a Russian bank hadn't been difficult. After all, the people squeezing him were Russian—most likely GRU. Not that he'd known that when this all started. He still wanted to kick himself every time he thought about it. How

"Obviously, you need to steer clear of the body, but you can see it over there."

The man pointed toward what was once the living room. On the floor lay Rita Salazar, or what remained of her.

Crispy was the first word that entered Hargrave's mind, and for a delirious second he had to fight the urge to bark out a laugh.

Samuel Chen asked, "Any ideas yet on how the fire started?"

"Nothing official yet, but do you see the kitchen counter over there? I believe those pieces are what's left of several jar candles."

Hargrave gazed around the scorched apartment, trying to run through the whole thing in his head. Salazar coming home late at night for a few hours of sleep, and she, what, lights a candle or two in the kitchen?

What the hell was Jade thinking?

Of course, Hargrave didn't know the woman's real name. He only knew her by the name she'd gone by when she entered Rita Salazar's life.

Sent there, like everyone else, by Sergei.

Three years ago, when this awful ordeal had started, Hargrave knew he needed to bring someone on as a fall guy. Even then, he'd foreseen the need to place the blame on somebody else if the occasion arose. He'd scoured several different agencies, trying to find the right person—not only someone qualified for the job but someone who also didn't have much baggage in their life.

Rita Salazar had fit the bill perfectly.

Though as time wore on, he wasn't sure he would even need her, what with Sergei having almost zero contact.

Until he'd begun to hear rumblings that the CIA suspected someone on his team may be selling secrets. And then, not too

42

At first the fire chief wouldn't let them into the building, let alone the apartment. It wasn't until Samuel Chen flashed his credentials that the man finally relented, though he insisted on being the one to guide them up the four flights.

"We evacuated the entire building despite the fact the fire appears to have been isolated to the one apartment."

The door had been busted open with a battering ram. The paint along the hallway wall near the door and the ceiling had bubbled and darkened, but beyond that, there didn't appear to be too much damage to the other apartments in the hall.

After the fire chief had them put on protective booties and N95 respirator masks, he led them inside a charred wasteland that had once been home to Rita Salazar.

"Detectives should be here shortly. I'm risking my neck by allowing you to come in beforehand, but I respect every three-letter agency we have. Except, well, the IRS."

The fire chief's strained chuckle sounded awkward coming through his mask.

Now we were here, more or less in the middle of nowhere, five miles away from the man I least wanted to see, and who I suspected didn't want to see me.

As Stephanie drove, she asked, "Are you finally going to tell me who this person is?"

She'd asked the question earlier and I'd shrugged it off, redirecting the conversation. Not wanting to get into it yet.

"A guy I used to work with."

I left it there, and five seconds passed before Stephanie shook her head.

"Could you be any more vague?"

"Back when I was in the military, he and I were briefly assigned to the same location."

"You mean the black site."

A statement, not a question. Stephanie had asked for the whole story, so I'd given it, though I hadn't gone into much detail about my time in the Philippines.

"That's right."

"What's his name?"

"Tyler Quinn."

"And he's a friend of yours?"

"I wouldn't say that."

Stephanie glanced at me in the rearview mirror again.

"So if he's not a friend, what is he to you?"

"Like I said, right now he's our only hope."

"You don't sound very hopeful."

I shrugged, settling back as I stared out my window at the gorgeous view.

"That's because the last time I saw Quinn, we got into a fight."

"A fight?"

"Yes. Quinn punched me in the face and told me if I ever crossed paths with him again, he'd kill me."

"No," he says, "no, please, don't—"

The car rocked and I jerked awake, blinking at the midday sun.

"Sorry," Stephanie said. "I hit a pothole."

I sat up from where I'd dozed off in the back seat, wiping the sleep from my eyes.

"How long was I out?"

"About four hours."

She paused, silently throwing me a cautious glance in the rearview.

"What is it?"

"You were talking in your sleep."

Remembering my dream, I asked, "What did I say?"

"I couldn't tell. You were mostly murmuring."

Hard to know if she was lying. I watched her face for a beat, then gazed out my window.

Deep-blue sky splotched with white clouds stretching to the distant peaks on the horizon. Rocky, brown country, interspersed with coniferous trees and sagebrush, spread out for miles and miles. Split-rail fencing running along both sides of the highway, presumably keeping in livestock, but there was none in sight.

"Where are we now?"

"We entered Wyoming three hours ago."

"Want to switch?"

"No, I'm fine. Besides, based on your directions, we should be there soon."

We'd been driving nonstop since leaving Los Angeles, trying to stay off major throughways, which is difficult when you get into the Rockies and all there are are highways.

I'd switched with Stephanie earlier this morning, wearing sunglasses and a hat to obscure my face, and drove for close to eight hours while Stephanie slept in the back.

After a beat, he starts toward the door. Opens it and steps out. I pause long enough to gaze at our latest prisoner begging for death, and then I exit and close the door behind me.

Quinn stands several paces away, his arms crossed. I walk up to him and wave the bloody pliers in his face.

"What the fuck is your problem?"

Quinn makes no reaction. Doesn't even blink.

"He doesn't know anything."

I scoff, shaking my head.

"You're going to believe him? The man's a fucking liar."

"He's not lying about this."

"How do you know?"

"Because I do."

Hearing our voices, Anne Kerberos steps out of the office down the hallway.

"Is everything okay?"

Staring at Quinn, I say, "No, everything is not okay. The newbie disobeyed a direct order."

Quinn says, "We're the same rank in here."

My grip, squeezing those pliers even tighter.

"Get the fuck out of my face."

Then I turn and call down to Anne.

"When Gene comes in, tell him I want to see him. I don't want to work with this asshole anymore."

I start toward the door leading back into the killing room but pause when Quinn speaks again.

"I may be an asshole, but you know I'm right."

My back to Quinn as I grip the doorknob, I say nothing. Just open the door and step back inside.

Silent, I approach the man strapped to the chair. The man who is still sobbing. Who now sees something different in my face.

Who sees my smile.

Standing off to the side by the table which contains several other tools, Quinn watches silently. He's a relatively new addition to the black site, having arrived a month ago. I don't know much about him as he doesn't speak much. Only that he's an army brat and had never lived in one place for more than six months. His father was a soldier, just as his father's father was a soldier.

I can't put a finger on the reason why, but I don't like the man.

"Quinn, hold his head steady."

In the killing room, we freely use our names. It's impossible to pinpoint when we started doing this. Probably after the first few prisoners had expired.

Tyler Quinn stands six feet two inches tall. Weighs 220 pounds, much of it muscle. A man with dark eyes and a steel jaw who was assigned here because he's one of the best at what he does, though so far I haven't been impressed.

When Quinn doesn't move, I slowly turn to look at him.

Silent, Quinn shakes his head.

In front of me, the prisoner whose name I don't know continues to sob.

"Please stop. Please . . . please, I don't know anything. I swear to you!"

I ignore the man, speaking directly to Quinn in a commanding tone.

"Hold his fucking head steady."

This time Quinn doesn't bother shaking his head. He holds my gaze as he answers with one definitive word.

"No."

My grip on the pliers tightens. My mind, racing.

Finally, I step back and motion at the door.

"Let me speak to you outside."

For a second, I expect the man to stay where he is. To continue standing there by the table with the assortments of tools. Defiant.

41

It doesn't take long before the man starts begging for death.

Tears streaming down his face, snot running from his nose, shouting so loud his voice reverberates around the small cinder block room.

"Please! I swear to you! I don't know anything!"

I stand before the man whose full name I haven't bothered to learn. A pair of pliers in my hand, dripping blood.

The man is secured to the chair. His arms, legs, even his torso—every bit is fastened in place so that he can barely move.

The only thing he can move is his head, which he'd shaken back and forth in agony when I tore off several of his fingernails.

The man continues to sob in his broken English.

"Please! I have nothing! My family—they are dead! Please . . . make it stop."

Sometimes inactivity becomes the most terrifying thing for these men. To stand there, staring back at them. Forcing them to look at their torturer. To see the lack of emotion in my face. To understand that in this room, I am their god.

PART III
CONTROLLED BURN